Ferris Jerome

High-Water-Mark

A Novel

Ferris Jerome

High-Water-Mark
A Novel

ISBN/EAN: 9783744662130

Printed in Europe, USA, Canada, Australia, Japan

Cover: Foto ©Andreas Hilbeck / pixelio.de

More available books at **www.hansebooks.com**

HIGH-WATER-MARK.

A NOVEL.

BY

FERRIS JEROME.

"The great moral combat between human life
And each human soul must be single."
OWEN MEREDITH.

PHILADELPHIA:
J. B. LIPPINCOTT & CO.
1879.

HIGH-WATER-MARK.

FIRST BOOK.

CHAPTER I.

"Dull, dull, dull !"

Burr Courtenay (an accomplished representative of a learned profession), tipped back in a revolving office-chair, with his feet elevated upon a round, rusty stove, in which an uncheerful fire smouldered, removed a cigar from his lips and made this return, in an indolent tone, to the above observation :

"Well, Mr. Burns, I expected something rather more original after such protracted meditation."

The first speaker wheeled around and came and stood with his back to the stove.

"Is it likely," said he, with some asperity, "that a daily prospect from that point of observation," indicating the murky window which looked out on the bleak main street of a very bleak prairie village, "is calculated to develop originality ?"

"Genius, Charles," said his companion, mildly, "is not dependent upon outward circumstances, it takes fire from within."

"It has got to have something to feed on after it has taken fire, has it not ?" said Mr. Burns. " I am not sure but it needs a little extraneous influence to kindle it. Though I pray you not to suppose," he added, "that I lay any claim to genius. I am at a loss to know why you mention the word in this connection."

"I mention it," said Mr. Courtenay, "because of your

having intimated to me some days ago that you intended to write a poem; and it was in my mind, as you stood there, that the poem might be in process of fermentation. But your remark dispelled the thought. By the way, Charley," he continued, "what do you suppose kindled the flame of the Scottish bard who bore your own illustrious name? Was it the Highlands, those poetic hills breathing the rhythmic name of Albion? Or was it the Highland lassies, adding their quaint beauty to the picturesque scenery, that inspired his pen? Or was it the ploughshare?"

"Perhaps it was—all of those," said Mr. Burns, with a faint smile, again throwing his melancholy glance from the window across the bare, brown, deserted street.

"There is a tradition in our family," he added, irrelevantly, "or was, before our family was reduced to its present insignificance, that Robert Burns belonged to our ancestry. But I repudiate it; I don't want to hang to any man's coat-tails."

The homely and trite figure suggested a literal fact to Mr. Courtenay.

"Charley," said he, with indolent apprehension, "you are in a fair way to ruin your own coat-tails; why don't you tuck your broadcloth under your arms when you stand with your back to the stove?"

"I wouldn't assume that boorish attitude for all the broadcloth in High-Water-Mark," said Mr. Burns, magnificently, moving away and seating himself on a high stool by the desk.

"I wonder," said Mr. Courtenay, whose mind was in that unoccupied state which catches at, and is willing to give a kind of inactive attention to, any trivial thought that floats by, as a feather or a butterfly is borne idly on the air, "what originated such a name for this village?"

"Spring rains, I fancy," said Mr. Burns.

"Ah, maybe so, I had not thought of that. I have heard that sometimes in the breaking-up of the ice and snow the river greatly overflows its banks. It may be that when they laid the town-plot they extended it just as far as the high-water mark, and hence the name."

"The river has never exceeded its banks much since

we have been here," said Mr. Burns; adding, gloomily, "and we have been here three years."

"Two years and a half, Charley," corrected his friend, deprecatingly.

"Well, we *shall* be here three years. I feel as if it would be all the same if we could project ourselves into the future ten, twenty, forty years, and look back upon them as already past. We shall probably go on and on, like Tennyson's brook, and the story will have, from year to year, a remarkable sameness. A feeling comes upon me that we are simply waiting for the years to tide over us and leave us, at last, stranded and dead on the beach. Noble souls! Burr, candidly, do you think it will pay, our sticking here all these years?"

Mr. Burns fixed his deep-set blue eyes, with the brows just now almost meeting above them, upon his companion with such earnestness and energy of expression as to make them appear, for the moment, intensely and brilliantly black.

Mr. Courtenay, quite unmoved, returned, "Pay? Why, of course it will pay! Won't there be a railroad through here one of these days? Isn't that what we have been waiting for?"

"It is what we have been waiting for, certainly; but the prospects for a road were just as 'immediate' three years ago as they are now. And in the mean time we are getting rusty. We are tinctured with Western habits and dialect. And then we don't have any practice, and when the railroad does come,—Heaven speed the day!—won't it bring troops of new lawyers, fresh from Eastern cities, and won't they have the preference?"

"God forbid!" said Burr, fervently. "I don't think they will, Charley; I have more faith in the people of this community than that. We are making heavy claims upon them by our long and patient residence among them."

"If they could only appreciate that!" said Mr. Burns. "My fear is that they may repudiate our 'claims' before the railroad comes. Two such accomplished barristers as ourselves is a considerable investment in legal talent for a village like this."

"I am certain of one thing," said Mr. Courtenay, getting up and dropping the stump of his cigar in the ashes, and then taking a turn around the room with his hands in his trousers' pockets,—"that if five hundred law-graduates were to immigrate to this town to-morrow, no two in all that number would be so well read, Charley, as you and I. I speak with modesty."

"No; we have done little else but read," said Mr. Burns. "But where is the good of it?"

"It will not be thrown away, Charley. You know that in the grand economy of Nature (and, too, of Revelation, I suppose, under which head I conclude Blackstone is classified) nothing is lost. You can follow the drop of dew through all its changing history and know that it cannot perish. Are not the gems of intellect as unquenchable? There is no death to the soul, or to anything born of the soul. If there were not a single Bible extant, or the vaguest scriptural tradition, I should still hold to the theory of immortality, basing it upon the indestructibility of things."

Mr. Courtenay, adroit diplomatist that he was, had hit upon a thought which he knew would divert his companion's mind from the gloomy prospect of remaining in a town destitute of railroads.

After a little silence he took it up and remarked, "The only immortality that I have any conception of as regards man—or rather, the only theory that my knowledge and reason accepts without a doubt—is the throwing out of influence that will last until its force is spent, like a ball pitched into the air. And there is a correspondence between that and your dew-drop; whatever form it takes it still adheres to the earth. There are a few men that lived centuries ago whose balls are spinning through the world yet."

"My dear Charley," said his friend (but I am bound to explain to the reader, who might otherwise, in the perusal of Mr. Courtenay's history, look upon him as singularly inconsistent, that he argued partly for the sake of argument, and partly because he loved to hold up a question like a prism, and catch as many rays of light as it was capable of reflecting), "if that is all the immortality we can count upon, it is hardly worth spending a lifetime for. What is fame, or anything, to a man if he dies and is oblivious?"

He paused in his walk, and repeated, in a voice deep and melodious, and whose modulation was perfect,—

> "'When the grass is green above me,
>   And those who bless me now and love me
>   Are sleeping by my side,
>   Will it avail me aught that men
>   Tell to the world with lip and pen
>   That once I lived and died?
>
> "'No; if a garland for my brow
>   Is growing, let me have it now,
>   While I'm alive to wear it.'

Or else let me have a conscious immortality after death. If fame—which is a mere breath blown over our graves— is the price to be paid for our grandest achievements, life, as I remarked, is not worth the living."

"Bah!" said Mr. Burns, with a shrug,—

> "'What is our life worth except in the giving
>   Of life to some aim? What's the good of mere living!'

You always go in for the individual, Burr. You never can identify yourself with a mighty movement, or merge your energies in a great cause and lose sight of self. *Burr Courtenay* is the grand object you have always in view. What is the difference which particular 'I' it is that accomplishes something for the good of the world, so that the something is accomplished? What matter who wrote the Iliad since it is written, or what do you or I or any man care for Homer,—the Homer who walked about, and ate, and drank, and slept? His personality died centuries ago; it is nothing to us or to the world. And because an inspiration was breathed through him upon the world, was he better than another? I have no particular reverence for the instrument on which a fine piece of music is played. I hate this detaching of oneself from the body of humanity, as though one particle were better than another."

"Perhaps one particle *is* no better than another," said Mr. Courtenay, "viewed by a disinterested party,—say a cherub or an archangel some leagues removed from us as regards both space and interest,—but you must allow me to discriminate between myself and the other particles. I have but one office to perform in life, I take it; and when I perform it perfectly, admitting even that I do it without reference to anything outside of myself, do I not chime in with the grand harmony of the universe? Is there any law in my being that clashes with my fellow-beings?"

"You lose sight of the question," said Mr. Burns, impatiently, "or, rather, you evade it. You are not thinking of the universe or of mankind, and of being true to them as the stars are true, or as Moses was true: you are thinking of yourself."

"Well, suppose I admit that," said Mr. Courtenay, good-naturedly. "The atom which I call 'I' is of vital importance to me, though perhaps to no one else. It is of moment to me whether I or another occupy such or such a position, or enjoy such or such an existence, just as it is of moment to me whether I or somebody else eat my dinner. Mind, I say it is of importance to *me*, not that the universe will suffer in the case. I and my neighbor are balancing like the two sides of an equation; it is of no consequence which of us takes from the other, the world remains the same. The Almighty has planted this dominant 'I' in every breast; and it is right. It is right that every man shall feel himself a king, and not be forever giving up his place in the meek spirit of self-sacrifice. Will you please reach me that document in the upper right-hand pigeon-hole?" he asked, turning away from the window at which he had been standing. "It is old man Jenkins's will. I see him crossing the street and heading this way. I presume he wishes to add another codicil. If he keeps on I shall have to pin a fresh legal-cap sheet to this instrument."

Mr. Burns handed down the paper, and Mr. Courtenay reseated himself grandly in the revolving office-chair. He was exceedingly handsome and majestic in appearance; rather massive about the head and shoulders, with a lion's mane of black, glossy hair curling about his coat-collar, a trifle longer than the fashion, perhaps, but strikingly becoming.

Nature had turned him out as complete a specimen of his kind as one will see in a lifetime; and art had finished him off with an exquisite polish in which there were many ingredients of good and evil. Some years ago when he first dawned upon Mr. Burns, his remarkable beauty of face and physique was even more dazzling and resplendent; being fed by the enthusiasm of youth, which alone can tinge the cheeks and fire the eyes and animate the whole being with a marvellous grace and glory. Moreover, he was finely educated, cultured, distinguished in appearance, and, though somewhat reserved and haughty in bearing, he was gentle and courteous in manner.

Long association had brushed off some of the outer splendor and revealed to the confident and appreciative friend more of the inner worth. Whatever seemed cold, or selfish, or biased in him (and it is true there was a good deal of such seeming) Mr. Burns thrust aside, or chafed at, as affectation, or, at the worst, as the fungous growth of circumstances. He had penetrated to the core of Burr's grand nature, and believed in him as he believed in all absolute good, and truth, and nobility. As for his vanity, which showed itself in his fine manners and graceful courtesy,—especially to women,—Mr. Burns cared nothing for that now; was a little contemptuous of it in fact (though it had helped to dazzle him once); being himself very free from mere outside polish. Whatever was pleasing and beautiful to others in him radiated from the centre of his being.

There was one thing, however, about his friend that was exceedingly unsatisfactory and sometimes absolutely painful to him. It was, that Burr never took him into his inmost heart to show him its hopes, its fears, its motives, its secret workings, nor ever revealed to him a glimpse of his past life except incidentally. Never purposely disclosed his tenderer and better nature, but continually baffled his affectionate sympathy, and, indeed, seemed to ward off, by a shield of triviality which he perpetually carried, any grave confidences which Mr. Burns himself might have liked to make to him. There was no getting at him somehow, or at the reality in him. In discussion, he took up any side of a question that presented itself to him without regard to any previous opinion he might have expressed concerning it ; declaring all things to be so many-sided that it was impossible always to take the same view.

"I look upon every subject as a landscape," said he, "which may be studied from many different stand-points and in many changing lights and shadows. One view may be as good and as true as another ; why limit myself to this or that ?" Which broad philosophy, though unobjectionable in itself, was sometimes very exasperating to his mercurial companion.

Personal elegance was a strong habit with Mr. Courtenay. He was a splendid creature and well worth being well kept. But he would have sat there with the office festooned with dust and cobwebs from one year's end to another if Mr. Burns had not flourished a broom over the walls and ceiling once a month or so.

Mr. Burns was fastidious as to his surroundings, and cared more for his own comfort than for the impressions he made on the minds of others. There was a principle running through his life that he endeavored to control his actions by, paying little heed to results.

Mr. Jenkins opened the door and let himself in with a modest air, as though he deprecated the liberty he was taking. Mr. Burns's utter indifference as he made his appearance, and Mr. Courtenay's imposing manner, justified the feeling that he *was* taking a liberty.

"Good-evening, Mr. Jenkins," said Mr. Courtenay, in a deep voice, a trifle reassuringly.

To which Mr. Jenkins responded, rubbing his hands over each other as if they were cold, and advancing into the room, "Good-evenin'. *Good*-evenin', Mr. Burns."

The deprecating air extended in particular to Mr. Burns, who was really the more formidable of the two, because of a certain fineness of nature and keenness of perception, which, linked with uncompromising principles, impressed upon the designer or the impostor the feeling that he was unmasked. There was no wavering in the direct glance of his steel-blue eyes.

He nodded distantly and pushed the visitor a chair

with his foot, after which act of scant courtesy he withdrew himself from Mr. Jenkins's spiritual atmosphere. He still maintained his position on the high stool by the desk; his hat, which he had a habit of wearing in the office, was pushed back from his forehead, and his mouth had a slight curve, which gave to his fine, classical face a half-contemptuous expression that was somewhat habitual.

Mr. Courtenay and Mr. Jenkins began conversation by speaking of the weather, perhaps the only common ground between them outside of the latter's business, which, of course, could not be entered upon without some such preliminary. Said Mr. Jenkins, " I've jist about made up my min' to leave this 'ere blasted cole country an go to a warmer climate. A man freezes the very marrer out o' his bones on these big prairies. I'd pull up stakes an' go in a minit if I could sell out."

"Go—where?" asked Mr. Courtenay, with a slight widening of his long eyelids.

"Why, down into Arkansaw. I've got a brother-in-law down there, been a wantin' me to come this three year. But ye see, what little I've got 's a'most all tied up in lan'. Not so very little either, he! he!" with a glance at Mr. Burns. "Wouldn't be a very easy matter to cut loose these hard times."

Mr. Courtenay discouraged emigration ; what the country needed was more men, women, and children. Though of course there would come a time, when the population began to thicken, for Mr. Jenkins—and others—to float off naturally, like the scum from a boiling kettle. But the time was not yet ripe.

"Do you not think," said he, in his smooth, polished manner, "that our cold, frozen winters are more conducive to health than those warmer latitudes?"

"Well, I dunno but they be," admitted Mr. Jenkins, readily. "Me nor none o' my fam'ly hev been sick a week, put it all together, sence we've been here, an' that's ten year. But then it's too cole fur a farmin' country. Why, they begin seedin' down there in Arkansaw while we're a settin' by the fire waitin' fur the groun'-hog to come out an' see his shadder."

"How many crops do they raise there in a year?"

asked Mr. Burns, severely, fixing Mr. Jenkins with his penetrating gaze.

"Eh !—how many crops?" he returned, struck, seemingly, by the newness of the suggestion conveyed in the inquiry. "Why, one, I 'spose,—the same as they raise anywheres."

"I thought perhaps they raised more than one, seeing they begin so early in the season," said Mr. Burns.

Mr. Courtenay, who was far more gifted in the way of sarcasm than his friend, had a velvet suavity that was careful, usually, to veil it from the object at which it was directed. He came to his client's aid and said, in a conciliatory accent, that he presumed Mr. Burns thought if only one crop could be raised in a year it did not matter greatly what particular time of year.

"Well, but," said Mr. Jenkins, who had a stubborn set of opinions, "ye see, the thing is to git yer crop in airly; there's a mighty sight o' difference in bein' airly an' in bein' late."

"It seems to me," said Mr. Burns, "about like the difference, longitudinally, between New York and High-Water-Mark ; the sun wakes them up a little earlier there, but their day is no longer than ours, and the morning is just as fresh when it reaches us as when it broke upon the Atlantic."

Leaving Mr. Jenkins to ponder feebly over this bit of mathematical geography, Mr. Burns again retired in a spiritual sense.

Mr. Courtenay sat intently scanning the will with its several codicils annexed, smoothing his glossy beard with one white hand and waiting for the old man to mention his errand ; whereupon he replied, promptly, "I happen to have the document in my hand at this moment; what is it you wish?"

"Well, as I tole ye afore," said Mr. Jenkins, "I didn't mean to will any o' the lan' to my dotter Sary Ann, bein' as she was engaged to Jim Sites that has a'most as much lan' as I hev myself. But, ye see, Jim an' her's fell out, an' she says she'll never hev him now, no how. She's purty high-strung, Sary Ann is, when she gits her dander up."

Mr. Jenkins leaned back in his chair and again glanced at Mr. Burns, who sat as deaf as a post.

Mr. Courtenay elevated his eyebrows without raising his eyes, and repeated, mechanically, "Fell out."

"Yes," said Mr. Jenkins, screwing his little, old, wrinkled face up into what was intended to be a facetious expression, and pointing with his thumb. "Ye see, the way of it was, Jim he got jealous o' Mr. Burns here."

Mr. Burns again fixed his eyes coldly on the visitor's face.

"'Twa'n't nuthin' o' no account," said Mr. Jenkins, fidgeting a little, "only, ye see, away las' summer when Sary Ann was a pickin' berries inside the garden fence, Mr. Burns, he comes along an' stops an' leans agin the fence to chat a spell, an' Sary Ann she gives him a han'-ful o' berries. An' same time Jim he comes a ridin' up the lane an' sees 'em there. Well, he's been a fussin' about it, off an' on, ever sence. 'Specially ef he sees Sary Ann a talkin' to or recognizin' them as *she* says is his betters."

By a peculiar chuckle and wink Mr. Jenkins made the latter part of his speech a personal compliment, including both gentlemen.

Mr. Courtenay made as if he would rather not be included.

"I hope you don't take no offence for the mentionin' o' your name, Mr. Burns?" said Mr. Jenkins, humbly.

"None whatever. I cannot see that the affair concerns me in the least," said Mr. Burns, with exaggerated indifference.

"Of course," the old man continued, hopefully, "Jim's good enough in his way,—got a better start 'n most o' the young men has aroun' here ; but fur all that, he's hardly the sort for Sary Ann. I've tole her so time an' ag'in. I've tole her to hold her head a leetle higher 'n that. She's twice as well-edicated as him ; she's got a certifiket an' 's a goin' to teach school this winter."

Mr. Burns, feeling a strong aversion to being loaded with any responsibility about the young lady, and strong indignation at the likelihood of such responsibility being thrust upon him, spoke out in reply to the old man's insinuations with—as Mr. Courtenay subsequently described it—great force and clearness.

"Mr. Jenkins, you may give my compliments to Mr. Sites, and tell him he has no cause for jealousy so far as I am concerned. You may say to him that I am not a marrying man. And it is my advice to you, gratis,—and it is not often **a** lawyer proffers his opinion so cheap,—that you had better get your daughter to make up with the young man. As you say, he has a better start than most fellows have, and I doubt if she can do better."

Mr. Jenkins was awed into silence by this unequivocal logic.

Mr. Courtenay, who had sat a silent listener, with an unreadable expression of countenance, hastened to bring forward the subject of the will. "You wish to transfer some of the property herein mentioned to your daughter, I conclude?"

"Well, yes," said Mr. Jenkins, somewhat relieved, hitching his chair a little nearer. "Ye see, bein' onsettled like, an' havin' no def'nite prospects afore her, as one may say, an' knowin' my liability to drop off enny minute" (Mr. Jenkins had a cheerful habit of predicting a sudden terminus to his career), "I feel 's if it's my duty to make some pervision fur her 's well 's the rest of 'em, ag'inst my demise."

"Certainly," acquiesced Mr. Courtenay, holding his pen suspended over the paper.

"Well, ye may jist change that last quarter-section we was disposin' of the other day, an' set it down to Sary Ann's credit; then they'll all fare purty much alike, gals an' boys."

Mr. Courtenay made the required alteration with despatch.

Mr. Jenkins got up and crossed over to give his admiring attention to the lawyer's dexterity of pen.

"Now, I couldn't make a scratch holdin' my pen atween my fingers like that," said he, with his head on one side and his hands in his pockets.

When the new addition or correction was properly approved, Mr. Courtenay asked, diplomatically,—

"Is there anything further, Mr. Jenkins? I am particularly engaged this evening, and if there is nothing more——"

"Well, I don't think of nuthin' more at present, I believe," said Mr. Jenkins, reflectively. "I guess Sary Ann's all right now, Jim Sites or no Jim Sites, he! he! That's what you might call a purty good dowry fur a young woman, ain't it?"

"Very good, indeed," said Mr. Courtenay.

"There's not many gals a gittin' married nowadays that's as well pervided fur, I'll bet a 'tater! A little money on the wife's side comes handy to a young feller jist startin' in life. My ole woman had a thousan' dollars, an' it gev me a mighty good lift. Ye see, when ye once git the ball a rollin' it doubles up pretty fast."

"I suppose so," said Mr. Courtenay, cautiously, reflecting that he had very little experimental knowledge on that head.

"Well," said Mr. Jenkins, finally, "I guess I'll hev to be goin'; it's about supper-time 't our house. Why don't you gentlemen call round some time an' git better acquainted? We ain't got much of a place, but it's not the house, I al'ays tell my ole woman, it's the people a body goes to see—an' the victuals, he! he! We've gen'ally got a little sumpin' t' eat. I sh'd think ye'd git awful lonesome stickin' here, year in an' year out, the way you do."

"It is a little lonely, sometimes," said Mr. Courtenay. And the visitor crossed over to the door and bowed himself out, just as he had bowed himself in, with,—

"Good-evenin', Mr. Courtenay. *Good*-evenin', Mr. Burns."

The last named returned the courtesy briefly, as before.

Mr. Courtenay remarked, glancing around, "Charley, you remind me very much of Poe's 'Raven.'"

"Wouldn't the likeness be more striking if I had a Roman nose and darker eyes?" said Mr. Burns, significantly.

"You misapprehend me, Charley," said his friend. "I meant, simply, that you brought the idea of the poem to my mind. I had reference to your expression only, which, had I spoken literally even, overcame entirely the color of your hair and eyes, and suggested that ominous bird. I hardly think," he added, deprecatingly, "that you could classify my nose as a Roman nose; to go back to the classics, it is more properly a Grecian nose."

"Possibly. I am not very well up in classical lore," said Mr. Burns.

After a little silence, Mr. Courtenay said, "By the way, Charley, can we not do something this evening? It is miserably dull, as you observed. Suppose we go up to the deacon's and spend the evening?"

Mr. Burns objected.

"Why not?"

"Burr, you and I don't intend to marry those young ladies."

"Admitted."

"Then we must let them alone. They put more stress on our trifling attentions than our motives justify. You know how it is, people expect us to marry; they keep looking out for it, and our little civilities, no matter in what direction, pass for much more than they are worth. The ultra-democracy of a newly-settled country puts us on an exact level with everybody. A little politeness to our wash-woman is mistaken for gallantry. We may as well put aside false modesty and face the question as it is. We are peculiarly situated."

"We are, indeed," said Mr. Courtenay. "But I don't see anything very disagreeable in the peculiar situation," he added.

"It is a fact," continued Mr. Burns, "that we seem to be preferred by the ladies of all classes here to any other two young men. I say it humbly, for it shows the remarkably poor status of society in this village."

"I suppose you mean the young ladies," said Mr. Courtenay. "I don't know of a single *mater familias* who looks upon us with favor."

"It is because we're so poor."

"No; I think they are in doubt respecting our intentions. Unlike you, I do not believe *anybody* expects us to marry. Did I understand you to say our popularity indicates a low state of society here?"

"I mean there is a *poverty* of society here; there is nobody for the young ladies to aspire to but us,—if 'aspire' is the word,—we get so ridiculously puffed up by being the lions of a small country village."

"Yes; you should have put it differently," said Mr. Courtenay. "Though, of course, it would have come to the same thing, however delicately worded."

"As to the deacon's young ladies," continued Mr. Burns, coming back to the point they had started from, "God grant they may bestow their affections more worthily than upon us!"

"You mean, I suppose," said Mr. Courtenay, "that it would be better for them to make an investment that would bring them some returns."

"Burr, for heaven's sake," exclaimed Mr. Burns, flashing round upon him, "don't treat the matter so lightly! You *do* possess the sense of right and wrong. Why *assume* such careless indifference?"

Burr shrugged his shoulders. "What shall we do?" said he. "Hermitize ourselves for fear of damaging some young lady's affections?"

Mr. Burns, curbing his temper, returned, "Did it ever occur to you, Burr, that you have a manner toward women—especially toward pretty women—which might lead almost any one of them to suspect you admired her?"

"No," said Burr, the least bit ruffled; "I am not aware of having such a manner and of employing it so promiscuously."

"Don't take offence, Burr; it is possible you may *not* know. But your experience must prove to you how irresistible you are to women,—God knows, I don't mean to flatter you!—and I should think you had tasted enough of the bitter fruits of indiscretion."

Mr. Burns's words seemed to ring up some memory of the past that was annoying to his friend.

"Oh, damn it! Charley, don't preach. What would life be without its sweet and bitter spices? A most insipid dose to me. Did not the bell ring? It must be supper-time."

He took up his hat and stepped out. Mr. Burns followed him, and they walked down-street to the one hotel in the village,—a long, two-storied frame building, commodious, but entirely without ornamentation.

As they ascended the steps up into the long porch that extended from one end to the other of the building in front, the two male employés of the establishment, Dick Gibson and "Nigger" Fred, came up to the pump to water a pair of tired stage-horses, the driver of which sprang down from his perch with a familiar nod and joke, and went around to hand out a rather lean mail-bag, with which he whipped across the street to the post-office.

High-Water-Mark was off the main stage-line, and got its mail only twice a week.

The landlord came out and rang the last supper-bell vigorously, and forthwith there came pouring in from every direction clerks, shoemakers, editors, apprentices, and various nondescript individuals,—all depending on this one eating and drinking institution for the wherewithal to sustain life.

Mr. Burns, in his gloomy mood, looked about him, and felt it a sort of degradation to be herding with all those people,—and ate no supper.

Mr. Courtenay, though fully as fastidious, had the happy faculty of standing aloof and ignoring what was repulsive.   He carried his own spiritual atmosphere with him.   Physically he was much more susceptible to disagreeable things than Mr. Burns.

CHAPTER II.

"Burr, what do you say to changing our boarding-place?"

They had got back to the office. The mail—not much to speak of, with the exception of the newspapers—had been duly examined, and Mr. Courtenay, ensconced in his favorite seat, was going over the latter.

"With a view to economize?" he asked, looking up.

"No," said Mr. Burns; "it occurred to me that it would be better for us, morally and socially, to obtain board in some nice, respectable family, where we could enjoy, in a degree, the pleasures and refinements of a home. Do you not think it would be an improvement on our present way of living?"

"It would, indeed," said Mr. Courtenay. "Have you thought which of the nice, respectable families in the place you would patronize?"

"No; I can't think of anybody that could take us," Mr. Burns returned, with a despairing accent. "I have been clairvoyantly — so to speak — prying into everybody's domesticity in the village, but the houses are all so small."

"And as densely populated as foundling hospitals," added Burr.

"Yes; I am afraid we'll have to give it up."

"I am afraid so. Unless the deacon's folks could be prevailed upon to take us in; there is plenty of room up there."

There was a levity in the proposition that grated upon Mr. Burns after the serious conversation of an hour before. He got up and thrust his letters—business letters in big, buff envelopes—into a drawer and walked to the window.

Uninteresting as was the view from there, the window yet had a sort of fascination for him, as though it were a connecting link between himself and the great, outside world beyond and the heavens above.

By and by, Mr. Courtenay threw the papers aside. "Well, Charley, what about your poem? Is it to be a little sonnet for the local periodical?"

"No; it is to be of considerable length. I'm glad you spoke of it. I think I'll begin it to-night," said Mr. Burns, turning away from the window.

"Have you got an inspiration?"

"No. I have got a volcano in my head. I am consuming in inactivity. Something must be done or there will be an explosion."

"So bad as that?" said Burr. "Well, you have hit upon an excellent safety-valve and a very harmless one. Have you the 'gift' of poesy? I don't think I ever saw anything from your pen that would argue your being endowed with the divine afflatus."

"I had a faculty for rhyming when I was a boy. I haven't exercised it since," said Mr. Burns.

"Charley,—excuse me if the question is impertinent, —were you ever disappointed in love?"

"No; not in the way you mean."

"Pray how many ways are there for a man to be disappointed in love?" Mr. Courtenay asked.

"There is such a thing, Burr, as striving for a prize and finding out after you have got it that it is not the thing you wanted after all. It seems to me the sort of disappointment you had in your mind when you asked me that question would be nothing to this."

"That is hardly like you, Charley; it is more in accordance with your friend's fickle temperament to experience the flavor of dead-sea apples," said Mr. Courtenay. "By the way," he added, with a candor that was customary between them, "it seems to me you ought to have got through with all this sort of thing long ago, Charley. Twenty-eight—I believe you tell me you are twenty-eight —is rather an advanced age to be still dabbling in poetry. Of course you will not understand me to imply that poetry should be left to school-boys; a genius who gives his life to it is the most glorious of men. He leads the van in the world's progress; he pushes forward the boundaries of thought and emotion and gives us what we most thirst for, and what seems to us a foretaste of the boundlessness of eternity,—freedom. And freedom, in all its significations, is the grandest word in the language of men."

"Freedom!" reiterated Mr. Burns. "Good heavens! we hardly comprehend it in any of its significations. If our limbs are unbound we glory in our liberty, though our souls are fettered with superstition, our intellect with ignorance. Society may rule us, poverty hamper us, circumstances control us, friends constrain us, enemies cut us off, and still we prate of freedom. There is no such state; it is only a word. I agree with you a grand word, which may have its definition, by the grace of God, in the great hereafter, but never here."

Mr. Courtenay seldom replied to any of his friend's outbursts, but held on serenely to his own line of thinking. He remarked, after a little silence, "How much we admire the man of superior skill who hits off a thought hanging like a ripe apple within our sight, but just out of our reach, and shares it with us! The poet gives expression not to his own idea alone but to ours. A test of your genius would be to waken thoughts and emotions that lie dormant in me; to strike a chord in my nature that I myself could have evolved no music from. We know little about our tone and melody until a masterhand plays upon us. Mind, I don't limit your genius to my capacity, or—for that matter—to the capacity of any age or people. Write your music and there will come, some time, an instrument to give expression to it. Human nature is wonderfully responsive when it is awakened. The past has shown that there have been poets who shot ahead of their time whole centuries; we have not come up to some of them yet, their light is still ahead, and shines back on our approaching footsteps. Genius is immortal. It can wait."

"But it is a drudge and has got to work for its immortality," said Mr. Burns. "I remember reading somewhere that if Shakspeare had never written a line he would still have been the immortal Shakspeare; he would have felt and lived in himself all that he wrote. What an absurdity!"

"It agrees with Byron," said Mr. Courtenay, and quoted,—

> " ' Many are poets who have never penned
>   Their inspirations, and, perchance, the best.
> They felt, and loved, and died, but would not lend
>   Their thoughts to meaner things; they compressed
> The God within them, and rejoined the stars
>   Unlaurel'd upon earth, but far more bless'd
> Than those who are degraded by the jars
>   Of passion, and their frailties linked to fame,
> Conquerors of high renown, but full of scars.' "

"I don't suppose Byron believed that when he wrote it," said Mr. Burns. "It is effort that makes men great. It is labor that makes their greatness effective. It is fine to talk about inspiration, and to fancy that the beautiful thoughts, exquisitely enfolded, that rain down upon us from the heaven of great minds, burst spontaneously from inspired lips. But I suspect Byron himself perspired over the very lines you just now quoted. Talk of soaring like the lark; that is pure sentimentalism. You have got to work like a slave."

"Why, then, do you wish to task yourself so heavily?" asked Mr. Courtenay, with mild irony.

"To drain off a little native and accumulated bitterness in my composition," said Mr. Burns.

"It seems to me your profession might serve as an outlet for that; there is something in vilifying your antagonist and browbeating witnesses, though, perhaps, it is not so safe—especially with reference to the antagonist—as the other valve, the poetry."

"Not when my antagonist is Burr Courtenay," Mr. Burns retorted.

It had been twilight in the office for some time. The fire burning up a little threw quivering spots of light on the walls and on the floor. But it was too dark for the young men to see each other's faces except in dim outline. A silence settled between them, and the air seemed to vibrate with unspoken thoughts. They were Mr. Burns's thoughts. Burr was only smoking and dreaming; perhaps feeling vaguely the pressure of the charged atmosphere. Mr. Burns broke the silence:

"Burr, you asked me if I were ever disappointed in love. As perhaps you inferred, I have been in love,—I suppose I was. I was once engaged to be married."

"With your principles," returned Mr. Courtenay, "the one would of course precede the other. Your being engaged would argue your having been in love."

"Not necessarily; one might deceive himself," said Mr. Burns.

"How?"

"Fancy himself in love when he was not, really."

"Or fancy himself not in love when he was—really," said Burr, smiling. "You are so cautious, so fearful of making a mistake, that you would be quite as liable to fancy the one as the other. You started out with great expectations; you wanted to get a great deal out of life, and were not easily satisfied. You would spoil the most beatific state with a doubt as to whether it were real and would last."

Mr. Burns groaned inwardly.

"You looked for something better than this world can give,—perfection. Let me give you a piece of advice. If you want to believe in anything, do not investigate, do not tear the veil from before it. Your mind is too analytical; you are always trying to get at the reality of things; you must grasp the rainbow. For me, I like to keep the down on my peach and the dew on my rose. I like to throw the halo of poetry around the beautiful, and stand at a distance from the sublime to admire its tremendous effects. Examine all things for enjoyment, as you do a picture. Put them in the best light, and don't come too near."

"But suppose you have something beside enjoyment in view?" said Mr. Burns. "Suppose you want to get hold of a principle?"

"Why, then," said Mr. Courtenay, "philosophers would tell you to dig deeply. There is a motive-power in the very centre of things corresponding to the outward aspect and action. A great man is a sublime mystery to us until we come face to face with him. That is the point of disenchantment. But if we stop there we are in danger of a warning from the illustrious Pope,—

'A little learning is a dangerous thing.'

If you are bound to investigate, for heaven's sake don't

stop until you have bored clear through to the centre. Anything short of that leads to skepticism and bitterness. You—you did not refer to Maggie, did you?"

"No," said Mr. Burns. "It was years ago. I don't know why, Burr, in all the years we have been together, I never told you."

A curious smile crossed Burr's face, unseen in the darkness. He was almost as cognizant of Mr. Burns's past history as of his own; though neither, in all their long intercourse, had unfolded himself to the other.

"How did the engagement come to be broken off?" he asked, after a short pause.

"It was not really broken off, it was dropped. I can't tell how, or when, or why the love I had—or thought I had—for that woman died out. As I regarded her then, and as I remember her now, she was incomparable among women,—sweet, amiable, talented. I don't understand how she went out from me. It all seems vague, misty. It was like the slow, unconscious fading of a day into night. It was like my youth: they both went together."

Impossible to tell the effect of this remarkable confidence upon Mr. Courtenay. After another little silence he asked, in a subdued tone,—

"And what of her,—the lady?"

"Heaven knows! She dropped completely out of the current we had both been sailing on so long together. I have never, for one moment, ceased to wonder, and to speculate, and torture myself about her. I have even tried to find her, to satisfy myself, but she left no trace."

"I can't see that you are to blame, Charley," said Mr. Courtenay, gently.

"To blame or not to blame, it is not a pleasant thing to reflect that you may have destroyed the happiness of a life,—of the very life you had intended and pledged yourself to bless."

Down in the bottom of his trunk, carefully wrapped up and preserved, Mr. Burns had a portrait and a bundle of yellow letters whose delicate tracery of penmanship had no tenderer meaning for him now than a parchment roll of Egyptian hieroglyphics would have had; albeit, he had once been thrilled to his heart's centre at sight of them. But that was long ago, when his youth was still fresh upon him and his cheek was tinged with an almost girlish blush as he unfolded the dainty sheets breathing the atmosphere of a tenderly loved presence.

He made a movement to get them for Burr to see, but restrained himself. What right had he to hold up the trusting heart that throbbed in them to Burr's criticising gaze? For even now he was not sure of his friend's sympathetic interest. Still, after an interval of silence, perhaps fancying he had paved the way in some small degree to Burr's heart, or—for he was far enough above prying curiosity—from whatever motive, possibly without any particular motive, he asked, "Burr, were you ever really in love?"

If he had thought to get a sympathetic answer the illusion was dispelled.

"A great many times," said Burr, with a movement as if to throw off a pressure and let himself up into his usual light atmosphere. "At the unripe age of fifteen I was desperately bent on marrying my preceptress, a lady of perhaps twice my years; but she discreetly rejected me. I am not sure but the romantic ardor of that attachment surpassed, in purity and intensity, anything I have ever experienced since. But the refusal was bad for me; I became a bitter skeptic while yet in my teens, and involved myself in no end of reckless flirtations."

"The habit has scarcely left you yet!" said Mr. Burns, ironically.

"Do you know, a few years ago, I had an opportunity to see that first love of mine," Burr continued, "by stepping a little out of my way; but I should have closed my eyes if she had passed directly before me. Not that any remnant of my boyish ardor remained, but she had grown old, they told me, and I could not bear to see the ravages of time on a face I had once idolized,—or idealized,—whichever it was. As it stands to-day, I am not committed to any lady."

"Not *committed!* How vastly people's ideas differ about certain things!" Mr. Burns exclaimed.

"Do you mean yours and mine?"

"Yes; yours and mine. If I beguiled any young lady into loving me, and believing I loved her, I should feel myself 'wholly committed,' as you say."

"Should you? And what would then be your course of procedure? For I fancy that is about the state of Miss Jenkins's mind with reference to yourself," said Burr.

The firelight shone up into his face, revealing an exasperating glimmer in his eyes. He took his cigar from his lips and held it, smoking, between his fingers.

Mr. Burns made a gesture of impatience.

Though in some respects the most tender-hearted of men, and easily moved to compassion by physical suffering of man, brute, or insect, there were certain kinds of worms Burr Courtenay loved to see wriggling on a hook. He not unfrequently impaled his companion.

"I at first had the impression," said he, "that the young lady only presumed on her intimacy with you as a means of coquetting with her lover; but it seems she has serious designs upon you, and her father appears anxious to further her claims. It looked like it, his coming in and laying the matter open and putting a premium upon her, so to speak, besides treating you with marked affability."

"Burr, you know as well as I," said Mr. Burns, flashing up, "that the old man has got upon the wrong track. It is you who have turned Sarah Jenkins's foolish, sentimental little head, not I. To speak with unvarnished frankness, I must say I cannot imagine the quality of your pride when you stoop to rivalry with such fellows as poor, uncouth Jim Sites!"

His severe way of putting the case was a little embarrassing to his friend.

"I think you are laboring under a misapprehension, Charley," said he. "I do not conceive that I have ever put myself into rivalry with Jim Sites."

Mr. Burns, unheeding the denial, resumed: "The Jenkinses have high aspirations, and they probably think it would be a fine thing to marry their daughter to an attorney-at-law! If it comes in my way again I shall take pains to effectually disabuse their minds of that impression."

"Don't be hard upon us, Charley," said his friend, good-humoredly.

"I will lay our poverty and general worthlessness before the old man in a way that will astonish him," returned Mr. Burns, as he went over to the desk, struck a match, and lighted a lamp with a very murky chimney and began taking out writing materials.

"Are you going to begin your poem immediately?" Burr asked.

"Yes; perhaps, by and by, you will aid me a little in the way of comment and criticism?"

"Gladly," said Burr, with a willingness that argued confidence in his ability for the office; but added, after deliberating a moment, "It occurs to me, Charley, upon reflection, that the position of critic and commentator is a rather difficult one, seeing that my criticisms and comments are to be made to you and not behind your back to the world. By the way, it strikes me this is hardly the age of poetry; every subject I can think of has been exhausted. Of poetical themes, take 'Morning,' for instance; it has been so abundantly bedecked with 'rosiness' and various gilding and coloring, from time to time, that if it should put on all its glories at one sitting it would rival the very shekinah. 'Evening,' too, with its gorgeous sunsets and its tinkling bells, than which nothing is more melancholy to my mind, as presaging the coming night; suggesting 'The curfew tolls the knell,' and so forth. 'Twilight' with its pensive hour,—everything, in fact. Not a school-boy but what has written an ode to Spring! Poetical description is exhausted."

"Hum! what a materialist you are!" said Mr. Burns. "Can you see nothing but what is suggested to your senses?"

"Well, take the graces and the virtues, haven't they been satiated with rhythmic laudation. As for Patriotism, does not every nation under the sun swell the music of its own anthems? And as for our warriors and our statesmen, is there a single illustrious name unsung? I contend that it is an exceedingly difficult matter to be a poet in this common-sense, matter-of-fact age. The same spirit of incredulity and investigation that has unmasked many sa-

cred and scientific mysteries, raises its unhallowed hands
and plucks off the ivy-wreaths and delicate frescoes with
which poetry is accustomed to bedeck itself, leaving the
naked skeleton of a fact, a tale, or a moral.   No matter
how beautiful or exquisite the shell, crack it, get at the
kernel.   No man has time to loiter among ancient ruins,
or beside pearly streams looking for stray gems.   Every
sentence that is spoken on the rostrum, in the pulpit, has
got to be pithy, no mere flowers of rhetoric; indeed,
rhetoric has little place with us,—the plainest, most con-
cise dress a thought can wear is the best.   A dash of wit,
a spark of brilliancy, a glare of humor may flash along
the page, or the sermon, or the oration, but it must be of
the keenest, and brightest, and, I might add, briefest.
We must wait until the great geniuses of the past have
been sifted like sand upon the public mind and earth is
mellowed with their ashes.''

   " Let me ask,'' said Mr. Burns, " if you consider that
Homer, Pope, Dryden, and all those ancients had been
so disseminated before—say Shakspeare's era, or Byron's
and Tom Moore's ?''

   " Certainly; and the latter were born of their ashes;
they were woven into the every-day lives of millions, just
as their contemporary philosophers and sages were woven
into the scientific life.   Why, let any one who has never
studied the classics turn to those old bards, and he will be
astonished to find himself almost as familiar with them as
with his own thoughts.   He might—in ignorance of their
antiquity—even accuse them of plagiarizing some of our
modern writers.   Every sentence (at least every sentiment)
has been made a text of, disguised, diluted, clothed in a
thousand different forms to mingle with our common literature.   There is but little originality afloat nowadays,
Charley; the most that we get comes to us with the familiar
odor of well-known flowers, hidden out of sight, it may
be, in a gorgeous bouquet of words, but still perceptible
to a cultivated mind.   Strange that the fragrance of an
inspiration should be everlasting !   There is a species of
immortality sweeter than that attained by the celebrated
Count Frangipanni.''

   " How is it to be attained by us poor mortals of the

present century," said Mr. Burns, "if we are to fold our hands and wait until the world has absorbed Shakspeare and nothing is left of Milton but a scented zephyr? I do not believe we are merely to wait for the uprising of the Phœnix, we are to work for it. We must help on toward the new era. No man lives for himself; in one sense no man is an individual, an integer, but a fraction of one stupendous whole."

"You are right," said Mr. Courtenay. "Take our oft-quoted Shakspeare. Ah! Shakspeare is a part of the universe,—the voice of it. My faith in him is pantheistic. If I were a spiritualist I would deny that William of Stratford was a mere man, and affirm that he was the writing-medium of all humanity."

"Spare him your eulogies," said Mr. Burns, turning again to his desk; "he doesn't need them. There he stands, as Webster said of Massachusetts, he speaks for himself."

"If you are going to write," Mr. Courtenay remarked, "perhaps I had better take a stroll and leave you to your inspiration."

"You will not be any constraint upon me," rejoined Mr. Burns.

"Nevertheless I think I'll step out," Mr. Courtenay persisted, and got up and lighted another lamp with a murky chimney, and went into a back-room. When he reappeared, gloved and equipped, Mr. Burns sat at the desk with a sheet of legal-cap spread out before him, poising his pen above it and contracting his eyebrows. His hair, light and curling, was brushed carelessly back from his forehead. His eyes were exceedingly bright, unsatisfied, and melancholy. It seemed as if the fire in them had consumed his youth and drunk up his youthful blood. His high, straight nose, slightly-curved lips, and pale complexion were responsible for a certain aristo-cratic air he had. In build he was nearly as tall and quite as symmetrical, but slighter, than his friend. The two contrasted strikingly in many ways. Mr. Courtenay showed a fulness of health and strength and physical beauty; Mr. Burns not a lack, but an absence of it, as though it had been,—as though it might be again. He was young; he was not broken, or wrecked, or decayed; only empty of the zest of living. His life might be re-filled like a goblet whose wine has been spilled. Burr, though some years his senior (he did not know just how many), was still in the enjoyment of his champagne, and still believed in its sparkling bubbles; he suffered no cloud to hang over his spirit. "Well, good-night, Charley; may the muse inspire you!" he said, with a just percept-ible elation of spirits, as he strode across the office to the door.

Mr. Burns responded moodily and without raising his eyes. Burr went out. When the door closed upon him, Mr. Burns got up, threw a picturesque blue cloak around him, took his hat and also went out. The night was dark, full of clouds and chilliness. Mr. Burns stopped and listened. He could hear Burr's footfalls on the frozen ground a short distance up the street, and he fol-lowed him.

"It's a mean, sneaking thing to do," he muttered, "track him as if he were a thief, but I want to make sure whether he goes there. That will be a bad piece of business yet."

On they went, the one behind the other, until they reached the summit of the hill upon which stood the proudest mansion in the village. It was Deacon Clyde's. Mr. Courtenay opened the gate, walked up to the front door, and rang the bell.

Mr. Burns, in the shadow of the fence and some shrubbery, observed through the low, lace-curtained win-dows of the parlor two young ladies sitting, one on either side of a small, oblong table, with a lamp upon it dangling with prismatic pendants. No other house in High-Water-Mark afforded so many luxuries and elegan-cies as Deacon Clyde's. The young ladies, Mr. Burns observed, were busy with some sort of fancy-work.

On the opposite side of the hall-door was a window half uncovered, revealing a scene similar to the parlor scene, except that it was an elderly couple—Deacon Clyde and his wife—who occupied respective seats at a small table with a lamp upon it.

The deacon had a newspaper in his hands, and appeared

to be reading aloud; for now and then he raised his eyes, and his wife glanced up from her knitting, and they smiled and nodded at each other over their spectacles. When the door-bell rang the deacon dropped his paper upon his knees, Mrs. Clyde suspended her knitting, and they both listened, then smiled and nodded, and resumed their quiet occupations.

The young ladies, meantime, exchanged glances, and then the taller one arose, and went out and opened the door. The light of the hall-lamp flashed in her face, revealing a pink flush blended with an ill-disguised, glad recognition, though she preserved a marked and quite charming dignity of manner.

The face in the parlor had an eager, expectant look, which Mr. Burns fancied changed to disappointment when Miss Clyde re-entered with Burr and closed the door, showing that he came alone.

"Poor little Maggie!" he said, with a sigh, and turned and went back to the office, resumed his seat and his pen, and began his poem.

CHAPTER III.

"BURR, are you awake?"

It was past midnight, and Mr. Courtenay had come in and gone to bed. But he instantly reported himself awake, and Mr. Burns took up the lamp and his manuscript and stepped into the back-room. He put the lamp down upon the wash-stand—splashed with soapsuds and loaded with toilet-utensils—and seated himself at the foot of the bed. His hair was rumpled, and had a pen thrust into it above his ear. His face was pale from excessive mental effort.

Mr. Courtenay's eyes had the appearance of being forcibly kept open. He professed deep interest in the poem, however, and Mr. Burns began, with an easy, swinging rhythm,—

> "Anon, at th' portal of life's pearly gate,
>   Youths and maidens in expectancy wait ;
>   And a rosy curtain is drawn aside,
>   And they catch a glimpse of a silver tide,—
>   (That is brighter than any stream that flows !)—
>   Upon its banks in luxuriance grows
>   The floweret that lovers love so well !
>   It has such a tender legend to tell."

Mr. Courtenay interrupted to ask, "You don't wish me to 'scan' it, do you? The mechanical part is all right, I suppose——"

"I care very little about the mechanical part," said Burns; "leave that to school-boys."

"Aha ! I like your independence," said Burr, "but they tell us that the highest freedom is in keeping the law. You must put your own will into harmony with the Superior Will."

"What has the Superior Will to do with my rhymes?" Mr. Burns exclaimed.

"Everything. The smallest thing you do is measured by a fixed and immutable principle. You are imperfect, inasmuch as you fall short of the measure. There are a good many principles even in rhyming; there is meter, for instance."

"I shall not be at very great pains to oblige meter," said Mr. Burns. "I am after the soul of poetry, not the body."

"Then you limit me in my office of critic and commentator," said Burr, patiently. "But no matter, so that we understand each other."

> "And when lovers part, as they sometimes do,
>   Believing each other divinely true,
>   It is meet to exchange a token then,
>   A souvenir until they meet again ;
>   She gives him a lock of her silken hair,
>   Which he puts near his heart and keeps it there;
>   And he—though assured of his happy lot—
>   He clasps in her hand a *forget-me-not*.

> "Now the impulse to leave a voice behind
>   To keep his mem'ry in the loved one's mind,
>   (And perhaps, too, to keep intruders out),
>   Shows distrust; or, at least, implies a doubt.

> She loves and believes, and has ne'er a thought
> That the beautiful dream may come to naught;
> She recks not the months, nor the years, I ween,
> All the changeful years that may intervene.
> For if change *should* come, why,—confident elf!—
> The change, of course, *could but be in herself.*
> And here is a text that's true to the letter:
> A change in oneself is a change for the better."

Mr. Courtenay made a gesture of dissent. "My experience goes to show that woman is constant," said he. "If anything, too constant."

"Your experience differs from that of most men," said Mr. Burns, dryly.

"Not from your own, I think," said Burr.

Mr. Burns read on,—

> "If harm ever comes to the sweet love-plan,
> The fault, you must know, is not in the man;
> It is she, it is she, the fickle and fair,
> Who gave him a lock of her beautiful hair;
> And who has in a casket, unforgot,
> A faded and scentless forget-me-not.
>
> "The life of that flower is frail and brief,
> But so long as a crumpled, withered leaf
> Remains, still to chant its sad, sweet refrain,
> Its tender plea is not made in vain.
> She may break her vow, and may prove untrue,—
> It is what the world expects her to do!
> 'Tis her privilege, too,—you cannot ignore it,—
> And society gives her license for it."

Mr. Burns paused to take up another sheet, and Mr. Courtenay started as though he had forgotten himself and what was required of him.

"It's a—a pastoral, isn't it, Charley?" he asked.

"A pastoral!" said Mr. Burns.

Mr. Courtenay, as critic and commentator, was a little crestfallen at having made the mistake.

"Ah! I thought it might be a pastoral,—from the forget-me-nots,—or a—a lyric?"

Unheeding the last venture, Mr. Burns read on. At the next pause Mr. Courtenay said, in somewhat languid tones, "It has a very dulcet rhythm, Charley, glides along like a—a—like a midsummer night's dream."

The comparison was so soothingly suggestive that the

D*

lids drooped over his eyes, and he felt an exquisite temptation to drift off into the land of sleep and visions.

"Are you getting sleepy?" Mr. Burns asked, a little suspiciously.

"Oh, no," said Burr, opening his eyes and staring resolutely. But he was drowsy to his finger-tips. "The light shines in my eyes," he explained, winking them pretty fast. "I believe my eyes are a little weak of late."

"I'll drop the shade over the lamp," said Mr. Burns. He did so, and then resumed the poem. A gentle snore arrested him, and he stopped and leaned over and peered into Burr's face, and a look of profound disgust curled his lip. He gathered up his papers, and took the lamp and went back into the office, looked at his watch, crammed the manuscript into the desk, and went to bed himself. As he crawled in behind Burr, that excellent commentator muttered, "Very soo—soothing, Charley; seems like a—a—seems—like—a—d-r-e-a-m."

Mr. Burns turned his face to the wall, with the feeling that one need never expect perfect sympathy in this world. In a little while he had gathered up his internal forces and resolved upon a philosophical self-dependence.

Meantime, the young ladies in the house on the hill,—neither of whom was the deacon's daughter, the elder, Evelyn Clyde, being his orphan niece, and the younger, Maggie Atherton, being his wife's orphan niece,—after bidding Mr. Courtenay "good-evening," an hour or so after that witching period of time is supposed by the vulgar world to merge into night, blew out the parlor- and hall-lamps (for the rest of the household had long been asleep), and tiptoed up-stairs, lighted by the moon. For the wind had swept the clouds aside, and the moon and stars were throwing their soft light in at the windows.

"What a lovely evening!" Evelyn exclaimed, still laboring under the delusion that the hour was not far advanced. She knelt by the window and drew aside the white curtain,—not to admire the night, that was an innocent little deception, but to watch the tall form gliding away through the still, white light, and to listen to his firm foot-falls on the frozen ground. Oh, beautiful moon, beautiful stars! can they make hearts so happy? or does the happy heart make night so beautiful?

He is gone. Out of sight, out of sound. And the night, and the light, and the stillness are left alone; except the soughing of the wind in the tall poplars stuck, at intervals, all around the deacon's premises.

Maggie has nothing for which to thank the night and the moon, and so she lights the lamp on the dressing-table and tucks her brown curls into a night-cap, and proceeds, sadly and in a quiet, matter-of-fact way, to get ready for bed. She kneels at the bedside and breathes an habitual prayer; and still Evelyn kneels at the window and breathes a different prayer, with more heart in it.

"Evelyn," Maggie calls from the white pillow on which she has lain her pink, sorrowful cheek.

"What, dear?" Evelyn springs up, and comes and stoops down and kisses her, rather in the exuberance of her own happiness and triumph than of affection for Maggie. Though she is fond of Maggie in her way, which is rather a proud and imperious way.

"Did you want anything?"

"No; but it's late," said Maggie, and shut her eyes, for there were tears in them, which she did not care to have Evelyn see.

So Evelyn turns away and goes to the dressing-table, and takes down and brushes her long, beautiful hair, feeling a vague thankfulness for her own beauty mirrored in the glass before her. Her heart beats, and her cheeks burn, and her eyes are more blue and intense in their brightness than the sapphire drops depending from her delicate ears.

She is beautiful, and very queenly in figure and bearing; wonderfully so to-night, Maggie thinks, watching her furtively and half envying her.

Though Maggie's faith in Mr. Courtenay was not so great as Evelyn's. She doubted the sincerity of his polished and courteous attentions. Sometimes she wanted to say as much, but Evelyn was too proud, and cold, and unapproachable on such subjects for her to venture.

Mr. Burns she knew to be the soul of truth. She could believe in every word and act of his. But, alas!

his words and acts in the direction of love-making to herself had been so few. She had weighed them all, and they were hardly sufficient to balance the smallest hope that he might care for her.

To-night she made a resolution founded on the conviction that he certainly did not care for her,—and clinched her plump hands in token of its fixedness,—that she would never, never think of him again ! And went to sleep with two bright tears tracking a pathway down her round, rosy cheeks.

The deacon and his wife had sat up a little later than usual, hoping the parlor visitor would depart, and leave the young ladies at liberty to come out and attend to the evening devotions,—a ceremony in which the young ladies took no very active interest. At last the deacon arose, and put away his newspaper, and Mrs. Clyde wound up her yarn and stuck the needles in the ball and put it away, and then pushed the lamp-stand a little nearer the deacon's arm-chair and laid thereon the family Bible. The deacon crossed over to poke the fire, and wondered if the girls wouldn't soon be out.

"Better not wait for 'em, father," said Mrs. Clyde. They called each other "father" and "mother" still, though there were none left of five children who had called them so, and who were all lying asleep in various places in the green earth, with white slabs above them. Two in a peaceful cemetery, hundreds of miles away, and three on a battle-field, where the grass grew rank above them, being fed with blood. "They do sit up so late when them young men come up from town," Mrs. Clyde continued, in a not displeased tone, being secretly proud of the distinction conferred on her girls by the attentions of the talented young men, but never compromising her matronly dignity by appearing to consider it a distinction. She was far too proud and too discreet for that.

"Yes, a *leetle* too late," the deacon responded, readily.

"Oh, well, young folks is young folks, they must have their day," said Mrs. Clyde, defensively. She might have added that they must also have their way, sometimes. Maggie was very docile and obedient, but was inclined to follow Evelyn's example. And Evelyn brooked little constraint. Though she never did anything more flagrant than staying home from church and absenting herself from prayers when she chose (some unguarded expressions of Mr. Courtenay's having led her to regard religion as old-fogyish,—and in which Mr. Courtenay was culpable, inasmuch as he took away from her a faith which she had leaned upon in an unquestioning, child's way, and gave her nothing in return,—a kind of swindling somewhat extensively practised in this land, though perhaps the perpetrators vindicate themselves by declaring their victims incapable of receiving what they would give). Miss Clyde also reserved to herself the right of going where she pleased, doing what she liked, and accepting attentions from gentlemen at her own discretion. In point of propriety there is no doubt Miss Clyde was perfectly competent to guide herself aright, owing to an inherent dignity of character that underlay all her motives and actions.

<hr>

CHAPTER IV.

THE Sunday following Mr. Courtenay's visit at the deacon's he proposed to Mr. Burns that they should attend church in the evening, adding that it was quarterly meeting, and the presiding elder would preach.

"Do you hold that out as an inducement?" Mr. Burns asked.

"I thought it might have some weight," said Burr.

"Well, you are mistaken; it has none whatever. The one item of Methodism I object to is the presiding elder. That is, I am passive in regard to the other items, but I am actively opposed to that. It has always seemed to me that that high dignitary was chosen with as much reference to his physical endowments as to his spiritual and intellectual."

"Well," said Mr. Courtenay, "it is true there are some fine-looking men in that body of divines; but why a man should be objected to, even for a sacred office, on account of a good corporeal development, is not plain to me."

"His corporeal development is not a thing to be considered in the question of a man's fitness for a sacred office," said Mr. Burns.

"Do you know, Charles, that the kings of Israel were chosen on that same ground to which you object?"

"The kings of Israel are swept off the boards; the world is done with them. They symbolized the highest idea of the people, no doubt, in their day; but now we don't care for the outside of a man, we are after what is in him."

"Waiving that," said Burr, "shall we go? It is time to be thinking of it, if we do."

After a moment's deliberation, Mr. Burns arose and went into the back-room and got himself ready. When they were about stepping out, Mr. Courtenay remarked, carelessly, "I thought perhaps we had better escort the young ladies to church this evening."

"If that is your intention you must excuse me," said Mr. Burns, and turned and threw his gloves upon the table and flung himself into a chair.

"Charley, what is the matter? What has come over you of late?" said Burr.

"Old memories."

"Damn old memories!" Burr exclaimed with sudden fierceness, as though he had them under his heel.

Mr. Burns looked up sharply, as though it might be possible to get a glimpse of his friend's inner consciousness at this moment through the crevice made by his sudden outburst.

But the flash of Burr's temper was like a flash of lightning in pitch darkness.

He bit his lip, and then said, a little sadly, "There is comfort to me in this, Charley; whatever we get, in this life, is probably the right thing. Or whether it is or not, we don't seem to have the sole ordering of our affairs. If we did, very few of us would be just where we are. However different our life might have been from what it has been, we should doubtless have old memories and regrets and remorse all the same. Then why not make the best of what is, and ' Let the dead past bury its dead ' ?"

" If one could !" said Mr. Burns.

" But even then I don't know as one should. There are some errors and mistakes we ought to suffer for."

" Deliberate errors and mistakes," said Burr ; " I admit one ought to be punished for intentional wrong-doing."

" There wouldn't be much wrong-doing if all the wrong done were deliberately planned beforehand," said Mr. Burns. " Not half the evil in the world results from cold-blooded intention."

" Well, however that may be," said Burr, "take up your gloves and come on. I will vouch for it that Miss Maggie is not going to break her stout little heart for you. Don't flatter yourself so much. You are getting morbid on this subject."

Mr. Burns got up. " Maybe you are right," said he.

A few minutes later, passing up the street on their way to the deacon's, they observed the resident clergyman of the Methodist order striding across to the place of worship to make sure that the lights and the fires were in proper trim ; fearing—possibly from some previous negligence—that the employé in the light and fire line was not to be implicitly relied upon.

" Poor fellow !" said Mr. Burns, with a sympathetic shrug, " he looks blue and chilly in his threadbare broadcloth."

" Not to speak of his ungloved hands," said Burr, who had a horror of numb fingers. " By the way," he asked, " is black broadcloth a church ordinance ?"

" I believe it has always been the canonical costume for orthodox clergymen," said Mr. Burns ; " but perhaps modern civilization will justify its being grown out of shortly."

The minister bowed clerically, that is to say, gravely, for it was Sabbath evening ; and besides, the young attorneys were of doubtful piety according to his reckoning, and it behooves a minister of the gospel to preserve the church dignity in his own person in presence of the worldly-minded.

They, on their part, gave the graceful military salute

habitual with them, though perhaps with an accent of mock deference, and passed on with their rapid, even strides.

"Who would be a fanatic!" exclaimed Mr. Burns. "I would rather be bereft of one of my five senses than have any part of my brain overcast or any faculty of my mind shackled."

"I venture to say that the fanatics have done more to push things forward in this world than the philosophers," said Burr. "Give one of them an idea,—they are essentially one-idea men,—and see how he will drive ahead with it. They are the working-men. If not exactly at the head of affairs, they are the tools that cooler and wiser men use in adjusting them. Fanaticism has been one of the boldest, most persistent, indefatigable, devoted, self-sacrificing powers ever set in motion upon the earth. It is like steam: all you have got to do is to get a steady-handed, clear-headed engineer to keep it going in the right direction. The philosopher sees all sides, his mind is a world of light; the fanatic's is but fractionally illuminated, but the darkened half is an added power propelling the one bright idea. Philosophy brings out all things; fanaticism throws out its head-light and shows us but one. In other words, it is concentration."

"I would rather not concentrate," said Mr. Burns, with a shrug.

"Fanaticism is apparently more consistent than philosophy," Burr continued.

"Consistent! I used to order my life by that word," Mr. Burns interrupted. "But I have repudiated it; it is treacherous and tyrannical. If you lay yourself out to be consistent, every step you take is a stake set up marking your boundaries; you will soon be completely hedged in. You make to-day the governor of to-morrow, and so on until you have narrowed your life down to the smallest compass. Of all things in the world I hate constraint, self-imposed or imposed by others."

"You are controlled by it more than any other man I know," said Burr, coolly.

"No; you mistake. Conscientiousness is not constraint. I hate a rule, but I believe in the law. No man shall handcuff me with his opinions; 'I'll not endure it.'"

"Regarding this idea of consistency," said Burr. "It is not necessary to carry it up into psychology; we are not governed by precedent in ethics as we are in logic."

They had arrived at the deacon's door and rung the bell. Bridget appeared, smiling all over her comely, Irish face, and ushered them into the parlor, which was vacant. The young ladies, she said, were up-stairs getting ready for church.

"Will you please say to the young ladies that Mr. Courtenay and myself wish to accompany them to church?" said Mr. Burns, with an assurance that Burr chided him for when the girl's back was turned.

"What's the use mincing the thing? they won't refuse," said he, moving about and examining the pictures on the walls.

"You might have put it more courteously," said Mr. Courtenay.

The prismatic lamp was burning on the marble-topped centre-table, and a comfortable fire glowed in the polished wood-stove. The room was very pretty, and had a cosy, delightful air that young ladies of taste can give to a pretty room. And these were young ladies of taste, though perhaps not much beside. They were very well bred and moderately educated, having spent a few terms at an academy before coming West. They had accomplished but little in music. Miss Clyde played a few set pieces, but never descended to jigs and hornpipes. And Maggie, being of a housewifely turn, was given to chirruping little snatches of old-fashioned song while going about her work in dining-room and kitchen, and seldom touched the piano, so that that beautiful instrument was rather an uninteresting piece of furniture in the deacon's parlor, being held in about the same respect as the tables and chairs. The young ladies were unacquainted with its wonderful resources, and the poor, cumbersome thing passed unappreciated, like many another poor thing that is pulsing with unheard music.

Mr. Courtenay seated himself luxuriously in a stuffed rocking-chair, and Mr. Burns, who had a sort of instinctive, tender sympathy with all musical instruments, though he had never cultivated their acquaintance much, sat down to the piano and began playing softly, "Those Evening Bells."

He was still drawing forth his little melody with a delicate and dreamy touch, when the young ladies' steps came lightly down the stairs. The door opened, and there was a rustling of silk, and the room was flooded with a faint perfume—and a presence. The latter belonged to Miss Clyde. Burr felt its magnetism, and towered up grandly from the rocking-chair.

There was, of course, a general recognition all round, but these two instantly absorbed each other.

Maggie, a little pale and tremulous, followed in Miss Clyde's wake, and Mr. Burns's eyes, as he turned around upon the piano-stool and stood up, sought her face.

Some eyes always have an earnest look whether they mean it or not, and whether from depth of soul or depth of color. Mr. Burns had such eyes, deep-set, glowing, intense.

Maggie blushed under them, and thought, "Oh, surely he does care for me!" and straightway suspended her fixed resolution never to think of him again.

How could she help it? He was magnetic to her, he thrilled her with an ecstatic delight in the very sound of his voice and touch of his hand; even in the outlines of his face and figure. He had once lent her a book from the office, saturated with cigar-smoke, and Evelyn had said, "Bah, how odious!" But to Maggie it was sweeter than patchouly. It was a breath from the atmosphere in which they lived.

"Is it time for church?" Mr. Courtenay asked.

"Nearly, I think," said Miss Clyde, seating herself, and drawing on her gloves.

Mr. Burns resumed the piano-stool.

"You were playing?" said Miss Clyde.

No one would ever think her at a loss for words to carry on a conversation. One rather suspected her of a good deal of reserved force. She was quiet and stately, and those qualities added to the idea of statuesqueness which Burr admired in her.

"I was drumming a little," said Mr. Burns.

"Won't you sing us something before we go?"

"We have hardly time, have we?"

"Oh, yes, please!" said Maggie, with eloquent eyes.

Mr. Burns could not often be induced to make an exhibition of himself, as he phrased it, but now he turned around and touched the keys and sang with thrilling pathos, "Come ye Disconsolate."

His voice had a rare, penetrating power, like his eyes. When he had finished he arose abruptly, and took up his hat. Maggie's eyelashes glistened with tears.

There was a general movement, and they started. Outside the gate Mr. Burns offered Maggie his arm, and walked fast to avoid anything like sentiment. Burr and Miss Clyde came on slowly, for the opposite reason. Not that Miss Clyde was sentimental,—she was rather matter-of-fact, and not at all subject to fine emotion, except the fine emotion of love.

The moon was shining, and hosts of glittering stars were pointing earthward.

Mr. Burns descanted on the most unpoetical of subjects: the bleakness of the prairies in winter, the fierceness of the winds, and the probabilities of a milder season than usual; all of which topics were of general interest, and could hardly fail of entertaining any young woman who had the good of the country at heart; and Maggie answered, yes, the prairies were bleak, and the winds and the winter storms were dreadful; but the Indian summer was beautiful, and sometimes it stretched to almost Christmas (Maggie was an older resident than Mr. Burns), and it was splendid to go nutting.

But, now and then, a little unconscious sigh fluttered up, and Mr. Burns, glancing down, felt an impulse to tuck the small gloved hand more snugly and warmly under his arm.

It occurred to him that Maggie was a little paler than usual, her cheeks seemed less rounded and rosy, and he ventured to remark upon it, and asked if she were not feeling well.

"I, not feeling well?"

The surprised brown eyes flashed up at him, brimming

with shy tenderness in the moonlight, and a pink flush spread itself over her face.   There was a great deal of prettiness about Maggie, the freshness and bloom of youth.

"Oh, yes.   I don't know what it is to be sick," she said, and the long lashes drooped again on the peachy cheeks.

Mr. Burns strode on a little faster.   They were nearing the place of worship.

High-Water-Mark had not yet advanced sufficiently in religious and financial importance to erect church buildings, and so devout services were conducted every Sabbath morning and evening in the village school-house,— the only available place.

Two ministers of different—and it might be added, incompatible—denominations (though the ministers themselves were upon excellent terms with each other) preached, on alternate Sundays, to about the same congregation.

A village school-house is apt to be an untidy and somewhat unhallowed place.   This one was.   But a janitor had been employed by the several boards of trustees of church matters to make a business of sweeping and dusting, and arranging the humble furniture every Saturday afternoon, with reference to the day following, thereby sanctifying the profane edifice for religious exercises.   The seats were rude, notched, pencil-marked, and otherwise marred and defaced.   Notwithstanding, there were a few aristocratic ladies—including the ladies at Deacon Clyde's —who spread their elegant folds of silk and cashmere upon them, and exhibited lovely bonnets in remarkable bass-relief to the background of disreputable black-board and dirty, whitewashed walls.

"I think we had better not wait for those two," said Mr. Burns, glancing back as they reached the school-house, and laying his hand on the door-knob.   By chance he seated Maggie and himself on the same bench with Sarah Jenkins and her lover, who, it appeared, had come to an amicable understanding.

Mr. Courtenay and Miss Clyde entered and took a back seat.   The back seats were usually left for the aristocracy, but sometimes a number of ungodly boys got into them.

It was so upon this occasion, but they scuttled away, speedily and with little noise, at the approach of "Lawyer Courtenay."

Soon the minister and the elder entered, and marched down the aisle, hats in hand and hands kid-gloved. The minister, "poor fellow," as Mr. Burns had irreverently called him, had assumed clerical dignity in the shape of a long buttoned-up overcoat.

Mr. Burns speculated on the difference between running over, in thin clothes, to poke the fires and trim the lights, and marching in stately order and full equipment of heavy garments to perform the solemn duties of the sanctuary.

The presiding elder was a man of fine appearance, with a military suggestiveness in his clothes and bearing. He was learned and eloquent, and was much praised and admired; though, perhaps, not well understood in his finest passages and best declamation by the greater part of his audience, but commanded all the more reverence for that; for it is true of our superstitious nature that whatever is a little mysterious to us commands our high regard. That which comes down to a level with our understanding, fails, in a measure, of our respect. Is this egotism or modesty? I am inclined to the latter on behalf of this congregation, for, surely, if they could go straight through the elder's sermon, from beginning to end, it wouldn't be much of a sermon! I don't know but the Roman Catholics are right with their Latin, after all; there is policy in it as regards poor, ignorant humanity.

The elder had selected for his text the remarkable declaration, "Ye must be born again," and treated it in much the usual manner. The discourse was not referred to on the way back to the deacon's, but when the door had closed upon the young ladies, Mr. Burns remarked, "It struck me, to-night, what an extraordinary injunction that is."

"The text?" asked Burr, who had the same thought in his mind.

"Yes. What a subject if he could but have handled it! But what a subject to preach to that congregation! One of the profoundest declarations in all Scripture."

"He simplified it, however," said Burr, smiling.

"Yes, he simplified it as some of our hard words are simplified by their no less hard definitions. Do you know, Burr, I have heard but a very few sermons in my life that did not outrage my feelings. Take this: The sins of the fathers shall be visited upon the children. I have felt my blood boil with indignation over sermons preached from that text; and yet, how just and perfect is the law when we understand it! If ministers could get behind this literalism and bring to light the soul-life of these texts! Every one of them is a rock which needs to be struck with an Aaron-rod to make the living waters gush. They preach 'Christ, and him crucified,' and every time they do it they crucify us. Mankind will never imbibe real, Christian principles merely through pity for Him who suffered. We do not accept the fact that the earth is round because Galileo was punished for declaring it. I hold that I am a Christian myself, and that Christ is the Saviour of mankind. His philosophy will stand the test of all ages and remain the foundation of all goodness, because it is truth. But I can never allow myself to be classified with those who are *technically* called Christians. They persist in offering sacrifice to Christ the Individual, and I wish to found myself upon Christ the Principle. The highest devotion is in observing and following the teachings of those whom we would honor."

When they got back home, the fire had burned low and the lamps were glimmering faintly. The law-office was not a room or suite of rooms in a brick "block," or other mammoth building, as is usual in more pretentious cities, but was a little independent structure, with a bedroom in the rear.

CHAPTER V.

MR. BURNS was an early riser. That is, he was much in advance of Mr. Courtenay in point of getting up.

The following morning being a sharp, bright November morning, shortly after Jack Wilds, a lad employed about the premises to make fires and bring in fuel, and feed and curry the horse in the stable back of the office, had performed these several duties and retired, he arose and underwent his usual copious ablutions at the wash-stand; after which he applied an energetic brush to his hair, which, it suddenly occurred to him, was getting rather long, and, being of a curly nature, rather troublesome. Then he went out into the office, took up his hat, flung the before-mentioned blue cloak around him, and, with his hand on the door-knob, called to Burr to get up and come on, he was going to breakfast. It appeared to be a mere matter of form, for, without waiting for a response, he stepped out and proceeded down-street to the hotel, and Burr slumbered on.

Breakfast over, he went into the barber-shop and got his hair cut, and returned to the office and entered upon his poem again with that vigor of thought and freshness of spirit that come with a bracing air and a fair appetite to the tolerably young.

Mr. Burns did not feel himself young; it seemed to him that he had been through everything, and was a good deal bruised and cut up. But he still possessed the power of throwing off his burdens now and then, and letting himself up into a freer air.

He was still scratching away with zeal when Burr appeared at the door of the little back-room, good-natured and handsome as an Apollo, with his black hair brushed back.

"Why didn't you call me, Charley?" he asked; and that being his standing morning inquiry, Mr. Burns gave it the customary answer without looking up.

"I did call you."

Burr returned, half skeptically, "I didn't hear you," and went back to complete his toilet.

He presently came out with his great-coat buttoned up to the chin,—he took excellent care of himself,—put on his hat (not a silk hat, silk hats were at variance with High-Water-Mark etiquette, except for the minister), and then *he* went down to breakfast.

Upon his return, finding Mr. Burns still busily writing, he inquired with sudden, renewed interest after the poem. Since that night they had not mentioned it; Mr. Burns had felt a little indignant and Burr conscience-smitten. That, however, was wearing off.

Mr. Burns held up an extended legal-cap sheet closely written.

"What! have you written all that?" exclaimed Burr. "Really, Charley, you are developing a surprising faculty."

"No; not developing, only exercising," said Mr. Burns. "My faculties all came to light years ago. I am not conscious of anything latent. Think I made as good rhymes at fifteen as I do now."

Mr. Courtenay lit a cigar and took up a newspaper.

Mr. Burns, turning again to the desk, wrote on until his poetic impulse was exhausted, and then came around to the stove, disposed to talk.

"I wonder if the 'Comet' will be out to-day?" said he. He referred to the local periodical.

Burr laid down his paper. "It is difficult to say; the 'Comet' is a luminary not to be depended on like the fixed planets. It is, as its name implies, of a meteoric character, appearing and disappearing at uncertain intervals."

"Given its appearances I can calculate to a degree of accuracy its disappearances," said Mr. Burns, with a laugh. He used the "Comet" to rub the windows and lamp-chimneys, it being printed on soft, pulpy paper, almost as pliable as a rag, and rags were scarce.

Just while they were speaking the printer's boy came in with a damp number of the "Comet" neatly folded. It was a courtesy the editor always showed the attorneys, sending their paper *per express*, instead of leaving it in the post-office.

Mr. Burns signified the customary "thank you," and the boy went out.

"Run over the locals," said Burr, "and see what has been going on in the neighborhood."

Mr. Burns read a few items about the weather,—Row in the Lim'rick Settlement,—Elopement in Winchester, "man of fifty runs off with hired girl, leaving wife and children."

"A striking commentary on the human affections,"

said Burr; "proves the truth of the poetic sentiment that the heart never grows old."

"Here is a railroad item," said Mr. Burns. "'Reliable information.' Humph! I have built too many delusive hopes on reliable information respecting railroads."

"Let's hear it," said Burr.

"'P. and Q. R. R. Company intend, as soon as spring opens, to begin work, and push through rapidly, on the North-Western line.'"

"Which route, I wonder?" said Burr; "though I suppose they will wait to determine that until they have ascertained who will pay the greater bonus. Is that all it says about it?"

"That is the gist of it; the editor appends some remarks."

"Never mind the editor's remarks; I hold them to be worthless upon any subject," said Burr.

"What is the good of continually imposing upon the people's credulity?" exclaimed Mr. Burns, throwing the paper aside. "The prospects for a railroad have been just as brilliant ever since we came here as they are now."

"Good heavens, Charley! have a little patience," said Burr. "Everything can't be done in a day."

"Something might be accomplished in a lifetime," Mr. Burns returned; "if a man had a dozen lives it would be different. But only one! and that slipping out of our grasp and we looking on quietly and letting it go."

Burr, apprehensive that his friend was bent on working himself up into one of his gloomy states, bethought him of the poem as a diversion, and requested to hear a few more stanzas read.

Mr. Burns presently went to the desk and took out his manuscript, and, ignoring the fact that his critic had probably slept through the last dozen lines or so, began where he had left off:

> " Ev'n Shakspeare, woman's most gallant defender,
>   Who praised the sex as so gentle and tender,
>   And otherwise lovable,—even he
>   Thought best with th' world on this point to agree;
>   Lamenting th' frailty of woman, that she
>   Is th' definition of ' Inconstancy.'

> " And how unjust that a person should be
> Adjudged, alone, by what others may see,
> Who see but the surface!   And then connect—
> As mathematicians—cause and effect."

" Are you sure that last is an entirely original simile?" asked Mr. Courtenay, interrupting.

"I could not swear to it," Mr. Burns admitted. "And just here let me state, once for all, that very frequently a thought glides off my pen that appears strangely familiar to me, though I have no recollection of any previous knowledge of it."

" Your position disarms criticism on the score of plagiarism," said Burr, feeling that his office as critic was becoming somewhat circumscribed. "However, it only proves the truth of what I said some time back: all paths are so trodden, and thought is so universal upon all subjects that are thought about at all, that there is no new thing to be said."

"Another thing that I have observed," said Mr. Burns, "is, that when I take up a subject and think hard upon it, and elicit—as I flatter myself—a new idea from it, I immediately begin to see it floating about in current literature, showing that other minds have been busy with the same thought."

"That is the result, Charley, of the uniform cultivation of mental soil. Each era in the public mind is marked with some general cast of thought. And when the people of any period bring their intellectual energies to bear upon a given question (which the people of all periods do), the natural deduction is that many of them will develop the same ideas. Every man's thought is a part of the capital stock of the age."

Mr. Burns fell into a speculative silence, which Burr filled up with smoking. By and by he remarked, " What we were speaking of a moment ago, Burr, our familiarity with a new thought, as if we had known it before, in our present consciousness, or in some pre-existent state——"

" Pray don't found yourself on a pre-existent state, Charley," Burr interrupted. "A future state is more than many of us dare aspire to in this day of skepticism. Though I have a theory," he added, speculatively, removing his cigar and blowing a slender column of smoke upward and watching its ascent, "that this essence which we call soul is simply the breath of the Infinite, blown now upon this instrument, and now upon that. It may be that this spirit within me has lived in a thousand others before me, and will still go on living after me."

"Do you suppose," said Mr. Burns, "that there can be a proper continuation of this life of ours if our personality is destroyed and our consciousness cut off? Why, there is nothing of us but our consciousness! If a dew-drop loses its identity when it is sucked up by the atmosphere and resolved into vapor, then I contend that the dew-drop is absolutely destroyed. So with us. If a man is to go through some change in which he loses his former self, it seems to me that this immortality which we so long for is no object to him, but merely to the Power that wishes to perpetuate existence in these changing forms. What puppets we are! Man's struggles are vain. God rules over all; it is his concern, not ours."

"Man's struggles, I suspect, are a part of God's plan," said Burr. "I should like to be enlightened as to what purpose they serve. Probably they belong to the refining process."

"I wonder if it would be any satisfaction to us," said Mr. Burns, "to account for all our grievances by believing that we thus help on toward some Higher Life which —though it might even be a sort of continuation and refinement of our own—we should yet have no actual consciousness of."

Mr. Courtenay laughed. "All the way up from the lowest insect," said he, "the animal creation are devouring one another. The poor beasts that suffer death to feed the lives of men have no realization of the importance of their office,—and I doubt its being any comfort to them if they had. So, perhaps (though in a far higher and finer sense), out of our miserable existence is extracted some purified form of being that we have no more conception of than the brute has of ours."

"That is what I am afraid of," said Mr. Burns. "If I could but believe that throughout the eternal ages I should still be *I*. Good God! it seems to me a soul—

a living, absorbing, conscious soul—is too precious a thing to be dropped into oblivion! That you, Burr (for instance), with all your splendid accomplishments, with your grand intellect, comprehending in its small but wonderful space the wisdom of centuries, should drop into the ground and become nothing!"

Burr shrugged his shoulders.

"Don't be personal, Charley," said he; "it isn't pleasant. By the way, I did not suppose you thought this 'I' of so much consequence. I remember when we were discussing a similar question the other evening, you took the opposite side."

"It was not a similar question," said Mr. Burns; "I meant then that I did not care for marked distinction among my fellow-beings, that it was of little importance where I was placed in the body of humanity. In my relation, as a human being, with the universe, I want to be *I.* I don't want to be smothered out of sight."

After a little silence he took up the poem again.

> " Let him who has never yet missed a bird
> That he aimed at, give his honor's word,
> If ev'ry result in life that he sees,
> With th' motive beneath it exactly agrees;
> If the outer garb is as nicely refined
> As th' beautiful warp and woof of th' mind.

> " The artist paints, and his soul is on fire;
> And th' world stands by to applaud and admire.
> Yet e'en in his triumph, for some hidd'n cause,
> His soul is unsated with th' world's applause.
> Still his hand and his brain are never at rest;
> Ah! he knows that th' world has not seen his best.
> There are finer gems in his artist-heart
> Than any picture in the Halls of Art."

"That is quite true," interrupted Mr. Courtenay; adding, frankly, "and as trite as it is true, if you will allow me to say so. Of course you express it very felicitously; but there has existed this vexatious fact in the mind of genius ever since a human soul was born, that an ideal can never be fully realized. A painting bears, of course, about the same relation to the artist's conception as a portrait does to the original. And to him—the artist—it is about as satisfactory as would be to you the photograph of the woman you love. The thousand varying shades of the great conception—like the emotions of the soul—are not portrayed. Only those who know the original can see the likeness; also, only those who by inspiration, as it were, or by kinship of soul, can make of the painting a gate through which to enter the artist's realm of fancy, can know the picture. The artist—and none the less the poet—at best, but gives the world a photograph. Genuine poetry is that which is lived; that which is written is but a description of it; and those who write it most often lack it in their lives! A soul must give out life to something, or in something, as a tree gives out leaves and blossoms, and fruit, and germs for other trees. It is oftenest seen in the social and domestic circles, of course; but lacking this, or soaring beyond it, the inspiration of living bursts through other channels, and we have poems, and paintings, and sculpture, and music, that are neither more nor less than souls photographed. And they are the mirrors in which we may behold ourselves,—the farthest stretch of the possible in us,—so that we sometimes exclaim, I, too, am a poet,—or a painter,—or a sculptor. Genius is not so rare a thing as we are inclined to think; the most of us have a spark of it hid away somewhere in our nature. Many of us obscure mortals bound up responsive, as soon as the magnet is held over us, showing that we have the faculty, if not the power, of genius. I sit here in my dingy office, little and unknown, and read Charles Sumner's speeches in the 'Tribune' and fancy myself as big a statesman as he. I may not be able to speak as well as Sumner, or write as well as Emerson, and yet, what these men, and other great minds, set forth, I may feel to be the measure of myself. And what would these men do without me to appreciate them? The world will advance through me as well as through them. We may not all be able to keep up with our leaders, but the next best thing is to follow close after them. It seems to me that the worst thing in the world to contend with is stupidity. It tears my heart, even at this day, to remember Socrates."

"Allow me to ask," said Mr. Burns, who had been for some time trying to sandwich a question between Burr's rapid sentences, "if, laying aside his attempts, mistakes, and achievements, a man is as great as his best thoughts?"

"You might as well ask if one would measure a river when it is swollen with spring rains! However, when you come to bridging it, you have got to bridge above high-water mark. You must judge an individual by his life and character,—the even flow of days and years. Still, when you attempt to measure his capacity you must allow for high tides; for a man, as well as a river, may go out of and beyond himself. Inspirational moments do not materially affect the even tenor of our lives, but they leave an impression always. Every soul that ebbs and flows will mark high-tide on the borders of its life. But go on with the reading, we have diverged."

Mr. Burns did not look upon himself as an inspired writer; his poem was not a spontaneous effusion such as Burr's æsthetic taste demanded, but a laborious undertaking.

There was a time when he had felt a good deal of poetic enthusiasm, but it proved itself to have been but the effervescence of youthful hope, ardor, and ambition. Thousands have experienced it, and drained it off like the froth from champagne before life has fairly begun.

He continued :

> "This conscious, mighty power of soul to feel,
> Beyond man's utmost power to reveal,
> Shows all the weakness—and the strength—of earth,
> And proves the soul is of immortal birth.
>
> "That point we reach where we cannot impart
> What we feel, to another human heart,
> Where the highest earthly intelligence
> Stops, and no cunning trick of mortal sense
> Can reveal to man what we might convey
> To spirit, uncumbered with mortal clay,
> Is the limit of earthly capacity,—
> The beginning of immortality.
>
> "Here is the germ of everlasting life,
> With which e'en savage, pagan hearts are rife;
> This longing after closer sympathy
> Than friend can give, however dear he be.
>
> "'Twixt spirits there is (at least there must be)
> A perfect and exquisite sympathy.

> Ev'n souls clay-embodied, and thus far concealed,
> Are oftentimes to each other revealed,
> In a measure. Oh, what rapture to feel
> The power to know what sense cannot reveal!
>
> " It is this divine power through which we see
> Something of love's most strange, sweet mystery.
> And love, oh, love is a beautiful thing l
> Perhaps it belongs but to Life's Young Spring ;
> For so many hearts are withered and old,
> And devoid of love, sear, desolate, cold.
>
> " If once the sweet buds of promise sprung
> About these cold hearts when they were young,
> And were snatched, and ruined. and trampled on,
> And the sad heart left with its pain alone,
> Could it take up the ' burden of life' again,
> And still live on, and outlive the pain ?
> Can one who has lost all the beauty of life
> Still join in the world's hard battle and strife,
> And grasp a pittance, 'mid the noise and din,
> Instead of the crown he had hoped to win ?
> Does life still go on when its zest is fled,
> Or the soul still pulse when all hope is dead ?"

"Do you propound these questions seriously, my dear Charles?" Mr. Courtenay inquired. "Because it is not right to look upon life in that desponding way. There is no occasion for hope to die or life to lose its zest. I maintain that every man is the arbiter of his own destiny."

"Not flattering to either of us," said Mr. Burns, with a bitter smile.

Mr. Courtenay continued: "If somebody knocks you down, get up again; the matter lies only between you and him, and the world moves on. If circumstances go against you, fight your way through them. Life is not made very easy for any of us, I notice. I will tell you where a thousand people fail; they get themselves into a groove too narrow for the contingencies of life, and when disaster comes and cuts off their one resource, the one little channel they have crowded their life into, they are undone. I have known a score of men who, being 'Christians,' have quarrelled with their particular sect, and gone out and straightway renounced their Christianity, simply because their whole idea of religion was embodied in a set of dogmatic principles laid down by a single church organization.　The current of life within us should be so broad and deep that the cutting off of one or more of our little tributaries would never turn the tide out of its course."

Mr. Courtenay ceased speaking, and when it appeared, by his lighting a fresh cigar and beginning to smoke, that he had no further remarks to offer, Mr. Burns resumed :

> "Oh, the world has many a fatal dart
> That—but the world ignores a broken heart !—
> Well, a broken purpose is all the same,
> Or a life that has missed a noble aim ;
> Or a ruined life that one can't reclaim.
> A life or a limb may be broken and lame.
>
> "Yet every dead hope will mem'ry outlast,
> And th' heart remain true to youth's beautiful past.
> Love lies far beneath all the outer strife,—
> Has chiefly to do with one's inner life.
> I mean that rare, delicate sentiment
> That fills the soul with a sweet discontent ;
> And not that regard of a coarser cast,
> That is knocked about in every blast
> Of temper that one's dearest friends may show ;
> 'Tis a different kind of love, you know,—
> A sensitive plant, a floweret rare,
> To be petted and nurtured with tender care.
> Oh, exquisite love !　But its fatal sting
> Can wither a soul to a lifeless thing."

"I don't know that I quite follow you," Mr. Courtenay interrupted.　"The poetry is very nice, but I can with difficulty distinguish between your true sentiments and your irony."

"I can with difficulty distinguish between them myself," said Mr. Burns.　"I am a mystery to myself,—I am full of contradictions."

"Perhaps we may set you down, then, as a philosopher who sees all sides," said Mr. Courtenay, facetiously.

Mr. Burns went on :

> "But the picture of life has two sides, of course ;
> We look to the sensible world t' endorse
> The plainer side, the more practical view,
> Seen from a point not romantic, but true.
>
> "To judge from this practical side 'twould seem
> That love, after all, is only a dream !

Yet th' world will agree that the dream is sweet,
And that earth is heaven when lovers meet;
Ay, that love is life, complete and whole,
The divinest dream of a poet's soul.
That a woman's life down that pearly stream
Would be sweeter still than a poet's dream.
Ay, sweeter far, and her heart is leal,
And true to the *dream*, but—
                         'Life is real.'
Some other considerations, you know,
Must be taken into account; and so,
Tho' th' heart be faithful, and loyal, and true,
Why, perhaps, after all, it wouldn't do
To be rash in the matter, or—as it would seem—
Sacrifice everything else to a *dream*.
Don't rashly declare her love has decreased,
Or that she's inconstant, ' to say the least;'
Or drink to woman's ' frailty' a toast,—
She is only prudent, to say the most.

" Twixt love and the world there's many a strife,
  The world having all the substantials of life;
  And love, though the very charmingest elf,
  Too often has naught to bestow but himself."

"Quite true," said Burr; "sentiment is frequently at variance with the practical concerns of life."

" Who would venture to sea with no visible boat
  Launched on the tide to keep him afloat ?
  Yet thousands embark on this stream of love,
  Nor ask if th' voyage may a safe one prove.
  All alike with hope's joyous wreaths bedecked,
  And happy, but, ah ! some one may be wrecked,
  And thrown back upon the deserted strand,—
  Not drowned, but powerless ever to land
  Again. What a terrible risk to run,
  The risking of life when life's just begun !

" The uncertain future no seer can foretell;
  The maiden but ponders the question well.
  She takes in her hand the withered flower
  In the last fluttering, changeful hour,
  And its sweet voice pleads and her eyes grow dim,
  And her heart turns wistfully back to him.
  To him the loved one,—the loved and lost,—
  For she has already counted the cost,
  And given him up.
                 But a sigh of regret
  Breathes th' heart's allegiance,—she cannot forget.
  ' I loved him,' she says; ' but, ah ! it would seem
  That after all it was but Love's Young Dream.'

c*

> "Yet love's young dream, strangely blended with truth
> In the very uncertain woof of youth,
> Is, even in one's advancing life,
> When one is a tranquil, contented wife,
> Serene in life's placid, calm September,
> A very beautiful dream to remember."

"It is so," said Mr. Courtenay, through his little cloud of smoke, with half-unconscious emphasis. "What! have you finished?"

Mr. Burns had collected his sheets together and laid them on the desk.

"Yes," said he; "I have run aground. I shall have to wait for a fresh impetus and a stiff breeze to fill my sails."

"I hope they will be forthcoming," Mr. Courtenay returned. "I was becoming deeply interested. I am anxious to know how it terminated with the youth. I suspect, however, the aroma of 'love's young dream' hardly lingered about the silken curl so long as about the forget-me-not."

CHAPTER VI.

Mr. Burns had been employed by Deacon Clyde to negotiate for some town lots he wished to purchase of a non-resident. He got the matter arranged, and said to Mr. Courtenay one evening,—

"I think I will walk up to the deacon's and settle this business," having the papers in his hand. "Will you go with me?"

Mr. Courtenay declined.

"Why not?"

"I thought, Charley," said he, looking up quizzically from a German paper he was perusing, "that you had cut yourself off—and wished to cut me off—from going to the deacon's for fear of injury to the young ladies' affections?"

"The young ladies," returned Mr. Burns, "are out of the question in this instance; our business is with the deacon."

"You are very transparent, Charley," said Mr. Courtenay. "I see you are not averse to meeting the young ladies; all you wish to avoid is the responsibility of appearing to seek them. So you smooth away the difficulty with those town lots."

"Of course," returned Mr. Burns, warmly, "I am not such an egotistic fool as to suppose our bare presence and social contact will tell very heavily upon the young ladies. There is no harm in meeting them, the harm is in giving them to think we care for them in a particular way."

"Well, go on," said Burr, resuming his paper; "you have got a fair excuse, make use of it."

There happened to be company at the deacon's. Mr. Burns, armed with his deeds and titles, was ushered into the parlor and introduced to the Rev. Mr. Kirkwood (the Calvinistic minister), his wife, and his wife's nephew, a young Dr. Webster just arrived from the East and newly fledged from a medical college. A worthy young fellow he subsequently proved himself to be, though just now a little offensive to Mr. Burns because of a certain perfume of "Eastern" style and fashion that hung about him, and that is always more or less disagreeable to Western nostrils.

"He'll soon get that taken out of him!" was our cynical attorney's mental reflection.

The doctor had come West to establish himself in his profession. Mr. Burns's first momentary sensation was chagrin at finding himself in such presence, and he was tempted to beat a retreat. But, being very cordially received (the minister and the deacon both standing up to shake hands with him), he gradually expanded. He was extremely susceptible to the influence of a warm social atmosphere.

Mrs. Kirkwood, by whom he found himself seated after the greetings and introductions, turned to him a refined, intelligent face, and launched at once into conversation, which turned finally upon the contrasts of East and West.

Mr. Burns took up warmly for the West, and quoted a little poetry upon it, which he said his friend Courtenay had composed once in an inspired moment, standing upright in a carriage and sweeping his eyes over a vast sea of tall, undulating grass. The only rhythm, he explained, apologetically, that he ever knew Mr. Courtenay to perpetrate :

> "There are many who can boast of a land of milder air,
>   Where bright birds sing more sweetly, and where flowers bloom more
>   fair;
>   Of green hills and snow-capped mountains,—but, oh! I love the best
>   The pebbly streams, wood-bordered, and the prairies of the West."

Mrs. Kirkwood smiled constrainedly, having a deep-seated prejudice against the unchristian author of the rhyme.

Both the attorneys, in fact, had a general reputation for skepticism in religious matters that precluded friendly advances on the part of conscientious church people, though Mr. Burns, it was believed, was the less dangerous of the two.

"Yes," Mrs. Kirkwood said, "one wouldn't forget to mention the prairies; one's whole idea of the West is that it is a great, vague expanse, with little more to be seen than is seen from the deck of a vessel in mid-ocean."

"Well," returned Mr. Burns (it was noticeable that Mr. Burns defended the land of his adoption to everybody except his friend Courtenay), "I like to be impressed with the vastness of things. I like the idea of expansion, it agrees with my theology. So much is said about mounting up, I want to widen out. I want to get where nothing, not even a church-spire, obstructs my view."

Mrs. Kirkwood glanced up suspiciously, and met his frank, straightforward blue eyes smiling at her. She replied literally and a little stiffly that she preferred the picturesque and cultivated to the bleak and barren.

"Oh, certainly, as a matter of taste," said Mr. Burns, "a prairie landscape would be nothing to speak of in the way of beauty. But after I had been here long enough to become accustomed to the prairies I went back East to the place where I was born. I had no personal recollection of it, my parents having come westward when I was but a few years old. I had the excuse of a little business for going, and I naturally wanted to see the skies my eyes first opened on. Well, it seemed to me that the whole valley of the Shenandoah wasn't big enough to hold me.

It cramped me, made me near-sighted; I had to hurry back to get a long breath and a clear sweep of vision. I tell you, madam, we Westerners are cosmopolitans; there is nothing local or small about us. We don't cling forever to old prejudices, we advance."

Mrs. Kirkwood looked up with a flash of her intelligent eyes, and a sudden determination to explore the dangerous ground of his "opinions" and perhaps air her own in the broad scope his mind seemed to present. She had always regarded him, as well as Mr. Courtenay, with a good deal of distrust. But his face, now that she had for the first time got near enough to him to see something of what was in it, disarmed her. She felt that between herself and him existed a bond of congeniality, and that, though they belonged to the separate ranks of two opposing forces, they might set up a flag of truce and become personal friends.

"If you do not cling to old prejudices you have adopted some strong modern ones," said she. Mr. Burns raised his eyebrows, smiling, and glad to have her defend her side. "Your 'broad views,'" she went on.

"What! you think my broad views are only prejudice?"

"I think every man has a set of opinions," she returned; "and if they are prejudice in one instance, why not in another? Your idea of expansion is opposed to some other person's idea of contraction; then, are you any more liberal than your neighbor? He cannot take in what you see; you cannot take in what he sees. Where is the difference between you?"

"Why, the difference is here," said Mr. Burns: "I try to examine all things; he is too proud, or too prejudiced, or too cautious·even to take them up and look at them."

"If one takes them up it is not easy to drop them again," said Mrs. Kirkwood, quickly. "Have you not found that true," she asked, "of many persons you have interested yourself in, as well as of many ideas you have examined?"

"Yes," said he; "but what of that? Shall we draw ourselves up like a turtle in its shell for fear of touching something unpleasant and that will stick to our fingers?

I want to get out of my shell and look about me. You
orthodox Christians, it seems to me, madam, labor too
much under the superstition that the world is full of snares
and pitfalls and enemies. You collect together in your
strong castles,—your creeds and churches,—and peer out
through your little loop-holes on a world of sin and de-
pravity round about. You are tender-hearted and generous, full of kindness and compassion, eager to succor
and to save. You stand at all the portals, in all the dangerous places, hooking in poor, perishing sinners, and
gathering them into the shelter of your strong walls.
Why not level them down, and stand out boldly, fear-
lessly, upon this green, beautiful earth God Himself has
made! You don't get near enough to humanity; you
don't let humanity get near enough to you. My dear
madam, it is your walls, in a thousand instances, that
divide God's people from each other! We mortals are
only divided by walls—of one kind or another anyhow—
of our own building. We are all His children."

Mr. Burns's blue eyes were eloquently lighted up. It
was a favorite theme of his, this thought that God was
the tender Father of all, ungiven to favoritism.

"You accuse me of having my one point of view, like
the others," he continued, but Mrs. Kirkwood interrupted
him, with a smile and a blush,—

"Pray don't take the accusation personally; I am driven
to making that broad assertion. I should be skeptical
of humanity if I disbelieved it, it would prove men to be
so dishonest. As it is, when I see people opposing one
another it is my comforting argument that they all have
different stand-points and are true to their convictions."

"You are very liberal, then," said Mr. Burns, looking
at her with his expansive smile, and thinking he understood her better than she understood herself, harnessed as
she was to her creed and dogmas.

"No, not liberal according to your definition of the
word," she returned; "all I dare profess is a little
charity."

"You only keep the old word, that is all the difference," said he.

"I sometimes think those people are the happiest,"

Mrs. Kirkwood said, "who really and honestly see but one side."

"And you are not one of those?" said he, a little quizzically. "Well, why should you try to be? You said a moment ago, one could not easily drop an idea he had taken up to examine; an idea is only hard to drop when we find a truth in it. Why not live up to our discoveries? Our lives are perfect in as far as they agree with the light we have."

Turning his eyes at this moment, Mr. Burns took in what was going on elsewhere in the room. Dr. Webster was giving the young ladies a graphic account of his trip westward. He was a vivacious talker, and they—at least Maggie—seemed highly entertained.

There was a hungry, restless look in Evelyn's eyes which he had often observed when Burr was not present. That, more than her manner toward Mr. Courtenay, proved how much she cared for him.

In Maggie's simple nature there was a vein of coquetry, and the situation was highly agreeable to her. She liked Dr. Webster's evident admiration of herself even while her heart was beating high at the proximity of Mr. Burns. And the innocent little double-dealer scarcely lost a word either of them said!

Mr. Burns thought he had never seen her looking so well; so white, and red, and bright-eyed.

Mrs. Kirkwood perceiving his divided attention, allowed the conversation to drop, and glanced around with delicacy, to see if there were not some opening she could glide into and so leave him to join the young people.

But Mrs. Clyde had stepped out of the room for a moment, and the deacon and the minister were afloat upon politics, that wonderfully seductive stream to the masculine heart. So she remained where she was, and Mr. Burns, being a little disgusted with the doctor's animation, presently turned toward her again.

"How do you like Western society?" he asked, having it in his mind that Western society was a rather loose institution when a young fellow with a glib tongue and a handsome face could step right into the best of it upon a mere introduction,—through relatives who probably knew nothing of his private character,—as this Dr. Webster was doing.

"We can hardly be said to have any, can we?" said Mrs. Kirkwood, smiling. "We have hardly organized ourselves yet."

"Well, who is responsible?" said he. "It seems to me we all have a duty in this respect, the elements of society are in us if they are anywhere; why don't we go to work? Of course," he added, a little sadly,—having reference to his own and Mr. Courtenay's solitary lives and not to the young doctor,—"we fellows who have no anchorage in home or family can't do anything. Don't you think, madam, we are the natural *protégés* of society, and ought to be taken better care of?"

Mr. Burns had a winsomeness that went straight to the feminine—and especially the matronly—heart.

"Indeed I do," said Mrs. Kirkwood. "You make me ashamed that we have been so remiss."

She inwardly resolved upon a different course of action in the future.

Mrs. Clyde came in presently, and sat down and began saying something which did not particularly interest or concern Mr. Burns, and he got up and crossed over to the centre-table, took up a late magazine (the deacon's young ladies affected first-class literature), and, seating himself on the sofa, began turning the leaves.

Maggie, mindful of a hostess's duties, excused herself from the doctor and Evelyn, and went over and placed herself beside him with a half-shy, half-coquettish air. He was looking at a poem by Whittier.

"Have you read this?" said he, and without raising his eyes for an answer,—he had long ago taken the measure of Maggie's literary capacity, and found her not much above milk-and-water novels,—began and read the poem through.

When he had finished, Maggie looked up brightly.

"I have heard that before!" she exclaimed.

"Indeed?"

"Yes; Eva and I were visiting at N—— City last week,—I suppose you did not know?"

"Yes; I heard you were away."

"Well, we heard a dramatic reader there, a Miss Stuvysant. Oh, you ought to have heard her read this poem!"

Mr. Burns shoved the work back to its place on the table.

"What else did she read,—Poe's 'Raven'?" said he, with a slight curve of his lip.

"No, she didn't read that, but she read 'Hiawatha.' I never could see anything in that before, but a queer jingle, jingle."

"And what did she make of it?"

"A gentleman who was with us said she made *poetry* of it."

"Indeed? Longfellow would be glad of that. What is this Miss Stuvysant like,—strong and masculine?"

"Oh, no! rather small and delicate. Everybody said her voice had wonderful 'depth' and 'compass' for so slight a creature. Her face looked like creamy-white lilies, and her eyes were large and dark, and seemed sometimes to have a far-off look, like—like Evangeline's."

A steel-engraving of that pathetic heroine, hanging in a small oval frame above the piano, had caught Maggie's eye and suggested the comparison.

"I heard some one say," she continued, "that she must have had a world of experience to be able to enter so passionately into the grand things she read; and somebody else answered, 'Humph! that is the power of genius, not experience.'"

So she prattled on, parrot-like; and Mr. Burns, with his elbow on the arm of the sofa, and his hand shading his eyes, looking at her, fell to thinking: "Of all poems, and pictures, and dreams, is not this the sweetest? This fresh, beautiful life in its dewy morning; the bright cheeks, the sparkling eyes, the radiant brow with its shining, waving hair?"

There is a charm in youth and bloom and innocent unworldliness that touches a tender chord in a man's nature. Mr. Burns felt the exquisitely sweet vibration, and knew that if he put out his hand this beautiful thing, with all its life and loveliness, might be his.

Maggie looked up presently, and threw a bomb-shell into the dreamy current of his thoughts. "There's going to be a dance next week !"

Mr. Burns started and, looking into the bright eyes she flashed up at him, repeated, mechanically, "A dance next week ?" But his thought arrested, asked, "What sort of a poem is it,—the 'Morning' with its 'rosy fingers' and 'pearly dews' ? What will be left of those bright eyes and glowing cheeks, the fair brow and shining hair, but husks after they have faded !"

To Maggie the most delightful break in the monotony of life was a ball. She prattled on about it, and Mr. Burns only half listened. He glanced at his watch presently and said he must go.

"Oh, don't hurry !" said Maggie. "It is not late."

Mrs. Clyde came forward, and said they were just going to have some refreshments, and he must stay.

"Pray, excuse me," said he, in the formal manner he and Mr. Courtenay were both in the habit of assuming, and which was the result, probably, of their mingling so little in general society. "I have an engagement which cannot very well be neglected. I merely came in to see Mr. Clyde on a matter of business. Perhaps you will step into the office in the course of a day or two ?" turning to the deacon, who assented, but began a strong protest against his early leave-taking, so that he had to make his excuses over again. When he had finally got clear of them all and bowed himself out, and the door closed behind him, he directed his steps rapidly toward the river and away from the village.

"It is true, as Mrs. Kirkwood said !" he ejaculated. "We have no society here, and I doubt whether we even have the elements. What could convert Deacon Clyde's young ladies into grand and interesting women,—such as I know there are somewhere in the world ? Education ? They have a little of that, but I don't see that it goes any deeper than the surface,—etiquette, polite language, and a rather refined style of dress and manner. Evelyn Clyde is a fine piece of statuary, with just soul enough to worship a brilliant man, without in the least comprehending the talents, education, and accomplishments that make him so. But, after all, it seems to me Burr sees no farther than she does; neither goes below the other's dazzling surface. He no more perceives her shallowness than she sounds his depths. If they marry, they will marry on the basis of a dream, that will flee away, and leave them strangers and aliens to each other. I remember'' (and Mr. Burns's thoughts went back a great way) '' how I, a man, was first captivated by the personal splendor, brilliancy, and eloquence of brave Captain Courtenay. And to-day I do not prize him for a single one of the qualities that charmed me then, though he still possesses them, and is still admired on account of them. I have taken hold of him by a stronger grasp than admiration, I have founded a friendship and a belief in him that his very faults cannot shake; albeit I do not like his faults. And it seems to me that the ' love of man and woman' is not so different from ordinary warm affection and esteem, but that a woman would have to find some of the same sterling qualities in Burr that I have found to be able to love him as well. I can think of no more damning misfortune than to marry a woman—to be taken into one's very innermost life—who can't comprehend, after she has entered it, the holy of holies. Heavens, what a desecration ! I want my whole nature to expand and blossom in the light and love of the soul I unite with mine. Miss Clyde would undoubtedly pierce through Burr's dazzling surface, for a small needle has a sharp point ; but I doubt if she could ever go much deeper than his faults.''

All this of Burr and Miss Clyde ; then his thoughts turned to Maggie. And what was Maggie but a schoolgirl, who, being a woman grown, was considered a woman finished. Her education had stopped, except as years and experience would teach her to be dextrous and economical in household affairs, perhaps patient and matronly and full of neighborly kindness ; for Maggie was amiable and industrious, and had strong natural feelings and affections, even if she had not the power of growth in other directions. As far as she went, certainly she was all he could ask. But he felt the need of a subtler companionship,—intellectual, moral, spiritual. If he could not find a being who embodied his whole idea of wife, why, then, he would not marry. Love, so often said to be incidental in a man's life, he felt to be essential—if he married—in his, as food for a part of his nature, like knowledge for the mind and religion for the soul,—the supreme thing, permeating all the rest. "Love is not simply a snare to entrap us into matrimony," he thought; "its chimes should ring down the whole journey of life, and strike as sweetly—more powerfully upon the ears of seventy than of seventeen."

Gradually his mind went back over a sweep of years, and he wondered what sort of woman had developed out of the little girl he had once believed that he loved. His memory, at least, was loyal to her virtues and her intelligence. He knew that she possessed a soul above the grovelling things of earth. Perhaps she was a grand woman now, nobly rounded and perfected. He wondered, vaguely, if she might not have power to charm him again if they should happen to meet in some of the crooked by-paths of life. The thought thrilled him. He would be glad if she could; it was very sweet to love and to be loved. Then Maggie Atherton's pretty face came up again,—as faces will come in dreams,—with its shy, bright eyes.

After all, people are strikingly affected by sense. It is the actual presence, contact, personal magnetism, that creates (and in most cases holds) the subtle, sweet emotion we call love. The absent for long years can have but little influence, however admired, esteemed, revered, compared with one who is present and can wield some personal attraction. *Could* she charm him again ? Alas, how ? since time and separation have swept away all the sweet influences of her presence and personality, and made her no longer the object of an active affection, which needs the daily bread of daily sight and touch and companionship to keep it aflame. Loved still, perhaps, with a softened tenderness like that we feel for those long dead and at intervals forgotten.

It was starlight and clear when he began his brisk walk and meditations. The road which he travelled led him into a strip of woodland skirting the river.

He was presently aware of a lulling sound in the tree-tops, and looking up, saw detached, ragged-edged clouds scudding across the sky and gathering darkly in the west.

He turned about to retrace his steps. Near the edge of the village stood a rude, dismantled fort, which the early pioneers had erected as a sort of protection against marauding bands of Indians in the neighborhood.

Coming near to this old fort, Mr. Burns espied, in the shadow of the wall, the figure of a man walking before him slowly in the same direction.

It was unmistakably the figure of Burr Courtenay; there could not be another form like that, with such graceful, gliding motion. Clinging to his arm—the arm next the wall—was a woman.

Mr. Burns stopped, confounded.

. What woman,—not Miss Clyde, surely?

Miss Clyde!—preposterous! This woman was short; Burr bent his head to talk to her.

She was enveloped in a large waterproof cloak; he could see its heavy folds flapping in the wind, and the huge frill of the uncomely hood gathered about her face as she turned it toward her companion.

Suddenly, out from a break in the wall, sprang another figure in front of these two,—the figure of a man with a gun upon his shoulder.

"Drop that girl's arm this instant, sir! or I'll blow the villain's heart out o' ye!" he exclaimed, and levelled the gun at Burr's breast.

Unlike most women in similar circumstances, this woman stood mute and motionless.

Burr also stopped, but did not drop the arm as commanded.

" I was not aware you had any claims upon this young lady, sir; if so, I beg your pardon; but presume it is optional with her to remain under my protection or go with you. The latter, it seems, would be the safer, seeing you go armed in this dreary neighborhood."

He glanced around and shrugged his shoulders with inimitable, good-natured contempt.

One thing Mr. Burns observed, that, though he was

not in the least moved by the man's angry threat, he gave the woman no encouragement to cling to him.

" *Your* protection !" exclaimed the man, half suffocated with anger, and took off his hat and wiped his forehead with the cuff of his coat-sleeve. After a short and hard struggle with himself he added, in a changed voice, that was both dogged and pathetic, "You're right; I haven't no claim on her; but neither have you."

"Then, as I remarked, the matter is at the lady's option," said Burr. "We are not far from the spot where I accidentally met her, and I should have proposed seeing her home if you had not so opportunely appeared. I presume, notwithstanding your incivility to me, you would be a safe enough escort for her."

The man, again clinching his hands with anger, hissed out, "A safe escort! *You* to call *me* a safe escort !"

He turned to the girl. "Are you going with him or are you coming with me?" he demanded, with both defiance and pleading in his voice.

The girl raised her eyes—imploringly Mr. Burns thought —to her companion's face, and then with a quick gesture of despair, or anger, or what not, dropped his arm, and Mr. Courtenay, with an inclination of his handsome person that had the finest touch of mockery in it, walked on and left the two standing face to face.

One instant the man turned and looked after him,— the splendid military figure moving off through the silence and dim light,—grasped his weapon and muttered something between his shut teeth, then threw it across his shoulder and offered the girl his arm.

She ignored it disdainfully; but they turned together and came in the direction of Mr. Burns, and were careless about keeping in the shadow of the wall; the faint starlight shone in their faces.

Mr. Burns crouched back farther into the darkness as they passed on.

The girl was Sarah Jenkins, the old man's "Sary Ann"; her companion, Jim Sites.

No need to keep in the shadow of the wall now ! She might walk with that man half the night and nothing come of it but a village jest.

How different to be found walking with Burr Courtenay!

Mr. Burns could not help hearing the conversation, which, for a time, was a monologue carried on by the man.

"So you've forgot your promise a'ready, Sally." There was wonderful pathos in the rough voice. "You said you wouldn't have nothing more to do with 'em, after we'd made up. As to Mr. Burns, it's proved to my mind that he's purty much of a gentleman. But this one, Sally, this one's a grand rascal. Maybe I've got you rid of him now; he wouldn't like to have a bullet put into him, if he ain't no coward. They say he was a good soldier and a good officer, and served all through the war, and fur that I wouldn't like to harm him. I just wanted to put him out o' your way, Sally. 'Twa'n't on my own account, neither, for I mean this to be the end of it. Since you don't care for me, Sally, I won't trouble you no more. But you keep clear o' Lawyer Courtenay, Sally, keep clear o' him. He ain't your kind. Not that you ain't good enough fur enny of 'em, and smart enough, too. But all sich fellows as them cares fur is to amuse themselves making love to every pretty girl as comes in their way."

His words penetrated to the girl's womanhood. "Did he not tell you himself that we met here simply by accident?" she demanded, compelled to put away the rigid pride she had assumed and defend herself.

"And what does that signify, Sally?" returned her lover, glad to have touched her. "Couldn't he have let you go your way an' him go his'n? What does he give you his arm fur, an' go promenadin' up an' down this old wall as sentimental like as if you was engaged?"

"What business is it of yours, anyhow, if I choose to walk with a gentleman?" the girl exclaimed, angrily, a round red spot coming into each white cheek.

She was ambitious, poor thing! and vain. She saw no reason why she should not aspire to win for a husband one of the dazzling attorneys if others did. She consciously felt herself to be superior in intellect, at least, to the young ladies on the hill, whose manner toward her was marked by a gracious condescension that was exceedingly exasperating. Why was she not as good as Evelyn Clyde, or that doll-faced Maggie? Why was it, my discriminating reader? She had a broader and deeper nature than either of those damsels. She had a sharper intelligence, a better education, and even a richer beauty. But she lacked some subtle quality,—or was it a quality? Perhaps it was simply the toning-down of all the qualities, a something which in music is the "touch," in painting the "tints" and "shading," the fineness of expression.

"You began with being jealous of Mr. Burns," she continued, rapidly. "Because he gave me a bunch of wild-flowers once that he had gathered in the woods, and because he took me up in his buggy one day when I had walked out to Aunt Jane's and the wind was blowing a hurricane. And now, because you saw Mr. Courtenay walking with me here——"

" I wouldn't mind, Sally," interrupted her lover, deprecatingly, "if he meant fair and honorable, but you know yourself he goes up to Deacon Clyde's, bold an' above board, an' pays attention to Miss Clyde,—takes her to meetin' an' places, an' acts as if he wasn't ashamed o' her. If he likes you the best, what's to hinder him from coming to your house an' talking to you at your own hearth-stone, or walking with you in daylight?"

He was silent, and the girl was silent too, with white, compressed lips. By and by they went off around the corner of the fort and disappeared.

CHAPTER VII.

Mr. Burns turned his steps slowly homeward ; he had a dread of meeting his companion. His companion, however, appeared to have no dread of meeting him ; he sat comfortably by the fire, feet elevated, taking a political view of the country through a late Eastern paper.

"I think the affairs of the nation are swinging around into something like order and settlement again, Charley," said he, throwing the paper aside and reaching to the table for a cigar.

"Do you think so?"

Mr. Burns stood warming his hands at the stove, looking down at the red coals in the grate. He felt little enthusiasm over the affairs of the nation just then.

"Yes," said Burr. "My interest in politics is reviving. In my youth I aspired to statesmanship, thought the acme of American ambition was reached in the Columbian Capitol. I limited my aspirations to Congress in those days."

"You were modest," said Mr. Burns, unsmilingly.

"But the war coming on destroyed all that," continued Burr.

"Or rather, the statesman was merged in the soldier," returned Mr. Burns, a recollection of his friend's past sweeping over him and relaxing the severity of his face a little. There was much in that past to call for admiration, and for the tender, chivalric love he had for Burr.

"I have been thinking, Charley, that you and I ought not to have come West," Burr said. "We should have stood our ground among the men we were educated with, locked horns with our equals, and fought an even contest with the world."

"Have I not said so a thousand times?" exclaimed Mr. Burns, aroused out of himself. It was so exactly what he had always maintained and Burr had always refuted, that he felt exasperated. Besides, if Burr gave up it was all over with them. He had accustomed himself to depend so much upon Burr, even against his own judgment. He continued, excitedly, "We came out here ahead of immigration almost; seized the one selfish right of possession, and are obliged to fold our hands and wait for everything else to come to us. There is something almost magnificent," he added, with a bitter laugh, "in this reckless throwing away of our youth and best energies! I feel that our vitality is dead, we are losing the best things we have got,—our youth, our strength, our ambition."

"I fancied we were saving up those things for the good time coming," said Burr, with his usual gentleness, that was hard for his friend to bear sometimes.

"And which never comes," said Mr. Burns.

"Except our youth," continued Burr, a little sadly; "I begin to feel that that is slipping away. See here! I am getting gray hairs, Charley."

He swept back the black waves from his temples, revealing fine streaks of gray.

"So am I," said Mr. Burns; "they are the laurels we won in the army. But I am not concerned about my gray hairs, except as they rebuke me for the wasting years, and show me that while the husk is withering the kernel also is shrinking into nothingness, whereas it ought to be bursting forth in the fulness and ripeness of manhood. I begrudged the four years we spent in the war, the waste of time, and brain, and opportunity; but a thousand times more I regret the three years since the war."

"Charley," said Burr, arousing himself to what he felt to be the necessity of the moment, "you have grown as much in these three years, I venture to say, as in any other three years of your life. When I first knew you you were a hot-headed, ambitious youth; confident, impatient, and egotistic (excuse me). You were eager to revolutionize the world and set it upon your own broad basis of free thought, liberal education, and general enlightenment. If you had gone on with such tremendous momentum as you began, you would have had a mere mushroom growth. You would have expended yourself in the froth of enthusiasm and had no good wine left in the bottom of your goblet. As it is, the froth has had time to settle."

"And stagnate," said Mr. Burns.

"A candle has just so much life to burn away," continued Mr. Courtenay; "so has a man. You were spending yourself too fast. Providence—as Shakspeare calls the overruling power that shapes our destinies—saw that, and so these quiet years were thrust upon you. The war itself was timely, with respect to you."

"You reason," said Mr. Burns, "like many other people I have known, who think the universe revolves around them, and that the Omnipotent Ruler occupies Himself with their smallest concerns; bringing about storms and sunshine, war and death, and pestilence and prosperity, all with direct reference to them! The sublimest picture of egotism the world can show."

"It seems so," said Burr, "and perhaps is in most cases. But, though I do not presume to suppose that the Supreme Ruler and Director of all things has a personal supervision over even the stars in the heavens, yet it pleases my geometrical mind to believe that every law and regulation and combination which He has established regarding the minutest things in creation is perfect in all its relations and bearings. This, of course, proves to us my comfortable doctrine that everything works together for our good, and we work for the good of all. The stars may have a particular reason of their own for shining, but they also perform the minor office of shining for us. The rain may come only because the clouds are full of it and are obliged to pour it out; but it blesses the earth and us. Can you not see the perfect law running through it all? I am filled with profound admiration; religion, in my mind, takes the form of perpetual praise to the Creator and Sustainer of this wonderful and sublime piece of machinery, the universe. But I am diverging. I was about to apply the weight of this stupendous argument to yourself. You know that an atom embodies in itself the whole principle which the bulk of atoms embodies. The bulk is simply the aggregate; what is true of one is true of all the others, and *vice versa.* What is true of the grand harmony of the universe is true of your life, unless you lay violent hands upon your own destiny. What a striking thought, that man is the only atom in all the harmonious creation who is capable of making a discord! It is the result I suppose of the gift of free-will to him."

Eloquent as Mr. Courtenay was when occasion demanded, he soon tired of a subject like this, involving so much effort of thought.

"Has anything especial happened to you, Charley? You seem depressed," said he, with a sudden change of topic.

"Not unusually, do I?" said Mr. Burns, with the feeling that it was his habitual state in these latter years.

"I thought so. Everything pleasant at the deacon's, I suppose?"

"Yes."

"Did you get your business transacted?"

"No; they had company. The Rev. Kirkwood and his wife, and that sprig of a doctor whom we have seen sporting a cane and a silk tile."

"Ah! A relative of the Kirkwoods', is he not?"

"Yes; a nephew.——Burr,"—Mr. Burns turned a grave face towards his friend,—"I took a walk down towards the river and came home by the fort after I left the deacon's."

Burr took his cigar from his lips, and knocked the ashes off the end of it carefully with his forefinger.

"Ah!" said he.

"I saw you walking there with Sarah Jenkins."

"And did you witness the tragic *finale* of the promenade?" he asked, without change of expression, except that the glimmer of a smile flashed athwart his dark, half-closed eyes.

Mr. Burns felt almost as helpless against his implacable coolness as poor Jim Sites.

"Why don't you let the girl alone, Burr? She might marry Sites and be happy."

"She will," said Burr. "That is, she will marry him, but she will not be happy with him. She is too smart for him."

"Well, let her alone, let her work out her own destiny. For my part, Burr, I stand appalled before the ruins men make of women's lives!"

"Charley, how often must I tell you that I do not step out of my way to interfere with any person's destiny? I hold that the sublime laws and regulations we have just been discussing will, in any case, control my course. So I move along as harmoniously as I can through all the complications of this wonderful world." Mr. Burns was too indignant to reply. "Anyhow," said Burr, changing his tactics, "the fellow is jealous and ill-bred, and needs a lesson."

" *You* cannot teach him," said Mr. Burns. "You only hurt him and hurt her. You may be laying up a sorrow for those two that will rankle for years."

"Nonsense, Charley!" Burr returned, with a shrug. "She will explain and they will make up again, and understand each other all the better. I met Miss Jenkins this evening by pure accident. After you went out I began to feel a little lonely and proposed a walk to myself, and put on my overcoat and started down toward the river. I passed by Deacon Clyde's and saw the windows all lighted up, and would have gone in if I had not discovered that there were strangers there. I spent some little time walking up and down the river-bank within hearing of the falls. Returning, I met Miss Jenkins coming out of the little hut occupied by old Mother Dexter, you remember, not far from the fort; and the evening being pleasant and I being lonely, and she being rather pleased to meet me (I thought), I turned and offered her my arm for a promenade under the shelter of the old fort."

"Sheltered from observation, I suppose you mean?" said Mr. Burns.

"No; from the wind. But where in thunder Sites could have come from is more than I am able to conjecture!"

"Perhaps he came on purpose to meet her, knowing where she had gone?"

"Perhaps; but how did he come to be armed?"

"I should think that would be a lesson to you, Burr; the fellow is excitable, he might have blown your brains out."

"I could easily have disarmed him," said Burr. "And now, Charley, I hope I have explained this mysterious circumstance to your entire satisfaction. Explanations are damnable! don't ask me for any more of them. If a man's life does not carry out his principles, no explanation of his actions will. That is Emerson's idea, by the way, but before he had expressed it it was my rule and guide. As you will find," he added, "if some 'spiritual medium' ever takes it in hand to write my private biography."

CHAPTER VIII.

THE ball which Maggie had made mention of came up for discussion in the law-office on the eve of it, by Burr's proposing to go and take the young ladies.

Mr. Burns, who happened to feel in a talkative humor, remarked that it was strange, seeing that dancing had met with so much disapproval from certain religious bodies as incompatible with a healthy spiritual growth, that so many people who have been church-members in the East, and consistent with church rules, consider themselves relieved of all restraint in the matter of dancing and the like the moment they cross the Mississippi.

"Yes," said Mr. Courtenay, "in that our Western emigrants differ widely from the Pilgrim fathers."

"You see," continued Mr. Burns, "that finding no civilizing influences in the West, it seldom occurs to us to create such influences among ourselves."

"All Christian religion," said Mr. Courtenay, "is of course founded upon the Bible. But how many Christians, do you suppose, take root in the truths of Scripture? How many who are not merely the outgrowth of churches and societies? People's lives are governed by circumstances; it is only here and there along the stream of religion or politics, or any social concern, that we find a man whose feet touch bottom. Very few act from principle, they simply follow where others lead. It is true that in most momentous things people have got to move *en masse*, but even then there is a difference in merely going with the tide and realizing an individual responsibility in the movement. I think it would be only fair and just to require every man to stand upon his own basis, and not blindly hang upon another."

"But," said Mr. Burns, "you can't get rid of responsibility by shaking people off. There are only a few who have stamina enough to stand alone, and they have got to take their weak brethren upon their backs. If you have light you must let it shine; many of us can only see a thing by having it pointed out to us. Herein lies both your power and your responsibility. We all like to feel that we have influence; but influence as controlling only men's actions is a weak thing. Point out a principle and you have accomplished something. A live seed planted in a garden is better than all the flowers plucked and strewn over its paths. I agree with you, that no man has a right to hang upon you blindly; let him make your principles his principles, and your motives his motives, if he will, and then you are free of him. You are accountable for your own life and actions, not for other men's. We must each act from a point within ourself. I do not doubt that it is a crime for many people to dance; it outrages their conception of religion and their most sacred feelings. If they persist, they will harden and demoralize themselves, because they go against conscience. People may sin against a law that exists only in themselves, nevertheless they sin. For our lives are only perfect in as far as they agree with our convictions of right. The law—I mean our learned profession—deals only in the broadest generalities, and touches men only in their extremity. The law *in us* is what must govern and control us, and we sin whenever we break it."

"You make every man's conscience, then, his rule and guide," said Burr. "How does that work when some devoted fanatic gets it into his head that it is his duty, and will be a benefit to society, to put a fellow-being out of the world? What did Virginia think of John Brown? What did the world think of Wilkes Booth?"

"They put themselves into juxtaposition with the supreme law, and were crushed by it. These things are not all properly adjusted, of course, or rather, we are not properly adjusted to the general law and regulations. I have a fancy that it took the stars and other heavenly bodies a good while to fall into their proper and harmonious places; even yet we are sometimes warned of danger to our earth by some unruly comet that has got out of its way and threatens to jostle us. Mankind is a universe, and every individual man, like every individual planet, has his orbit, and no one has a right to crowd him out of it."

"Well, what about the dance?" said Burr.

"I don't think I shall go," Mr. Burns returned.

"Why not; have you any scruples?"

"Yes. I scruple to make myself ridiculous. You and I, Burr, are getting pretty well up in years to be still 'tripping the light fantastic toe.' When nature has added to our manhood the dignity of gray hairs, it seems to me high time to give up youthful follies. And I mean to do it gracefully."

"Teach me how!" said Burr, with mock humility.

"Certainly. Rise superior to them. Dismiss them with a wave of your hand and say, 'I have done with you.' Don't wait until the next generation sweeps you off the floor; save your dignity while you can, by stepping up higher."

"There is time enough yet for that," said Burr, a little uneasily; any reference to his years touched him in a sensitive spot.

"I don't think, Charley, we ever did much dancing in the 'light fantastic' manner!" he said.

"No; it is too active an exercise," laughed Mr. Burns. "I have walked through a few cotillons, but never essayed a 'round' dance in my life. But you," he added, "used to waltz, you remember, when we were in the army, or rather when we were in camp."

As though the remark had touched some unhappy reminiscence, a silence followed, and a cloud settled on both the young men's spirits.

By and by, Mr. Courtenay arose and shook it off. It was growing late.

"Well, what do you say? Shall we do ourselves the honor of escorting the young ladies? If so, we had better go up this evening and invite them."

"I shall not do myself the honor," said Mr. Burns.

"In that case, I think I will venture to invite them both, and trust to you to change your mind and take Miss Maggie off my hands."

"My mind is irrevocably made up," returned Mr. Burns. "It seems to me," he added, as Mr. Courtenay made himself ready to step out, "that you are rather late with your invitation."

But Burr, whom much adulation had made a little vain, like Napoleon Bonaparte, made his own conditions. He went up to the deacon's, but did not commit himself to the avowed purpose of going to invite the young ladies to attend the dance, but ostensibly to spend the evening. His manner was the farthest remove from Mr. Burns's outspoken bluntness. He scrupled to make his attentions to Miss Clyde appear pointed, even to herself. He rarely escorted her to places of public entertainment, but contrived in his diplomatic way to take advantage of whatever occasion offered him the pleasure of her society,— and her preference.

Her preference, however, was not marked, except by a proud acceptance of his attentions and equally proud indifference to the attentions of other gentlemen; a distinction very gratifying to Mr. Courtenay's vanity. He was an epicure in such matters, appreciating the most delicate shades of flattery, and relishing what was especially rare and sweet.

As he sat in the deacon's parlor the subject of the ball came up, and he remarked:

"You attend, I presume?"

"No," said Maggie, laughing and blushing, and looking across at Evelyn; "one might as well be frank, we have nobody to take us."

"That is lamentable," said he. "If an escort is all that is lacking, I might presume to offer myself."

Maggie was overwhelmed by the effect of her audacity.

"Oh, Mr. Courtenay! I didn't mean to make you ask us," she said, helplessly. "I didn't think how it would sound."

Will any one doubt that Mr. Courtenay himself had brought it all about, exactly as he had planned? Having made his point he swept the subject aside gracefully, helping Maggie out of her embarrassment.

Nothing further was said about the ball until he was taking leave of Evelyn at the hall-door. He had stepped out and turned to say "good-night."

"Shall I come and *chaperon* you to-morrow evening?" he asked.

"Why, yes, if you please," Evelyn returned, a delicate

D*

flush mounting her cheek.   She stood straight and slender
and tall in the door-way, with the moonlight streaming
over her and softening her beautifully cut features.   It
was her lily-like stateliness and maidenliness that Burr
admired.   He would no more have broken through the
thin fibre of delicate reserve that divided them than he
would "brush the down from the peach or the dew from
the rose."   He put out his hand and took hers and held
it a moment lightly, and then said "good-night," and
walked away.

It was the nearest approach to familiarity he had ever
allowed himself to make toward her, and he enjoyed the
thought that no one save himself could presume so much,
even, as that.

CHAPTER IX.

THE dancing-hall had been lighted up some hours
(there is always a share of the populace who like to begin
a thing early and get the most of it), and the music
floated across the street to where Mr. Burns sat alone in
his office, endeavoring to ignore it by assiduous study.

But life must be seasoned a little, and we have got to
take what spices we can get.

Had Mr. Burns been living in New York City he
doubtless would have displayed a fastidious taste; he
would have flavored the evening with something fine, a
Booth or a Beecher.

As it was, after—as I have said—some hours of difficult study, he was moved to go up and look on at the
dancers.

The "hall" was up-stairs over a dry-goods store.

He flung on his cloak and, crossing the street, ascended
a flight of steps running up on the outside of the building, intending to remain among the bystanders, who
always clustered around the door and sat upon the steps
of the orchestral platform.

But he was endowed with too delicate an organization
for tobacco and coarse slang, and soon detached himself

from the motley throng and wended his way to the upper and more exclusive end of the hall, where stood Burr with Miss Clyde and Maggie, they having come in at a late and fashionable hour.

Of all the things that travel in the train of emigration, etiquette, perhaps, keeps nearest the van; and fashion, and style, and all those high-toned divinities, hold up their sceptres on the plain and in the wilderness.

Mr. Burns approaching Burr's group, hat in hand, threw back his cloak and paid the usual compliments.

Maggie bowed to him with a poor little attempt at stiffness, which he made no effort to dispel.

Dr. Webster was there and appeared to be paying some attention to Maggie. Mr. Burns inwardly determined to encourage him in that. Looking at the young doctor dispassionately, he could not help considering him a very good match for Maggie.

However, when he offered her his arm with an easy, deferential assurance, and led her away to join in the Lancers just then forming on the floor, Mr. Burns gave a contemptuous shrug, and went over and sat down upon a long bench against the wall and watched the dancers, with curved lip and the Poe's Raven expression.

Of all ridiculous dances the Lancers appeared to him, at that moment, the most so. The profuse bowing was burlesqued by the many ungraceful figures engaged in it, and the whole scene seemed, to his disenchanted eyes, the silliest farce. He thought of what De Quincey has written; that from the spectacle of certain dances he derived "the very grandest form of passionate sadness which can be derived from any spectacle whatsoever."

At one time in his life Mr. Burns had been grateful to De Quincey for giving expression—and countenance—to his own elevated emotions amid dancing and festal music. Had the scales fallen forever from his eyes? Was he no longer capable of fine elevation of feeling?

The dance ended, they all came up and gathered around him, making him a sort of nucleus for their exclusive little party.

They praised the music, which was unusually fine,—a clarinet being added to the local string-band, played by a grave, handsome young man whom nobody seemed to know.

Burr inquired—at Miss Clyde's instigation—of a dry-goods clerk who approached the group, anxious to secure Maggie for the next dance.

"Don't know his name,—he's from Winchester. Splendid player,—ain't he?" said the young fellow.

"He does very well," said Burr, distantly.

"Well, sir, they say he was nothing but a blacksmith's 'prentice a few years ago!"

"Impossible?" said Mr. Burns. "Pray, what raised him to his present elevation?"

"Genius, I s'pose. He never had any teaching; just got him a horn and went at it."

In the mean time the young man had come down from the orchestra, leaving his instrument, and button-holed a manager and whispered something in his ear. Whereupon the manager brought him up and introduced him to Maggie, whom he solicited for a waltz.

Maggie was not taken wholly unawares; she had caught the stranger's eyes several times and thought them like Mr. Burns's; which that haughty young gentleman would doubtless have resented.

She took his arm, with a blush, and moved away.

The dry-goods clerk, having lost his opportunity, sauntered off, chagrined.

"Did you catch his name?" asked Miss Clyde, turning to Mr. Burns.

"No," said he. "And I suppose it does not matter; he is some young fellow who knows nothing but his music, doubtless."

"You are mistaken," said Burr, to whom the manager had been speaking. "I have just ascertained his name to be Dale, of the 'Winchester Independent;' he is an editor, you see, as well as a musician."

"It is all the same," said Mr. Burns; "he blows his own trumpet in either case."

Dr. Webster, turning to Miss Clyde, and offering his arm, said, "Shall we try this?" and led her away to join the circle of waltzers.

Proud Miss Clyde, she was called far and near; the most

beautiful figure, the most graceful waltzer of all the whirling throng. Burr sat down beside Mr. Burns, his eyes following her. The music was a full, undulating harmony that seemed to sweep the light forms off their feet, and bear them along with graceful, rhythmic motion. Oh, power of beauty and of music! Never before as in that reeling, dizzying, graceful, enchanting motion had Miss Clyde so touched the heart (or imagination) of the man she so longed to win. Was it love? A thousand marriages have been born of a waltz. Even Mr. Burns was impressed.

"A very pretty exercise for young persons," he remarked, sagely. "We all have to pass through the realms of enchantment once in our life, I suppose. Though I must say, my fairyland seldom took the shape of a ball-room. I remember only one or two occasions when I was carried away with a thing of this kind."

"Well," said Burr, "I don't mind confessing to you, privately, that I never got upon the floor in my life, and began to spin around like that, that I did not feel it a sort of stepping down from the dignified estate of manhood."

"Do you confess so much?" laughed Mr. Burns. "I never experienced that feeling until the thing was over; my enthusiasm carried me through."

"I never could get up any enthusiasm," said Burr.

A few moments later Mr. Burns arose and gathered his cloak around him.

"I am going home," he explained.

"No?" said Burr. "Stay, and take Miss Maggie over to supper."

"I don't think my services are required," said Mr. Burns, significantly.

The waltzing had ceased, and the interesting stranger was slowly leading Maggie back to her place, his head inclined toward her, busily talking.

Some fellow in Mr. Burns's vicinity remarked, in an audible voice, "That 'ere chap from Winchester, 'at plays the clar'net, 's a married man."

"Well, what ef he is?" said a companion.

"Oh, nothin'; only he seems purty sweet on Miss Atherton."

Mr. Burns glanced angrily around at the speaker, who returned his look with a blank, good-natured stare. The manager called out "supper," and Burr brought the young ladies' wraps, having to go across the street to the hotel for refreshments. The Winchester gentleman was still hovering around Maggie. Mr. Burns made a sudden resolve, and went up and offered her his arm.

"Will you allow me to take you over to supper?" said he, not in the gentlest tone, utterly ignoring her companion, who immediately bowed himself away.

Maggie looked up with a glad heart-bound and assented, her little air of stiffness vanishing in the sunshine of his presence. Returning to the ball-room after supper, Mr. Burns at once excused himself and went home.

CHAPTER X.

Mr. Burns turned up the light in the office, and threw himself into a chair, sickened and disgusted with the sawing of the violins and loud "calling" of the leader of the band across the way. It helped him to see—this paltry ball, by its miserable mockery of pleasure, or rather by its cheap imitation of what many people hold to be the highest pleasure—the poverty and emptiness of this world.

If pleasure—light, fantastic enjoyment—could wear a covering so complete as to hide the skeleton beneath, it might be endured. But this wretched make-believe was unbearable. When Burr came in an hour later, he sat wakefully by the fire.

"Why, how is it," Burr asked, cheerfully, glad to feel the warmth of the office, "that you are not in bed?"

"Who could sleep with that damned fiddling going on over yonder?" Mr. Burns returned, with unwonted profanity.

Burr drew a chair up to the stove, and sat down. "The fiddling wasn't bad," said he.

By and by, Mr. Burns remarked: "I have been thinking, Burr, that it is a misfortune for a man to leave all the friends of his youth behind him in the march of life. The tenderest associations we ever know are those that cluster round our boyhood. But as we advance we think it is smart to outgrow them, to launch ourselves upon the wide world and cut loose from our early loves, and say, with so much wisdom (never thinking how crushing the words may be to those still living in the dream we have awakened from), 'Time flies, dreams vanish, and bubbles burst.' As if there is anything more beautiful, or more substantial, even, in this earth, than those dreams and bubbles! I would to God I had mine back again."

"A foolish wish, Charley," said Burr; "you can't keep them; they are too fleeting; they go as the years go."

Mr. Burns got up and went to the table, and took out of his portfolio a little scrap of printed paper and read,—

> "'When all the world is young, lad,
>   And all the trees are green;
> And every goose a swan, lad,
>   And every lass a queen;
> Then hey for boot and horse, lad,
>   And around the world away!
> Young blood must have its course, lad,
>   And every dog his day.
>
> "'When all the world is old, lad,
>   And all the trees are brown;
> And all the sports are stale, lad,
>   And all the wheels run down;
> Creep home and take your place there,
>   The spent and maimed among;
> God grant you find one face there
>   You loved when all were young.'"

"Very pretty—in spirit," said Burr, "though a little homely in garb."

"It contains the whole poetry of life," Mr. Burns asserted, and sat musing long after Burr had gone to sleep. He dropped his head in his hands, and his memory went back to the little village where his boyhood had been spent, alive with scenes and faces, and friends whose truth had inspired him with faith in God and man. Not one was left to him.

SECOND BOOK.

CHAPTER XI.

[It is rather bungling to break off the thread and tie a knot in the skein one is winding, but take my word for it that in this case it is expedient, my kind reader.]

SNUGLY cuddled out of the reach of high winds among low, sandy hills covered chiefly with scrubby red-oaks and hazel-brush, in a certain section of that vague, vast country called the " West" in a wholesale way (but about whose latitude and longitude it is not needful to be precise), a few hundred miles beyond where the sun sets over the Blue Ridge and Catskill Mountains; and so old, and so settled and populated, that " West," as applied to it, was no longer synonymous with " new,"—so old indeed that civilization had folded its hands and dropped asleep as having nothing more to do, rustled the little town of Hazelville, to which Mr. Burns's memory in its sad pilgrimage went back. It was not distinguished in its appearance from many another small town in its vicinity; it had the same sleepy, general expression, the same settled, satisfied, changeless air. Architecture had not touched it, nor painter's brush marred the sanctity of wall, post, or sign-board for a generation, except in one instance where dry-goods and notions were advertised in new and glaring colors upon an old building.

The school, built of hewn logs, bore—upon the outside at least—no sign of progress; and the squatty, old-fashioned church commanded the same veneration it did in its earlier and palmier days, and was filled to overflowing of a Sunday, though its battered walls resounded to no new thing in the way of preaching, any more than they resounded to the stroke of hammer in the way of repairing. Perhaps one would have been considered as sacrilegious as the other.

A couple of peaks rise above the sandy hills surrounding Hazelville, and are christened respectively—and suggestively—Big and Little Twin, or, banded together, Twin Points. There are some points of difference between them: where one is grassy and slopes far out into surrounding meadows, inviting to cool, shady nooks on its terraces, the other is steep and rocky, and discouraging to Young Ambition aspiring to its summit (except initiated Young Ambition which knows a meandering path leading to the topmost crag through many inspiring difficulties). And where one spreads out many a broad, low oak, like an umbrella in the sun, the other rears its bleak, bald head against the sky, defying sun and storm.

There is a little silver stream winding in and out among the hills barely affording water for a mill-race. Across this small stream is a dam of brush and stones that has to be crossed to reach the twins. The race is bridged by a couple of logs thrown across it.

In the early autumn twilight—twilight comes very early down in the hollows, though the sun still gilds the hill-tops—we may discern two people, one a man with a boy's smooth face and stripling form, the other a young girl, crossing the dam hand in hand.

"Come," said the youth, grasping the girl's hand with a tighter pressure and striding forward, "let us make haste or the sun will be down before we reach the top of Little Twin, and I don't want to miss it to-night; it is my last chance for a good many months, you know. I shall not have time to-morrow night. You can come up here any night," he added. "You and Fred, or Miss Barker." The last with a half-humorous, half-sarcastic curl of the lip.

"I shall not come here again until you come home," his companion returned, decidedly.

"I should think you would, Wilma!" reproachfully. "I know I should. I like to look at your picture and everything that can remind me of you when I am away from you."

"Oh, but I don't need anything to remind me, Charley; I think of you all the time anyhow."

She clasped his arm suddenly with both her little brown hands, and looked up with such a pretty mingling of shyness and frankness, a vivid blush spreading itself over her face (and besides it was such a gratifying thing to have said), that the young man, with a quick, responsive glow, bent his rather proud head and kissed the lips that said it.

Hitherto one might have thought him a brother, carelessly kind, helping her not very gently—not so very gently as a lover might—over the stones. Now, however, a sudden tenderness drew them together.

Charley half forgot his hurry, and they walked lingeringly and in silence, feeling that exquisite nearness to each other that comes only at intervals even between lovers, especially lovers of several years' standing like these.

The young man felt his pulses thrill with an unusual gladness. Wilma seldom gave him so frank an assurance of her loyalty, thinking perhaps, with maidenly reserve and it might be a dash of maidenly coquetry, that it was his part to do the love-making. He had had many misgivings about her depth of feeling, and believed with keen regret that in the mutual interchange of affection he gave much more than he received. He had strong faith in his own power of discernment, and was sure that his eyes pierced to the bottom of Wilma's soul; and though it pleased him that the pool was clear and pure, and that its sweet waters had no outlet but in him, he regretted that it was not deeper, and felt with some bitterness that the depths of his own tenderness would never be fully known because of her incapacity. It never occurred to his loyal heart that he might break his boyish contract and seek for a wife one who could be more to him than she could be. He would as soon have thought of replacing his mother with some other woman.

As for Wilma no misgiving disturbed her. The current of her days and years swept as smoothly on as a meadow brook, and Charley's love was security for all her future. It was the green banks hemming in the narrow, happy stream of her life; the flowers growing on its edges all the way down to where it widened into a mystic eternity; the stars shining above and the blue sky. Charley's love was all this.

But perhaps she accepted it too much as she accepted the sunshine and all natural blessings, with a deep, silent gratitude that she herself was scarcely conscious of. And Charley did not like to give his heart's wealth and have it taken as a matter of course.

Love is a costly gift, and however carelessly accepted, there will come a time when the receiver will learn the value of it.

Wilma was a dreamer, as perhaps most of us are, and it would take a shock to waken her. And shocks will inevitably come when there is anything to be unearthed. Pity that they must so rack and unnerve us, leaving us forever after with a stinging sense of our weakness.

It is a very ingenious saying, He tempers the wind to the shorn lamb. It is so true of each of us that just such storms will come as are needed to unfold us. "He tempers the wind to the shorn lamb," but He tempers it to the oak sapling as well, and it is tossed and buffetted, and it grows and develops.

Perhaps a human being differs from an oak sapling in this, that the former invites the storm by its own tossing. Or (for we know that the tempest sweeps over the whole forest) perhaps the tempering is in the heart and fibre of the tree itself. And it may be that the same winds blow over and search out all hearts alike, only that some have deeper caverns and longer and louder echoes.

So He does not temper the wind, He tempers us. He does not leave us more helpless than the vessel that adjusts its sails and has power to right itself when the billows roll.

By and by Wilma said, looking down, "Charley, you don't know how I dread going off to school!"

"What! Not discouraged?" said Charley, surprised.

"Oh, no! Of course I want to go; I have dreamed about it all my life, you know. But to think of the great, strange school; I shall feel so awkward and out of place."

"Little goose!" said Charley, laughing and pressing her closer to his side, while, with a sort of patronizing affectionateness, he slipped his slender, student fingers under her chin, and bent his head again to kiss the cherry-red lips. "My little jewel only needs polishing to make it the brightest of gems," said he. And Wilma, accustomed to such pretty compliments and unspoiled by them, took it as a matter of course that Charley should say so, without the least vain consciousness that it was so. There was not any danger of her overrating herself; her home-training had cultivated her in the opposite direction. Her mother, fearful of encouraging vanity in her children, constantly depreciated instead of praising them.

Wilma had not a doubt that in the academy she was about to enter she would be the least brilliant of all the students. They crossed the race upon the logs, and again Charley tightened his clasp of the hand, and drew it within his arm with a tender impulse.

"No, no, darling, you must keep a brave spirit! The great, strange school will not seem such a formidable thing after you have entered it. You have no idea how the mountains dwindle away when you come close up to them. I know just how it is; I had that same feeling myself before I went to the university."

"And now you are one of the 'most promising young men' there!" said Wilma, looking up at him proudly. "I heard the minister tell mother that."

"Nonsense! What does the minister know about it?" said Charley. "I look upon these school-days of ours, Wilma, as the bridge that divides us from each other and our sweet by and by."

"It is a very long bridge, Charley," said Wilma, and again he felt his pulses thrill at the unusualness of her emotion. Could it be there was more depth than he had imagined? Did she really care so much for him?

He wound his arm gently about her waist. "It is a long bridge, darling; but then you know I love you always, and am looking forward to the happy future I am trying to make for you,—for us both. I am shaping my life to that end. But we must ''bide a wee': this long separation is as hard for me as for you, my dear."

Close following the words was the pungent reflection that it was perhaps harder, and he ended with a sigh.

They climbed on in silence till they came to the top of
the hill.   Charley instinctively uncovered his head, and
turned his face to the setting sun, his golden curls lit up
by the red beams, and his face aglow with light shining
through out of a poet soul that leaped up and soared beyond the sunset.   Wonderfully buoyant things are these
souls that have wings !   Wilma admired the sunset, too;
but loved better to watch its reflection in her lover's eyes.
She stood looking up at him with a kind of awe, as
though his spirit were unveiled before her, her face as
rapt as his own.   A spectator would have said she worshipped him.

"Is it not grand, Wilma?"   He drew her nearer to
him with the arm that was round her waist, but did not
take his eyes from the glowing west.   "It doesn't seem
as if we are very far off from heaven standing here—does
it, darling? If that great crimson curtain were lifted just
a little way we would be on a level with the golden gates
and could look right through."

"Oh, Charley !" said Wilma.

"And why not?" said Charley, smiling.   "Do you
see how motionless everything is down below?   There is
something so solemn in the hush of the wind just as the
sun goes down, as though a voice whispered, ' Peace, be
still I'   And look yonder, where the sun breaks through
and shines upon the water, was ever anything more tran-
quilly beautiful? How I love water ! I wish I had a boat,
—though I would not dip an oar down there to-night to
break the charm ; it would be sacrilege. We shall have a
boat some day. I mean to live near some beautiful body
of water, and get as much poetry out of life as I can.   I
don't see how people can be content to pass their lives in
barren places.   This sunset is a grand poem, Wilma ;
and you and I are studying it together, just as we will
study all beautiful things in the sweet future. I shall
never forget it, darling."

A little while longer they stood and gazed, while the
red was slowly fading.   Then the spell was broken, the
soul receded backward from Charley's eyes, and a sigh
fluttered on his lip, which might have meant that he felt
himself to have been alone on the greatest of those

heights, and regretted that Wilma's perception of the glories of the Invisible was not so fine or so keen as his own. For Wilma had scarcely spoken ; she had felt, but had kept silence ; her brown eyes widened, and were full of wonder and subdued, sweet joy. The moon came up with a stealthy "bo-peep" behind them, so that when they turned it was looking full at them with its bland, demure smile,—as though secretly amused that it had stolen a march upon them,—seeming to have risen out of the thin, broad sheet of water that lay far down among the hills, like a rosy-faced boy coming out of his morning bath. Charley linked Wilma's arm through his own, and they began to retrace the long, downward path.

CHAPTER XII.

Wilma's family was an odd mixture in the relation of its several members to one another.

It consisted of the widow Lynne, its one head ; Frederic, her stepson ; Wilmingard, her daughter by a former marriage ; and Blanche, half-sister to the two last named.

There was also a Miss Amelia Barker, who boarded in the family, and had had her home in it ever since Blanche, whose existence measured a little more than seven years, could remember ; and she was likely to continue in it so long as she continued in her character of village schoolmistress, which would probably be until some radical change took place in educational matters. For the good, easy citizens of Hazelville were averse to change, and had a great reverence for time-honored institutions.

And Miss Barker's reign was a time-honored institution. The smaller children were as much accustomed to her authority as to that of their natural guardians.

She was a little past the first glow and freshness of youth,—not confessedly so on her own part, but inferentially so on the part of other people,—but still held on to the last pretensions to bloom and beauty, with that reluctance to give them up which we all feel more or·less, according as we outgrow our frivolities, and other things take the place of bloom and beauty.

Miss Barker was a power in the Lynne family; a firm, strong, decided sort of person. Which, of a woman, may sound a little harsh.

There was no compromising with her; she adhered strictly to accepted facts and never indulged in speculation. Astronomers and scientists and theologians could not impose their guess-work upon her.

· Mrs. Lynne was held to be in easy circumstances. The statement, of course, requires modification according to locality. The reader has an inkling of what it would signify in Hazelville. The chief source of her income was a small farm a mile or two out of the village.

Wilmingard, always spoken of as Wilma Lynne, had inherited a small fortune and an old Knickerbocker name from her father, neither of which she had come into actual possession of as yet.

The fortune was fixed for a day when she should have arrived at a discretionary age. The day was now not far distant.

As to the name, Wilma had many times had vague dreams about going to New York and hunting up her family connections, who, as her mother expressed it, were somewhat "high-flown," and had always looked down upon poor little Mrs. Lynne, especially after her second marriage (immediately after which she had quitted the metropolis and emigrated to the West), which was far beneath the Knickerbocker pride.

Wilmingard stood in great awe of that side of her house; even of her father's picture, a stately painting hanging curtained in her mother's chamber.

Her first marriage was the romance of Mrs. Lynne's life. She had been taken from a little country town to a pretentious city home, and was tenderly loved by a noble husband, a little too grave and too great for her, it may be, though he did not live to learn it.

The romance only lasted two short years, and then she

went out a widow from among her husband's coldly patronizing people, back to the little country town.

Wilmingard, pretty, delicate, and brown-eyed, upon whom they had bestowed their pet family name, they begged to be permitted to adopt and bring up; but without success.

When Mrs. Lynne with her husband and their two children were about to emigrate Westward, a fine carriage drove up one day, and two fine ladies, whose soft, dark hair was mixed with gray, got out and came with rustling silks into the little parlor where she was sitting, and renewed their supplications for the child, who stood by with her shy, wondering eyes.

Meeting again with a distressed but firm refusal, they took Wilma in their arms and kissed her, and told her that when she grew up she must come and see them.

One of them gave her a little gold locket, and the other a Bible with clasps; then they touched her mother's hand with the tips of their slender, gloved fingers, and went away sorrowfully, as from a funeral, with tears on their thin white cheeks, which they dried with their delicate cambric handkerchiefs.

Wilma did not understand the scene, but it left a deep impression on her young mind: an impression which was the cue to all her after-speculations about her father's family.

CHAPTER XIII.

Wilma's lover (whose identity I do not doubt the reader already suspects) left that young lady at her mother's gate upon coming down from seeing the sunset.

A gentleman was approaching the gate from within; a gentleman who was professedly courting Miss Barker, though it is to be feared without serious intentions. He bowed deeply upon meeting Wilma, to which she returned an inadequate little nod, showing—without her intending it—the exact degree of respect in which she held him, and passed on.

Outside the gate the gentleman walked briskly to overtake Wilma's lover, upon which he slackened his pace, touched his hat and asked with a smile, which was all a smile could be in the way of trying to make itself agreeable and insinuating:

"I have the honor of addressing Mr. Burns, I believe?"

Mr. Burns looked up, and then bowed, coldly.

"We business men, you see," said the gentleman, in no way disconcerted, "have a better chance of knowing strangers than they have of knowing us. Though I take it you hardly call yourself a stranger. He, he! Think the name would apply better to myself, doubtless. I beg your pardon, sir."

"There is no apology necessary," said Mr. Burns, with dignity.

"It is true," continued the gentleman, "that I have not lived here a great while; but then, while I have been growing into the place, you, sir, have been growing out of it. Sorry I didn't have an opportunity of making your acquaintance sooner; been East on business. Understand you leave us again in a day or two?"

Mr. Burns bowed again, coldly.

"I suppose you don't recollect seeing me once before?" The gentleman put the question as he might a puzzle.

"I don't think I have ever had the honor," Mr. Burns returned.

"Well, sir, you were in my store this morning. Elston's old stand, you remember; new sign,—Dry Goods and Notions. You came in on a little matter of trade,—cigars, perhaps."

"I don't smoke," said Mr. Burns, expressing as much disapproval of the practice as could be crowded into so brief a sentence.

"Ah! my mistake. Beg pardon. My clerk waited upon you. Well, sir, I took advantage of the occasion of your coming in to make some inquiries about you, of gentlemen who were sitting around; which, permit me to say, were answered in a manner highly creditable to you."

Mr. Burns showed his appreciation of this compliment

by kicking, with some vehemence, a small stone off the sidewalk.

"But, sir, I beg your pardon! I had forgotten to introduce myself to you. He, he! My name is Smith. Popular name, isn't it? Not much danger of its being soon extinguished. He! he! he!"

It was a stale joke, which he had perpetrated many times before. Nevertheless, he laughed enjoyably, his mirth in no way lessened by the fact that he laughed alone.

"Town changed considerable since you were last here?" he inquired complacently, after they had walked along for some distance in silence.

Mr. Burns replied uncompromisingly that he had not observed any remarkable changes, at least in the way of improvement.

"O, come, now; that's too bad! The place seems a little dull just now, because a good many have pulled up stakes and gone West. Leaves an opening for a few wide-awake chaps to come in and take their place. Should think you'd quit college now and go into business. Splendid opportunity with your stock of learning. Might start a hardware store or grocery. It doesn't pay to spend all a fellow's worth getting an education, especially that sort of education that can't be turned to account in trade. What's the use of science and languages to fellows like us who haven't got a fortune to back us? There's no money in them! I'll tell you what, there is one kind of schools I like,—these commercial colleges. They fit a man for business. Nothing ornamental about them, it's all useful. It's true, I'm something of a dabbler in literature myself; was educated that way, you see. Read the poets now and then, and scribble a little occasionally. But if I had a boy to bring up I'd send him to a commercial college."

Mr. Burns's dignity suffered tortures; especially as it was of that fine quality which disdains reply to stupidity or impertinence. He took advantage of the first convenient street-crossing to step aside with a superior air and very formal "I bid you good-evening, Mr. Smith."

The impressiveness was lost on the pachydermatous

Smith, who, thus suddenly pulled up, responded cordially, though in a tone of slight surprise, and walked on soliloquizing, "Hum, queer chap! A *leetle* hard to get acquainted with. Young, though ; hasn't seen much of the world yet, I take it."

CHAPTER XIV.

MEANWHILE, Wilma went into the house and sat down with the family in the best room, which was a very plain room, with a faded carpet, cane-seated chairs, and coarse white curtains at the windows. The only thing that attempted ornamentation was Miss Barker's little rosewood melodeon with its carved legs. Before it sat that lady, not performing, but looking over a little work on thorough bass that was upon the rack. Blanche was seated near her with her feet drawn up on her chair-rung, her short dress reaching scantily below the knees, contracting a pair of precocious eyebrows over a slate and an arithmetic.

Mrs. Lynne looked up from her knitting when Wilma entered, and asked with mild reproof, "Isn't it rather chilly to be out so late, Wilmingard ?"

"Oh, no," said Wilma, a little shrinkingly, the question grazing the edge of her ideal world, of which Mr. Burns was the centre, and of which she never made any mention in the presence of her family.

They knew of her engagement, but of all the tender hopes and plans of the two young hearts they were quite ignorant. The engagement, which, notwithstanding their extreme youth, was already of long standing, wore a very matter-of-fact aspect to all outsiders, except, perhaps, Mr. Burns's mother.

"You wouldn't mind if your fingers and toes were a freezing, so long as my Lord Lofty's around, would you, Will ?" said Fred, who sat with his elbows on the table and his chin dropped in the palms of his hands, looking out sleepily from under a great shock of light, frizzly hair.

Mrs. Lynne glanced up reprovingly. She was fearful —like many a poor woman left alone to bring up a house-full of children—of having her authority trampled on, and so continually held it up like a banner before the eyes of her subjects. Resulting from which, it is not strange that it was sometimes treated with a disrespect like that paid to Gessler's cap by the indomitable William Tell.

Fred was silent a moment, and sat winking drowsily at his mother's knitting-needles. By and by, he looked across at Wilma again, his tantalizing spirit unsubdued.

"Why didn't 'Squire Burns come in and spend the evening, Will? Couldn't condescend, eh? There ain't any of the rest of us high-toned enough, I s'pose."

Mrs. Lynne again waved her banner by flashing at.him another grieved, reproving look, which he affected not to notice. Blanche, with a world of indignation in her black eyes, shot a glance at her brother over her slate-rim.

"You think you're dreadful smart, Frederic Lynne!"

"Why, sis, who'd 'a thought you'd 'a spoke!" said Fred, turning around with mock surprise.

Blanche figured away in sarcastic silence. She had great respect for Mr. Burns, whose rather proud bearing and dignified reserve accorded with her young ideas of a gentleman. Frequent skirmishes on his behalf were carried on between herself and Fred, all pretty much upon the same plan and all ending in Fred's discomfiture.

Wilma never took any part in such combats. She was too keenly sensitive where Mr. Burns was concerned even to defend him, though the blood tingled in her very finger-ends to hear him assailed.

Blanche presently slid down from her chair, put by her book and slate, and going up to Miss Barker asked, coaxingly, "Please sing something, won't you, Miss Barker? Sing 'Annie Lawrie.'"

Miss Barker complied with a smile (Blanche was a favorite of hers), and touched the keys. A tender prelude glided from under her slim fingers and prevailed over the silence. Frederic's head had dropped upon his folded arms on the table, Mrs. Lynne plied her needles industriously, and Wilma had taken up a book,—a book of poems left by Mr. Smith for Miss Barker's edification.

Miss Barker sang with a queer, half-affected pathos, which Blanche, much admiring, tried her best to imitate, and the chorus, especially, was very plaintively rendered:

> "And for bonnie Annie Lawrie,
> I'd lay me down and dee."

"Oh, Lord!" groaned Fred, raising his sleepy eyes toward the singers.

Blanche flashed round upon him with intense disdain.

"Frederic, what do you mean?" demanded Mrs. Lynne, with much sternness.

"Oh, nothing, mother. I mean that I don't mean no offence to Miss Barker; but to think of a fellow that 'ud lay him down an' die for a girl!"

"Oh, we all know you wouldn't put yourself out for anybody," sneered Blanche.

"Yes, I would," said Fred. "I don't mind putting myself out a *leetle*, say to beau a girl home with an umbrella of a wet evening, or trot half a mile to fetch her rubbers when she's come off and forgot 'em, or some such reasonable inconvenience; but come to putting myself out *altogether*, blamed if there's a girl in Hazelville I'd do it for."

"Nor anywhere else," said Blanche, incisively.

"I beg pardon, Blanche, and you, too, Miss Barker," said Fred, humbly (though Blanche doubted the genuineness of the humility). "Don't be offend d, go on with your interlude, and let's have the rest."

But Miss Barker had emphatically ceased to play, and arose from the instrument with an offended dignity which she evidently believed would express itself best in silence. And a very ominous silence accordingly followed. It was too much for Fred; in his own language he began to feel "mean," especially when he inadvertently encountered his mother's sorrowful eyes fixed on him in solemn reproach, as much as to say, "See what you have done."

He made a strong resolve to hold his peace, and with

that dropped his head upon the table again. His attention was next attracted by Mrs. Lynne saying something
to Wilma about her wardrobe, having reference to her
going off to school.

" 'Most ready to go, Will?" looking up, his bright
eyes twinkling underneath the bushy hair.

" Yes, I am quite ready," said Wilma, "unless I happen to think of something else."

" I suppose you'll keep on, when you get started, till
you know as much as my learned and lofty brother-in-law
that is to be? Well, that's right,—go ahead. Here's
poetry for it :

> " A little learning is a dangerous thing ;
> Drink deep——"

" Oh, poetry, poetry !" sneered Blanche. "You're
always quoting poetry."

" Blanche, my small sister, you are much too sarcastic
for your years," said Fred. "You are developing pre-
maturely in that particular direction."

" I am afraid she owes that to you, Fred," said Wilma,
who was secretly more in sympathy with Fred than the
others supposed. There was a stratum of sense and good
nature in him which she liked, though she realized as
much as any of them that he must not be upheld in his
odd ways. She never laid up against him anything he
chose to say of Mr. Burns, knowing that it all came out
of a spirit of mischief that loved to tease her. Outside
the family circle Fred himself defended the young colle-
giate with all the boyish eloquence and confidence he
possessed, which was not a little.

Blanche, always industrious, got her little morocco-
covered Testament and began studying her Sunday-school
lesson. After a time she looked up with a puzzled expression and asked (she had a very old head for a little
girl), " Ma, where did the Bible come from?"

Mrs. Lynne glanced up, surprised and disconcerted.

" Huh! I sh'd think everybody 'd know that," said
Fred.

" Do you know? Perhaps you can tell us then!"
Blanche retorted.

"Why, it was handed down," said Fred, lucidly.

"Dear, how smart you are! Handed down where from?"

"Well, that's what we don't know," Fred returned, candidly. "There's some things we don't understand, and it ain't likely we ever will; but we're to believe 'em all the same, for all that. That's faith,—don't you see?"

"No, I don't see," said Blanche. "I don't understand what faith is."

"Why, it's believing what folks tell you whether it's so or not," said Fred.

"Oh, Fred!" exclaimed Wilma.

Miss Barker, horrified, felt that it was time for her to speak.

"Faith," she began, addressing Blanche, to the utter exclusion of Frederic, "means that you are to accept and believe just what the Bible says."

"Yes, I know," said Blanche, with her baby brows precociously contracted, "but there are lots of things that the Bible doesn't say!"

"You are not to trouble yourself about what it does not say," returned Miss Barker, severely, stopping inquiry with authority instead of satisfying it with explanation, which is perhaps not the most effectual way to lead young minds into the right belief. "It says enough for everybody's salvation if they choose to accept it."

"Or for everybody's damnation if they don't choose to accept it!" said Fred, with a sudden inspiration, anxious to impress Blanche with the sufficiency of the Scriptures.

Miss Barker raised her hands and turned her face aside to ward off the blasphemy.

"If we could clearly understand about the judgments spoken of in the Bible," interposed Wilma, "as well as the rewards, I suppose we should find them to mean nothing more than the natural consequences of sin, or of righteousness."

"That's a fact!" said Fred. "Though I suppose we get it at second-hand from you, Wilma."

Wilma blushed, as she always did when betrayed into giving any of Mr. Burns's opinions.

"I think, Frederic, we have heard enough from you this evening," said Mrs. Lynne, with unusual severity. "You may go to bed."

Fred obeyed, thinking to himself as he went up-stairs, "I'm sure I've heard it preached in the pulpit that the most of us are to be damned, and I've given myself up for lost every time. If there's only room for a few, I say let the ladies go ahead as they do at Masonic funerals. I know I ain't good, and I ain't so very particular where they put me, either. I expect there'll be others in the same boat, and I can stand what the rest can. That's a pretty good idea of Will's—or young Burns's—that we've just got to suffer the consequences. Of course it stands to reason that the punishment won't be greater than the offence, if we are to believe in the Almighty's justice. If He ain't disposed to be fair, why, we can't help ourselves, as I see, anyhow. It's my belief, though, that a fellow can pull through, some way or other." With that the philosophic Fred, relying more upon his own stoicism and ability to "stand the consequences" than upon the Supreme Father, tossed his boots into a corner and turned into bed.

The other members of the family were variously affected by the occurrences of the evening. All except Blanche, who, forgetful of everything weighty, went and got her big china-faced doll and arranged it in its white night-gown, a duty she never neglected. Miss Barker felt personally offended with Fred. Wilma believed he would come out all right, he had at bottom such a good, honest, kind heart. Little Mrs. Lynne, deeply distressed, lay awake half the night praying, planning, hoping, despairing for her wayward boy, who was as much hers to guard and care for and love as either of the other children. Poor, tender, mother-hearts, what burdens they carry! Selfish, and yet sublimely unselfish in their great love.

CHAPTER XV.

THE following evening was Mr. Burns's last in Hazel-ville, as he was about to return to his university. It was too precious to spend anywhere save with Wilmingard. Notwithstanding he lingered in his mother's little sitting-room and seemed reluctant to start, for the sweet-faced old lady who sat by the fire with her knitting appeared to watch apprehensively every movement he made. By and by he got up and took his hat.

"Are you going out, Charley?" she asked.

"Only to bid Wilma good-by, mother; shall you be lonely?"

He came round to the back of her chair and bent over and touched her faded cheek with his lips.

"No, I am used to it, you know, my son. Put on your scarf and keep your throat warm. I think it is raining a little. The umbrella hangs in the kitchen."

She got up and took the lamp to get it herself. Poor mother, it was his last evening. He put on his hat, but-toned his coat, and half-regretfully opened the door and stepped out.

"I won't be gone long, mother," he called back, with his hand on the door-knob.

"Very well," said Mrs. Burns, cheerfully, but sighed the moment the door closed, and listened as her son's quick footsteps went ringing down the stone pavement, and then drew up the stand that held the lamp and the family Bible. She took off her spectacles and wiped them on her white handkerchief, and even then could hardly see for the blurring.

Human nature is so rich in resources, and yet how many lives run in a single narrow channel. It seems as if there ought to be more general development of human faculties. Would it not be well, for instance, if parents would cultivate something beside parental affection? Some resources within themselves, some interests not centred wholly in their offspring. Old hearts are very desolate

E*

in the deserted nest after the young birds have flown, as fly they must and will.

A dismal little rain was spattering the pavement as Mr. Burns wended his way to the Widow Lynne's. He found to his extreme annoyance that Mr. Smith, of the immortal family, had preceded him, and was familiarly seated with the family in the best room. Miss Barker and he were engaged in a discussion upon education, in which the former had shown herself in favor of it upon any terms, compulsory or otherwise, and in which Mr. Smith had rather gone against it, giving as his objection to the public school system the immense taxation to keep it up. Moreover, farmers' sons, he declared, and farmers' daughters should not be educated above the plow and the dairy. Else, what will the country do for its bread and butter, by and by, when our boys are all doctors, and lawyers, and preachers, and our girls all fine ladies, who read novels and play on the piano. Miss Barker suggested immigration as a means of recruiting the laboring ranks; but Mr. Smith was opposed to immigration also, though it was evident he had not thought of a way of stopping it.

Mr. Burns upon coming in had seated himself apart from the debaters, and although he at first lent a polite ear to the conversation he forbore participating, and soon drifted into an undertone aside with Wilma. "I wonder how many of us are capable of education?" said he. "So many accumulate knowledge without being really educated. So many appear to think they have no mental faculty but memory. For my part, I have no wish to cram my head with a mere mass of facts, dates, events; what I want is expansion and development. I want to get hold of the best there is in me and bring that out. I believe there is enough of good in every human soul to make a grand character, if only the best was cultivated. Do you observe the mistake these people (nodding toward the group at the other end of the room) have fallen into, of assuming that every man who educates himself must necessarily quit his farm and his quiet occupations and get into public notice?"

Wilma smiled. "After all, that is natural, isn't it?"

"I suppose so, but it is needless. No man who is a thinker and a worker need trouble himself about his obscurity. You know the very desert is traversed by men, and a grand character in any obscure corner of the world is sure to be sufficiently known and admired. I'll tell you what I want, my dear. I want comprehensive rather than accumulative faculties, and the power to bring my mental and moral forces to bear in actual living and working. I don't care to put the world's past in my memory; it is enough to have it in my library for reference or for leisure hours. I want to make a workhouse of my mind, not a storehouse. What good is a human cyclopædia? History is better—more accurate and more lasting—in a book than in a man. Flesh and blood are too costly a binding for statistical records. I could never be a historian to gather up and preserve the implements, the vehicles that men have used in carrying forward the world's progress. I want to be one of those who go forward into the unknown."

"What if everybody were like you, Charley?" said Wilma, looking up, archly.

"True! we should soon have no foothold in the past, should we?" Charley returned, a sudden expansive smile breaking over his rather grave face. "Somebody has got to keep history going, I suppose. If all were like me the world would soon get into a very chaotic state. But, thank Heaven! we are not all cut after the same pattern. I want to pick out of the great bundle of work that which suits me. I claim it as my right to have a choice. I want knowledge, I want education, only as a lamp to use on my way through life, to light me into the unseen. Do you understand me, Wilma? I want all the helps I can get toward living and working. And this I call education. When my faculties are trained to do what I wish to accomplish, I shall be educated. We have splendid possibilities, my dear; but ah! the waste of human material— human souls. And it is all the result of ignorance; you have no idea of the low, animal life among the mankind of our large cities. Mankind! It is a burlesque upon manhood, upon womanhood. It makes me heart-sick to look upon the suffering, degraded women. It is the saddest picture the world can show.   And in view of it all, one. pair of hands are so powerless.   I thank God, my darling, that it will be my sweet privilege to bless one woman's life, to keep the glad song of love in her heart, the beautiful light of happiness in her eyes always."

Mr. Burns, reaching this climax of beautiful devotion, paused a moment in contemplation.   He had the most tender and chivalric nature, and felt himself to be true and unchangeable.   Wilma's heart thrilled with infinite love and trust.

"I am so glad you are going off to school, Wilma," Charley continued.   "You will learn so much, not merely in books, but in many ways beside.   Of course, I should love you all the same, darling; but I think we shall be better and happier and more useful by being largely and uniformly developed in mind and heart."

"Oh, Charley! I could never know as much as you if I should study a thousand years," Wilma exclaimed.

"Oh, yes, you will, my dear; not the same things, perhaps; I want my wife" (and here the young collegian plumed himself a little) "to know just as much, or more, than I.   Only a little different knowledge, more delicate, more refined, just as a woman's mind differs from a man's, being more gentle and beautiful "

It must be allowed that Mr. Burns's tone and bearing sometimes justified Fred's criticism of him, if we judge him from Fred's standpoint.   A few college years had lifted him above ignorance, but he had not yet acquired that broad, charitable wisdom that makes a man tolerant of—I had almost said of *all things*.   He could hardly help looking back with contempt on the grovelling lives he had left behind him.   The little, quiet town whose pulse never quickened to the beat of the world's great drum; he had shaken its dust from his feet.   However, that youthful egotism that despises the lower life while aiming after the higher, is not a bad thing viewed by the philosopher stationed a little farther on in the way of life; by and by, when it has risen clear of the dust itself, it will acquire a broader vision and expand with a softer charity.

Charles Burns was very much awake upon the great life

problem, and felt a high degree of personal responsibility.
Well, the enthusiasts are the men that move the world.
They give the impetus.

By and by, Miss Barker and Mr. Smith got into a con-
troversy about the poets, and the latter appealed to Mr.
Burns. "I say, Burns, don't you think Tom Hood was
a great poet? Miss Barker, here, is inclined to dispute
his laurels."

Mr. Burns replied, a little stiffly, that it was perhaps
a matter of taste, education, and cultivation, whether he
would be considered "great." Remarking, that there is
a market for literature the same as for other produce, and
that it is changeable and fluctuating all over the world.
In certain localities Hood might rank above Shakspeare ;
in others, fall below Widow Bedott. Just as, in some
places, the superior article of food is rice ; in others, corn ;
in others, potatoes.

"Oh, of course," Mr. Smith returned, uncertain
whether the young collegian sided with him or not : indeed, Mr. Burns had purposely left that point obscure.
"Of course, everybody has his own opinion."

"On the contrary, very few have," said Mr. Burns,
taking him up unceremoniously. "We usually borrow
other people's opinions, without taking the trouble to form
our own. In the matter of books and authors, the critics
decide for us. Popish rule takes the Bible out of the hands
of ignorance, fearing misconstruction; none the less, we
have a priesthood to interpret all our books."

Mr. Smith was a persistent talker, and might have continued the discourse indefinitely, having succeeded in getting Mr. Burns launched ; but he had an engagement that
could not well be put off, being an engagement with a
debtor who was coming in to "settle up," and so he was
obliged to take his departure, which he did with reluctance.
He approached Mr. Burns to bid him good-night and
good-by, and Mr. Burns got up and bowed, with his hands
behind him. Shortly afterward he himself took leave of
the family, and Wilma went with him down to the gate.
It would have been impossible for her to have kissed him
"good-by" in the presence of them all.

It could hardly be called a sad parting with so much

love and trust on both sides, though there were tears in Wilma's eyes. Charley said, tenderly, his strong arm clasping her waist, and his smooth cheek pressing hers, "It will not be for long, Wilma; be brave and patient, and trust the future all to me, my little one. I shall think of you and love you all the time, darling. Good-by, good-by!"

He turned and walked away rapidly, and Wilma leaned over the low gate and looked and listened as long as his footfalls echoed through the night's stillness, big slow tears dropping silently and unheeded. Then she went back into the house and up-stairs to her own little chamber and closed the door, feeling that there was a sacredness in this hour in which she had parted from her lover, perhaps for a whole year, which must not be intruded on. She liked being alone, though she was fond of people. She liked to speculate about them, and invest them with wonderful histories. The self-consciousness going on in every soul was a deep, romantic mystery to her.

By some one of the many seemingly singular affinities in this world (what outwardly conglomerate assemblages there would be if there were no obstructions in the spiritual currents that draw people together!), Wilma had contracted a strong friendship with a family consisting of three elderly maiden sisters, whom Fred impiously called the three Black Crows, because of their having peculiar bird-shaped faces and always dressing in black. These ladies were much in advance of the village in point of breeding and cultivation. They were very isolated and not very well liked, being considered proud, because, poor ladies, they did·not know how to put themselves on a level with coarse minds. Mrs. Lynne, though not coarse, had no key with which to unlock their different nature, and so shared in the general dislike.

Wilma went to them under a sort of protest of her mother and Miss Barker, and the whole village, in fact. Indeed, most of the things Wilma liked to do—and did do, for, though she had little combativeness and would have been better pleased to drift with the tide than to stem it, she had a keen intuition of right, and a strong disposition to follow it—she did under protest. Being

naturally amiable and obliging she would have been easily
led and controlled, without this innate principle which
made it a difficult thing for her to be pushed into a corner and kept there by others' prejudices.

Wilma's friends, the Shermans, had seen better days,
as their surroundings and belongings testified. They had
books, and pictures, and fine old lace-curtains, and ancient, stiff, silk dresses. They lived in a rambling, low-
roofed old·house, unpainted and moss-covered, shut in
by trees and clambered over by vines; a curious and
romantic place from which almost all the villagers, envious
of Wilma's freedom of it, were shut out by their own
unkindly regard and awe of its inmates. The three sisters, quaint and delicate and shrinking from contact with
their neighbors, sat among their old luxuries, and looked
out a little shiveringly upon the cold, unsympathetic
world. And Wilma was the only bit of fresh young life
that penetrated into their home and hearts. And it was
only when safe in the midst of them, with their kindly
and lively sympathy stirred for her, and their sweet,
home-like atmosphere surrounding her that Wilma freely
expanded. They gave her a freedom that nobody else
who acted upon her life—even Charley—allowed her.

On the walls in the Shermans' parlor, and in the folios,
were some fine paintings and engravings. What interested
Wilma most among them were the portraits of eminent
men and women,—men and women who had thought
and suffered, and whose faces were books. Charley had
often said to her in their rambles through the woods
and over the hills, "I love nature, Wilma!" And once
she answered, laughing, "And I like folks." "Well,"
said he, "we shall see which love is abiding, nature's
or man's."

Ordinarily Wilma was not brilliant in looks; there was
only now and then a flaming out of the inspiration within
her to color her cheeks and illumine her eyes. She had
a soft, brown, fine-textured skin, and an abundance of
light hair, some of it short, and curling in little ringlets
about her face. Her eyes were much darker, large and
brown, and sometimes limpid and bright as the shaded
brook in the heart of the woods.

The morning following Mr. Burns's last visit was very hard to be got through with. Miss Barker put on her bonnet and started to school at eight o'clock, so as to be there betimes to sweep the room, and dust, and set the children's copies before the legalized hour for beginning the day's work. In half an hour Blanche followed. Fred hitched up in the one-horse cart and drove out to "the farm," and Mrs. Lynne and Wilma were left to do up the morning work. Wilma went about with a brain full of thoughts and a heart full of emotions that her busy mother had no conception of, being occupied with her own affairs.

At nine the stage would start from the hotel and she could see it from her chamber window. She had dwelt upon that anticipation all the morning with such a concentration of longing for one more glimpse of her lover that it seemed as if her mother must read it in her face. At last she was at liberty and flew up-stairs, her heart throbbing as though some great crisis was at hand. Only to see Charley a quarter of a mile distant. She put aside the curtain and looked off eagerly in the direction of the hotel. She could see the barn, and they were bringing out the horses. Two or three travellers were standing on the stoop in front of the hotel waiting. But no Charley. Her eyes ran swiftly down the street in the direction of his home, shut out of sight by the hills and trees. In a moment he came leisurely around the corner, carrying his travelling-bag. Wilma's heart bounded and the blood rushed up into her face at sight of the splendid figure, broad-shouldered and athletic, full of elasticity and strength, and the perfect health and vigor of youth. She longed intensely to be with him for one moment, just one moment, to feel the clasp of his hand and say "good-by," again. Her eyes were full of passionate tears. The morning had been long enough, why had he not come? She remembered that she had not asked him to come, and, for all his tenderness, he was so proud. It seemed to her, as he went up into the porch and stood among the other men carelessly talking, that he was leagues away from her. There was nothing in his manner that had any reference to her.

Suddenly her heart thrilled; he walked to the end of the long porch, apart from the others, and looked away to the top of Little Twin. Then she knew he was thinking of her, and they were again united.

The stage rattled up, and he turned and walked back and threw his travelling-bag into it, and sprang up on the seat with the driver. The others got inside. A sudden thought occurred to Wilma; she might at least meet his eyes once more; there was a turn in the street as it left the village only a few rods from Mrs. Lynne's. There would be a few moments' delay at the post-office, and in the mean time she could walk up that street and go and see her friends, the Shermans, and she would be sure to meet the stage. She felt a guilty little pang at the deception she was practising upon herself,—about the Shermans,—to cover up what seemed to herself, and what she knew Miss Barker and her mother would denounce as a great piece of immodesty.

She flew down-stairs and got her hat and walked rapidly up the quiet, unpopulous street, under the thick shade of the trees that bordered the narrow, steep sidewalk. Just as she reached the foot of the hill on the other side, the stage came banging round the corner. At first she thought, in an agony of suspense, that he would not see her. He was looking straight before him, smiling and talking with the driver. But the intense magnetism of her eyes attracted him. He turned his head suddenly, and a flush of glad surprise broke over his face. He bent forward and kissed his hand to her in the quick moment of passing. It was but an instant, rattlety-bang went the old stage, and he was out of sight. Wilma stood still for a moment, too deeply moved to give a thought to the Shermans, and then turned and went slowly back home.

For many miles the picture of her walking there like a brown, wood fairy under the trees, with the gorgeous autumn leaves above her and under her feet, filled Mr. Burns's thoughts and kept his heart throbbing. "I wonder if she was not there on purpose to see me?" he speculated again and again, feeling more and more tender toward· her as he tried to convince himself that it was so.

The morning had seemed interminably long to him;

he had got up early, in time to see the sun rise, and his mother had set out a dainty breakfast, and he had eaten with hearty relish, partly to please her, and was in fine spirits. But when he had got himself all ready for his journey, even to the locking of his valise and putting the key in his pocket, and looked at his watch to find that he had an hour yet to wait, he began to think of Wilma and to grumble because he could not see her again. Why could he not see her again? What inexplicable something was it that stood in the way of his going over and bidding her "good-by" again? He picked up his hat and went out for a short, brisk walk up the hill back of the house. When he got to its summit he looked across in the direction of Mrs. Lynne's. "Why didn't she tell me to come back this morning?" he ejaculated. "There's plenty of time. I have half a mind to go anyhow." He pondered the thought a moment with knit brows, and then shrugged his shoulders and turned on his heel. "No, confound it! I will not. Probably she wouldn't care to see me again so soon; it would take all the sweetness off the parting last night. I would be a fool to go rushing back! Wilma is afraid of her folks," he supplemented a little contemptuously, as he slowly retraced his steps down the hill. "I have an idea they tease her about me,—that Fred, at any rate; and she is such a sensitive little thing." With that he came back to thinking more tenderly of her, and when he picked up his travelling-bag and kissed his mother good-by, he said, "Be good to my little Wilmingard, mother dear." Showing that between himself and her there was no reserve on this delicate subject.

"You forget that I seldom see her, my son," said Mrs. Burns.

"True, I don't see why she never comes here; I have begged her to come so much." Knitting his brows and then suddenly expanding them again. "But she will some day. God speed the time!"

The first opportunity he had after leaving Hazelville he wrote to her, and said,—

"Tell me, darling, was it accident that brought about that flash of a meeting as we came around the corner, or did you (tell me truly) care enough about me to come on purpose to see me? I have tortured myself with the query ever since. You can't think what a pleasure it was to me, Wilma; that vivid moment photographed a picture of your sweet self upon my mind that can never be erased." .

Wilma, who had been educated in a practical, matter-of-fact school that rather frowned upon the silliness of love-making, answered him back jestingly and coquettishly, and really unlike herself,—

"To think you would suspect me of *designing* to get another glimpse of you, you conceited Charley! I had started to go over to the Shermans."

Mr. Burns replied,—"So my pretty fancy is exploded. Better suspense sometimes, I find, than certainty. It *was* conceited in me, wasn't it? Well, I beg your pardon for the bold suspicion. I'm desperately jealous of those Shermans. To think I should flatter myself all that long journey with such an empty delusion!"

<hr>

CHAPTER XVI.

An omnibus, coming from one of the Eastern trains, backed up early in the evening against the stoop of the Crawford House, in an academic town of that name; and a spruce clerk, with white cuffs and spotless shirt-front, and with a pen behind his ear, came out and handed down, one after another, half a dozen giggling, laughing girls, who, as soon as their flounces were properly shaken down, went tripping off up the street as if quite at home with the place. Last came a little gray figure, which the clerk carelessly assisted to alight, at the same time exchanging jesting remarks with the beflounced damsels, with whom he appeared to be on easy terms. Not until they had all turned their backs upon him and ran, laughing, away did he observe that the small figure standing timidly beside him on the steps was waiting for his returning attention. Then he looked down and asked, quite kindly, if she wished to "stop." Being answered affirmatively, he opened the parlor-door and ushered her in. Before he had quite shut it again she, Wilmingard (to dispense with what may appear like a mystery), asked with deference if she might send a letter to the principal of the academy, and drew it from her pocket. Miss Barker had written it in the character of her former teacher. The clerk took it unceremoniously and disappeared.

Wilmingard took off her hat, and seated herself at one of the front windows and looked out. Crawford was not a large town, but to eyes just opening upon the world it seemed very imposing. The church-spires were much taller than the church-spire in Hazelville. The business blocks were large and high and compact, and the dwellings—what few came within range of the window—were elegant beyond any she had ever seen before. Grander than ·all, in the distant, upper end of town, loomed up the bulky brick proportions of the academy, whose shining pewter dome was just now ablaze with the reflection of the sun far down in the west. The streets of the little city were remarkably broad and smooth, and an occasional carriage full of smiling faces and gay draperies went rolling along. The sidewalks were gravelled and bordered on the outside with rows of maple-trees and little square patches of thick green sod enclosed by a low white railing. Everything wore a sort of holiday aspect. Young girls in jaunty hats and gay jackets sauntered by in groups, talking and laughing. Good-looking young men struck their boot-heels sharply upon the pavement, and walked briskly as if life meant something decided.

It was all new and beautiful and wonderful to Wilmingard, the wide-awake town crowded with gay and happy-seeming human life. It was always the humanity part that touched her. The beautiful town itself, its fine buildings, its trees and tinted autumn leaves, and its boundary of low hills lighted up by a golden sunset, was but the gilt and rosewood framing-in of the exquisite picture of human life. Most of the young people Wilmingard made sure were students, and devoured their faces eagerly as they passed along, thinking with great trepidation how soon she would be among them ; but

never of them,—oh, no! She looked down at her plain
gray dress and sober little hat, and smiled. She could
never be so jaunty. Well, she did not care to be; she
reassured herself by going back into her own little world
and remembering the dear ones that comprised it. Crawford meant nothing to her but education. She did not
look for it to take hold upon her in any other way. She
had hardly speculated even upon what her teachers and
classmates might be to her or how they would affect her,
except that she had dreaded being plunged into a world
of strangers. She had no more thought of enlarging her
life socially, and letting a stream of new people into it,
than Lake Erie has of opening its arms and embracing
the ocean, if one may make so grand a comparison in
reference to so small and obscure a person. She was satisfied with her own little sphere.

Perhaps there is little danger of shipwreck so long as
the heart has a safe anchor grappling it to something,—a
mother, or a brother, or a sister, or only a memory or a
steady hope. Without it a human soul is in peril, unless
it have an inner strength of its own that enables it to
drop anchor in any sea and live in any storm. There
are brave souls rocked in mid-ocean that need no helps
from outside; the *God in them* is stronger than all that is
round about them.

Watching the crowd on the street, Wilmingard singled
out a figure walking rapidly down the opposite sidewalk,
—a tall, distinguished-looking man, dressed in black,
magnificent in form and carriage compared with all the
other passers-by. He bent his head downward like
people do who have a good deal to think about, and knit
his black brows. ·He had more than ordinary momentum
(in whatever way the word may be taken), and people
made way for him, and young men lifted their hats as
they passed him, which courtesy he briefly acknowledged.
He crossed the street, and Wilmingard lost sight of him
around the corner of the hotel, but in another moment the
parlor-door opened and he stood on the threshold.

The clerk, having hold of the door-knob, swung himself around in sight and announced, "The principal,
Professor Ingraham."

Wilmingard got up with palpitating heart and stood trembling before so august a personage. It seemed to her that Miss Barker's prim, laboriously-composed letter of introduction had brought about a tremendous consequence which she could never have foreseen. The piercing eyes under the knit black brows transfixed her, but in an instant a smile—with which the mouth had little to do, being hid by a black beard—scattered the sombre expression and illuminated the fine, dark face.

He crossed the room quickly and held out his hand, retaining Wilmingard's in a strong, magnetic grasp, while he asked a few rapid questions. Was she alone? Had she just arrived? Did she want a boarding-place? She felt completely taken out of her little world and introduced into a new, strange, but not disagreeable atmosphere. The principal, despite the magnitude of his presence, had a peculiar personal winsomeness. A sense of how his students who were near to him by long association must love him, pervaded her first impressions of him. He seemed so protective. He was just that sort of strong, broad-shouldered, great-hearted man to be loaded with everybody's burdens and to bear them easily. He had a wonderful faculty for smoothing other people's paths; Wilmingard felt that intuitively in the grasp of his hand. "My sons," and "my daughters," he called his students, and held them all by their heart-strings, which is about as strong a hold as you can get upon human nature.

"I will take you home with me to-night, Miss Lynne," said he; "we have no boarding-house proper, as I suppose you know; our students all board with families and in private boarding-houses. The preceptress will find some good place for you to-morrow. You have a trunk?"

"Yes; it is outside somewhere," said Wilmingard.

He stepped to the door and gave some directions about it.

"Now, come," said he.

Wilmingard put on her hat and they stepped out. After they had crossed the street and got upon the other side where the crowd was thicker, the principal looked down and drew her hand within his arm, walking rapidly. He talked very little, seeming preoccupied. Two or

three times he paused to speak a few words to persons
they met, relating to business matters, and it seemed to
Wilmingard that he quite forgot her as he strode on
again. Half-way up the main street he stopped and
opened the gate leading up to a pretty, Gothic house.

"Well, here we are," said he.

"Is this your home?" Wilmingard asked, feeling that
it was an unnecessary question, but possessed of a desire
to make herself as agreeable as her small powers would
permit.

"This is my home," said the principal, concisely.

A little shrub-bordered path, gravelled like the sidewalks, wound around to a side door facing the south, and
in a small portico partly protected by a mass of slightly
frost-bitten vines sat a pale-faced, severe-looking lady,
with a scarlet shawl around her, who looked up without
a smile. Her presence was singularly chilling.

"Why, Leah," said the principal, "is it not too cold
for you to be sitting here?"

He spoke in a tone both cheery and solicitous, or in
that venturous tone that is doubtful of the mood of the
person addressed and tries to be conciliatory.

"Where have you stayed so long?" she returned,
coldly.

"I went down to the hotel to fetch this little girl,
having met her messenger on the street. There! I have
forgotten your medicine," striking his hand on his breast-
pocket.

"Oh, well, no matter, seeing you had more important
business to attend to," she replied, in the most cutting
and yet the quietest tones.

"I'll send James for it as soon as he comes in," said
he, ruefully; and then, seeing Wilmingard, "This is Miss
Lynne, from H—— County, Mrs. Ingraham."

Mrs. Ingraham gave the merest recognition, and then
the principal took her on into the house, and told her to
be seated and to take off her hat, and there his hospitable
civilities ended,—men having, as a general thing, small
knowledge of such matters. Then he stepped to the
dining-room door and told a girl, who was setting the
table for tea, to call Miss Belmont; after which he placed

his hat on the table and seated himself in a large arm-chair, leaned back and passed his hand once or twice across his forehead, as if to smooth out the deep lines upon it, and ran his fingers through his hair, which was very black and heavy, and slightly streaked with gray.

Wilmingard felt that she might study his face as openly as she liked, so oblivious he made himself as he sat waiting. He seemed to her much older and more care-worn than at first, and she felt a sort of tender pity mingling with her spontaneous affection for him.

In a few moments a quick, light step came down-stairs and along the hall, the door of which was ajar. Mr. Ingraham got up quickly and went forward, the sombre expression of his face breaking away and an eager, relieved look coming into his eyes, that made the fair face of the woman who entered flush a pale pink.

"Here is a new student, Miss Belmont; Miss Lynne, from H——— County. Miss Lynne, this is your preceptress."

He turned Wilma over to her, just as a man so often turns over things to a quiet, clear-headed, strong-hearted woman on whom he has the greatest reliance, and went out into the portico.

Miss Belmont justified his reliance upon her; Wilma unconsciously felt it the moment the blue eyes beamed upon her face and the white hand closed over hers in a firm, kindly clasp. She had been on the borders of home-sickness the moment before, and felt, just now, that it was not of half so much consequence to get an education as to gain a friend, in this new world upon which she was suddenly launched without, in one sense, the least preparation. It was her first experience in loneliness, though she had spent a large share of her young life alone; and she was surprised into a knowledge of the before unthought-of fact, that the presence of strangers makes one's isolation felt.

Miss Belmont was neither very young nor very beautiful; but there was something about her more charming than youth or beauty. It had speedily lifted the cloud from Mr. Ingraham's brow, and it comforted Wilma inexpressibly.

Mr. Ingraham came in, in a moment, with his icy companion, and they all went out to tea. The latter was certainly not open to genial influences. She seated herself at the table with cold stateliness, and made such serious business of table etiquette that Wilma, poor child, who had a voracious appetite after her journey, felt under too great constraint to eat, and left the table almost as hungry as she had sat down to it.

Nowhere else did Mr. Ingraham labor under such great disadvantage as in his own home—in the presence of his own wife. As Wilma subsequently learned, she had brought him a fortune, and he had somehow lost it ; and she had no hesitancy in saying she had thrown herself away upon him. She had had children ; their four smiling faces looked down upon her from her bedroom walls but their little pattering feet and prattling tongues were silent. Altogether her life had gone wrong, and she was "soured."

One is sometimes tempted to ask, Is the leaven of sweetness in us, or in circumstances? Could we be any better or worse, any happier or more miserable, if fate had ordered our affairs otherwise?

Mrs. Ingraham was said to be bitterly jealous of her husband ; jealous even of his fatherly regard for the young ladies of the academy ; and some shrewd persons hinted that she had need to be. Others said, Bah ! he had a genial, affectionate disposition, and the natural outlets of his warm, generous heart being cut off by the death of his children and the coldness of his wife, other channels had to be opened, and it was a good thing he had charge of young people. He was tender-hearted and exceedingly sympathetic ; thought it no compromise of his manhood to be deeply affected at a play, or a funeral, or anything sad, or tragic, or pathetic. I have said he had unusual momentum, and whichever way he turned he was sure to go with a certain force, putting his whole soul into what he did. He was a fine dramatic reader, and could personate a great variety of characters.

The day following Wilma's advent in the school, she heard him read Shylock, and thought nothing could be more hideous, and at the same time more fascinating, than his dark, swarthy, and rather handsome face con-

torted into a representation of the despised Jew. Passing
directly from that, he repeated, with the happiest change
of expression :

> " When breezes are soft, and skies are fair,
>   I steal an hour from study and care,
>   And hie me away to the woodland scene,
>   Where wanders the stream with waters of green ;
>   As if the bright fringe of herbs on its brink
>   Had given their stain to the waves they drink," etc.

At home he spent a good deal of time among his books ;
piles of books, on the tables, on the floor, on chairs ;
and he was so fond of a listener—some one to share the
things which he liked—that he seized on whoever came
in his way. He made endless demands on Miss Belmont.
But Miss Belmont, though secretly in sympathy with his
fine literary tastes and keen intellect, had marked out a
line of duty, as well as of study, for herself, and it did
not often run parallel with Mr. Ingraham's wishes.

Mr. Ingraham was not troubled by conventionalities ;
the little politeness and suavity that varnish most men's
manners, he was quite free from. He wasted no time ; he
took a man by the hand, and went straight at what he
wished to say ; his mobile face expressing whatever feeling
was uppermost.

After tea, they all went back into the sitting-room,
which Miss Belmont made cosy for the evening by letting
down the curtains, drawing out a small table, and arranging the lamp and the evening's mail, which James, the
errand boy, had just brought in, upon it, and opening the
grate in which there was a little fire to melt the chill of
an October evening. Mr. Ingraham went across the hall
into his study, put on his dressing-gown and slippers,
then came back and drew up his arm-chair, and settled
himself in it preparatory to looking over the papers. But
he was presently visited by some students, whom he carried off into his study, because student-visitors annoyed
Mrs. Ingraham. So his big easy-chair, that had an air of
belonging exclusively to himself as though imbibing some
of his personality, stood empty, and made a vacancy
keenly felt in the small circle, at least by Wilmingard.

Mrs. Ingraham sat gloomily by the fire, with her shawl

around her in which she appeared always to wrap herself up along with her troubles. Miss Belmont tried to interest her in a magazine article, but met with so little encouragement that she laid the book aside and took up some needle-work, and turned her attention to Wilmingard, whose open heart and mind were taking in a world of new impressions almost unconsciously. Our consciousness is the last thing to waken ; years after a certain set of images pass before us, we wake up to the meaning of them. Just as when we are children, we read a grand poem for its musical rhythm, and see nothing else in it until we are gray-haired, maybe.

Wilmingard took in a few disconnected ideas respecting the various members of this singular family,—Mrs. Ingraham's utter disagreeableness, Miss Belmont's wonderful gentleness, tinged with a faint sadness, and even the principal's well-governed impatience at the unreasonable constraint put upon him. But the workings of the combined domestic machinery were a mystery to her that remained obscure for years.

Miss Belmont was Mrs. Ingraham's step-sister, and owed her education to her and lived under the weight of the obligation. She was housekeeper in Mr. Ingraham's domestic establishment as well as preceptress in his academy.

At last Mrs. Ingraham got up and left the room, barely having the grace to say "good-night" as she closed the door. Miss Belmont sighed, and presently put aside her work.

"We will go up-stairs now, my dear. I presume you are tired and sleepy, and would like to go to bed," she said to Wilmingard, who did not object.

As they were about leaving the room Mr. Ingraham came back, having dismissed his visitors, and looked surprised to find the little circle broken up so soon. He asked if Mrs. Ingraham had retired, and then added, "And you two are going to desert me, also?" Knitting his brows and frowning and smiling at once,—his face being capable of an endless variety and combination of expressions,—"Come back and sit down !"

The preceptress shook her head in some slight embarrassment; she had that sort of delicate, transparent complexion that is quick to flush and pale.

"Our little friend is tired and must go to bed," she explained, glancing at Wilmingard.

"But you are not," said he. "You will sit up half the night poring over those dry books; bring them down here by the fire."

He spoke with a mixture of imperativeness and persuasion; but the preceptress was resolute, and leading Wilma out into the hall, said, "Good-night," and closed the door, leaving him standing alone on the mat in front of the stove, with his hands behind him and a roof of black hair, which he had been running his fingers through, projecting over his forehead, adding to his look of grim disappointment. He had a tyrannical will, and hated to be frustrated even in little things. His remarkable government in school, that had won his academy an enviable reputation, lay chiefly in his strong personal magnetism. He did not instil principles so much as he infused himself. His students did not obey purely because it was right to obey, but because it was he that commanded. He exercised little visible control over Miss Belmont, and yet there were times when he seemed to read in her flushed face that his magnetic power was felt even by her, and the suspicion pleased him, though he felt chagrined that she set up her quiet, resolute will in opposition to him.

He remained standing a moment, and then betook himself to what were available: namely, his arm-chair, the papers, and a foot-rest, and forthwith forgot that he was alone or lonely.

Miss Belmont took Wilmingard up into a little white room opening out of her own, and touched her lips with a good-night kiss and went out, leaving the door ajar, and set her lamp down on a table piled high with ponderous books. Not a paper or magazine; no gilt-edged leaves or ornamental bindings; all grave-looking volumes bound in calf. Seating herself, and opening one of them, she began to study earnestly, absorbingly, as only those can who have learned the art of close application.

Wilmingard, watching her through the open door, felt

that her own and Miss Belmont's consciousness, mingling a moment before, and creating a little world in common around them, were divided now, and each was alone. She began to realize all the new sensations of being for the first time in her life among strangers, surrounded by strange white walls and unfamiliar objects. Not unpleasant sensations; the two rooms, Miss Belmont's and her own, had an exquisite air of purity from being absolutely clean. An air that extended to Miss Belmont herself, who was daintily neat in person.

Wilmingard had a good opportunity now to study her face as she had studied Mr. Ingraham's. She had a broad, low, projecting forehead, and her light, silken hair was parted and combed carefully above it and coiled behind. Her skin was without speck or blemish, and delicately fair. Her face was too short and broad for beauty, though it was fine in intelligence and expression. She had small, firm hands, short-fingered, not soft, but white and smooth. Mr. Ingraham called her "The Little Woman," and it seemed to imply that she had wrapped up in her small person a great deal of the dignified, admirable quality which we call womanliness. A firm, energetic, determined character was hers, softened by the gentlest—almost timid—manners.

Wilmingard lay watching her sleepily until her eyes involuntarily closed. Long afterward Miss Belmont sat studying, and all the while the red coals glowed in the sitting-room stove, and Mrs. Ingraham's cushioned chair stood empty and open-armed. (Of all people in the world, Mrs. Ingraham was not jealous of Miss Belmont.) And Mr. Ingraham would have been glad of just her silent presence. Not that he preferred Miss Belmont's presence to that of any other intelligent, companionable person, whose silent thoughts (even) were in harmony with his own. He hated the solitary evenings and wanted somebody to talk to occasionally, and to read to, to take an interest in what interested him. It chafed him to be left alone. Even if he were busy studying or writing, so that he never looked up, or spoke, or showed by any sign that he was conscious of another presence, he yet liked to feel that some other was there. Mrs.

Ingraham was never available, preferring the solitude of her own room and the companionship of the four smiling baby faces on the walls. So he looked to Miss Belmont; but Miss Belmont would not amuse him.

Under different circumstances (if Mr. Ingraham had been an unmarried man), it might have been attributed to womanly pique; for he seldom took any notice of the preceptress in society, or even in the academy, where among all the teachers and professors she was the staunchest pillar, being the profoundest scholar, the deepest thinker, and most indefatigable worker of them all. She was a philosopher, a constant seeker after the abstract and hidden, and delighted in tracing the analogy of all things to all things, and in bringing all investigation to bear on the great problem of human life and destiny. Though living, in her inner consciousness, the most solitary, isolated life, she had the warmest, tenderest, most charitable love for mankind. She had the finest moral and spiritual perceptions and æsthetic tastes. If people had taken the trouble to know her they would have called her fastidious, and stood in fear of her verdict. As it was, nobody was offended by her critical judgment. The merest chit of a pianist would dash off a piece of music in the most soulless manner and expect her to admire it, or, at most, not care whether she admired it or not.

How we shallow, conceited creatures would writhe under the lash of these silent, terrible judges, did they but apply it! Our safety lies in their nobility, that will not stoop to criticise us by so much as a sneer.

Miss Belmont did not assert her own individual, grand nature. She was simply the preceptress. She wore that garb, and it concealed her as effectually as the black dress conceals the personality of the nun. She surveyed men and things from.a far-above, disinterested standpoint, her mind spreading out like a clear intellectual and moral sky above the petty contentions, egotism, and prejudices of men. It is not strange she was not appreciated; our appreciation of a thing is commensurate only with our understanding of it.

When Wilmingard came to know her better and to study her face, she seemed to reveal much of her grand nature through her eyes; such poor eyes, too, they were, in form and color, but wonderful in light and expression. She was not popular in the academy, she did not shed around her the sunshine that was radiated from Mr. Ingraham. Hers was one of those deep, subtle natures that only a few people find out and worship as they worship truth and honor and heroism. The influence of such persons is certainly more far-reaching and wide-spreading in the end than the magnetism that attracts to itself simply.

Wilmingard awoke with a start the following morning to find herself surrounded with so much strangeness. The shutters were open, but a jasmine clambering up outside the window covered it with a thick, green shade. Nevertheless, she saw that it was daylight and heard the preceptress moving about in the next room. She got up, her whole being quickened with that sense of expectancy one feels when stepping within the borders of a new life, and washed and dressed herself and then pushed open the door and went out. Miss Belmont stood at the window and beckoned to her. Wilmingard went up to her, and she put her arm around her and said, "Good-morning," without turning her head. The window was open from the top half-way down. The sun was peeping up over a long line of many-hued hills stretching away to the east. Wilmingard was forcibly impressed by the spirit of beauty breathed through the scene, and stood silent.

"I always thank God for a morning like this," said Miss Belmont. "I mean spontaneously,—as the birds sing for joy and gladness."

Wilma glanced up into her face; it had a little different expression from the night before,—less sad, more hopeful. She seemed lifted above the clogging circumstances around her. In solitude Miss Belmont gathered up her forces daily, and braced herself for her daily work.

"Should you like to take a short walk before breakfast?" she asked. "I am going out to mail some letters."

Wilmingard assented, and got her hat and shawl and they went down-stairs. No one was astir below except a servant or two, in the far back regions of kitchen and stable. Miss Belmont turned the key in the hall-door and they stepped out. The grass and the trees and shrubbery and fences were all whitened by a thick frost, on which the early and not very powerful sunbeams glistened. The streets were silent, the village looked like a picture of still-life. In a few moments doors began to open and gate-latches began to click.

"Do you like getting up so early in the morning?" Miss Belmont asked.

"I have always been used to getting up early," Wilmingard said; but as to the question of liking it, her mind ran back to numberless occasions when her mother's voice (alas, it gave her a pang to remember it) had aroused her from sweet, reluctant dreams.

Miss Belmont smiled.

"It is natural for the young to sleep," she said. "But it seems to me the morning is our best time; our thoughts are freer, our intellect clearer, and life a little fresher. The night and sleep throw over us a gentle influence like this delicate frost-work on the trees, and when the morning and consciousness break upon us we come out like the day, with a certain vigor and newness."

They went down street several blocks and entered the outer room of the post-office, which stood on a street corner. Miss Belmont dropped her letters in the box, and they turned to go out again.

"Oh, maybe there is a letter for me!" said Wilmingard, with a sudden hope.

Miss Belmont turned back and tapped a little silver bell that stood on the counter. Immediately the postmistress, a woman with a broad, square chin, and mouth firmly locked, as though nothing were ever to be got out of her, came in through a back door and awaited orders.

"Any letters for Miss Lynne?" the preceptress inquired.

The woman turned automatically, and took down a handful of letters from the box marked L, and shifted them rapidly through her hands. She was near-sighted, and held them close to her face. The last one, in a large white envelope, with a bold superscription upon it, Wilma instantly recognized as Charley's. The woman glanced at it a second time and threw it upon the counter. Wilma caught it up with a glad heart-bound that sent the dark red blood into her dusky cheeks, and put it in her pocket. It seemed almost as if Charley himself were beside her, banishing all the newness and strangeness, and throwing around her his own dear, familiar presence. He put so much of himself into his letters,—into the very chirography of his letters.

Mr. Ingraham was out on the steps when they got back, in dressing-gown and slippers, his hair uncombed and projecting over his forehead, as was often the case.

"So, Miss Belmont got you out early, did she, Miss Lynne?" said he, looking quizzically at Miss Belmont rather than at Wilmingard.

"Miss Lynne got herself out," returned the preceptress, the pink flush suffusing her white face again.

Mr. Ingraham smiled, looking at her narrowly as if piercing the delicate reserve with which she hedged herself around. It was as though he said, Come, now, I know you are glad to see me, I know you rather like me; why not give up and let it appear so? But the letting it appear so was where Miss Belmont took a stand and set up a principle. So long as she could preserve the thin partition of unacknowledgment between them, she could preserve her own dignity and command his respect. Perhaps one strong prop to her firm principle was this, that if she lost his respect she would have nothing left.

She passed him on the steps and went in.

"Come into my study," said he, following them into the hall and opening a door opposite the sitting-room door. "It is not breakfast time yet," taking a massive gold watch from his vest pocket. "I want to read you a little scrap from Dr. Holmes. Come!"

"Please bring it into the breakfast-room," said Miss Belmont. "I have a little work to do there."

Mr. Ingraham frowned portentously, and obeyed.

Mrs. Ingraham did not appear at breakfast, which Wilmingard felt to be an immense relief. It seemed to her things would go on much better without that severe lady. The house was remarkably pleasant; it had luxurious furniture, deep bay-windows, pictures, shells, stones, busts,

F*

and no end of books.　Mr. Ingraham's library and study were both in one, but his books were by no means confined to it ; they had the freedom of the house and were scattered about everywhere.

As soon as breakfast was over, Mr. Ingraham went into his study.　By and by the boy "James" drove around in a one-horse topped buggy, and he came out dressed, carrying an armful of books, and got into it and drove away.　A little later, Wilmingard, having gone up-stairs and read her letter by the jasmined window in her little white room, put on her hat and started to walk to the academy with the preceptress,—the distance being nearly half a mile.

The academy enclosure was a large park set with trees and covered with thick, green grass, broken by several gravel walks leading from the building to the different gates.　Miss Belmont opened a gate at a corner of the park and went up to the front entrance, Wilmingard beside her all a-tremble with excitement and anticipation. A group of girls stood in the long hall on the second floor, talking and laughing boisterously.　They drew aside and bowed respectfully, looking a little confused, as Miss Belmont passed.　Immediately a side-door opened and Mr. Ingraham came out with his portentous frown, that did not altogether conceal a certain good-humored gleam in his eyes.　All the girls exclaimed in a breath, "Oh, there's Prof.," and surrounded him and got possession of his hands and began proffering some very earnest petition, looking up to him, towering above them, with the most affectionate admiration.

"Breaking the rules," said he, ignoring their request and moving up the hall.　"What is all this noise about?"

"Oh, we didn't know *you* were in there!" they answered, saucily.

Wilma, glancing back as they turned to ascend a flight of stairs running at right angles with the hall, felt the scene grate upon her somehow, and observed that Miss Belmont's face gathered an expression of almost severe disapproval.

CHAPTER XVII.

WITHIN a day or two Wilmingard was settled at Mrs. Woods's Boarding-House for Students (as a neat inscription above the front door described it); Miss Belmont having been at some pains to secure the best place she could find for her. Mrs. Woods was an elderly lady of strict respectability, who lived quite alone, excepting her boarders and a German girl, Rachel, who helped cook for them. Her boarders were her " family," and she took more care and responsibility upon herself concerning their welfare and behavior than is usually included in the contract between a boarder and his landlady. She was jealous of the reputation of her house, and required the most circumspect conduct on the part of each member. She knew the academy rules and regulations by heart (and kept a copy of them posted up in her dining-room), and reported scrupulously whatever violation of them came under her observation, with such honesty of purpose that no one could accuse her of malice or evil intent; simply rigid justice. She performed her own duty always with careful exactness, and expected the same of others. She would not wrong her milkman out of a half-penny, neither would she allow him to defraud her of a drop of milk.

When Wilmingard was taken over and introduced to her by Miss Belmont herself (a fact that placed her high in Mrs. Woods's respect), there were already five boarders in advance of her,—three young ladies and two young men. She had an opportunity to study their faces the first evening, as they sat around the common study-table; a common study-room and table being Mrs. Woods's plan to economize light and fuel.

The young men were good-looking, bashful fellows, fresh from some out-of-the-way country place, evidently, like Wilma herself. They had been hard-working young men, farmers probably, and now were prepared to be hard students, having a conscientiousness in the matter which " town boys" seldom feel, being " brought up" on learning, rather than work, and consequently more or less satiated with books. They had already a good foundation of arithmetic and other solid branches for an education.

The young ladies were entirely different. One of them, Nellie Beach, had a beautiful face,—though there was not much in it,—a solid, compact little figure, and taciturn, good-natured disposition. She was hard to get acquainted with; there seemed to be nothing in her to fasten to. You might admire her to your heart's content, and she would only smile in her slow way, and give you to feel that no amount of flattery could make her vain, so you flattered her all the more. Every day of her life somebody told her in a spontaneous burst of admiration how beautiful she was. The girls were forever twining her chestnut curls around their fingers and sticking rose-buds among them, and squeezing her little, soft, white hands, and praising her Cinderella foot. And Nellie went through it all with a stoical good nature, and plodded on through her studies with a hopelessness of ever knowing anything. It would make anybody's heart ache to see the slow tears force themselves into her pretty eyes over some incomprehensible text-book mystery. The other two young ladies called each other "Miss Allen" and "Miss MacIvers" with punctilious politeness. It was plain to be seen that the former was only tolerated by the latter because they happened to be thrown together in the same house.

Of Miss MacIvers, Wilmingard stood in profound and admiring awe from the first moment of seeing her. She was the most elegant person she had ever met, exquisite in feature, and indescribably majestic in form and carriage. She had a certain hauteur that blended in a queenly way with her grace and loveliness, but which sprung from pride of intellect rather than pride of beauty. She was a superior scholar, being somewhere in the mysterious labyrinths of Greek and Latin and the higher mathematics. She was a favorite with Miss Belmont because she competed successfully with the advanced class of young men, which few other young ladies did; and Miss Belmont had some pride of sex, and believed in the even balance of masculine and feminine minds, other things being equal. Miss Belmont, whose great mind was capable of weighing so many other minds, felt that Miss MacIvers was deserving of some credit for her intellectual exertions in view of her great beauty, which would have satisfied so many smaller ambitions. She was a great favorite with Mr. Ingraham also, being in every respect an ornament and an honor to the school. But she took no advantage of his partiality, and was not in the least compromised by it. She was very correct and high-principled.

As soon as the young men got through with their lessons they closed their books and went up-stairs, saying, "Good-night," awkwardly, as they left the room, to which only Miss MacIvers, rigidly polite, responded. Shortly afterward the young ladies pushed back their chairs, Nellie giving a weary little sigh.

"Poor child," said Miss MacIvers, pettingly, with a light laugh, "discouraged, are you?"

Nellie smiled sadly, and replied in her slow way, "Oh, yes; it is my natural state. I was born so."

"Too bad. Can't I help you?"

"Not unless you could give me a thimbleful of brains. I don't know why I was cut off with such a short allowance. If I just had enough to put me through this binomial theorem of Sir Isaac Newton's, I think I should be satisfied."

"You can't expect to have everything, Nellie," broke in Miss Allen. "If I had your curls I would let Newton and his binomial theorem go to—— Halifax."

"The curls would help you a good deal on examination day," said Nellie.

"Oh, do you know we are going to have a new music-teacher?" said Miss Allen, abruptly, turning to Miss MacIvers, who looked up with slightly-contracted eyebrows; she always regarded Miss Allen a little coldly to keep down a rising familiarity, to which that young lady was somewhat prone unless reasonably checked.

"A new music-teacher! What is to become of Mrs. Bramen?"

"Oh, she is to remain all the same. Prof. couldn't dispense with her, the little beauty," Miss Allen returned, with a sneer.

"I do not see why she should be thought indispensable to Mr. Ingraham," said Miss MacIvers.

Miss Allen reddened.

"Of course everybody knows he admires her. Did you never see him, when she comes in and goes sweeping up to the rostrum with her long trains, and shawl trailing over her shoulder, get up and hand her a chair, as if she were the Queen of Sheba? A courtesy he never shows the preceptress."

"The preceptress does not invite it. Besides, Mrs. Bramen only comes into the chapel occasionally, and is a sort of visitor. What were you going to say about this new teacher? Where is she from?"

"From the East," said Miss Allen, laughing. "Isn't that definite? It is all I heard. Her name is Percy. Aint it a pretty name? She is going to board at Pettibone's."

"At Pettibone's!" Miss MacIvers elevated her eyebrows.

"Yes; the Pettibones are going to take lessons of her."

"I thought they went East for their accomplishments."

"This is the same thing, the East is coming to them," said Miss Allen. "It seems that this Miss Percy was recommended to them through their Episcopalian bishop, or somebody of immense consequence, and of course 'Congressman Pettibone' has a mighty influence with 'Principal Ingraham,' and so it is all settled. She is to teach only advanced scholars; so I suppose she is away up among the 'old masters,' and has ripened out of the 'new school,' and all that sort of thing. I mean to take of her."

"You?" said Miss MacIvers, with a slight curve of her lips.

"Yes. I detest that Mrs. Bramen so much. Anyhow, I don't think a woman who is divorced from her husband ought to be taken into society as she is."

Punctually when the clock struck ten, Mrs. Woods opened the study-room door and came in. It was the signal for the young ladies to pile up their books, light their several small fluid lamps, that stood on a little shelf in one corner of the room, and go to bed. ˙

Mrs. Woods was a tall, spare, strongly-built woman, straight and broad-shouldered, with a form like a man's. She was perhaps sixty years of age. She wore her "back hair" twisted up in a little coil behind, and the front made into two short, iron-gray curls, put smoothly back behind her ears. She had sharp, coal-black eyes, looking through a pair of spectacles. She said not a word, but stood with her back to the stove and rapped her snuff-box gravely, and took a pinch of snuff while the girls were getting ready.

Miss Beach and Miss MacIvers went up-stairs. Miss Allen said, taking up her lamp, "Come, Miss Lynne, you and I are to be room-mates, I suppose."

Their room was in a wing of the house opening out of the study-room. There was still another room beyond it. "That," said Miss Allen, nodding toward it, "used to be Miss MacIvers's room, but she took a notion to go up-stairs this term. I can't say I'm sorry."

"Why?" said Wilmingard, opening her eyes.

Miss Allen laughed. "You might have observed that she is not the most agreeable person one could have for a neighbor."

"I think she is very beautiful, don't you?" said Wilmingard.

"Beautiful! Of course. My dear girl, you don't know what a common remark you have made; everybody says that. That is, all the new people say it; the old ones have got used to it."

Miss Allen, herself, was not beautiful, but she had a finely developed figure; such a perfectness and robustness of physique, that, as she stood before the looking-glass at the dressing-table, combing out her braided hair, Wilmingard instinctively threw back her shoulders.

"What is your name, Miss Lynne?" she asked, abruptly. "Your given name. If you and I are to live together we don't want to be 'missing' each other all the time."

"Wilmingard; but I would rather be called Wilma."

"Aha; so should I. 'Wilmingard.' What a funny

name! Dutch, aint it? My name is Evangeline, but I prefer Eva,—with the long sound of E, you know. Dear! What a stupid set of boarders we have here this term. The boys I mean.''

'' They are strangers, aren't they ?'' said Wilma.

'' Yes; and likely to continue so,'' said Miss Allen, laughing, and proceeding to unlace her shoes. '' They're not bad looking, but there's no ' get-up' to them; they're afraid to look you in the face. By the way, how did you happen to stop at Ingraham's?''

'' Mr. Ingraham came down to the hotel and took me there to stay until they could find me a boarding-place.''

'' Ah! And how did you like Mrs. Ingraham?''

'' I didn't see much of her,'' said Wilma, evasively.

'' No; I suppose not. I've heard them say she's very *reserved.* I have never had the honor of an introduction. Don't aspire to it. I suppose you fell in love with Miss Belmont ?''

'' Oh, yes!'' said Wilma.

Miss Allen laughed. '' I just thought that of you. I suspect you are a conscientious little Christian, after her own heart. Except that I don't think she's a Christian; that is, a *denominational* Christian. Come to think of it, she reads the Bible, though,—reads it beautifully some mornings in chapel. But it is my impression she doesn't belong to church.''

'' How could one be a Christian and not belong to church?'' said Wilma.

'' How could one be a Christian *and* belong to church ?'' said Miss Allen. '' I might be ever so good a Christian, but when it came to church I wouldn't know where to put myself. The churches, you see, my dear, must tear down some of their partitions and dividing walls, and open out, like our parlors with folding doors, before I consent to enter any of them to remain faithful ' until death do us part.' ''

Wilmingard had gone to bed and lay watching Miss Allen's movements. She felt a little shocked and bewildered, and did not reply.

CHAPTER XVIII.

A SHORT time after Wilmingard was established at school and at Mrs. Woods's, the academy was favored with a visit from the governor of the State, and his wife and daughter. The ladies were very stiffly and richly dressed, and wore that peculiar style of bonnet known and admired some years ago as the "Sky-Scraper" (the word defines itself to the uninformed), the fair wearer of which rolled her demure eyes beneath it as if pleased with the magnitude of the achievement, and innocently unconscious of the speculations that might evolve from a philosophic and artistic mind regarding either its utility or beauty. They were accommodated with seats on the rostrum, and sat looking down upon the students like grand pictures in elegant oil-colors. Very urbane, agreeable pictures; the governor had a benign countenance with a few deep lines about his eyes, and a few more circling away from his mouth upon his cheeks that gave his face the appearance of perpetually smiling. The wife, though similar in general appearance as husbands and wives well mated usually are, seemed more energetic and wide awake. One could not help thinking—looking at them—that she was probably the "power behind the throne" that had lifted him into eminence. Besides their daughter they were accompanied by another young lady, a little older, who did not seem to be one of them exactly, but appeared like a cheap imitation done—or a little overdone—in water colors. Her bonnet was a trifle higher, if anything, and the roses in it more vividly red. Her dress was just as stiff perhaps, without the satiny appearance of very fine silk. As for her bearing, that was haughtier by a good many degrees than the bearing of any other member of the party. Her *rôle* in life was the "poor relation;" too proud to be the recipient of pecuniary aid, but ambitious to rank with her grander friends, and inclined to be a little envious and spiteful, and to stick for her rights. (I do not go behind the scenes to give this explanation of the young lady; it was all apparent to the observer.)

Eyes, of course, were raised furtively and respectfully, as in all well-regulated schools, and immediately dropped again. All but Wilmingard's,—after the first timid glance she could hardly withdraw hers from the face of the governor's daughter. It was such a pure, transparent face as to complexion; such a highly expressive, animated face, with large, droll, black eyes, and a mouth that curved a littlë as if meant to be satirical, but was far too sweet and too mischievous.

After they had sat awhile Mr. Ingraham took them out and escorted them over the building, exhibiting the various apartments and departments as if it were some sort of museum. Finally they went up into the observatory, which was a dirty, dusty, disreputable little look-out, though it commanded a magnificent view, and then came back to the chapel and gave their admiring attention to a few general exercises; after which the governor was requested to address the school, which he did in a pleasant, off-hand way, making his remarks both encouraging and complimentary, as school-visitors are expected to do. Following this they took their departure, Mr. Ingraham accompanying them down-stairs, whereupon there was a general buzz and confusion until the preceptress entered, following the classes from below, and hushed it up with the quiet authority of her presence.

Of all the faculty, Miss Belmont was the most rigid disciplinarian, and, in consequence, was not a general favorite. There was a certain severity, not in Miss Belmont herself, but in the exercise of her office as preceptress, that was effective in government, but not in winning the popular affection. She seated herself at the desk, and gathered up and put in order all Mr. Ingraham's books and papers, and then, though conscious that the little clock tacked to the wall above her head was pointing to twelve, leaned back in her chair, and commanded five minutes study, sure that they would all know what the penance was for. The room became at once breathlessly still, except for the loud tick, tick, tick, tick, that checked off the seconds one by one. No one knows the length and value of moments until they are thus measured for him. Three minutes passed, and then Mr. Ingraham came in, walked up to the desk, glanced at the clock, and literally swept Miss Belmont out of the way, and tapped the bell, to the infinite and open exultation of many of the students, though he could see at a glance how the matter stood. Miss Belmont's face crimsoned, and tears of mortification forced themselves into her eyes.

"It is a shame!" Miss MacIvers declared, with indignation, outside in the hall.

"Served her right!" Miss Allen retorted. "She had no business to keep us after twelve; she is always doing something on her own account."

That evening Wilmingard went home a little in advance of the others, which she almost always did, not yet being on locking-arm terms with any of the girls. She walked into the study-room, and had just put her books down on the table, when a rustle near the window startled her, and she looked around. There stood the governor's daughter, just arisen from a chair. Her black eyes, directed to Wilmingard, were red and swollen, and her whole face presented a tearful appearance.

"Did I frighten you?" she asked, with a gleam of amusement.

"Yes—no. You startled me a little," said Wilma. "Are you—are you alone?"

"No; Miss Morris is here;" nodding toward Wilma's bedroom door.

"Ah! you have come to school and are going to board here?"

"Exactly. You fathom the whole mystery of me at a glance," laughing. "Do you know, I feel a little acquainted with you. I met your eyes several times this morning, in school."

"Yes," said Wilma. "I remember."

"Seeing there is nobody here to present us to each other, you must tell me your name."

"Wilma Lynne."

"'Wilma Lynne;' that is musical. Mine is Belle Raymond."

"You are the governor's daughter?" said Wilma, her

consciousness adjusting itself to the dignity of the young lady's position. "They said one of the young ladies was the governor's daughter, and I was almost sure it was you."

"Because I look like my papa, I suppose."

"Were you feeling homesick just now?" Wilma asked, sympathetically.

"A little. I have been crying."

She laughed, and brushed the tears away with her hands. The quaint, unnecessary admission was so odd and funny that Wilma laughed, too.

The governor's daughter was not very formidable, in tears, at least. She was a very small pattern of a young lady, divested of her bonnet and wraps, though evidently some years Wilma's senior. She was very fragile and delicate, and yet had a spirited expression and bearing that seemed to overcome her frail stature. Even her wet eyes had little dampening effect on her lively, animated face.

She had a quaint, peculiar dignity and primness in her manner and in her dress that strongly individualized her. She was one of the few people who give character to their clothes and possessions,—whose gloves and books tell who they belong to.

"I suppose I may call you Wilma, may I not?" she asked. "You are quite a little girl beside me."

Wilma opened her eyes.

"Oh, yes, I'm small!" adding gravely, "but I'm old." From that time she assumed an attitude of kindly guardianship toward Wilma, based on her seniority. "You may call me by my given name, also," she said. "I suppose I ought to tell you I was christened Arabella, but I am never called so except by my brothers, to tease me, or by my friend, Matilda, when she wishes to be particularly impressive."

"Is that the young lady who is with you here?" asked Wilma.

"Yes; that is Miss Morris."

Just then the young lady, who resembled a picture in water colors, made her appearance, and Miss Raymond presented her with an air of parade which she usually affected toward her friend. Miss Morris nodded coldly, and made her way to a large arm-chair that conspicuously occupied the middle of the room, and seemed to be always offering itself to the most important personage present. She had a weary, exhausted air, as though she had sorted over all the things life offered, and found nothing to her taste.

"Tell me the names of all the boarders; how many are there?" said Miss Raymond, unconsciously lowering her voice out of an unacknowledged deference to Miss Morris, which her presence seemed to command.

"Five, beside me," said Wilma, and named them, while Miss Raymond mentally checked them off. "Miss MacIvers (always first and foremost), Miss Beach, Miss Allen, Mr. Gray, and Mr. Liebenwald."

"Liebenwald? What a pretty name, and those German names always mean something."

"Yonder they come," said Wilma, glancing from the window.

The three young ladies were coming in at the gate; following them the two young men.

"Dear me! Can you get me through an introduction to all those?" said Miss Raymond.

Wilma laughed, and said she would try. She was saved the ordeal. Miss MacIvers came first, and was duly presented, after which she swept Wilma aside, and went through the ceremony with the other four herself. Then Miss Raymond brought Miss Morris into notice with another flourish, and the whole party began to assimilate.

In chemistry it is found that certain ingredients will not mix without the aid of certain other ingredients. It seemed that the governor's daughter was just the element needed in Mrs. Woods's household to make it harmonious. In the academy, also, she came to be a leading spirit. Whether it was that she unconsciously presumed upon her station a little,—not noticeably or disagreeably,—or whether from much petting and adulation resulting from her fragility and winsome prettiness, or because of an amusing and childlike confidence and assurance, she seemed to take it for granted always that people would like her as a matter of course. And so they did like her, and she came to rule in an artless, kindly way. She founded a fellowship with all around her on the broadest basis. She was as many-sided and as bright and transparent as a prism, and turned a sunny face to every one. There is no disparagement in that; many of us are like pictures, fair upon one side but blank on the other. She thought no one with whom she was thrown unworthy her best efforts to entertain. If a bashful, shrinking girl sat beside her in class or walked with her from the academy, she was all kindness and adaptation. If a higher-department young man offered her polite attention, she met it with lady-like grace. Even Gray and Liebenwald—bashful fellows that they were and never aspiring to the notice of any other young ladies—employed secret strategy against each other for the privilege of carrying an umbrella over her when it rained, or doing any such small service; though neither of the good souls ever suspected the other of such petty meanness!

She was an inimitable mimic, and had a remarkable talent for amusing and entertaining an audience. Now and then of an evening the spirit of acting came upon her, and she would put the whole little circle around the study-table into such an uproar of laughter that Mrs. Woods would throw open the door and appear on the threshold—her little iron-gray curls fairly jingling—to see what upon earth was the matter!

To Wilma, however, there was something exceedingly pathetic in her mirth; she was so appealingly delicate and frail in body, though determinedly buoyant in spirit. Many times she exhausted all her small stock of strength to entertain, and then sank back in her place at the table and dropped her head in her little blue-veined hands, and fell to work gravely to make up for lost time, for she was conscientiously studious and industrious.

• One evening she invited Wilmingard to go with her to call upon Miss Belmont, a thing none of the other young ladies had ever thought of doing. They rang the bell, and Mr. Ingraham came along the hall in slippered feet and opened the door, his hair rumpled as usual, and a pen in his hand.

"Well," said he, a smile breaking out like a ray of sunshine from under his cloudy brows.

He took them each by the hand and drew them towards his study-door.

"I don't know where anybody is," said he; "so come in here."

"Oh, we called to see Miss Belmont," said Miss Raymond. "Isn't she at home?"

"Miss Belmont!" said Mr. Ingraham, with his peculiar combination of frown and smile. "I am getting jealous of Miss Belmont."

"Oh, don't begrudge her such a poor little portion as us!" retorted Miss Raymond. "You have all the others."

"Oh, no; you flatter me. Well, do you wish me to send for Miss Belmont? I presume she is up-stairs."

"Perhaps we might go right up?"

"I see! You want her all to yourself. Be off with you then; Miss Lynne knows the way."

He laughed and went into his study and shut the door. As they turned to go up-stairs, they were startled by the apparition of Mrs. Ingraham, who had opened the sitting-room door and stood looking out. Wilma bowed and they passed on.

"Heavens! what was that," said Miss Raymond, half-way up the stairs: "a ghost or a lunatic?"

"It was Mrs. Ingraham," said Wilmingard.

"You don't tell me! What a cheerful domestic establishment this must be with such a head! I have heard whispers about it; but I never listen to whispers."

They knocked at Miss Belmont's door, and her voice said, "Come in." She was seated at her table with her books before her. She sprang up apologetically, and went forward holding out a hand to each, her eyes beaming.

"I beg your pardon. I supposed it was James bringing in the letters."

She led them over to the window. The sun was almost down, and it was growing dusky in the room.

"Now, we have broken in upon your studies?" said Miss Raymond, ruefully, glancing at the table.

"Oh, no; at least it is no matter. I am glad to have them broken in upon so."

"I always want to know my teachers personally," Miss

Raymond went on by way of apology for intruding. "You see, we don't get very near to you in the school-room."

"I know," said Miss Belmont, smiling. "There is a kind of conventionality in the relation of teacher and pupil that acts as a sort of barrier between them. I am glad you think it worth while to step over the barrier and come a little nearer to me. It is you who must do it, you know, my dears. We teachers feel a great delicacy about thrusting our grave presence upon our pupils out of school."

"Oh, think of it !" said Miss Raymond. "And we feel a proportionate delicacy about forcing our frivolous selves upon you. We shall have to strike a happy medium somewhere."

"Perhaps so," said Miss Belmont, laughing. "I have just been making a call," she continued presently, "upon our new music-teacher, Miss Percy."

"Ah ! has she arrived, then ?" asked Miss Raymond.

"Yes; she came this morning. Do either of you intend to take lessons ?"

"I do," said Wilma. "But I suppose I shall take of Mrs. Bramen. Miss Percy is only going to teach the advanced scholars, I have heard."

"Yes, I believe so. Have you a great taste for music, or a great desire to learn it, my dear?"

"I should like to learn it," said Wilma; "I don't know about my taste."

"She sings sweetly !" exclaimed Miss Raymond. "Do you know, my dear Miss Belmont, Wilma is the most wonderfully and variously gifted young person I have ever met. She can draw beautifully, and she can write poetry, and improvise lovely little airs on the piano, and do anything she turns her attention to. I believe she could win distinction in any given direction if she would narrow down to it."

"Don't you persuade her to 'narrow down' to anything !" said Miss Belmont, smiling and shaking her head. "There is time enough yet for that. Few persons possess more than one dominant talent or faculty; and it is sure to come out, and give the key to their life all in good time. We must begin by cultivating our whole mind and nature uniformly. The starving of one faculty will never feed another,—for this reason, that each particular faculty requires its own particular nourishment. You cannot take from one and give to another. Every branch of art or science we master is the opening of a new window letting in light upon the soul. Before you give yourself to a specialty, better open all the windows possible, and get a strong light upon what you wish to do. You can accomplish very little, my dears, until your whole understanding is awakened."

"Why," said Miss Raymond, laughing, "I have always thought one ought to begin life by marking out a path, and travelling in it with scrupulous exactness, never deviating from it. And you can't imagine how many paths I have laid out for myself! I have taken music-lessons and drawing-lessons, and lessons in oil-painting, and in all kinds of fancy work, and given myself to each particular thing unreservedly, for the time being, with a solemn resolve to pursue it faithfully through life. There is consistency for you !"

Miss Belmont laughed. "I should hardly call it inconsistency, my dear. It is right to give one's whole attention to the thing in hand. But, perhaps, not all of us need ever mark out a special path, or follow a special pursuit."

"Who of us ought, and who of us ought not?" asked Wilma.

"I suppose only those who have genius need follow some particular bent," interposed Miss Raymond.

"Then if one have the gift of poetry, you would say he must write it?" said Miss Belmont.

"Why, certainly."

"These faculties or talents of ours," said Miss Belmont, "all endow us with innate power and strength. Shall we give out this power and strength always through pen or pencil? May we not simply live beautiful and grand things, the conceptions of which are born in us, rather than try to represent them outside of ourselves? Not every poet can write, not every artist can paint. There are only a few who can make the world vibrate ; the most of us have only power enough to be felt by a little circle around us. Shall we not rather give out the best there is in us in our daily work, than concentrate our life in a poem or a picture, and throw it out on the world's wide sea, maybe to float and be picked up, maybe to go down and be forever lost? Ah! the lives that have been wrecked, the noble hearts that have been broken, the eyes that have grown weary with watching and waiting for tidings of the little waifs sent out on the wasteful waters! Even those to whom glad tidings have come so often, feel them turn to ashes on their lips."

The sun had gone down. Miss Belmont rose and lighted a lamp that stood on the table, and turned to say, with a smile, "I beg pardon for making you such a long speech. I forget myself, and think I have a class before me instead of some young lady visitors."

Her eyelashes glistened with tears; she did not brush them away, perhaps did not know they were there.

"Oh, pray do not apologize!" said Miss Raymond. "You don't know how glad we are to have you talk to us outside of text-books! It brings us so much nearer to you, somehow."

"That is the grand *humanity* principle, my dear," said Miss Belmont. "Through it we wield our strongest influence. We come nearer to people as individuals than in any other way. As I said, not many of us can so transfer our souls to a picture or a poem, as to come into closest communion with other souls. But nearly all of us can, by individual presence and personal intercourse, touch some hearts and better some lives."

"I am going to begin to look for the meaning of everybody!" laughed Miss Raymond, rising as she spoke. "I am going to say, See here, madam, or sir, what are you living for? And I will make them teach me their lesson. Why not study people as well as books? A life lived must be as interesting as a life written."

"Not everybody—and not every book—has a meaning," said Miss Belmont, smiling. "Must you go?"

"I think we must; the study-bell will soon ring," said Miss Raymond.

Miss Belmont went to the door with them, and said good-night, and returned to her books—but with a heart too deeply stirred for study—a smile on her lips and a light in her eyes. She had spent her strength for that night in something outside of books, and felt the better for it.

CHAPTER XIX.

"DOES it strike you that Miss Belmont is a little bit self-contradictory, Wilma?" Miss Raymond asked, going home.

"How?" said Wilma.

"She warned us so solemnly to-night against narrowing down to any one thing; and you know she often preaches to us in school about having an aim."

"Oh, but I think," said Wilma, "the one refers to our education and the other to our life and character."

"What rare discrimination, Wilma. Tell me you are not 'gifted'! Now I, with my beclouded brain, that can't see a thing unless somebody shows it to me, should have meanly accused that grand woman of inconsistency! I beg her pardon. Of course you are right. A person's character is not dependent on his pursuit. But do you think we ought to live to illustrate a principle, and every word we speak and every act we do be charged with it? What stiff machines we would be! Oh, heavens! How I have despaired over that terrible sentence,—'For every idle word spoken ye shall give an account in the day of judgment.' What a formidable array will be brought up against poor little me! Sometimes I have tried to imagine the scene. The awful question is propounded,— 'Arabella Raymond' (of course I should be called 'Arabella' in a blood-curdling way), 'what did you mean by saying so and so?' repeating some of my most meaningless remarks. And I, trembling and stammering, try to set forth some good and sufficient reason, and signally fail. What then? Alas! Imagination stands appalled. Oh, Wilma! What do you suppose will become of those men who have preached these dreadful things to us and frozen our hearts, without bringing forward the all-merciful love of the tender Father, who cannot look angrily on the playful gambols of his little children any more than on the sports of kittens and lambkins, and the music of birds and falling waters!   And yet, I suppose those men believed what they said, and in all kindness gave us warning.   The same Father that pities us who are hurt by their harsh interpretations, also deals kindly with them. How much we all stand in need of the Divine Love! We all err on this side or that.   As for myself, I believe I should rather err on the broad side than on the narrow."

"I suppose," said Wilma, "the better way is to look after our motives, and see that they, at least, are good. I believe they are the law we shall be tried by."

"Why, you little liberalist!   Will you let every man set up his own tribunal?   It is true that if the heart is pure it does not matter much about the little rivulets that bubble through our lives in words and acts.   Wilma, I think those people are the best who never have any personal ambition, or wish to accomplish certain things for themselves, but just go on doing, and doing whatever comes in their way, losing themselves in others.   We sometimes say their lives are wasted, and we praise the men and women who have achieved greatness for themselves.   But it seems to me that in the hereafter those wasted lives will be gathered up and made into the brightest crowns.   There *must* be an even balance somewhere.   Take me!   Oh, Wilma!   I am a poor little piece of drift-wood on the stream of time.   What shall I be on the great ocean of eternity!"

Her hand trembled on Wilma's arm and her whole little frame suddenly shook with sobs.   She recovered herself in a moment and laughed, and replied to Wilma's expression of pain and pity: "Oh, I am not underrating myself, dear; don't you look so shocked and grieved!   I flatter myself I am just as strong and brave, and of as much consequence as anybody—in spirit.   If only I were not cooped up in such a poor little shell of a body!   There is where nature has been unfair with me; she hasn't given me a chance, you see.   But then she saves me a good deal of trouble and effort.   Instead of responding to the invitation to be up and doing, which is liberally extended to all mankind, I sit still and send in my regrets with this grave apology: 'The spirit is willing but the flesh is weak.' Oh, that little word 'if,' Wilma! What a comforter it is and what a flatterer. It gives us room for so much self-gratulation! It is such a strong, invulnerable wall that no suspicious doubt can creep through it to wound our vanity. I can shelter myself behind it, you see, and boast what I might do with all the more valor because I shall not be put to the test. What grand things we could accomplish if——! Oh, my dear, it has stood in the way of far more glorious battles than have ever been fought."

Wilma was silent, wondering whether she was in earnest or not. It was difficult to tell, her tone was so light and her eyes gleaming full of drollery in the moonlight, and her red lips curved with a half-mocking smile. Yet her words seemed to tremble with a weighty earnestness.

The other girls, when they got home, were discussing the new music-teacher. The young men had betaken themselves up-stairs.

"Has anybody seen her?" Miss Raymond asked.

"I saw her on the street with Ella Pettibone," said Miss Beach; and Miss Allen took the subject away from her: "Nellie says she is wonderfully fair and has heavenly blue eyes, and dresses in pale gray."

"Miss Beach has remarkable powers of observation," said Miss Morris, with languid irony. "I had an introduction to this extraordinary person this evening, but I failed to discover the color of her eyes; all that impressed itself on me was the coldness of her face."

"You, Matilda! When and where, pray?" said Miss Raymond.

"I had occasion to go up to the academy after tea," Miss Morris proceeded to explain. "I had forgotten some of my books. The janitor hadn't shut up yet. Mr. Ingraham and Miss Pettibone and Miss Percy came up and went into the ladies' hall to superintend the putting up of a new grand piano."

"I heard there was to be one," parenthesized Miss Allen.

"Miss Turner was with me," Miss Morris added, "and Mr. Ingraham introduced us. She looked at us as if we were a different variety of the *genus homo* from any she had ever seen before."

"Why, Matilda, is she a supercilious person?" Miss Raymond asked.

"I don't know what you would call it; she is as distant as the North Pole."

"Did she play?"

"No; she swept the keys to see how the instrument had stood its journey, and said it was out of tune. For my part, I don't think it is."

"Why?"

"I think she was simply too disagreeable to gratify our curiosity to hear her."

"Is she disagreeable?"

"Dreadfully.   Did you not think so, Miss Beach?"

Poor Nellie, wounded a moment before by Miss Morris's sarcasm, returned, with a little effort at the same thing herself, "I am afraid I was not penetrating enough to discover it. I thought she had a sad, sweet face, and looked too young and innocent to be alone in the world, as somebody said she was."

Miss Morris smiled, well enough pleased to have her small fire take effect. Nothing suited her better than a clashing of arms. Miss MacIvers laughed. She and Miss Morris had long ago openly declared war.

"The needle attracts the loadstone," she remarked. "Nellie is not the sort of magnet, perhaps, to draw out 'disagreeableness.' "

"A body with no polarity neither attracts nor repels," retorted Miss Morris. She was not especially spiteful toward pretty, quiet little Nellie; she cut them all up as occasion offered.

"Who of us are interested in music?" Miss Raymond asked, to change the subject. "Shall you take lessons, Matilda?"

"Certainly not," said Miss Morris, with emphasis. She was a fine scholar; superior even to Miss MacIvers in some things, and felt above mere accomplishments.

"You will, I suppose, Miss Allen?"

"Oh, yes," said Miss Allen. She always took music lessons and carried about a ponderous instruction-book and rolls of sheet music, though nobody ever heard her play.

"Miss Percy, I hear, is also a fine elocutionist," said Miss MacIvers to Miss Raymond, whom she usually addressed. "She intends teaching a class, I believe."

"Does she? Oh, that will be grand; I shall vote myself a member of that class," Miss Raymond returned.

"You read very well now, Arabella," said Miss Morris, patronizingly.

"Yes; I have been told I have a shrill voice and tolerably distinct enunciation. Girls, would you like to hear me declaim?"

She got up and stood in the middle of the floor, with her hands down at her sides, in the stiffest attitude.

"Ahem !

> "'Tis not enough the voice be sound and clear,
> 'Tis modulation that must charm the ear!"

She gave the whole piece in ringing, metallic tones, all the girls laughing until the tears came into their eyes, except Wilmingard, who seemed preoccupied.

"Well, Wilma, my dear; you don't applaud," said Miss Raymond.

"I beg your pardon, I did not hear," said Wilma.

"Is the child deaf?" exclaimed Miss Allen.

"I mean I did not listen," said Wilma, blushing.

"What a wretched compliment !" said Miss Raymond. "Oh, I know ! Wilma would rather hear me sing."

She crossed her small hands demurely and began chanting, in a doleful strain, "The Lake of the Dismal Swamp."

"Oh, don't ! please don't !" said Wilma. It seemed ghastly to her.

Miss Raymond instantly desisted, and took her place at the table.

"I shouldn't think Prof. would give up his elocution class to anybody else," said Miss Allen. "He prides himself so much on his own reading."

"With good reason," said Miss MacIvers. "I think he renders some things better than any professional elocutionist I have ever heard. I like him especially in the tragic and pathetic."

"Oh, yes!" exclaimed Miss Raymond. "He might have been a Booth or a Forrest, if he had taken to the stage. He has touched some chords in me, I know, that were never attuned before."

"Oh, by the way, Wilma; I was down to the post-office this evening and got a letter for you," said Miss Allen, tossing it across the table. "I came near forgetting it."

It was from Charley, and Wilma's face flushed. She was not expecting it. Charley made it a point of writing at a stated time, once a week. This was an "extra."

She waited until the study-hour was ended and the others had all left the room, and asked Mrs. Woods's permission to remain long enough to read it,—which was conditionally granted.

"If you'll be sure an' blow the light out, an' not set the house a-fire when you git through," Mrs. Woods said, "you kin stay as long as you want to. It's my bed-time."

She went out, and Wilma had a few delicious moments to herself, which, these days, did not often occur. It seemed as if her little, quiet world was dropping far behind the broader, busier school-life. Of course she would go back to it again, she believed, never thinking how like a river life is, flowing on and on, growing wider and ·wider.

One thing is true; that if we stretch our boundaries they will never spring back again. We ourselves may shrivel and our lives not fill the channel we have cut, but we cannot narrow the lines our broadest experience has drawn.

Charley's letters were an outlet into even a bigger, busier world than Wilma lived in. He was a bold seaman, striking out vigorously into all depths,—except that his element was thought instead of water. He touched all boundaries, it seemed to her,—if he did not go beyond them! And he sketched for her, with his rapid pen, all the beautiful things he felt and saw. And her heart quivered with the ecstasy of the thought,—He is mine, this grand, noble spirit is mine by the supreme right of

love ! He was ambitious for her as for himself. He tried
to keep her soul keyed to the world's thundering march.
But Wilma's life had not risen out of its prelude yet.

CHAPTER XX.

MISS PERCY seemed to be in no haste to commence her
duties at the academy. Days passed and she did not
make her appearance, and in the mean time endless
rumors were afloat concerning her. Her beauty, her
coldness, her repelling haughtiness, and her marvellous
accomplishments all were fruitful themes which, coupled
with her being taken up by the exclusive and aristocratic
Pettibones, made her an object of much curiosity. Regarding her personal history and antecedents there was
nothing but unfounded speculation. If questioned closely
the Pettibones themselves would have had to admit they
knew nothing about her.

At last, one morning, she made her advent in the
chapel in time for prayers, Miss Pettibone accompanying
her, which was something, in itself, in the way of deepening the impressions already conceived of her. For
Miss Pettibone had always held herself aloof from the
academy students, as much as to say, This country school
may do for you, but I patronize Eastern institutions. A
little of her pride and dignity seemed reflected on Miss
Percy. Only for a moment, however. Miss Percy rose
above it, eclipsed it by her own superiority of presence,
and threw Miss Pettibone quite into the shade. Mrs.
Bramen had come in a few moments before and created
the customary sensation, sweeping up to the rostrum with
her long train and graceful wrap thrown around her shoulders, compelling Mr. Ingraham by some invisible magnetism to rise and proffer her a chair. She was a handsome woman ; languid, with a creamy complexion, smiling
mouth, and large dreamy eyes with drooping lids. Miss
Belmont unconsciously drew away from her. It seemed
to her that under all that smiling softness was a cruel

G*

heart. When Miss Percy entered, Mrs. Bramen's eye-lashes quivered, and her sleepy eyes shot forth a wicked gleam. She was not at the head of her profession, as had long been patent to some of the more advanced young ladies who were ambitious to progress in music, and she was spitefully envious of those who were. She accepted the coming of a superior teacher as a personal affront.

Mr. Ingraham, on the point of commencing the morning exercises, advanced to meet Miss Percy, and made a place for her and Miss Pettibone in the semi-circle of teachers on the rostrum. She was a slender, fragile-looking creature, with a perfectly white, transparent face and soft, shining, dark hair. She was elegantly dressed, and her garments seemed as much a part of her as the plumage is a part of the bird.

As soon as she was seated, and looked abroad over the scores of upraised faces with an unconsciously exploring gaze, her blue-rayed, starry eyes riveted every other eye. Yet she repelled quite as much as she attracted. Her glance drew yours by a cold fascination, but her lips had an indescribable curve that seemed to scorn your admiration. She raised a singular conflict of feeling; she appealed to all your chivalry and tenderness, and you felt that you could be a friend to do and die for her, if need be, but that she would not accept your devotion; that she put you in the attitude of an enemy, and it seemed as if, against your will, you were so. But that if some strong, inconceivable power outside your will compelled you to slay her,—as Othello his Desdemona,—you would yourself, like Othello, be the most despairing mourner. She had the beauty of transparent, ethereal things. If a summer sky, deep blue with white clouds in it, could be also icy cold, Miss Percy's effect upon you would have been the same. There was a delicacy of finish about her (as it were) that gave you the impression that she was finely cultivated, and that the blood in her veins came purified through many generations of high-bred, high-toned ancestry. She seemed costly and precious; if anything happened to her, if she should be broken from the slender stem on which her young life was growing, it would be as if Michael Angelo's masterpiece were destroyed, or something else equally rare were lost to the world. It would be so great a pity.

She remained only a short time on this first occasion of her coming up to the academy. A day or two after, she came before Mr. Ingraham's large class in elocution in the ladies' hall, and gave a reading previous to entering on the office of teacher in that department. Her power was something wonderful and impossible to describe. If the description of anything grand could equal the thing itself we might all be capable of grand things. It is the power of genius to rise above description. There was nothing teacher-like about her, no sympathetic telegraphy between herself and her pupils. She seemed to be cut off, in the matter of sympathy, from all her kind. Yet she made her art so beautiful and attractive as to seem to be the chief thing, and to banish, for the time being, all other aspirations but the aspiration to be an accomplished elocutionist, able to grasp and to express the meanings of the sublimest thinkers and subtlest poets.

"Words, what are they?" she said, in a little lecture to the class. "Only empty moulds in which to fashion our thoughts. The power, the life of language lies not with him who has written it, but with us who utter it."

For the hour in which she read and taught everything was forgotten by the class except the thing in hand. The impassioned spirit seemed to work a spell upon them; they went out from her presence dazed by her power and brilliancy, but no nearer to her than before. When she turned away from a recitation she was, as Miss Morris had said, "distant as the North Pole."

She was discussed one evening at Mrs. Woods's. Miss Morris said, "The idea of a music-teacher wearing brocaded silks, and diamonds, and point lace! I don't believe she is a teacher at all; I believe she is playing a part."

"What part could she possibly play in this obscure Western village?" said Miss Raymond.

"One can't tell that. But mark my words, and see if it doesn't turn out that she is masquerading here for her own amusement or somebody's displeasure."

"I'll bet," said Miss Allen, who could not eradicate certain rough adornments from her dialect, "that she has been an heiress and has lost her fortune."

"Romantic," said Miss Morris.

"I should like to hear Miss Belmont's opinion about her," said Miss Raymond. "I wonder if she doesn't know something of her history. It seems to me, always, that she looks at her in a kind of compassionate way."

"Compassionate!" sneered Miss Morris, with a laugh. "The elegant and aristocratic Percy snubs the preceptress."

"That would make no difference with Miss Belmont," said Miss Raymond.

"Why not? You must think Miss Belmont very saintly."

"She is too great-minded to be biased in her estimate of people by their opinion of her."

"Ah! what a sublime philosopher."

"You might well call her a sublime philosopher, without any of your sweet irony, Matilda," said Miss Raymond, warmly.

Whether Miss Percy accounted it a misfortune or not, she made many and bitter enemies. Miss Allen went to her to take music-lessons, but showed herself to be so dull and backward, that she was dismissed with the indignant outburst, "I am not here to teach beginners; go to Mrs. Bramen."

Red with mortification and anger, Miss Allen went, and Mrs. Bramen, in her turn, waxed wroth and set her white teeth and bit her smiling lips at the implied depreciation of herself.

Miss Percy herself had risen so far above the mechanical as to have almost forgotten the laws governing her two beautiful accomplishments, making her perception seem intuition and her power supernatural. Nothing could equal her impatience when a pupil seemed to be laboring under the law. "I want you to work by rule, of course," she said; "but above all things, don't let the rule appear in sight. One's greatest endeavor should be to cover up these geometrical lines and angles, as nature does in all her beautiful works. Think of it!

Men have been for centuries trying to ferret out her laws; but so intricate are they, and so gracefully intertwined, as to be, most of them, past finding out. Mathematics enters into music and poetry as well as into the universe, but only as a skeleton to be elaborately draped.''

She never placed herself beside the pupil at the piano, but walked restlessly about the room possessed of a spirit laboring intensely and suffering—so it seemed—acutely, until the pupil had risen out of the physical or mechanical into the spiritual. Then she would throw off the violent effort with which she *constrained* (as it were) the pupil,—as the clairvoyant throws off the spell he has labored under,—and her *spirituelle* face would become almost transfigured. It is impossible to imagine a creature more impassioned and yet so cold. She seemed suspicious of everybody, except, perhaps, Mr. Ingraham, in whom she placed a shy, childlike confidence. Miss Belmont had tried to approach her, feeling sure there was some trouble clouding her young life, and anxious to show her there was yet some tenderness in the great world she looked on with so much dislike and fear; but Miss Percy repelled her. She was skeptical as a child who has been once deceived, and could not bring herself to believe the preceptress's goodness genuine. Besides, though so delicate, fragile, and alone, and apparently utterly ignorant of the world, she had an independent and proud spirit that would not brook compassion.

One evening, Wilma and Miss Raymond, delaying a moment in the chapel after school, came down-stairs and heard Miss Percy singing in the ladies' hall. They stopped outside the door and listened. Wilma had never heard anything to be compared with it. She would not have thought it possible for a human voice, controlled and swayed by a human spirit, to so rise, and swell, and tremble, and float, and die away, carrying one's very soul with it. Yet it seemed like the answer, the fulfilment of some vague, wild dream or longing, making her wonder, when she thought of it again, if there is not in the vast universe a response to all our questionings; or whether there is something yet farther beyond toward which each new and wonderful experience is but a step. Who can measure a soul, since with every expansion comes the power of still greater enlargement?

By and by, Miss Belmont came out, closing the door softly. "I have been in paradise," she said, smiling, with wet eyes.

"And we have been just outside the gates," Miss Raymond answered, wittily. "She sings exquisitely, doesn't she?"

"Exquisitely," repeated Miss Belmont.

Wilma felt that she could not have ventured to make any comment upon what had so far transcended any previous experience or conception. Comment was commonplace; it seemed to bring down the wonderful and ideal to plain matter of fact, and to measure it by the common standards. Wilma had a fine sense that could have understood and appreciated Miss Percy's curl of the lip, when she heard either words of praise or criticism on her wonderful powers. Surely nothing can equal the fine scorn of a smile on the lips of conscious greatness, pecked at or patronized by inferior critics and commentators.

"Miss Belmont, tell us what you think of Miss Percy," said Miss Raymond.

"I think," said Miss Belmont, "she is far too delicate to be knocked about the world. She ought to belong to some one who would keep her tenderly and not let the winds buffet her roughly. She certainly has been, she must have been, carefully shielded all her life until now. Some strange freak of fortune evidently has set her adrift."

Just then Miss Percy opened the door and came out. She glanced coldly from one to another, bowed to Miss Belmont, and then turned to Wilma, who was standing a little apart. "Will you come with me, Miss Lynne? I believe you go my way," she said, in her abrupt manner.

Wilma, taken by surprise, complied. She had frequently met Miss Percy's eyes fixed upon her with their half-vague, wondering expression, but she had never directly addressed her a word before. Indeed, it was the first advance she had made toward any one in the academy.

When they reached the gate leading out into the street Miss Percy stopped and said, "Suppose we go into the woods, Miss Lynne? The ground is dry and it is not cold to-day."

Wilma would hardly have had the power to refuse anything she might have asked.

They turned off up the street toward a thick wood that lay along the edge of the town at the foot of the hills and partly covering them. Miss Percy walked fast and Wilma kept silently beside her, with a feeling that her companion might almost be a creature of some other world, so detached she seemed from all the interests and busy, practical concerns of this earth.

"I have brought a book with me, Miss Lynne," she said, when they had reached the wood and penetrated some distanec into it. "And if you care to hear me we will sit down on a log somewhere here, and I will read aloud."

Wilma said she would like it above all things.

"Yonder is a log for you, then," said Miss Percy, stopping and glancing around. "And here is a stump for me. We shall be a little way apart, which is better."

She seated herself on the low, mossy stump, a tree near by throwing out a crooked limb for her to lean against, and drew a small volume from among the heavy folds of her dress and opened it.

"If you get tired presently, you can get up and walk away," she said. "I sometimes lose myself in reading. But don't go off and leave me; I should be frightened to be left alone in the woods."

"I shall not get tired," Wilma said.

The volume was Longfellow, and she read extracts from the Golden Legend, principally Lucifer's monologues, and finally the story of Irmingard, as related to Elsie by the abbess herself. Wilmingard held her breath when she came to the dreadful pursuit:

> "How I remember that breathless flight
> Across the moors in the summer night!
> How, under our feet the long, white road
> Backward like a river flowed,
> Sweeping with it fences and hedges,

> Whilst farther away, and overhead,
> Paler than I, with fear and dread,
> The moon fled with us, as we fled
> Along the forest's jagged edges!"

Miss Percy's patience gave out before she had finished the recital.   Reading the lines,—

> " But the same passion I had given
> To earth before, now turned to heaven
> With all its overflowing fulness,"——

she closed the book with a bitter smile.

"To think of healing a wounded heart in the solitude of a convent!"

"I would rather than almost anything else in the world be able to read like that," said Wilma, in a low voice.

Miss Percy had almost lost consciousness of her already. She looked up.

"Would you? Well, you may; it is not a very difficult accomplishment. There is one requisite, however."

"What?" Wilma asked.

"You must have all these things burned into your soul by the cruel iron of experience. You must taste joy first, unalloyed, pure joy (I think it always comes first), and then you must be racked and tortured, and made to feel with the sharpness of actual pain all there is in your nature to feel of suffering. We know nothing of what it is to be wounded, to be hurt, until the real shock of a blow is felt by our own self. Would you like the experience for the sake of what it would bring?" she asked, mockingly.

"I don't know," said Wilma, recoiling. "It seems to me," she added, "that I should be willing to suffer a good deal if I might so come into the deeper meanings of things."

Miss Percy shrugged her shoulders, which gesture seemed to say, eloquently, "How ignorant you are; you don't know what you say."

Ignorant and romantic. She had studied so many great faces in the Shermans' little cottage at home, and they all had the lines of suffering upon them, and that halo of refinement and intelligence born of suffering and the wide knowledge of experience, that she had come to think the enlightenment and perfect awakening of the soul worth any price within the power of this poor earth-life to pay. There have been people, she thought, who have borne all that could be borne,—for there must be limits to suffering,—and could not I? She had something of Fred's stoicism. It might be that the greatest strength of both lay in their ignorance of what suffering really was. She had never tried to picture to herself a possible affliction. The sorrows of others which she had read about all had the coloring of romance and the softening effects of distance. Looking through the telescope of a hundred years at things that have been,—at combinations of circumstance surrounding a particular object brought out into bold relief, all other things being cut away or pressed into a sombre background,—what life but has had its poetry, its passion, its tragedy? Alas! that affliction in its day should be so real and unromantic.

"Come," said Miss Percy, rising. "We will go now. Would you like," she asked, as they neared Mrs. Woods's, "to come to my room sometimes? I will send for you now and then, if you care to come."

She appeared to be afraid of seeming to ask or want a favor.

"Oh, yes," said Wilma, gladly.

She went on down the street, and Wilma crossed over to the gate. Miss Raymond spread the door open and exclaimed, gayly, "Come in, my distinguished young friend! We are dying to hear all about it; how did you get so intimate with her, you sly little thing?"

"I am not intimate with her," said Wilma. "She never spoke to me until to-day."

"Did she not? Well, I'm sure she made a pretty bold advance upon you. Where did you go?"

"Off into the woods. She read Longfellow to me."

"Oh, girls! do you hear?" said Miss Raymond. "Wilma is getting ahead of us all, she is taking private lessons in elocution."

"No doubt she will profit by her opportunities," said Miss Morris, scornfully.

Wilma's next letter to her lover was full of the strange

music-teacher.   Charley, when he read it, rumpled his curls, and got up and fumed a little.   "Those people are turning her foolish little heart," said he.   "What do I care about her Miss Percys and her Miss Raymonds!   I must tell her I want to hear more about herself, and not so much about Tom, Dick, and Harry."   But he recovered himself soon, and sat down and took up his pen. "It is natural for her to be carried off her feet a little at first," he reflected.   "The current is pretty strong up there, I warrant, for a little thing who has seen nothing of the world but a bird's-eye view from the top of Little Twin!   After all," he added, with his expansive smile, "so long as her friends are all of the feminine gender, I don't know as I have any reason to grumble."   So he wrote a long, and kind, and tender letter as usual, and only remembered to add at the end of it, "Don't let your new friends quite eclipse the old ones, Wilma darling."

CHAPTER XXI.

Some time after this Wilma wrote Mr. Burns an unusually elaborate letter.   "I must tell you," she said, "more about my dear Miss Percy; for, though I don't seem to know her any better, I love her more, and feel more and more sorry for her.   Is it not strange, Charley, that she should take to me of all the students?   I think it is because I am so little and unimportant, and so detached as it were from all the others.   I often go with her into the woods, and sometimes up to her room, at Mrs. Pettibone's.   She reads to me a great deal, and from many books I never saw before.   She says books are our magnifying glasses through which we may see people and things much clearer than with our own unaided understanding, because they reflect so accurately and interpret so truly.   I happened to speak of this to Miss Belmont one day and she seemed alarmed, and said, 'I don't want you to be wholly educated by books, my dear; keep your eyes open and make use of your own faculties instead

of leaning wholly upon others, even the best and greatest.'
That same evening she took me with her to the cottage of
a poor family whose little daughter was dead. We went
into a poor, plain room where, stretched upon a board
supported by two old chairs, lay the sweet, wax-like figure.
The mother silent, but oh! so broken-hearted, came forward to receive us in a dumb, anguished way; a crippled
boy with the saddest face I ever saw sat near the window
with his crutch beside him. The father came in, big and
broad-shouldered and awkward, but made dignified by his
great sorrow. Oh, it was heart-rending! I sobbed aloud.
When we came out Miss Belmont said, 'Do you not find
here, my dear, a reality of sorrow greater than in the story
even of Dickens's Little Nell?' I saw then why she had
taken me there. 'Great writers,' she said, 'can better
express what you feel than you could express it. But
don't depend upon them to tell you what you may see
with your own eyes. There is danger of cultivating false
sentiment by dwelling too much on imaginary pictures of
life. Many people weep over fictitious stories of wrong
and suffering who never see the actual tragedies going on
under their very eyes. More than that, I have known
people to hug a volume of descriptive poetry to their
hearts, and delight in it, and bury themselves in it, who
never look up to admire the real beauties of earth and sky
around them. Be sure that you are living all the time,
my child, and not dreaming.' I know nothing about
Miss Percy's friends or her past history; but people must
have been very cruel to her some time or she could not
say, as she often does, that she has no faith in human
nature, or belief in any human creature. When she talks
so I cannot keep silent and let it seem as if I think so
too, and so I tell her about my dear friends, and especially about my dear Charley. (I don't know how I first
came to speak of you to her; I never have to any one else,
not even Miss Raymond.) And she listens to me, and smiles
and shakes her head as if it were a fancy your loving me
and my believing that you do. She says we deceive ourselves in such matters as well as each other. Yesterday
evening, after school, Miss Belmont asked me to stop in
her room a moment. There was a letter lying on her desk

with an Eastern postmark. She said it came from a clergyman, and was in reference to Miss Percy. It stated
that Miss Percy had suffered a grievous wrong,—he was
not at liberty to explain the nature of it,—and that it had
shocked her moral nature and almost overthrown her
reason ; that she was a great sufferer both bodily and mentally, and that the greatest good that could be done her
would be to convince her of the love and goodness there
is in human nature by being a friend and helper to her in
spite of herself. Miss Belmont said, when she had explained it to me, 'I have no way of helping her, my
dear, but through you ; Miss Percy allows no one else to
come near her. I only want to encourage your friendship
for her ; you may do her much good. Not that I wish
you, my child, to feel burdened by any great responsibility about her,—you are too young for that. But by
being very tender and kind to her, and showing her in
many little ways that you love her, which I think you do,
Wilma?' I said I did, dearly. Then she went on to
say that there was one thing more, which was that I must
not allow any thing Miss Percy did or said to poison my
mind and make me doubtful of the goodness of my fellow-
beings ; but that I should keep in mind always that there
are such things in men and women as truth and honor and
love. She said she could not conceive of a greater calamity happening to people than the having their faith shaken
in these things, and that it often came about from our
being disappointed in people and not finding them to be
what we took them to be. , She said we should never go
so far in our worship of an individual—seeing that mankind is human and fallible—as that we cannot separate
him in our judgment from an infallible principle,—like
truth,—fearing that if we are deceived in him we will cry
'there is no truth.' That we should accustom ourselves
to contemplate great principles and make them our standards of judgment, so fixed in our understanding that if
the whole world were to fall away from them, they would
still be our strength and support. 'In a word,' she said,
'we must not confound frail humanity with Divinity, nor
our imperfect theories with the grand abstract principles
of virtue.' After this we walked down street together,

and she spoke of the frost that had hung on the trees all day, and told me to look far down the street to where the two sidewalks with their two rows of trees came together. It looked like a grand hall in a crystal palace. The sleighing is very fine now, and Miss MacIvers is going to have a ride with one of the higher department young men. I wish you could see her; she has just come down-stairs in her beautiful velvets and furs, and Miss Raymond calls her the princess. There! the bells are jingling now, and Miss Raymond says, 'Come, quick, Wilma, let us take a peep through the blinds.'"

The day following a messenger came for Wilma to go to Miss Percy's room. She was well enough acquainted with the Pettibone house by this time to pilot herself up-stairs, and, when the servant let her in below, she ran up and knocked at Miss Percy's door and entered. The bed, draped in white, was drawn out into the middle of the room, and Miss Percy, also white, with the delicate blue veins outlined upon her temples, lay upon it with her eyes closed and the long dark lashes sweeping her cheeks. Wilma had never seen her so before, and approached the bed surprised and alarmed. Miss Percy opened her eyes and smiled, and held out her hand feebly. It was a mere baby hand, transparent and perfect, and glittering with a heavily-jewelled ring. Wilma took it tenderly. "Dear Miss Percy, I did not know you were so sick."

"Oh, it is nothing," Miss Percy returned; "I am always an invalid more or less," and withdrew her hand a little impatiently.

"Is there anything I can do for you?" Wilma begged.

"Yes, you can read to me; that is why I sent for you. My eyes are too weak for me to read much, and I can't lie here and think; it would kill me. Raise me up a little, please, and put that other pillow under my head. Thank you."

There were some elegantly-bound books on the table. She pointed to them. "Bring the one in purple, and come and sit by the bedside," she said.

Wilma did as she bade her.

"Open where the mark is," she languidly directed.

Wilma opened at "Childe Harold." After a time Miss

Percy opened her eyes and became interested in watching Wilma's face. Soon she put out her hand and stopped the reading.

"Close your eyes a moment, dear; how prettily your eyelashes curl up! Did you ever think you were pretty, Wilma?"

"No," said Wilma, blushing a little; "I am too dark."

"Humph! there are handsome dark people as well as handsome fair ones," said Miss Percy. "You are different from most people, child; you are more beautiful than your mirror tells you. Your finest expressions are not photographed on a looking-glass. There, read on."

She closed her eyes wearily again, and Wilma resumed. Often Miss Percy interrupted her, and made her read a line or a stanza over again. Sometimes she repeated whole stanzas herself, and they seemed to throw her into a state of such wild excitement, that at last Wilma felt that the reading was at an end and closed the book.

Miss Percy seemed to feel no responsibility about Wilma; no fear as regarded her youth and susceptibility that the influence of her unhappy views of life and people might be hurtful to her. Nor was it. Wilma's anchor of faith was in her lover, and grappled her to the best side of human nature and to a firm belief in it. Notwithstanding Miss Belmont's injunctions, which, without her knowing it, bore so directly upon Wilma's own life, she could not separate her lover from all things good and true. He was boundless and infinite to her. She saw nothing beyond him. She saw everything through him.

Miss Percy bewailed bitterly her lost happiness. And Wilma asked, timidly, "Dear Miss Percy, is not happiness in us?"

Poor Wilma! She had learned the forms of speech which we all use upon occasion, but she had not grown into the meanings of them, and could scarcely match her trite little sayings (though there did begin to bud a certain truth in them to her alert understanding) against Miss Percy's bitter experiences.

"Happiness in us!" said Miss Percy, scornfully. "It is the misfortune of some of us to find that it is in things as hollow as empty tombs."

"What things?" Wilma asked.

"Well, say friendship,—*love!*"

Wilma had so often tried to prove that there was truth in those things, and failed, that she was driven to a different stand.

"Well," she said, "you wouldn't think it right to put one's whole happiness and one's whole life in those things, dear Miss Percy? I mean that it is not best, is it, to depend so much upon people, or upon anything outside of us, as to make us either happy or miserable?"

"What else in this world have we got to depend upon, child? You don't know what you say. Wait until all your props are taken away, and see if you have innate strength enough to stand alone! Heavens, how easy it is to talk! There are certain grand virtues attributed to mankind, and we are apt to think we see them in our friends. But when one after another proves false and empty, cannot you see what a wreck it makes of our faith? So long as people don't sin against us, we can't see that they sin against anything. If the devil smiles on us, we smile on him, though we know he has just slain our brother; but let him turn against us, and how we rise up in our wrath! A fault in friendship or in love is the most grievous of all faults; we can stand anything better than that. How often you hear a man say, self-congratulatorily, of some known villain, 'Well, he never harmed me!' As though we have each got to fight our own battles against our personal foes alone, and not make common cause with each other in fighting evil. Bah! I am sick of the selfishness of human nature that stands aloof with its arms folded looking on while its fellow-beings are torturing and killing one another. I hate the calm looker-on in the world's fierce battles; I am glad when he gets a blow! It is amusing to see him arouse himself to a sense of the horrible situation when he himself is the victim!"

"But all people are not false and selfish and cruel," said Wilma, determinedly, and yet in the gentlest manner. She felt it incumbent upon her, in view of many true-hearted friends in whom her faith was firm, to defend the better side.

"Human nature is just human nature," said Miss Percy.

"It is the stuff we are all made of. If only one person were false in a hundred, it would prove the possibility of all becoming so under various temptations."

Wilma returned quickly, that if one friend were true under all circumstances, was there not an equal likelihood that all might have the element of truth?

"No," said Miss Percy, sadly. "We start out with the supposition that all are true. My faith was once just as blind and persistent as yours, Wilma. Oh, child! our happiest days are those in which we lean upon our friends. To be freed from a higher power that guided and directed us brings a responsibility worse than slavery. It is terrible to feel you have no arm stronger than your own to lean upon."

She grasped Wilma's hand suddenly and held it, as if in her weakness she felt the need of something strong to cling to. As if, too, she recognized strength in Wilma. She shut her eyes to keep back the tears springing into them, and her slight frame shook. But in a moment she controlled herself and looked up. No eyes could show more fulness of interest and sympathy than Wilma's.

"You are a faithful little creature, Wilma," she said, in softer tones. "Not simply faithful to me, but to better things than I, and faithful to them in spite of me. Even when you do not speak, when I hush you up by my violence, there is a something in you looking out of your eyes that steadily opposes me and disproves my miserable theories. What is it, Wilma? Is it faith in your lover? Oh, take heed to it, my child, and do not build your beautiful young life on the foundation of any man's truth and honor! The world is full of stronger things than love. When I was a little child I was left, an orphan, to the guardianship of an uncle, who had charge of a large fortune for me. Through all the years we lived together I idolized him. But my idolatry was destined to end in hate and loathing. I was obliged to fly from him as from my worst foe: my fortune squandered, I friendless, alone, a fugitive. Can you understand a grief like that? No! there is only one way to learn what misery is, and that is to feel it. But I—— Oh, God! I have suffered even greater wrongs than that."

She turned her face to the wall, sobbing bitterly. Wilma, deeply moved, knelt by the bedside.

"Dear Miss Percy, don't be so unhappy, don't grieve so. Do you not look up to God and heaven? If this life is all spoiled for you, why, is there not another and far better life to look forward to?"

"Another life!" exclaimed Miss Percy, and caught up the book which Wilma had dropped, and read with terrible force and clearness,—

> "Is't not enough, unhappy thing! to know
> Thou art? Is this a boon so kindly given
> That being thou wouldst be again, and go
> Thou know'st not, reck'st not to what regions, so
> On earth no more, but mingled with the skies?
> Still wilt thou dream on future joy and woe?"

Throwing the book from her, she sank back upon the pillows utterly exhausted. Her eyelids dropped, and she lay still and white as marble. Wilma, alarmed, caught up a fan that lay on the foot of the bed and began fanning her. After a little she revived and looked up.

"There, kiss me, Wilma, and go. I am tired. I am going to sleep."

Wilma touched the white forehead, with its little ringlets of dark hair lying damp upon it, with her lips, and then went softly out with a heavy heart, whose burden she could not shake off. She was one of those whom other people's griefs lay hold of with a vital grasp. In all Miss Percy's horizon she saw no light; and only in a lesser degree she carried Miss Percy's weary load and felt no hope.

Passing up the street on her way home she met Miss Belmont at a street corner, and they walked together as far as Mr. Ingraham's gate. Miss Belmont had a wholesome mind that was wonderfully reassuring when one felt inclined to lean toward the gloomy side of life and to doubt the goodness of human nature. Not that Wilma doubted the goodness of any human nature with which she was connected; none of the shafts Miss Percy threw touched her idols. But they must strike somewhere, and they struck the vague, remote world which took shape as a cruel monster to Wilma, just as it does to all of us when we separate ourselves from it and look at it in the cold distance. When we go near to it, into it, and make ourself a part of it, and learn to judge it leniently, charitably, its monstrosity wears away, and the great, busy, bustling, wicked, prowling, designing world is our brother and our sister, with a heart like us, and affections and passions, and wounds and suffering and disappointments.

"Well, how did you find your friend, Miss Percy, my dear?" asked Miss Belmont. "I suppose you have just come from there?"

"Yes. I found her miserable," said Wilma.

"In health, or in spirits?"

"Both."

"The one follows the other, I think," said Miss Belmont. "I believe if Miss Percy were stronger physically she might rise above her mental troubles. But then, to reverse it, if she were stronger mentally she would not, perhaps, be so broken in health; her mind preys upon her body. I am sorry she takes such morbid views of mankind. She accuses people of systematic and designing cruelty, whereas their culpability lies chiefly in being humanly fond of self and unmindful of others. We are all sticklers for our rights and dignity; things of mighty importance to us, but of little consequence to anybody else. No wonder we get hurt! People are not absolutely wicked, my dear; only thoughtless and careless and selfish. Do you suppose any of us realize how often we pain somebody else? If my little personality is wounded I try to rise up and look down upon it as the all-seeing, dispassionate One might do, comparing it with all the other ills and vexations that go to make up the sorrows of a world. If we are small in anything, my dear, it is in our afflictions. We can't get above our own petty calamities. Think of the great, slow ox that steps upon a worm. Of course the worm is enraged because it can only understand what it feels; but man, who is superior to both ox and worm, can't blame the ox for all he pities the worm. People jostle us and hurt us all the time, and pass on unmindful; and the great Eye above us looks down and sees all, and pities all, and forgives all."

When they reached Mr. Ingraham's gate Miss Belmont went in, and Wilma hurried home. Some of the girls had been to the office and brought the mail; there was another "extra" from Charley, a cheery, gossipy letter, written in his lightest vein. He had recently entered the law school, and wrote graphically about it, describing mock-court and all the interesting and amusing things connected with it, dashing off his sentences in a vigorous, rapid style peculiar to him. Toward the last the letter ran on to say:

"I've had my hair cut, Wilma, and my chum Ben says to tell you it looks like thunder; a meaningless slang, if not profanity. We are going out this evening (which explains my visiting the barber-shop, though I am not sure my appearance *is* improved). We expect to meet a young lion lately arrived from the East, who is making something of a sensation here. A lawyer, by the way; we heard him plead a case very eloquently the other day in court. Absolutely the handsomest man I ever saw; his name is Courtenay. It seems funny to speak of a man's beauty, doesn't it. There is nothing more contemptible than masculine prettiness; but real masculine beauty, which includes grace, strength, symmetry, is something rather glorious, and, I must say, not often met with. Ben is hurrying me, says it is time to go, and I am not dressed yet. What uniform creatures we men are. Here are Ben and myself, with our white vests and neckties, as much alike as two clothes-pins, setting aside a little difference of feature. By-by."

Later.—"Back again and at my desk to scrawl another line to my darling. Have had a very lively evening, but am disgusted with myself and all concerned on account of it. Saw but little of the magnificent Courtenay; the ladies monopolized him, as might have been expected. They monopolized me, too; kept me playing cards and talking nonsense for three hours. Three hours! Three precious, golden hours. How poor I feel after wasting so much of my capital! I might have been reading Shakspeare all that time, and gleaned many a fine thought and expanded my brain. I am not going to spend any more evenings with young ladies who have to entertain

me with cards. Three hours, ugh ! Three hours would
have saved the field of Waterloo to Napoleon Bonaparte.
However, I have one small comfort, my time is not so
precious as Napoleon's was on that occasion.   My letter is
getting too long, darling, and besides it is past midnight.

"With tender love,

"Your CHARLEY."

CHAPTER XXII.

THE holidays were at hand, and in consequence, a
short vacation ; but so short, that but few availed themselves of the opportunity it offered to go out of town.
There was to be a "sociable" in the ladies' hall the
last evening of the term, as had long been the custom at
Crawford Academy.   Immediately after tea, on the event-
ful day, Mrs. Woods's young ladies retired into their respective rooms to make preparations. Quite elaborate
all of them were but Wilma's ; what she should wear was
not a very broad question to Wilma, being limited to one
or two "best" dresses and a few simple ornaments.   She
had just combed out her long hair ready for braiding,
when Miss Raymond came in already dressed, with her
quaint little air of primness and dignity, and turned herself round to be inspected.

"How do I look, Wilma?" she asked, with her pretty
artlessness.

"Beautiful," said Wilma ; but the word did not express half the admiration in her eloquent eyes. Miss
Raymond, pleased with the compliment, whose genuineness it was impossible to doubt, smiled and seated herself
on the bedside and gave her attention to Wilma's opera-
tions.

"You have such lovely hair, my dear," she said. Her
own shining black braids were coiled like a coronet round
her shapely little head, daintily poised on its slim, white
stem of a neck.

"A good many people here speak of my hair," Wilma

returned; "at home we never thought much about it except that it was hard to comb, because it is so thick and long."

"Let me fix the braids and fasten the bow on," said Miss Raymond, and stood on tip-toe to do it, and then stepped back to consider the effect.

"Did any one ever tell you you looked well in pink ribbons, Wilma?"

"Yes, Charley," said Wilma, and stopped, blushing.

Miss Raymond was again intent upon the hair, touching it up here and there.

"Charley who, your brother? You have never told me anything about your folks, Wilma. I have told you all about my two brothers, Starr and Waddy, and everybody else I know."

Before Wilma had time to reply, Miss Allen came in, and as soon as her toilet was finished, she and Miss Raymond went out into the study-room where Mrs. Woods and Rachel were waiting to see the young ladies' dresses.

"Oh, Miss Raymun'! sie vill al'ays look so sweet," Rachel exclaimed, clasping her hands ecstatically, and turning for confirmation to Mrs. Woods, whose grim smile expressed as much approbation perhaps as Rachel's utmost enthusiasm; each regulating the scale of feeling according to her own standard, as different thermometers are regulated.

Wilma's attire, though pretty and effective, Rachel ran over with a rapidity and completeness of comprehension that larger brains might have envied, the light in her face gradually subsiding. But it blazed up again when the other young ladies made their appearance. Miss Morris, as usual, had fashioned herself upon the model of her friend, and came out gloomy and repellent, as upon most occasions when her poverty was contrasted with others' abundance. Miss MacIvers was resplendent in amber-colored silk, and soft laces and jewelry. Miss Beach was dressed as became her dumpling figure, dimpled shoulders, and baby arms, in low neck and short sleeves, with a gold necklace and bracelets. Miss Allen, the gayest of all, had flowers in her hair, and an immense, fan-shaped train. The latter she spread out like a peacock's tail, and glanced over her shoulder to observe the effect, and was rapturously praised by the enthusiastic Rachel in broken English. Rachel stood in great awe of Miss MacIvers, and merely clasped her hands and looked her unbounded admiration of that regal young lady, having an instinct that anything more demonstrative might be resented. Gray and Liebenwald came down-stairs in stiff white collars and fresh cravats, and passed through the room, raising their eyes timidly and with much deferential respect (they would not have presumed upon admiration) toward the young ladies.

Shortly after there was a knock, and Rachel and Mrs. Woods hastily retired. Miss MacIvers went to the door. She had a promised escort from the department of Greek and Latin and the higher mathematics,—a Mr. Haviland, —and that gentleman now made his appearance. It is reasonable to suppose that Mr. Haviland had enjoyed many more of the advantages of polite society—he being a Congressman's son—than Gray and Liebenwald ; yet even he looked slightly disconcerted at finding himself alone, in one sense, in such a magnificent company of ladies. Miss MacIvers exerted herself to put him at his ease.

"It is early, is it not, Mr. Haviland?" she asked, and Mr. Haviland appealed to his watch, and replied that it was a quarter past eight.

"Oh, it is quite too early to go !" said Miss Allen.

Presently there was an imperative knock at Mrs. Woods's door, which was the main entrance from the street, and Rachel, shuffling along the hall in a pair of old slippers without heels, ushered into the study-room two young men and announced, "Some visitors for Miss Raymond."

Miss Raymond started up and ran forward, and was lifted quite off her feet by one of them,—a young gentleman with a downy upper lip and smooth, boyish face, a masculine copy of her own.

"Waddy, let me down ; don't you see the room is full of people !" she exclaimed.

"Waddy" set her down in mock haste, and lifted his hat to the roomful of people with an impudence that

would seem unpardonable to any one not witnessing it.
Those who did witness it laughed. The other gentleman being older—to the extent of a luxuriant moustache
and chin-whiskers, which he took in his hand while waiting his turn to be greeted,—was considerably more dignified and undemonstrative. He bent his head gravely,
and Miss Raymond grasping his two hands, stood on
tip-toe to kiss him, after which she introduced to the
company, with sisterly pride, her two brothers, "Starr"
and "Waddy."

"Oh, please set me up properly, Arabella!" begged
the younger, with his hat in his hand, in the attitude of
bowing.

Miss Raymond laughingly explained that Waddy was
"short" for Warren.

"And an exceedingly undignified abbreviation it is!"
said the young man.

Miss Morris crossed the room with unaccustomed alac-
rity, and gave her hand to the elder Mr. Raymond with
extreme cordiality. The greeting between herself and
Warren was less warm, and on his part tinged with a
ceremoniousness very much like his sister's. When the
sociable was mentioned, he expressed himself as delighted,
and inquired what was considered the fashionable hour to
put in an appearance.

"Perhaps your brother Starr doesn't care to go, Arabella," said Miss Morris, feeling that for her part she
would be satisfied to remain at home and entertain him.

But Starr hastened to assure her that nothing could
give him greater pleasure, and the young ladies went out
to get their wraps.

Miss Raymond turned back to speak a confidential
word to her brothers. "You will have to do the agreeable and escort some of the girls," she said. "Of course,
Matilda will expect to go with you, Starr."

Warren hastily echoed, "Of course!" and Starr shrugged
his shoulders.

"But I shall go with you, too," she added as an offset.
"And you, Waddy, must offer yourself to some of the
others."

Warren begged to know how many. "You know,

Arabella," he said, "two are all a gentleman can wait upon handsomely. And, by the way, can't you contrive to make that little, black-eyed beauty one of them?"

But Miss MacIvers had Magnanimously invited Miss Beach to "go with us," and Wilma and Miss Allen fell to Warren's share.

The night was quite mild and still; the moon shone softly on the snow, and the stars glimmered faintly through a thin, delicate mist Warren insisted upon not following the others, but going around a block or two to give him an opportunity to see more of the town; said he was already familiar with the main street, he and Starr having paraded up and down it some half-dozen times that evening trying to find their sister. When they reached the academy and proceeded to the ladies' hall, —after leaving their wrappings in a little room outside,— the rest of their party were already upon the floor promenading to slow music which somebody was playing on the piano.

"Would it be agreeable to you to fall in?" Warren asked. He had one of his companions upon either arm, and it being agreeable to them, at a convenient opening they edged into the procession.

The music, the lights, the warmth, the hum of voices, the numerous and graceful figures in rhythmic motion, had a pleasing effect on the senses. It was Wilma's first sociable, and her cheeks flushed with excited enjoyment of it, and her heart swelled with a longing for Charley to share it with her. Never an emotion stirred in her soul, of pain or delight, but she turned instinctively to him for sympathy.

There were two circles of promenaders moving, one within the other, in opposite directions, and presently Wilma encountered Miss Percy on Mr. Ingraham's arm, smiling and radiantly beautiful.

"That majestic individual is your principal, I take it?" said Warren.

"Yes," Miss Allen answered.

"And who is the lady?"

"That is Miss Percy, our elocution and music teacher."

"Indeed!" turning his head to look after her. "Arabella's letters have been full of her. A very remarkable looking lady!"

"Beautiful, don't you think?" asked Wilma.

"Angelic!" said Warren.

Farther up the room sat Miss Belmont, talking with one of the ministers of the place.

After making one or two rounds of the hall, Mr. Ingraham seated Miss Percy, and Wilma, asking to be excused, went up to her.

"I never saw you looking so well as you do to-night, Miss Percy," she said, with fervent admiration.

"I am trying to fancy myself happy, to see how it will seem," said Miss Percy, with a half-pleased, half-mocking smile. "I have put on one of my old party dresses," glancing at the folds of sheeny silk that swept around her, "and my jewelry, to try to make myself think that things are just as they used to be, and that there is no such thing as sorrow. The night I last wore these things I had never known the meaning of the word; and now I can scarcely realize that there is such a thing as happiness!"

Wilma wondered vaguely whether happiness and unhappiness *are* real, tangible things, or only phantoms; the one an ignus-fatuus which we follow, and the other a hideous nightmare which follows us!

What are these unseen influences that fasten upon us and make us happy or miserable? Have they any real, sovereign power and right to rule over us, or are they mere superstitions?

If Wilma had been inclined to doubt the reality of Miss Percy's settled grief, she might with equal cause, perhaps, have doubted her own happiness.

Though we seldom do have any doubts about our own state; it is only other people's joys and sorrows that wear an air of romance.

"Now, if it were a possible thing to forget," said Miss Percy, narrowing her gaze and looking through her long eyelashes, "if memory were not always tugging at one's heart-strings and pumping the zest out of life, one might be happy in this world; there is enough in it, one would think, and each of us has enough for our needs. Any philosopher would tell us that, I suppose. Miss Belmont doubtless thinks we have more than we deserve. But it seems to me there is a mistake somewhere; either we ought to be more like the lower animals,—satisfied with physical blessings,—or else there ought to be less precarious provision for our higher wants. Which do you think it ought to be, Wilma? As it is, the better part of us is too often starved!"

Wilma had gathered some confused ideas from Miss Belmont about building one's life upon a solid basis, and leaning upon the strong arm of the great fundamental laws underlying the universe; one of which bore strongly upon the physical condition of man, commending to his particular care the house we live in.

"You will never find a thoroughly healthy, strong person in a continued morbid, abnormal state of mind," Miss Belmont said. "Keep the body robust and vigorous, and sentimental griefs will vanish like clouds before the sun."

But would Miss Percy admit that hers was a sentimental grief that she might throw off if she had a good digestion? Hardly. It takes a disinterested party to say whether we have good cause to weep. And even he cannot convince us, and only makes himself disagreeable. Sentimental sorrows are as stubborn as any other sorrows, and perhaps appear more blind and exasperating to those who undertake the office of comforters.

"Perhaps," said Wilma, with a mental struggle to get hold of something to say, "there is enough in the world for all our wants if we could get the right things."

Miss Percy laughed, bitterly.

"A beggar might console himself with the same reflection. Though I suppose your words have a far deeper meaning," she added, mockingly, "whether you see it or not. You got them from Miss Belmont, I suspect."

Wilma reddened.

"How little either you or Miss Belmont know of these things," Miss Percy continued, with her narrowed gaze.

"Surely Miss Belmont knows," said Wilma, who could not conceive of Miss Belmont's being in the dark upon any subject whatsoever.

"Why? Because she professes to be a philosopher?

She is a mere bookworm, a mathematician laying out her life by the square and compass. She seems no more human or sympathetic than the stars in the heavens. She has not a particle of interest for me."

Wilma had seldom seen Miss Percy so excited about anything not pertaining to herself. Her cheeks glowed and her eyes flashed defiantly. But her very vehemence disproved her professed indifference to the preceptress. Miss Belmont had an interest for her, inasmuch as she aroused in her a spirit of angry resistance.

Wilma had a dim perception of the attitude of the two toward each other. Miss Belmont, calm, strong, clear-headed, understood and pitied Miss Percy's unhappy condition. The preceptress did not dwell upon and lament the innumerable sorrows of mankind; the important thing with her was their effects upon individuals. Miss Percy was keen enough to see that not her afflictions, even had they been known to Miss Belmont, but their results in her were compassionated. And this sort of compassion, though generous and broad, was yet unconsciously tinged with contempt for the weakness and wilfulness that would not rise above the accidents of life. And it stung Miss Percy into asking herself the startling question, "Am I exaggerating my suffering, and are my sorrows not real? could I get above them and take hold of life anew?" Arousing her momentarily out of the luxury of her grief and making her ashamed, as a drunken man brought suddenly to sober consciousness in the presence of clear-minded people, who feel a certain fine scorn for his weakness, might feel ashamed. Miss Belmont, in her strength and wisdom, seemed to so sit in judgment upon her and draw her out of her abandonment. And she did not want to be drawn out of it; she was like a morbid, sick person who shuts the blinds and will not let the sun come in with its cheer and brightness.

Miss Percy had scarcely ceased speaking when, glancing across the room, she met Miss Belmont's eyes fixed upon her with a half-sad, wistful expression, and to Wilma's surprise she got up abruptly and went over and sat down beside her in the place which the minister had just vacated.

"What do you want me to do?" was her sudden, un-expected question. "You have something in your face when you look at me that seems like reproach. Do you think me wicked, weak, worthless?"

Miss Belmont met the flashing, defiant, yet half-relent-ing face without any pretence of not understanding her.

"What do I want you to do?" she asked. "Gather up your forces and live."

"My forces are spent," said Miss Percy, bitterly.

"No; they are not spent," returned the preceptress. "Some of them are even too strong. Your imagination never sleeps; it carries away your reason and judgment, and destroys all interest in reality. My dear, your feet are not fastened to any spot; you take hold of nothing tangible; and humanity is so weak when it stands alone."

Large tears gathered slowly in Miss Percy's blue eyes.

"You need not have told me that," she said, tremu-lously, but with a strong effort to keep up her pride. "I once had friends in whom I trusted, but I have learned the sad lesson that one cannot rely even on one's friends."

"There is a still sadder lesson," said Miss Belmont: "that one cannot rely on oneself. We know not what forces may develop in us under the stress of circum-stances. I had a motto given to me once, to fit a certain event in my life, that I have endeavored to guide myself by in all my relations with others. It is this, 'Be true yourself and let time shape the rest.' My dear, there are few things which we greatly need that will not come to us by being true and waiting patiently."

"You preach like all the rest!" said Miss Percy, curl-ing her lip. "Why don't you preachers and teachers say, Do this or do that? I can do, but I cannot wait."

"Because no one dare lay down a special law for an-other; each must be a law to himself," said Miss Belmont.

"What! not even you who live so far above us and have no part or interest in the affairs of weak mortals?"

Miss Belmont winced.

"If I had no part or interest in the affairs of weak mortals, I should indeed be a poor sympathizer and teacher," she said, her great heart quivering for a mo-ment; for, under all her philosophy, Miss Belmont was

tender and sensitive. Her philosophy only helped her
to bear and to hide her hurts.

"Consider me a child, irresponsible, and without discretion to exercise free will; and take me in hand," said
Miss Percy, with a smile and half-sneer, as doubting
whether anything could be made out of her case.

"Well, the first thing I should do with you," said Miss
Belmont, smiling, "would be to put you on a mental
diet. I would take away your books and your music for
a time and allow you no unwholesome reflections. I
would wake up all your faculties that are asleep, and lull
to sleep all that have been on too long a strain."

"My books and music?" said Miss Percy, opening her
large eyes. "They are my only comforters."

"But they are morbid comforters," said Miss Belmont.
"I sometimes wish no books were written to sympathize
with our selfish sorrows and so exaggerate them. We
should have books that would take us out of ourselves
and interest us in things more worthy our thoughts than
our own petty troubles, which we are always too prone to
magnify. Believe me, my dear Miss Percy, this sorrow
which you are hugging to your heart, and which is drain-
ing all the good out of your life, is not so gigantic as you
think it is, if you would but thrust it away from you far
enough to enable you to look at it dispassionately. People,
I believe, are more selfish and more blinded to duty—
more reckless—in their sorrows than in their joys, or even
their pleasures and dissipations. Everything must give
way to the majesty of grief. I cannot but think that one
of the reasons why people yield to it so completely and
with so little compunction, springs from the old belief
that there is merit in being miserable, a sort of sacrament
in self-inflicted pain. For really, my dear, many of our
heartaches are self-inflicted; and there is, after all, a sort
of satisfaction or luxury in them that gives our yielding
the character of indulgence, and makes it a crime to waste
our lives in vain regret and sorrow."

Miss Percy's eyes were downcast, and her lips had lost
something of their usual haughty curve. Miss Belmont
was watching her narrowly. She continued speaking in
the kindest, most persuasive manner.

"I know how hard it is to turn about and right oneself after a great shock; a trouble comes upon us and revolutionizes the world for us, and after that every other way seems barred except the narrow channel of sorrowful memory and bitter regret. And this narrow channel comes to be, finally, scarcely more than a habit. The keenest griefs, by and by, lose their strong emphasis of pain, and the most we have to do is to break up habit, and herein lies our duty."

"Duty," said Miss Percy, sneeringly, and yet with a tremulousness that showed how painfully and throbbingly her heart vibrated. "What duty can one have who stands alone,—cut off from all the world?"

"My dear, no one can be so cut off; family ties may be severed (and, indeed, we are apt to place too great a stress upon these), but there is our common humanity which nothing can destroy, and which is forever creating duties for us toward our fellow-men. Besides, there is something you owe to yourself which you should not defraud yourself of. You have a fine nature to be developed and cultivated; you have talents that ought to be employed. You have it in you, by your genius and accomplishments, to shed abroad on those around you great spiritual warmth and light. You hold in your hands a power to elevate and refine that the fewest possess. My dear, our duties correspond exactly with our abilities, and in the grand book-keeping of life ought to balance."

Miss Percy was growing restive, and Miss Belmont was warned that she had fallen into the common, tiresome habit of preaching. She checked herself with a sigh, and Miss Percy got up abruptly and walked away with a haughtier step than usual. She spoke to Miss Pettibone and the two left the room together. After that her manner bore even a more marked coldness toward the preceptress, which that patient heart bore as it did all the hard, unkind things of life, without protest.

In the mean time, Mr. Ingraham, frowning and smiling more than ever, and diffusing a very genial influence everywhere (his presence seemed to radiate to the farthest corner, no matter how large the room), came up with Miss Raymond upon one arm, and invited Wilma to take the other. Wilma had lost consciousness of her surroundings and sat still, thinking. Mr. Ingraham's voice aroused her, and she got up gladly and took the offered arm, feeling the old sense of protection with which he had inspired her on their first day's acquaintance,—a feeling that Mr. Ingraham was able to call into play at will.

"How much I should enjoy this, now, if we could dance," said Miss Raymond, her face radiant. Some one else had taken the piano-stool and was playing a delicious waltz.

"Pooh, pooh," said Mr. Ingraham. "How does dancing differ from this? A mere acceleration of motion, like when one's horse breaks into a gallop."

"Well, who wouldn't rather gallop than walk?" said Miss Raymond.

Mr. Ingraham shook his head.

"Pray, did you never dance?" said Miss Raymond, looking up at him archly.

"Did I never dance? Yes; and I have seen the folly of it."

"Oh, well, we want to see the folly of it, too," she said, saucily.

Mr. Ingraham laughed. "Do *you* want to see the folly of it, Miss Lynne?" he asked, looking down.

"No," said Wilma, quickly; "I would rather stop short of that."

"Good!" said he, throwing back his head. "Better not wear things out; stop while they have a pleasant taste and will leave a sweet memory."

He had become suddenly grave, and knit his black brows. But Wilma was too young and inexperienced to wonder whether he had not tasted some bitter dregs. A moment later she dropped his arm abruptly and stood still. Looking down and following her glance, he saw framed in the door-way they were just passing, a handsome young stranger standing with his hat in his hand. Wilma took a step forward, and the stranger advanced with a smiling, expansive expression of face and held out his hand.

"Oh, Charley! how you startled me," she said. Her eyes as she looked up at him were full of tears.

"Did I?" said he. "It was stupid of me to come upon you so abruptly. I really could not avoid it, though; that is, it was impossible for me to let you know beforehand. But do you know, I had it in my mind that surprise adds something to the joy of meeting!"

The current of promenaders swept by, they drifting a little to one side. Miss Raymond, comprehending the situation with her accustomed quickness, had drawn Mr. Ingraham away. Mr. Burns, annoyed by the many pairs of curious eyes levelled at them by the promenaders in passing, drew Wilma's hand through his arm and fell in with the procession.

"I might have known it would be a shock to you," he said, ruefully; "but I had no time to write after I had made up my mind to come."

"Don't think about it," said Wilma. "It is all over now, and oh, I am so glad to see you."

Mr. Burns was very susceptible in some respects. A pleased flush spread itself over his boyish face, and his blue eyes kindled.

"Are you?" said he, pressing her hand close against his side. They moved on for a little while in silence, each feeling a rush of tender emotion to which the music seemed to play a happy accompaniment.

By and by the current began to crystallize into little knots and clusters, and Wilma, observing Mr. Ingraham in the centre of one of them, said to Charley, "I must introduce you to somebody, must I not? To Mr. Ingraham?"

Mr. Ingraham was a great man to Wilma, who did not in the least comprehend Mr. Burns's view of him. Mr. Burns's life had widened out much more than Wilma's, and principals of country academies occupied no very high rank in the social and intellectual world which his broad consciousness embraced. He lost sight of that which he himself advocated, that a man can make the most of himself just where he happens to be placed. Perhaps he hardly believed in the truth of his own theory (so many of us unwittingly preach one principle and act upon another), or else had little faith in its ever being put into practice. People so often justify in their lives being placed by fortune (or what not) in modest positions that perhaps a young man of Mr. Burns's limited observation could hardly be expected to look for anything but a schoolmaster in a schoolmaster. He had a suspicion (and in it lay, secretly, a flattering hope such as most ambitious young men feel) that greatness will eventually show itself at the front; whether forcing its way there by its own volition and momentum, or borne there by circumstances, was a question with which he sometimes wrestled, the two sides gathering weight, alternately, from such illustrious examples as Bonaparte, William the Conqueror, Shakspeare, and others. He did not care particularly to be introduced to Mr. Ingraham, he said, but if it came in the way he had no objection.

It did come in the way, Mr. Ingraham himself advancing to shake hands with the stranger with great cordiality. True to his prejudice, Mr. Burns was not favorably impressed; he disliked an overflowing manner, and intrenched himself all the more strongly with a dignified reserve. His pride was of a very sensitive sort; there was something presumptuous and not altogether respectful, to him, in the easy familiarity with which many people approach us.

He had hardly got through the introduction, however, when Mr. Starr Raymond came up to them and grasped his hand.

"Why, how do you do, Burns?" said he. "Who would have thought of meeting you here. Why didn't you tell us you had friends here, and come with us?"

"How did I know *you* had friends here and were coming!" retorted Mr. Burns, laughing. "Though, by the way, I did know. You have a sister?"

"Yes."

Miss Raymond had come up on her brother's arm. At this moment she stood a little in the background. Mr. Raymond brought her forward.

"Arabella, I wish to make you acquainted with a highly-esteemed friend of mine, Mr. Charles Burns."

"I think I must shake hands with one so impressively introduced," said Miss Raymond, with her usual readiness. "Besides, you appear to me in the double character of my brother's friend and Miss Lynne's friend, Mr. Burns."

Mr. Burns said he considered himself happy in being so well recommended.

It turned out that Mr. Raymond was also a collegian and a senior, and a member of Mr. Burns's law class. They stood talking a moment,—something about the route and the train each had taken to reach Crawford,—and Warren came up and begged Wilma and his sister to go with him to the other end of the room, where some sort of amusing game was being played creating a good deal of merriment. Warren was already familiar with most of the company.

Finding themselves alone, Mr. Burns and Mr. Raymond locked arms and made a slow circuit of the hall. Neither of them seemed to be made of the stuff that mixes readily with a crowd.

"Is Miss Lynne a relative of yours?" Mr. Raymond inquired, not curiously, but by way of showing a polite interest in his companion's affairs.

"No,—a friend," said Mr. Burns.

"This is a large school, if these are all students," Mr. Raymond remarked.

"Yes; and there are some very interesting faces among them," Mr. Burns returned, glancing around with the air of one whose judgment is mature. His eyes rested upon Miss MacIvers. Young Raymond also had singled her out.

"How beautiful she is!" said he. "I have been introduced to her, and I believe I will try to cultivate her acquaintance a little."

"Now is your opportunity, then," said Mr. Burns.

Miss MacIvers was sitting a little apart and alone. He turned aside and joined the group where Wilma and Miss Raymond were standing, and Starr approached Miss MacIvers.

"May I presume upon my introduction to ask you to take my arm?" said he, with that gallantry that seems at once so natural and so graceful in the young; and Miss MacIvers arose.

"Yes; it is stupid to be sitting still," she said, with a

laugh, laying one hand upon his arm, and adjusting her train with the other.

"Though this promenading is but mildly exciting," said he, smiling back at her, their eyes on a level.

At the opposite side of the room, Miss Morris sat watching them with spasms of anger. "She has been trying for that all the evening," she said to herself, fiercely, and felt a bitter regret that it was not Mr. Burns who was her victim. "He would have suited her quite as well as Starr," she said, without intending any disparagement of Starr.

Perhaps she was right. Miss MacIvers had keen discrimination, and though Mr. Burns was not strikingly handsome, he had a fine figure, an intellectual face, and extremely noble, dignified bearing. Miss MacIvers was quite capable of setting him up beside Mr. Raymond and drawing the lines of difference between them. "Not quite so smooth, but has more character, more energy; will make a better figure in the world," was the sum of her mental calculation.

Meantime, Mr. Burns, who had little thought to bestow upon anybody but Wilma, said to her, "Haven't you had enough of this? Suppose we go and take a walk down these pretty streets of yours. It is beautiful out-doors, and it seems to me it will be pleasanter walking alone by moonlight than promenading among all these people by lamplight."

"So I think," said Wilma, glad that he had proposed it.

They went out into the little anteroom where she had left her wrappings. There was no light but the moon shining in softly.

"It *is* beautiful!" said Wilma, glancing from the window.

The town, snow-enshrouded, lay white and still below.

"Yes," said Charley; "the moon has on her misty bridal-veil to-night, something like my Wilma will wear one of these days."

He was helping her on with her things,—tying her hood-strings under her chin,—and he took her round, radiant face in his hands and kissed it.

"You have grown more beautiful than ever, my darling," he said.

"I beautiful? How can you say so after coming out from yonder!" said Wilma, nodding toward the hall, but nevertheless blushing with pleasure.

Charley shrugged his shoulders.

"What are all those to me?" he said. "You are my Wilma ; so long as I have you, let the wide world wag as it will."

They went down the long halls and stairways, dimly lighted, and through the wide doors standing open. Outside all was quiet, and only the pleasant sounds from above came, subdued, through the closed windows. The white snow-crust, covering the ground and glimmering in the soft light, was unbroken except by the several distinct paths leading down to the different gates and hard-beaten by the tread of many feet.

CHAPTER XXIII.

"I FORGOT to ask, Charley, how you happened to come?" said Wilma, after they had got outside upon the path, and were walking slowly with arms interlocked, both feeling delightful thrills of gladness at being together again.

"Because I wanted to see my Wilma," said he, looking down and twining his arms around her lovingly. "My eyes were longing to behold her, my arms ached to clasp her, my heart was hungry for her. You see," he added, playfully, "I can't get along without you, my darling, any more than I can get along without several other things that go to make up the sum of human happiness, I will not say human existence ; we can exist, you know, under very adverse circumstances. I possess a good many things—you among them—that I shouldn't like to give up; but I suppose if some unexpected disaster were to sweep them away (for instance, if some other fellow were to come between you and me and carry you off), I should go on eating and drinking and living all the same. The animal, you see, my dear, predominates to the last, and holds on to life after the affections and all the finer qualities of the being are vanquished."

He tried to meet Wilma's eyes, but she did not look up. The bare possibility of her ever being lost to him, or divided from him by any of the accidents of life, hurt her. She wanted to believe that their relations to each other were like the relations of the planets in the universe, fixed and unalterable. She disliked the idea of change. She wanted to believe in all the old traditions. The saddest of all things to her was the thought that any life should be built upon an unreality, or that any one's firm hope should be fixed upon a thing that would never be. And to have Charley set up, even in jest, so dreadful a possibility,—he had a habit of setting up possibilities, and of maintaining that the world was full of them, and that no one ought to be surprised at their unexpected realization in whatever quarter,—was a cruel jar to her faith. There was no balm to her in the thought that his existence would be spoiled without her, and that, though divided from her, he might still be true to her; if they were ever separated, therein would lie the utter ruin of all happiness and joy. She could conceive of no compromise with a destiny that would take him from her. Nor is it remarkable that, without experience, she could not take into account the thousand little attendant circumstances that at last will make the most aggravated sorrow bearable. She had still much of a child's tenacity of affection. Of course Charley could not know what feeling his words stirred in her; we are such short-sighted mortals, we penetrate such a little way into the soul's solitude of those nearest us! That Wilma should have a deep inner life of thought and emotion apart from him, and yet in which he was held with such strength of devotion, he did not suspect; and, being of a rather playful disposition, he liked to tease her sometimes.

"I did not intend to come quite so soon," he explained, as they walked on. "I intended to run down, by and by, and spend a day with you. But yesterday I had a letter from my mother, urging me to come home. The letter alarms me ; it is very short and written in a feeble hand. Oh, Wilma, the thought of losing my mother is almost more than I can bear! You never knew her, Wilma; you don't know what a good, good mother she has been to me. She has been an inspiration to me all my life, leading me onward and upward. And I have been so contented away from her. I have left her in her lonely old age with cruel thoughtlessness. How selfish we are, how blindly we go on, and deceive ourselves into thinking we are doing our highest duty! I always wanted to make the most of myself for my mother's sake. At least I told myself so ; and I wanted to be worthy of her pride of me that always seemed to have a sort of prophecy in it for my splendid future which was to be the delight of her old age. My love for her at the very commencement of my life was my strong motive-power. My wish to please and satisfy her has influenced me always. How we lose sight of our aim and miss it in the very pursuit of it! It is like toiling to reach a certain goal and finding at the end that the goal is gone,—has been removed out of our reach. We never think how time, too, is rushing on and may change all things for us. There is no such thing as marking out a straight path in life and gaining a direct end. We trust too much to the absoluteness of things. Time is treacherous, deceitful, changeable."

"Oh, no, Charley," said Wilma, "don't say so. Time gives us only the present moment and promises nothing more."

"In one sense, I suppose so," said Mr. Burns. "But the present is not big enough for a man to live in. There are very few present moments in a lifetime that satisfy us. We have got to be reaching out, reaching out, though we know that at the last, when we are about to lay our hands on the thing we have struggled for, it may be snatched from us."

"But, Charley dear," Wilma said, gently, "don't you ever think that you are gaining something every day that you live and work that cannot be snatched away from you? Don't you think we talk too much about great ends and aims, thinking that our lives are wasted unless we accomplish them?"

"Oh, yes; it is true we are gaining something for ourselves," said Charley; "but I was thinking of my mother and of how I have deceived myself into believing I left her for her good, and for the final happiness and satisfaction she would derive from my making the most of myself. I begin to think that through all I have thought much more of myself than of her. I ought to have devoted my life to her as she has devoted hers to me."

"And do you really think, Charley," Wilma said, "that she would like to be paid back in kind? I don't think so. I believe you are much more of a comfort and satisfaction to her as you are than you would be if you had stayed with her and devoted yourself to her, as you say. I think I know just how a mother—a large-hearted mother—would feel about that. Dear Charley, I know how even *I* feel about it. I don't mind your being away from me any more, knowing that you are growing into a great man. I don't mind anything, so that you love me."

"No; you women are such unselfish creatures!" Charley exclaimed, winding his arm around her again and drawing her close to him. "Unselfish and generous. And how men impose on your unselfishness and generosity! How many men are skeptical of it. I thank God that my faith in womanhood is so firmly rooted,—through my mother and through you, my darling!"

"And do you think your faith would need that positive evidence?" said Wilma, looking up with a smile.

"I don't know," said he, shaking his head and tossing back his curls. "I am a lawyer, you know, and I demand proofs. My mother and you are my witnesses."

"And you love us," said Wilma, "and it is your love that gives the verdict. If you found us false, what would become of your judgment then?"

"I shall not find you false," said he, "and so my judgment will stand, strongly supported to the end. I suppose one couldn't have a well-grounded belief in the goodness and purity of womanhood without having known some good and pure women."

"Miss Belmont argues differently," said Wilma. "She says we must leave individuals entirely out of the question, and place our feet upon a solid foundation of principles.

She says the qualities which *ought* to make men and women do exist as absolutely as God exists. But that we ought not to expect to find them, or be disappointed at not finding them, in the men and women we love. And, dear Charley," Wilma added, "it is so hard for me to do that; it is so hard for me to see abstract things. Take Honor, Truth, Goodness,—they are all unreal to me; they are all mere sentiment, until I fasten them to something. I fasten them to you, Charley, and then I see and understand. Miss Belmont says the reason why she would detach principle from personality is because human nature is changeable and fallible. But you are not, Charley!" Clasping his arm suddenly with both her little hands, and looking up with a passionate earnestness, startling to him, her eyes brimful of tears.

"I hope, in God, not in a way to destroy your faith in those things!" he said, fervently. "You humble me, Wilma; you must not bound the attributes of God by the little measure of man!"

"Oh, I do not," said Wilma. "Cannot a man be truthful, honorable, noble?"

"A man may change," said Mr. Burns; "or, rather, he may grow out of one thing into another, and so appear to change. We cannot tell what the future will make of us. Our promises to-day may not be binding upon our consciences to-morrow. Our own self is a mystery that we cannot unravel—that we cannot vouch for. I can imagine such a thing as this, Wilma, that though I could never love anything else in the world so well as you, yet there might be circumstances in which I would feel bound to give my life to something else rather than to you, though I have pledged it to you. I can only hope, and trust, and sincerely believe that no such appalling duty will ever come between us."

Wilma winced again under the dreadful possibility. Simple absence from Charley had no pain for her now, as she said; but separation, division of heart, of interest, of life, took all life away.

"You will not always feel as you do now, dear," Charley continued. "I am glad and proud to embody your ideals—or principles—for a little while; they will soon outgrow me. By and by, when your mind grows bigger, and your wings are fledged, and your practical little feet that cling so desperately to tangible things let go of earth, and you soar up into space and stand alone in the presence of the absolute, your soul quickened to a perception of principle rather than example, unaided by men and women and the blush of physical beauty and the music that is audible to the senses; seeing all goodness, truth, beauty, with the spiritual vision, you will not need to find me enthroned upon the heights, exquisite as a rose, beautiful as a rainbow, and mighty as an archangel to convince yourself that these are grand things in the world."

"Don't laugh, Charley," said Wilma, so appealingly that he took the sweet, earnest face in his hands again, and kissed it affectionately.

"It is true, darling," said he, smiling and shaking his head. "This buoyant thing, this soul that is in you, and which I cannot touch or hold, will rise far above me and will find that its Charley does not fill all space, one of these days. Do you know, Wilma" (very seriously), "that you would be placing a heavy responsibility upon me, in what you have just said, did I not know that you inevitably will soar above me,—I mean above the human in me? If I fall you must not. I dislike that sort of dependency upon one another. I would like you to believe in me, of course; and I would like you to think as I do upon all great and important questions; but not *because* I do. I would like you to harmonize with me and yet be independent of me. There is no growth in us when we simply follow and imitate, without thinking. It is like scattering grain in a soil so shallow that it is thrown up next day to bleach in the sun. Better sunk a fathom under ground and not a sprout appear for a score of years. I am not alarmed about you, Wilma," he added, smiling, "or weighted with any great responsibility about you; but do not fancy, darling, that I do not appreciate the solemnity of my relation to you. No man could realize more fully the preciousness of a woman's love given into his keeping than I. But I know that you will find your way whether I lead you or not. And I love you all the more for being able to feel this confidence in you. By the way, Wilma, it has always seemed to me that your Miss Percy must be rather a weak sort of person. I would not envy the man that has wrecked her tiny boat. Of course it was a man! Has she never told you about any false lover?"

"Oh, no," said Wilma, a little hurt.

"I did not see her, did I?" said Mr. Burns.

"No; she went away before you came."

"I should like to have seen Miss Belmont. Your Mr. Ingraham, Wilma, is a small tyrant, who domineers over you, and makes the balance even by a good deal of petting. I suppose," he added, "Miss Belmont doesn't patronize sociables?"

"Oh, yes; she was there a little while. She never stays long. She says she doesn't think the young folks need her when it comes to amusement."

"Oh! And all her acts are mere matters of duty. I like that spirit of self-importance!"

"Charley! What makes you so sarcastic?"

"Sarcastic, am I? Well, it seems to me we never cut so ludicrous a figure as when we set ourselves up to do nothing but what has the air of duty, and put a value on everything we do and say, and are fearful of spending our worth upon an unworthy object or occasion."

"You don't understand Miss Belmont, Charley," said Wilma, firmly. "Indeed, I am afraid I describe people very poorly, since you get such impressions of them."

"There! now, I beg your pardon, Wilma. I didn't mean to offend you. Your descriptions are perfect. I am afraid the fault all lies with me; I suspect I am jealous of your friends."

They had reached the farthest limit of Main Street, the point where it was merged into the country highway, and crossing over, went up on the other side. When they got to Mrs. Woods's gate, Wilma stopped and Charley looked up at the house and said he meant to photograph it upon his mind, so that in future he could picture her there, seated at one of the windows. Wilma told him which window was hers. A naked jasmine-vine clambered over it.

"By the way, Wilma," said he, "I have not told you

my errand yet,—at least not all of it. My mind has been so full of it that maybe you have guessed it, though. I want to take you home with me. Can you spare me a few days?"

Wilma looked up with a sudden leaping of joy in her eyes.

"Home, Charley? Oh, is it possible? It is such a short vacation they did not expect me to come home this time."

"We will surprise them," said Charley. "Have you never been the least bit homesick, Wilma? I could never gather from your letters that you were."

"But I was at first," said Wilma. "After I got accustomed to things here, I wouldn't let myself think of home,—that is, in the way of wishing myself there."

"You are a little philosopher," said Charley. "Well, I suppose you must go in; it is getting late. I will come for you to-morrow morning at nine o'clock; the train leaves at a little past nine."

He went with her up into the porch and bade her "good-night," and walked back to the hotel.

CHAPTER XXIV.

THE following morning, when Mr. Burns came to take Wilma to the train, he met a young gentleman—Miss MacIvers's escort of the previous evening — at Mrs. Woods's gate. He had driven up in an elegant livery sleigh to take that young lady out riding. Exchanging the formal salutations of strangers, they walked up into the little porch together. Mr. Burns, being foremost, knocked, and Miss MacIvers, in plumes and velvets and furs, opened the door, and was a little taken aback upon meeting his face instead of Mr. Haviland's, and blushed; then bowed with her usual superb grace, and, catching sight of the higher department young man over his shoulder, came forward royally, and was escorted to the sleigh, with its bright linings and robes, and whirled away with a joyous jingling of bells, than which nothing seems more in keeping with youth and cold weather and fine spirits. Mr. Burns turned his head and looked after her as she passed him and went down the steps.

Wilma coming to the door to meet him, he asked, "Who is that beautiful creature?"

"Why, that is Miss MacIvers," said Wilma.

"Oh, the belle and beauty of Crawford! Well, she certainly deserves the title. Are you ready?" he asked, passing into the study-room; "we haven't much time. There is the hack already."

Wilma hastened to put on her hat and cloak.

"I have nothing but this valise to take," she said. "I thought it wouldn't be worth while to pack my trunk."

"No, you will be back within a week," said Charley.

Home! home to mother, Fred, Blanche, Miss Barker, and her quaint old friends; home to all Hazelville, to the old church and school-house, and the race and the mill and Twin Pionts. What a thrilling, thrilling gladness to feel the first rushing motion of the train, homeward bound, after a school-girl absence of three months! I know it is trite to describe it.. But how many, many trite and common things are forever bubbling up new and strange and sweet in young hearts!

Mr. Burns did not share the feeling. Though usually buoyant and hopeful, and determined to look on the bright side, he could not shake off the sad foreboding that his mother's letter had awakened in him. Whenever the train stopped so that he could talk, he told Wilma of his childhood that had been so tenderly protected by his mother's love. Things long forgotten came up and flooded his memory, and magnified her gentleness and goodness to him.

It was new to Wilma, and it endeared him to her more than ever. He had always been extremely reserved, even to her, regarding this side of his life. She knew that between him and his mother there was an unusual tenderness, and so sacred that he hardly ever touched upon it. She felt grateful that he did so now in his sad apprehension.

It was not many hours' ride; the distance was barely a

hundred miles. But there was a change of cars and some delay, which they took advantage of to get a lunch at a small station and to walk about, the day being pleasant.

Charley had telegraphed that they were coming, and so now at home they were all watching and waiting. And in a darkened chamber lay Charley's mother watching and waiting, and asking in a faint voice, "Will he come soon?"

Two or three women moving noislessly about answered soothingly, "Yes; only be patient a little while longer, he will soon be here." And put something moist to the dry, thin lips, and laid their hands on the damp, wrinkled brow, and glanced at each other, shaking their heads.

But he came too late. When he reached home and ran up from the gate and laid his hand eagerly and tremblingly on the door-knob, and pushed open the door, his mother was gone. For a time he knew nothing; his limbs gave way, the color left his face, and he sank into a chair utterly overcome by the shock.

By and by he awoke to the realization of his great sorrow, but to nothing else. Wilma and all other things were as completely crowded out of his life as though they had never been. He went back to his childhood and was alone with his mother. He remembered nothing but that he and she were all the world to each other, and now she was gone, gone. She had been his first, his only incentive once, toward a high career. When he was a little boy his great ambition to be great was to please her. Latterly, he had lost sight of it, but now he went back to it and thought he had nothing to live for. For now she was dead. Oh, was she dead? They had told him so, but was it true? He got up and went into her chamber,—her pretty chamber! No one else was ever so carefully neat and tasteful as his mother. There on the white bed, with her waving, silvery hair parted smoothly above her broad forehead which, in spite of its wrinkles and its age and the stamp of death upon it, was very like his own, she lay rigid and still. He sank down upon his knees and covered up his face and groaned aloud, so that the women who were busied about the room left their solemn work and went out with streaming eyes.

CHAPTER XXV.

DEATH cuts off all the little resources that other afflictions have of hope, or lingering expectation, or doubt
even.   There is no extenuation, no compromising with
this sorrow, or putting it off.   It has got to be met.   In
all its abruptness, in all its enormity, in all its hopelessness. He is dead. There is nothing beyond that. There
is the end so far as concerns our relations and intercourse
with him of whom this grave sentence is written.   There
is a final giving up and putting away, out of our lives, of
something that cannot be brought back.   Perhaps there
is something merciful in the absoluteness of it; we are
reasonable creatures, and however sorely we are wounded,
we must and will finally see the great necessity of adjusting ourselves to the irremediable change.   Nothing else
is so compulsory.   In answer to all other discouragements
and sorrows we say, " While there is life there is hope."
And so we go on through all the wearisome years with
sickened hearts, forever torn and forever bleeding.   Death
makes but one wound, and when it is healed it never
reopens.

Charley's mother was dead.   The sad rites and ceremonies were all over, and a new snow had covered up
the new grave, and Charley sat with Wilma in Mrs.
Lynne's little parlor.   It was hard for him, he could not
reconcile himself to it.

"There is no use," he said, again and again, with a
burst of tears.   "I can't give her up.   It tears my life
up by the roots.   Oh, Wilma, there is something so terrible in this thing death.   It is such a fatal, final thing.
It is such a destroyer of one's hopes and plans and ambitions.   It takes all the zest out of life.   It sickens me.
I hate the sight of books and the thought of school.
Everything seems so empty, living and working so useless.   What is life anyhow?   What is the final end to be
gained by all this striving?   My mother lived and labored
and suffered for sixty years.   And this is the end.   I do

not say her life is wasted; her best years were given to help and comfort others who, themselves, are long since dead. But it seems to me a faithful life of sixty years is worth some permanent good thing."

"Dear Charley," said Wilma, gently, "does not your mother's life go on in you? And will not your actions, inspired first by her, be a sort of reward to her? Perhaps nothing is really permanent in this world. But lives may be good while they last, and running on into other lives make a continuous good, and the world grows better. Surely, Charley, from the grave where your mother lays down her work you can take it up and carry it forward. Is not that a beautiful thought?"

"You are a good little comforter, Wilma," Charley said. "What is there, after all, to do but go on! Perhaps it is enough simply to help each other, even though man's beginning and end are centred in this poor, fleeting earth. That is a sad view to take of life, is it not? We can hardly go about with cheerful faces and hopeful hearts, thinking that this is all! And yet, who knows? Oh, Wilma!" he exclaimed suddenly, coming and seating himself beside her and taking her hand, "you are all that is left to me now. I have made very few friendships. I have not cared to make any. Do you know I am tempted, sometimes, to take you and go away to some sunny clime and try to forget this busy, struggling life that, after all, only ends in death! Why should we hurry and fret? Why not drift as peacefully down the stream as we can, since the end is the same?"

"We cannot, Charley,—we cannot go away and forget," said Wilma. "It makes no difference where we are; we carry our own little world with us everywhere. Besides, it is not right,—is it, dear Charley, to turn aside from the path we have marked out for ourselves, and which our friends have marked out for us, in our calmest and wisest moments?"

"No, no, no!" said he. "I talk at random. I am not myself. Let us go and walk; or, stay, the snow is too deep for you; I will go myself."

He put on his hat and greatcoat hurriedly; and his heart ached when he remembered how many, many times in such weather his mother had cautioned him to wrap his scarf around his neck and keep himself warm.

"Poor mother,—poor, poor mother!" he said, with a groan, and went out.

He set his face against the north wind and walked briskly several miles into the country. When he came back in the edge of the evening, with ruddy cheeks and a keen appetite, the morbidness of his sorrow was gone, though it was many months before the conscious aching went out of his sorely-wounded heart.

CHAPTER XXVI.

THE spring following the death of Mr. Burns's mother, Mrs. Woods's boarders were all back in their old places, with the exception of Mr. Gray, who had "gone West." His place was taken by a Mr. Langworthy, a higher department student.

One afternoon, when Wilma had finished her recitations at the academy, she got permission to leave the building and go down to see Miss Percy, who was again an invalid; Mr. Ingraham always being more than willing to grant such permission. When she came back at tea-time, Miss Raymond met her with the delightful information that to-morrow was May-day, and Mr. Ingraham had granted the school (upon petition) a holiday They were to go into the woods, "to those hills away over east of town," Miss Raymond said, "which look so beautiful in the distance. Mr. Ingraham says there is a stone-quarry there, and we will have a chance to hunt fossils. Then there is Miss Belmont's botany class."

"Oh, do you suppose there are any flowers?" Wilma asked. "Maybe I can get some for Miss Percy. She was wishing for some wild-flowers to-day."

"She is a wild-flower herself," said Miss Raymond. "You are always thinking of her, Wilma, though I don't know as we should quarrel with her about that; she has few enough to think of her, poor thing. But it is her own fault. I have put forth my best efforts to be agreeable to her, and she repulses me continually. I should think she had no taste or penetration whatever, if she didn't like you; that one spark of discrimination redeems her in the eyes of your friend Arabella, my dear; and I am constrained on that account to be civil to her still."

"Thank you," said Wilma, laughing.

Everybody was jubilant over the holiday plan; even Miss MacIvers discussed it enthusiastically with young Langworthy, who was trying to eclipse Mr. Haviland in her regard.

Early in the morning, before it was time to start, Wilma ran down to see Miss Percy again. She found her much better, though looking very fragile and delicate, and proportionately lovely. Her complexion was never a sickly pallor, but a clear, beautiful transparency; and her large, bright eyes were unfathomably blue and deep. Her pretty silken hair curled about her white neck and forehead in delicate little ringlets, and was loosely caught up at the back. There was a peculiarly happy and childlike expression upon her face that only appeared at rare intervals—when she was free from bodily pain and forgot, momentarily, her mental suffering.

"You see I am much improved, Wilma," she said, cheerfully; "I am going to get up to-day. How is it out-doors?"

"Beautiful!" said Wilma; "and the birds are singing among the trees as I have not heard them sing before this spring."

"Open the shutters, please," said Miss Percy; "you have no idea how I long for summer skies. I have spent a great part of my life in Florida, and I hate these cold Northern winters."

Wilma put by the crimson curtains and threw back the blinds, and let in the fragrant breath and sunshine of May. Away beyond were the woods just budding into delicate greenness, and all things seemed bent upon a resurrection of freshness and beauty, such as would blot out even the remembrance of last year's decay. The very air had a strength of life and buoyancy that lifted the spirit heaven-

I*

ward as if borne on invisible wings.   Wilma turned from the window intending to speak of the holiday.   Miss Percy was opening her lips to say, "Is this Friday ? Yes ; I recollect.   I wish it were Saturday, so that you could stay with me all day."

A quick thought shot through Wilma's mind, and its shadow crossed her face.

Miss Percy had keen perceptions.

"What are you thinking about ?" she asked, smiling. "One can *see* the images that pass behind your transparent face, but cannot wholly define them."

"I was thinking whether I might not stay with you anyhow," said Wilma, blushing.

"Do you think your preceptress"—curling her lip— "would give you permission ?"

"Dear Miss Percy, Miss Belmont would give me permission to do anything that would be a pleasure or a benefit to you !" said Wilma, earnestly.   "Shall I go and ask her if I may stay with you ?"

"Yes ; if you will be so kind," she said.   "The days are so long, and it kills me to stay here alone ; and I do not care to have the Pettibones sit with me, they are so stupid."

Wilma tied her hat-strings and started down-stairs. Miss Percy called to her, "Will you please tell them to send Bridget up here ? I hate these country houses with no bells."

Wilma tapped at the sitting-room door, and was bade to "come in."

"Miss Percy," she began, advancing the name as soon as she opened the door, as a sort of apology for her intrusion,—for she stood in considerable awe of the aristocratic Pettibones,—"says, if you please, she would like to have Bridget sent up to her."

"Is it possible," said Miss Ella Pettibone, breaking into a laugh, and looking across at her mother (they were the only occupants of the room), "that Miss Percy sends so courteous a request ? Or are we indebted to you, miss, for the politeness ?"

Wilma blushed, but did not reply.

"You just step out into the kitchen and speak to

Bridget, will you?" said Mrs. Pettibone, good-naturedly, nodding toward a side door.

Wilma complied, and passed through a large dining-room, and opened another door which let her into Bridget's domain. That worthy domestic was busy washing up the breakfast dishes. Wilma had already made her acquaintance in Miss Percy's room. She delivered her message, and Bridget straightway wiped her hands and prepared to go up-stairs.

"The purty dear!" she ejaculated. "It's her breakfast she'll be afther wantin' now, I suppose. Though it's precious little she'll ate when she gits it."

Wilma went out the back way and hurried home. Miss Raymond was waiting for her; the others had all gone up to the academy, from whence they were to start.

"You are all ready, are you not, Wilma?" she asked, meeting her in the porch. "We must hurry or we shall be late." Wilma had not thought of anybody's disappointment but her own.

"I am not going," she said, bravely.

"Wilma!"

"I am going back to stay with Miss Percy. I came to tell you."

It was hard for her that Miss Raymond reproached her so with her eyes, and said no word. Great tear-drops welled up and rolled down her cheeks. She went on hurriedly, her lips trembling, "She is sick, you know, and lies there all alone; and I couldn't bear to leave her. And so I told her I would stay with her."

"And she was selfish enough to keep you!" said Miss Raymond, with flashing eyes.

"Oh, no, no! She doesn't know there is a holiday. She would not have consented if she had known."

"Then I shall go and tell her, and make her release you."

"No, no!" Wilma laid her hand upon her arm. "She would be angry with me; you can't understand how she would feel about it."

"Do you understand how I feel about it?" said Miss Raymond, coldly. "You knew I depended on you today, the other girls are all gone."

"Oh, what shall I do!" said Wilma, deeply distressed. "Miss Percy is sick and weak; she can't reason as stronger people do. I depended on you,—on your kind good nature, not to be hurt and offended; and you are hurt and offended."

"I am a wicked wretch!" said Miss Raymond, throwing her arms around Wilma's neck. "You depended on me, and I have shown myself small and mean. As though it were not hard enough for you to give up your holiday, without my making it harder."

"Yonder comes Miss Belmont," said Wilma; "let us run across the street; you can go up to the academy with her."

They crossed over and met Miss Belmont on the sidewalk.

"Don't you think, Miss Belmont," said Miss Raymond, "that Wilma can't go! She has to stay with Miss Percy."

"Oh, no; don't say it in that way," said Wilma. "I don't *have* to stay. I offered to stay of my own accord. And it seems treacherous and deceitful in me to want to go all the time and not to tell her."

"You did not tell her?" said Miss Belmont, raising her eyebrows.

"No," said Wilma; "she wouldn't have listened to my staying if I had told her."

"But do you think it was quite right, dear, to place her under such an obligation to you without her knowing it? She is so proud and sensitive, I am afraid she would hardly take it as a kindness."

Wilma had not thought of it in that way. "What shall I do?" she said, with tears in her eyes. "I cannot go back and tell her now."

"No," said Miss Belmont, taking her hand and holding it kindly; "you cannot go back and tell her now."

Wilma, to cut the matter short, withdrew her hand hurriedly, smiled, and said "good-by," and ran away with the tears in her eyes.

"The dear child," said Miss Belmont. "What would she not do for Miss Percy?"

"What would she not do for anybody?" said Miss

Raymond. "She is the most generous, unselfish little creature I ever knew. I hope Miss Percy appreciates her."

"Whether she does or not," said Miss Belmont, "Wilma's own good heart rewards her; she never will suffer the bitterest pains that mortals can feel."

Wilma gave herself no time for regret, but hurried back to Miss Percy. She ran lightly up-stairs and opened the door and found her—she had been up and got herself dressed in some soft, gray fabric—lying across the bed asleep. Sleeping like a little child, with her lips parted and wreathed with a smile. Wilma went softly to the window and sat down on a low ottoman, and looked away to the hills where the school was going for its holiday. Her tumultuous thoughts and heart-throbbings were greatly at variance with the stillness of Miss Percy's room. By and by, her gaze dropped into the street back of the Pettibone premises, and there went the school, teachers and students, in all the happy abandon of holiday freedom. There were so many voices talking and laughing that the distant murmur of them floated up to her without carrying any intelligible words. Most of the young men bore lunch-baskets. Mr. Ingraham, with his tall hat, was surrounded, as usual, by half a dozen merry girls, who had conspired together to keep off Mrs. Bramen. Mrs. Bramen was therefore reduced to the escort of one of the uncomely professors, which, however, as a polite woman, she accepted with grace. Mr. Langworthy had outgeneraled Haviland, and walked beside Miss MacIvers and carried her parasol. Haviland, who was gentlemanly and not resentful, accepted the situation and dropped back with Miss Belmont and Miss Raymond, who still kept together. Once Wilma saw them glance up at the window where she sat, and was tempted to raise the sash and flutter her handkerchief. Changing her mind, she drew back a little so that they might not see her. In a few moments they had turned down another street and passed out of sight; and Wilma, sitting alone in the silence, soon lost all regret and recollection of them, in a long, delightful revery, such as she used frequently to indulge in before the era of these busy school-days. She had no conception of the length of time that had elapsed when Miss Percy called to her.

"Wilma? Why, how long I have slept. I didn't mean to go to sleep. I was so tired after dressing myself that I thought I would lie down and rest. Will you look at my watch on the bureau, please, and see what time it is?"

Wilma took the little jewelled watch off its velvet cushion, and said it was nearly twelve o'clock.

"So late?" said Miss Percy. "Then our carriage will soon be here. Do you know, I have ordered a carriage for you and me; we are going to have a holiday. I would always rather walk than ride, but I have not strength enough to walk now."

Wilma's face flushed guiltily.

"Bridget will bring us up some lunch," Miss Percy continued. "I think I hear her coming up the back stairs now."

She walked across the room and opened the door; and Bridget, shuffling along the hall in her working slippers, came in with a great tray of dainties, which she set upon a little table that she had previously cleared of books and various articles not rightfully belonging to it; Miss Percy having rather careless habits.

"An' ye think ye will go for the ride, do ye, ma'am?" she asked.

"Certainly, Bridget," said Miss Percy, smilingly.

"Mistress Pettibone thinks it's a great risk, indade."

"Oho!" laughed Miss Percy. "A great risk. Tell Mrs. Pettibone it will be a great benefit."

"Well, cud ye think o' anything more as I cud get for ye now?" Bridget asked, with her hands on her hips, surveying the table.

"Oh, no; you have thought of everything — and more than I should have thought of, Bridget. Thank you," said Miss Percy. She was very kind and gracious to Bridget; she was altogether good-natured and amiable to-day, and Wilma was charmed with her; and would have been happy, but for the generous deception she had practised upon her. Bridget said she must go down and spread the luncheon for the family. In less than half an hour she came hurrying back again to say that the carriage was waiting.   Miss Percy wrapped herself up carefully, and Bridget half carried her down the stairs and saw her comfortably seated among the cushions, with Wilma beside her; and then stood shading her eyes with her hand to watch them off.

Away they went, whirling up the long main street, smoothly graded, past all the beautiful houses with their green yards and budding shrubbery. The sun shone and the birds sang, and the wind blew soft and warm from the South.   The woods were getting green, the lilac buds were swelling, and the wild plum and crab-apple trees were blossoming out in delicate pink and white.   There was beauty and fragrance and gladsomeness everywhere.   They splashed through a shallow, clear little stream with a pebbly bottom and clean, white, sandy borders, and scared the birds twittering in the bushes; and Wilma put out her hand and caught it full of white, sweet-scented blossoms and gave a spray to Miss Percy, and scattered the tiny leaves like snow-flakes over the scarlet lap-robe.   They came to cross-roads and the driver called back,—

"Which way now?"

"Oh, no matter," said Miss Percy.   "The road to the right looks rather the more inviting, doesn't it, Wilma?"

"Yes; it is the *woodiest*," said Wilma, leaning out.

They turned down a long, green lane with farms and farm-houses and abundant shade-trees upon either side of it.   Men were ploughing and women making gardens all along.   From the lane they passed into a winding road through a stretch of woods, and going for some distance in a southerly direction, Miss Percy leaned out of the carriage and looked away to the left, where there was a long line of hills stretching away in the distance.

"Look yonder, Wilma, there's something waving there on the brow of that hill," she said.   "It looks like a flag."

"It is a flag," said Wilma, "and people are moving about.   I wonder—— oh! it's the school."

"The what?" said Miss Percy.

"Why, it's May-day," said Wilma, in confusion. Miss

Percy looked at her so that she was bound to explain. "Mr. Ingraham gave the school a holiday."

"And why did not you go?"

Wilma was silent.

"You thought you would be self-denying, and stay with me?"

Miss Percy's blue eyes dilated, and her red lips curled scornfully.

"I don't demand any sacrifices, Miss Lynne. I will not accept them."

"Oh, Miss Percy!" said Wilma, inexpressibly pained. "Pray, don't be offended. I wanted to stay with you. I would rather a thousand times please you than please myself."

Miss Percy, leaning out, called to the driver, and asked if there were a road leading up to the hill where they saw the flag waving.

"Yes'm," said he, pulling up; "there's a road t'other side o' the hill, windin' up in there som'ers."

"Find it, and drive up there," said Miss Percy, and leaned back in her seat again.

Wilma, shrinking into her corner, was silent, feeling crushed and miserable. But yet, in all her little troubles (how little they would look in the breadth of later experience, and yet how stinging they were then!) Wilma had one infallible comfort. It was Charley. The thought of him brought always and ever a sweet, consoling balm. How deeply she could trust in him, how securely lean upon him! He loved her; he was never, never unkind to her. Tears came into her eyes, but they were tears of tenderness as much as of grief.

Suddenly Miss Percy exclaimed,—to Wilma's unbounded relief,—"Look yonder, Wilma! Is not that Miss Raymond's brother?"

Wilma looked and recognized "Waddy" approaching from another road on horseback.

"Ho!" said he, drawing up alongside. "Why, is it you, Miss Lynne?" lifting his hat, with a smile. "I believe I have lost my way," he continued. "I am hunting Crawford Academy; they told me it was out in the country indulging in a *fête champêtre* to-day. I saw a flag waving before I got into the woods, but I have lost it now, and don't know exactly where to go."

"Keep right along 'ith us; we'll come 'thin sight of 'em purty soon," said Miss Percy's driver.

"Thank you!" Warren returned, and said to Wilma, "Then you are bound for the picnic, too?"

"No, I think we are too late for that," said Wilma; "but we are going to drive up there."

She presented Warren to Miss Percy, who bowed, but could not be induced to talk, though Warren appealed to her many times with his bright, admiring eyes as he rode along beside the carriage. In a few minutes they came to the scene of rural festivity, and Miss Raymond came flying up, overjoyed to meet her brother.

"And you, Wilma!" she exclaimed. "Is it possible? You sly little thing, to think of your getting us all off, trudging on foot through the heat and dust, and then following in this magnificent style!" A look in Wilma's face checked her, and she added, "I am so glad you have come! Hasn't the day been fine? How do you do, Miss Percy?" she said, her manner taking an unconscious touch of formality.

"I am very well, thank you," said Miss Percy, coldly.

"Do you know," said Miss Raymond, turning to Wilma again, after looking around and discovering that her brother was conversing very earnestly with Nellie Beach, "we are talking of going home already. We have gathered all the flowers we could find and all the petrified remains we can carry, and oh, you don't know how tired we are! Miss Belmont has sick headache, too, and is hardly able to stand."

Wilma glanced at Miss Percy, who, without looking at her, said to Miss Raymond, "If Miss Lynne wishes to walk back with you, Miss Belmont can have her place in the carriage."

Wilma arose gladly, and Warren came up and helped her out. She and Miss Raymond went to hunt up Miss Belmont, whom they found sitting under a tree, leaning her head against its trunk, and looking very white and sick.

"Ah, so you came after all, did you, dear?" she said,

smiling faintly and pressing Wilma's hand. "How did it happen?"

"Miss Percy got a carriage for us to take a ride. When we got out of town she saw the flag waving here, and I had to explain. She is very much offended," said Wilma.

"Well, don't grieve, child," said Miss Belmont, "it will all come right; Miss Percy is impulsive. Leave it to time and your own sweet faithfulness."

Miss Raymond had gone to fetch Miss Belmont's hat and parasol. Wilma could not tell these things to her, because her affection for herself would bias her judgment. But Miss Belmont was broad enough to take in everything and do justice to both Miss Percy and herself. When Miss Raymond came back, Miss Belmont got up and walked slowly to the carriage. As it rolled away, she leaned back and closed her eyes, being too sick to talk, except to thank Miss Percy for her kindness.

The students and professors, with one impulse, began to gather up their baskets and other belongings, and set their faces homeward in clusters of two, and three, and half a dozen. Warren threw his horse's bridle over his arm and walked with Nellie Beach, and Miss Raymond and Wilma followed at a little distance.

THIRD BOOK.

CHAPTER XXVII.

I HAVE no desire to connect this history with the history of the Great Rebellion, inasmuch as the latter has been, already, the groundwork of so much romance. Inasmuch, also, as that nothing which is written can equal in interest and intensity what was the common experience of all in those sad times. But in the beginning of Wilma's second school year civil war began to be loudly talked of, and I am obliged to touch upon it in so far as it concerns the lives of personages in this narrative. Wilma's first serious consideration of it came about through Charley's letters, which by rapid degrees took a high tone of patriotism, and inspired her with—not so much enthusiasm as dread of war. Starr Raymond wrote gravely to his sister, and Warren declared himself ready to enlist under the first banner hoisted, and at the tap of the first drum. Suddenly, as we all remember (for great shocks come suddenly, however long anticipated), it came,—the call to arms, the quick response.

Mr. Langworthy got into the habit of reading the daily papers aloud of an evening, the boarders being all seated around the study-table anxious to hear. One evening he began an account of a thrilling volunteer speech made by a famous young attorney at the capital. "At the close of which," ran the paragraph, "one hundred young men, the flower of the city,—chiefly from the senior class and law department of the university,—headed by the talented and promising *Charles Burns*, stepped out of the ranks of scholarship and entered the ranks of volunteers. It was a thrilling scene. The meeting was held in the large assembly-room, which was densely crowded. Enthusiasm mounted to the highest pitch. Men cheered, women fainted and were carried from the building. The eloquent recruiter was himself elected captain, and Mr. Burns first lieutenant of the splendid company."

As Mr. Langworthy, with kindling eyes, read the glowing account, Wilma, at the other side of the table, sat as if turned to stone, her eyes blank and staring, her lips compressed and bloodless.

"Wilma!" Miss Raymond exclaimed, affrightedly.

The exclamation aroused her, and she started up with a wild look and cry, and ran toward her bedroom door. The other young ladies staring at one another blankly, arose, after a moment, with one impulse and followed her. The young men sprang to their feet, ready for any emergency, but not knowing what to do.

"Is it a fit?" Miss Allen had asked, and Liebenwald caught at the idea and looked to his companion.

"Go for a doctor?"

Langworthy shook his head. "Wait and see," he replied.

"Wilma, dear Wilma, what is it, what is the matter?" Miss Raymond cried, throwing her arms around her.

Wilma had taken down her hat and shawl, and was trying with trembling hands to put them on.

"Charley! Charley has gone to the war!" she said.

"But what are you going to do, Wilma, dear? You cannot go to him," said Miss Raymond, persuasively.

"No, no. But he must have written; he wouldn't leave me to find out in this cruel way. I must go to the post-office; it's raining and no one has been there to-night."

"Oh, I know!" exclaimed Miss Allen, in a whisper, in Miss MacIvers's ear, a liberty she would not have taken or Miss MacIvers allowed under less exciting circumstances. "It's that Mr. Burns who was here once, long ago, you remember?"

"So I think we have all inferred," said Miss MacIvers, haughtily, withdrawing her ear.

"Well, dear me. Send one of those fellows out there to the post-office, can't you?" said Miss Morris. "I wouldn't think of going out in this rain."

"Oh, no, no," said Wilma, "I must go myself."

"Of course," said Miss Raymond, "it is better she should go, and I—or some one—must go with her."

" Not you, certainly, Arabella," said Miss Morris with emphasis, she being a sort of guardian of Miss Raymond's health.

Miss MacIvers, much to everybody's surprise, stepped forward. "I will go with her, myself," she said. "Wait, Miss Lynne, until I get my wraps."

It still rained a little when they stepped out, and the night was dark and chilly. Miss MacIvers tucked Wilma's hand under her arm, and spoke comfortingly to her, but without much effect. Wilma was so sorely wounded as to be quite reckless about what was due to anybody's dignity and importance, but walked along with her head bowed and her tears falling fast, hardly conscious of the august being beside her, upon whom she had always before looked with so much awe. As for Miss MacIvers, her haughty lips curled with mingled contempt and envy. That that Mr. Burns, whom she had once seen and admired as so handsome and intellectual, whose fine, earnest eyes she had met,—the remembrance of which made her cheeks flush even yet,—should belong, in his affections and in betrothal, to this simple little goose! In her secret heart Miss MacIvers felt that she would like to exchange places with the simple little goose, and go with a proud heart for the expected letter which, sure enough, was waiting. For it was a time when maidenly ambition pointed to military heroes. Though maidenly love, such as Wilma's, shrank with terror from the thought of giving up their lovers to make military heroes.

Happy news is well enough conveyed in letter, but sad news can come in no more crushing form. There you are alone with it. It is like a stab in the dark; the hand that strikes you is hid from you. No arm to steady you, no eye to look pityingly upon you. Nothing, nothing but the cruel, wounding words.

The woman who handed out the letter went back to the domestic quarter of the establishment, and Wilma and Miss MacIvers were left alone in the outer office. In justice to Wilma be it said that she did not presume to open and read her letter in that presence without first asking permission, which being accorded, she retired a little to one side and broke the seal. Miss MacIvers, with an instinct of delicacy, also turned aside and walked to the window to watch, by the light of a few street lamps, the rain still pattering on the sidewalks and in the muddy streets. A carriage, shining wet, went splashing by, and an omnibus and men and boys. Now and then she glanced furtively at the little figure quivering with choked sobs; and, having a tender spot in her nature,—as the hardest of us have,—tears sprang into her own eyes.

Turning around when she had read the letter,—it was not a long letter,—and regardless of her wet cheeks, Wilma held it out and asked, timidly, almost apologetically, "Would you like to read it, Miss MacIvers? It is all about the volunteering and that Captain Courtenay who made the speech. Oh, I wish there were no Captain Courtenay!" with a burst of tears. "I never let any one read his letters before, but now it seems like —like as if he were dead, and—it—don't—matter now."

"'There, there; don't cry so, dear," said Miss MacIvers, soothingly. "It is not so bad as that; not nearly so bad as if he were dead."

She put her arm around Wilma and drew her close to her side, while she looked over the letter.

"Why, surely," she thought, "there is nothing here to call for tears, unless they were tears of pride and joy at having such a lover!"

The letter breathed the most inspiring, soul-stirring sentiments; such as dried her wet lashes and made her fine eyes flash with patriotic fire.

"I know that it will hurt you, darling," he wrote; "I would have come and told you if I could, instead of writing. I will come soon and see you, Wilma. I tried to prepare you a little in some of my preceding letters; but I know that it will be a shock to you, all the same, to know that I have enlisted. Be brave, my little one. I know you will; and believe this, Wilma, that whether collegian or soldier, I am the same to you always, my darling, your   Charley."

CHAPTER XXVIII.

CRAWFORD ACADEMY was not deaf to the call to arms. Nearly the whole department of Greek and Latin and the Higher Mathematics drew off at the beck of Miss MacIvers's especial escort, young Haviland, and donned government uniforms, and shouldered government muskets, and went into camp. Not that it was much comfort to Miss MacIvers. Mr. Haviland was not her lover in an accepted, or even in an offered sense; and showed no disposition to become so, notwithstanding that she came down from her pride and dignity and manifested some womanly and even tearful emotion in view of his departure for the dangerous scenes of war. She actively interested herself in a flag, which was to be presented to his company by the young ladies of the academy, and was appointed to make the presentation speech, to which he responded, expressing the company's gratitude in a brief, heart-felt acceptance of the gift, which they emphasized with three tremendous cheers. Afterward he thanked Miss MacIvers, personally, for her great kindness to, and interest in, a young Union volunteer like himself. And pressed her hand with much warmth and fervor, and looked eloquently into her dark eyes that were humid and tender. But it was in the spirit of a soldier, rather than of a lover. She was so superior, so exalted, and he so modestly unpresuming, that he would never have suspected her of the weakness of any personal feeling for himself.

Just previous to their going away—Captain Haviland's company—Mr. Ingraham permitted another sociable in the ladies' hall in their honor; and on this occasion consented to have dancing. For how could the strangely compounded enthusiasm of the time confine itself to any milder form of expression than the delicious excitement of a ball-room, with its music and rhythmical motion? It happened again, strangely enough, that Mr. Burns came the very day of the sociable. Wilma's first letter, after the crushing news of his enlistment reached her, carried with it a shock of surprise to him that she should be so greatly affected by it, followed by a tender pity that was eager to soften the blow to her. In the excitement of patriotism that had hurried him into the ranks he had scarcely thought of her. War was a something that concerned the men of the nation, and a something beside which all the private and personal affairs of life became small and insignificant. Perhaps it was this very thought that was so crushing to Wilma. She who had always been supreme in her lover's life, and consulted regarding its smallest interests and changes, saw it rushing by her in a great sweep and leaving her behind. And the thought (very narrow and selfish, no doubt it was) striking her so sharply and reflecting itself back to him in her complaining letters, aroused him to a view of the case from her standpoint. He had written that he would come soon, but there had been so much delay that Wilma's terrified heart began to doubt whether he would come at all. And in reply to her fears he wrote, in extreme tenderness, "Let me take your hand in mine, darling, across this wide stretch of forest and prairie, and help you to wait."

And he came at last, unexpectedly. Wilma, on her way down street, met him a little way from Mrs. Woods's gate, with a burst of tears.

"Why, why," said he, stopping and taking both her hands, "what is the matter? You have a very sorrowful welcome for me. Come, come! why, I counted on your being a perfect little Spartan!"

"I don't think you thought of me at all," said Wilma, weakly, in a hurt voice. But her heart was so sore.

Mr. Burns's brows contracted. He was eminently good-natured and sunny, but still capable of sternness. He had come very tenderly disposed toward Wilma, and felt the hardness of parting from her. But she, in her blindness (pain will make us blind), somehow repelled him; made him almost wish he had not come. Still holding her hand, he turned her about to walk back with her.

"Are the students in there?" he asked, nodding

toward the house, and thinking it would be awkward to go in just now if they were.

"Some of them are there," said Wilma.

"Then let us go and take a walk in the woods," said he.

He wore his uniform, and in Wilma's eyes looked the most nobly beautiful being upon the earth. He had a tall, lithe, symmetrical figure and graceful bearing. His bright hair curled about his white temples. His face was radiant with a new light ; his eyes flashing, his soul at high tide for battle and for glory. Not that he or any of those enthusiastic young volunteers rejoiced in the great calamity of the nation ; but it had come upon us, and we *must* fight. So, hurrah ! If there's glory in it, we'll win the glory. The Union is to be preserved, and we will preserve the Union though we die for it. That was the spirit of the times. It was Charles Burns's spirit, but very hard for Wilma to catch ; it called upon her for so great a sacrifice. But, then, was it any harder for her to buckle on her lover's sword and send him to battle, to danger, to death, than for many a maiden who had no lover to buckle a sword upon ? It may not be a fair question or one that anybody can answer impartially, because we all speak out of our own experience. We who have loved and buried our loved ones, in one way or other, apply this pathetic philosophy to our wounded hearts,—

> " 'Tis better to have loved and lost,
> Than never to have loved at all."

And we who have never loved, or, loving, have not lost, smile, superior to such melancholy sentiment.

Wilma felt that her lover was almost as good as lost (so to speak). It was agonizing to her to look upon him, her brave, beautiful, chivalrous Charley ! It seemed as if her heart must break with grief and tenderness. Now that he no longer belonged wholly to her, but was being borne away from her upon this great public wave, he seemed more dazzling and splendid to her than ever before.

They went into the woods, and Mr. Burns did his best to inspire her with some of his own enthusiasm ; but failing in that, and his good-humor coming back, he attempted to throw it all off lightly.

"What does it signify?" said he. "I shall probably come back in a few months with the gratifying and exalted sense upon me of having done something for my country. A feeling that is calculated to make a man think better of himself for the rest of his life. I know whereof I speak, Wilma," he added, laughing; "for haven't I heard some old soldiers recount their heroic deeds? And heaven knows, I think we wretched beings have need to be stimulated into thinking well of ourselves sometimes!"

Wilma felt that he was only parrying her fears, trying to soothe her into unconsciousness of the dangers of war, and still clung to her own dark side of the picture. So that he finally came down to an honest *view* of the subject, which was better, and owned that, as to his life,— the possibility of losing it,—that had no place in his thoughts. He had given it already, and no longer reckoned upon it. An admission that chilled Wilma's blood and made her lips dumb. For what could she say after that? His generosity, his grandeur of soul, humbled her. How many leagues he had gone beyond her!

His real self, he said, his conscious being, he believed would live on, and go on thinking and working and loving all the same. He told Wilma that he saw no difference in being on this side, or that, of the wall between him and eternity; except, perhaps, that the society over there is better than here, and one can mingle with it more freely by not being borne about in a clumsy body. "I have a great curiosity about that other side of life," he said, "of whose glories it hath not entered into the heart of man to conceive. Do you know, Wilma, that after hearing so much about heaven, one is a little surprised, upon going through the scriptures, to find so little said about it there! Of course there is a heaven to answer to the cravings of men's souls. There *must be* a heaven in which are gathered up the jewels that melt away from earth. I should like to know what Shakspeare and all those grand souls have been about over there all these years! Something, I've no doubt, that will be for our good when we get there. I'll tell you what, Wilma, if some rebel puts a bullet through my head, or my heart, I'll just embrace the opportunity to slip out of this mortal prison-house, and I'll go and explore the unseen land against you come; and when you come I can take you by the hand and lead you all through the wonderful regions. It strikes me that heaven must be a safe place to put one's friends, Wilma! There is not half the danger of losing them there as in having them straying about this earth, where there are so many snares and dangers and pitfalls. The mother is sure of the baby that is taken up in Abraham's bosom; she is not sure of the one that is left to wander here."

"You speak of heaven, Charley," said Wilma, looking up with a struggling smile, "as you might of Italy!"

"And why not?" said he. "I have never seen either place. My imagination pictures the one, my spirit penetrates, almost, to the other. I sometimes fancy that in each of our souls is wrapped up the germ of our heaven. I don't want any man to make my heaven for me; let Milton and Dante confine themselves to their own kingdoms. I want to fashion mine. I want it to grow out of myself. My idea of it is that it will be no more and no less than we can each of us fully appreciate and enjoy. There may be much more of it than we know, of course; but *for us* there will be just what we can take in. Just enough of freedom, of unconstrained thought, of peace, of love. Here we have not enough, you know. We are never quite full of the things we like. Something hinders us; we can't go far enough, or high enough, or deep enough. We can't get much farther than our bodily senses can take us. Sense is the outer wall built up around our souls, and beyond that we can go but a very little way without getting wofully mystified. Still, we have a pretty wide range, we men and women have; see how much we know! bah, see how little we know. At all events I am satisfied, both with this world and the next. I believe in them both with all my heart. It's a grand scheme, this scheme of life! I have no fears."

Wilma was silent. A new world seemed opening. Her lover stood revealed to her in a largeness of mind and thought—nay, of actual life—with which she had not kept pace, of which, until this moment, she had had no conception.   How small, how narrow, how selfish were her complainings compared with his pure motives and grand aims!   And she had tried to bind down to herself, and to her little world, this great, generous nature.

They had strayed away, out of town, to the little pebbly stream that, a year ago, she and Miss Percy had crossed in their pleasant drive.   Wilma was reminded of it by the pink and white blossoms on the trees and the birds twittering in the bushes.   Charley gathered a handful of the blossoms and tucked them in her hair.

"I don't know which are most becoming to you, Wilma," he said, smiling, "the pink or the white blossoms, or the green leaves.   I'm not much on effects; think you look well in any of them.   You are a sober little thing, Wilma," he added.   "Why don't you wear some gay colors, blue for instance?"

"Like your uniform?" said Wilma, smiling, and laying her hand on his sleeve.

"No; a brighter blue," said he.   "More like the sky. Was ever anything so blue as the sky?"   Glancing up through the trees.

"Your eyes, Charley," said Wilma.

"And yours are brown,—aren't they?   Contrast," said he.   "I like contrasts.   Did you tell me you drove through this rivulet when you went a-maying that time, you and Miss Percy?"

"Yes; and everything looked then just as it does now, except that it is a little later in the season now."

"You are very fond of riding," said Charley.   "Are you not?   I like to walk.   Contrast again.   Though that is hardly the sort of contrast to make a harmony, is it? We want to travel together, you and I, and we must adopt some mode agreeable to us both, when we begin our journey, Wilma,—eh?"

"If we ever begin it!" said Wilma, with tears starting afresh.

"Nonsense!" said Charley.   "We shall journey together through all eternity. And, by the way, Wilma, there comes in another of the delights of heaven,—perfect congeniality of souls!   How often we hear this question, Shall we know each other there?   Whether we will or not depends very much on whether we know each other here. Shall I know my mother, with the earthly tie of mother and son broken and dissolved between us? We must keep in mind that all things earthly perish; that death breaks all relations, except the relation of soul to soul. If you and I keep close to each other, darling, in mind, in thought, in spirit, we shall know each other there. Will not that be a beautiful recognition?"

They had sat down together upon a fallen tree, and Charley had been busy making a wreath.

"There, Wilma! now take off your hat, and let me put this on your head; we'll play it's May-day, and I'll crown you Queen o' May. There; you've no idea how pretty it looks. Can't you step down there, and see yourself in the water? You look like a fairy."

"A brownie!" said Wilma.

"Well, a brownie; that is a fairy all the same. Say, to come back to a dropped subject, why don't you wear some gayer colors?"

"I don't know. I will, if you want me to. You spoke of blue, but Miss Barker would never allow me to wear blue, I'm so dark. I have worn pink a good deal, you know."

"And looked as pretty as a rose," said Charley.

"But who will care how I look when you are gone?" said Wilma.

"My dear, I shall care all the same. I shall see you in my thoughts and in my dreams."

"And in your thoughts and dreams you can deck me as you like."

"I must have a picture of you, Wilma," said Charley. "A good one. I will send you one of mine when I go back. By the way, are we not staying out here a good while? I see the sun is getting low. Do you remember how often we used to watch the sun set from the top of Little Twin? I have not been to Hazelville since my mother died. I have always intended going. It would be a sad sort of pleasure to me to stand once more beside her grave; but I am afraid I shall not be able to do it. Poor mother, she never thought her boy would be a soldier!"

They had arisen, and were walking slowly back toward Mrs. Woods's.

"What a revolution circumstances make in a man's life," continued Mr. Burns. "In all my ambitions and plans and aspirations, I never took this circumstance—war—into account. I thought, somehow, in spite of all that was said, that, as a nation, we had done with bloodshed,—had got above it. That, however much the foreign heathen might cut and slash each other, we were superior to it. Alas, we are all made of one common clay! What a vain conceit for any of us to fancy ourselves bright exceptions to the general rule! I have looked across the ocean at men killing one another, and felt that sort of pitying contempt we entertain for inferior creatures. Now these same creatures are in the ascendant, and will stretch up their necks, and look across at us. Bah, what wretches we are!"

"Then, why do you go?" said Wilma, as one catches at a straw.

"One can't escape. I belong to a period; I must act with the times. I don't approve of war, but it's not a time to proclaim it when the country is in arms and the enemy in our midst. The mistake is here: we are not diligent enough in times of peace to elevate ourselves above the possibility of war; we are working up to it, and in the mean time we must do the best we can."

When they reached Mrs. Woods's gate, Mr. Burns looked at his watch. "It is five o'clock, Wilma. I will go down to the hotel and eat my supper and then come back if you want me, and stay until time for this sociable you speak of. I always happen here in time for your festivities."

Wilma assented and went in. The tea-bell was jingling, and as soon as tea was over she went into her room to dress for the evening. Miss Raymond helped her.

"You are to be the belle of the evening," she said, "because you have such a handsome lover."

She braided Wilma's hair and wound it about her head; and looped up her white muslin dress with bows of pink ribbon and tiny sprays of clematis, and then pronounced her lovely. Which she was, with her pretty, oval face saddened a little, and her sweet, brown eyes looking as if there were tears back of them.

"Hark!" said Miss Raymond, peeping from the window. "I hear some one coming,—and it is that lieutenant of yours. What a soldierly figure and bearing he has, Wilma! I suspect you are very proud of him!" tapping her cheek. "There, you must go out, now; he has come up into the porch."

Wilma went out and opened the door. There was no one in the study-room, and Charley took her in his arms and bent down and touched his lips to her forehead, almost with solemnity. There had always been in his affection for her, and in his treatment of her, a great deal of reverence.

"My Wilma!" he said, tenderly, "how can I leave you? You are dearer to me than anything else in the world, except those abstract things we call honor,—principle. I told you once—you remember, do you not?—that it might be I should some time be compelled to give my life to something else rather than to you; and the time has come, darling. And I am hardly prepared for it. Just now I feel unstrung at the sight of you and the thought of leaving you."

"But if you love me, Charley," said Wilma, with a sad little smile that showed the heartache beneath it, "if we have each other's affections, that is having the best part of each other, is it not? So long as you live I shall feel that you are near to me. But if you fall——"

Her lip quivered and her eyes filled with tears.

"If I fall," interrupted Charley, "your life must blossom all the more; it must blossom for us both. I know it will. I know something of the spirit that is in you, my darling! It will not be easily crushed. You know what I have always aimed at, Wilma, for you and for me. If I never come back to you, make your life what I would have it to be. Can you promise me that?"

It was a moment of as great solemnity as either had ever experienced. Wilma's heart was too full for utterance, and she answered by a pressure of the hand.

One by one the young ladies came out, dressed, and flooded the little sitting-room with bloom and elegance.

Captain Haviland, and one or two other gentlemen in uniform,—among them Starr Raymond, Captain Courtenay's second lieutenant, who had arrived on the evening train from the capital, and whom his sister greeted with a flood of tears, which she immediately dashed away, her disposition being a good deal like an April day. Mr. Burns was introduced to all that were new to him, and shook hands, cordially, with those whom he had met before, and made himself delightfully agreeable.

Miss MacIvers, hearing him remark that his regiment was encamped, for drill, at the beautiful little city of R——, one of the loveliest places in the West, he declared, turned to him and said, with a charming smile, "Do you think so? That is my home."

"Indeed?" said he, turning to look at her, and feeling strongly attracted. Presently he drew his chair near to her.

"I shall regret," he said, his eyes lingering upon her beautiful face with frank admiration, "that you are not at home when I go back to my regiment!"

"Oh, but I shall be there then, I presume," she returned. "I intend going home to-morrow."

"You do? And I return to-morrow," said he. "I hope you will not think me presumptuous if I contrive to take the same train?"

"Oh, no," she answered, laughing, and added—arching her exquisite brows—something about its being fitting, "in these per'lous times," for ladies to travel with armed knights. She went on, her color rising and her beauty growing upon him, to tell him about her home, its situation, its elevation upon the summit of a terraced hill, and its distance from the camping-ground. And, looking into each other's eloquent eyes, and making delightful excursions into each other's consciousness, they were both mutually pleased.

"I think I remember the place you describe," said Mr. Burns. "We have passed it occasionally in our evening walks. I remember the fountain and the terraces and the image of the Newfoundland dog. I hope you will be so gracious as to invite us to come and see you?"

"Oh, yes, certainly," she answered, laughing. "If

the war does no other good it ought certainly to develop hospitality in us toward the defenders of our country."

Mr. Burns's face flushed pleasurably.

"You say 'us?'" continued Miss MacIvers, raising her eyes.

"Yes; I included Captain Courtenay," said he. "He and I usually stroll out together."

"I have heard of Captain Courtenay, frequently," said Miss MacIvers. "The papers speak very flatteringly of him."

"The papers cannot do him justice," said Mr. Burns, quietly.

"Why not?"

"Because nobody can describe him. One must see Captain Courtenay; his presence, his manner, his looks, voice, gestures, bearing, create an effect upon you that no description could give you a conception of. If you saw him you would comprehend what I mean. It seems to me he has it in him to be *great*, more than any other man I have ever met; but whether fortune will make him an Alexander or Napoleon Bonaparte, I can't say."

"In what direction is he capable of greatness?" asked Miss MacIvers. "As a soldier?"

"As a soldier, or statesman, or orator, or anything he might turn to," said Mr. Burns, smiling. "I see you are incredulous, so I'll say no more."

"Oh, yes, go on. What else? I am deeply interested."

"Well, then, he is the most magnificently handsome man I have ever seen. You will think that a great stepping-down, I suspect, to pass from a man's splendid capabilities to his mere looks."

"Ah, I suspect you meant to deepen my interest in your gallant captain," laughed Miss MacIvers.

"And so persuade you to let me take him to call upon you," said Mr. Burns. "Maybe you are right."

"Oh, of course, you must bring him to see me."

"Thank you. You plant an oasis in the desert. I dreaded the tedium of camp life."

Some one said it was time to go to the academy, and Miss MacIvers glanced at her little, diamond-studded

*K

watch and arose.   Mr. Burns started up and crossed over to Wilma.

On the way to the academy Miss Allen remarked to some of the girls, "If Wilma doesn't look sharp, Miss MacIvers will get her handsome lieutenant away from her."

"So I think," said Miss Morris. "And no great wonder. What the young man can see in that little Miss Lynne to admire is more than I can fathom."

"Matilda," said Miss Raymond, warmly, "if you can't see anything noble or beautiful in Wilma Lynne yourself, go and ask Miss Belmont. to describe her to you."

"Pray excuse me," said Miss Morris, sneeringly.

The ladies' hall was beautifully decorated with leaves and flowers, and festooned with flags. Two immense chandeliers overhead flooded it with light, and a full band of music was playing and lading the air with a passionate joy and sadness. The soft, warm wind drifted through the open windows. The night was magnetic and subtle and strange. Voices were subdued, eyes were beaming, cheeks glowing, and hearts beating high with the tumultuous glory feeling that war brings.

Wilma, coming in on her lover's arm, was conscious of the strange vibration of the atmosphere, and seemed to feel, under all the music and the hum of voices and the lights and beauty and fragrance the far-off booming of battles; and above the sublimity of an eternity and of grand lives budded in earth, amid all its strifes and tumults, expanding in everlasting life and bloom. Charley had so opened up and brought near to her wonderful spiritual regions. She determined to get up on a level with him and look abroad. Ah, she could do that, with her hand upon his arm, thrilled by the magnetism of his touch, his voice in her ear, his face bending above her ! It is certain she was lifted up above all the small, practical affairs of her little life. All the hopes they had had, all the plans they had made, sank into nothingness. What mattered anything but that he loved her and that in heart they were united ! After all, what were earthly ties ? They might kill her Charley, but—though the bare thought

made her heart bleed—they could not take him from her!
Brave little Wilma! She was coming up grandly, as Charley had said she would. She had given up his life just as
he himself had given it up, and was standing on the
heights with him as they had stood together on the top
of Little Twin.

Many couples were promenading to the heavily-charged
music. A number of soldiers were there in uniforms not
yet stained with blood; officers with shoulder-straps and
swords dangling, supporting upon their arms fair partners
whose eyes beamed with a softened radiance; for when
men are brave women are more tender. A little group
collected and stood talking together, and, at its breaking
up and falling into line with the promenaders, Captain
Haviland offered his arm to Wilma, and Mr. Burns turned
to Miss MacIvers; and for the first time in her life Wilma
saw him detached from herself and giving his smiles and
the dear light of his eyes to another, who answered back
with glances charged with electric power. They walked
before her, and his head was slightly bent toward his companion. It flashed upon Wilma that she had as yet taken
but one step in grief,—a very baby step. Charley was
going away, and she had cried as a child might cry whose
toy was broken. The heart can be quickly educated.
In a moment it came to her that this sort of separation,
though it were to last till death, was nothing, nothing
compared with soul-division. To lose Charley was
nothing; to lose his love was all the world. And the
possibility of losing it was dimly shadowed forth in his
frankly apparent admiration of Miss MacIvers. Mr.
Burns himself did not dream of the possibility; he believed that he needed Wilma as much as he ever needed
her. But it is true his world was widening out. He had
not changed in respect to her; she still held the same
safe corner of his heart. But many other corners had
been opened up. Certainly life was larger than he had
once thought it. The world had more interests for him than
he had counted upon,—many interests which she did not
share. It would have surprised him to have been brought
suddenly to face the thought that she was not indispensable to him. It would have been a shock to him no less

than to her, and perhaps not less painful to him than to her.　He would have lost confidence in himself; he would have been hurt and humiliated.　But just now he was saved from it; he felt himself to be true and loyal. He was happy; he was fearless; launched upon a great wave of public enthusiasm.　It is not often in our lives that we can throw ourselves forward with the tide; usually we must stem it.

CHAPTER XXIX.

THE following morning Mr. Burns came to bid Wilma good-by and to take Miss MacIvers to the train.　Miss Mac-Ivers's great trunk was packed and strapped, and standing in the porch waiting to be carried to the depot.　Miss MacIvers herself came down-stairs in an elaborate, pearl-gray travelling-dress, with some bits of rose-color here and there to set it off.　And again the electric fire that flashed between her own and Mr. Burns's eyes the night before, lighted up both faces when they met.

Though Miss MacIvers was not a coquette.　She had too much dignity to descend to vulgar flirtation.　She disliked coarseness.　She rather scorned the admiration that is based upon mere physical beauty.　She felt that she charmed Mr. Burns by something more than that, and she liked the homage he paid her with his eloquent eyes, which seemed to explore her mind as well as her face. She liked the intellectual intercourse with an understanding like his.　They could measure each other.　Both of them had read a good deal, and partly in the same direction.　She was, perhaps, the more polished, but he had thought farther.

Most of the students were in the study-room, and there was no opportunity for Wilma to speak to Mr. Burns aside, though her heart ached for some tender parting word.　A dray came for Miss MacIvers's trunk.

"I did not order a carriage," said Mr. Burns.　"I did not know what your arrangements were."

"Oh, I intend to walk to the train," said Miss Mac-Ivers. "It is only a step."

"Then perhaps we had better start," said he, looking at his watch. "We will have barely time."

Miss MacIvers arose, and Mr. Burns turned to Wilma, who was waiting with trembling heart for the leave-taking. All her courage had ebbed away.

"You will go to the train with us and see us off, will you not, Wilma?" said he.

Oh, why were all these people here to witness this supreme parting? Why could they not have one little moment alone? A little while ago she could not bid Charley "good-by" in the presence of her own family. Now, she felt reckless enough to throw her arms around his neck before them all; but that he himself seemed constrained.

"Let me go with you, too, Wilma," said Miss Raymond, "so that you will have company back."

As they passed out the gate, which Mr. Burns held open, she slipped her hand through Miss MacIvers's arm and said, significantly, "We will walk on and leave the lovers to follow at their leisure."

Mr. Burns, with the charm of Miss MacIvers's presence still upon him, could hardly recall himself at once to the old attitude of tenderness toward Wilma.

"What a fine morning!" he said, alighting upon the commonest of topics. "I am going to begin cultivating an extra affection for old mother nature, now that I am to be turned out of doors, with her green sod for my carpet and the blue sky for my roof! I don't mean to spend much of my time cooped up in a little soldier's tent, I can tell you. I have a sort of reckless feeling about all the duties and obligations of life, like a boy let loose from school."

"But do you think it is right to feel so, Charley?" Wilma asked, merely because he paused there.

"Oh, no; I suppose not. A soldier is morally responsible, the same as anybody else. But I am upset. I am jostled out of my course. I shall be all right by and by, when I get settled. I hope so."

"How long will you be in camp at R——?" Wilma

asked, not without reference, in her thought, to Miss MacIvers.

"I don't know. It will depend, partly, on how fast our regiment fills up,—a couple of months, maybe. I have gained something by coming to see you, haven't I?" he asked, nodding toward Miss MacIvers. "I shall have a place to visit while I am in camp. What a charming person she is!"

"Yes; she is very beautiful and accomplished," said Wilma.

They had no time to spare at the depot; the train was coming in. Mr. Burns had to attend to Miss MacIvers's trunk. Then he shook hands with Miss Raymond, kissed and embraced Wilma hurriedly, helped Miss MacIvers up the steps, and sprang up after her, waving his hand as the train moved off. Wilma stood looking after it with streaming eyes, and Miss Raymond put her arm around her gently, and drew her away. A number of by-standers were lounging about, to whom a soldier's leave-taking was no new thing.

Mr. Burns, standing on the platform outside, pitying the pain in Wilma's face, turned as soon as they were out of sight of the town, and said to himself, with a sigh, "Poor Wilma! well, it can't be helped;" and went into the car and looked about for his companion, and took a seat beside her with the air of a "natural protector;" the little cloud that had settled upon his face vanishing rapidly in the light of hers. People looked curiously and admiringly at the handsome pair, and wondered if the beautiful lady were the soldier's bride. And Miss MacIvers enjoyed the situation; she liked to triumph; she liked to hold an advantageous position before the world. In that she differed from Mr. Burns. He did nothing for effect; he was not concerned about anything people thought or said; he did not imagine that folks could be interested in speculating about him.

They stopped at a small station, and a woman with two children was gathering up her bundles to get off. Mr. Burns, observing her hurry and confusion, went and helped her courteously, and then came back and sat down again.

"You are very gallant!" laughed Miss MacIvers, mockingly, and, though it grated on Mr. Burns's finer sense, he smiled back at her.

"Gallant is hardly the word, is it?" said he. "Call it a little act of humanity."

"Oh, very well!" She turned her head and looked out of the car-window, and presently exclaimed, "What a blank, aimless stare the people have who congregate about these depots!"

"Yes," said Mr. Burns; "I suppose it is curiosity that brings them here, and yet their faces show very little of that."

"And they all belong to our species," said Miss MacIvers. "Now, if we could classify them in some lower order; but we can't. Humiliating, isn't it?"

"Well, I don't know," said he; "I hate to think about it. One is inclined to fall in with an article of the Buddhist's creed,—which is, that we are not all immortal beings; only a few can attain to the sanctified state they call *Nirvana*."

"But Buddhists are not predestinarians, are they?" said Miss MacIvers. "The 'chosen few' are not elected; their immortality depends on themselves."

"Every man is elected at his birth," said Mr. Burns, "to a certain heritage. He has within him the germs of his own fate."

"I fancy our destinies are written upon our faces," said Miss MacIvers, laughing, and still looking from the window. "See, what a dreadful old woman! Do you not think such faces are fated?"

"What is fate?" Mr. Burns asked. "My opinion, as I have just intimated, is that it is a something within us, and which shapes us, rather than a something outside overruling us. But we must be careful," he added, "and not judge people altogether by their outward seeming; we may not be able always to read the signs correctly."

"Of course not. People are not answerable for their looks; it is the moral nature we may criticise and find fault with."

"May we, really?" said Mr. Burns, looking at her with his smiling eyes, and a charming curve about his lips—(which you and I, reader, know deepened, in after-years, to almost a sneer).

"Are we any more responsible for our moral nature than for our faces? For my part, I think our physical nature is quite as much under our control as our moral."

"How can that be?" said Miss MacIvers, opening her eyes.

"We can educate the expression of the face, but the features will remain the same; what more can we do with the mind? We can cultivate it, we can tone it down, but we cannot change it."

"You teach me a broad charity," said Miss MacIvers.

"Charity for others, and for ourselves, too," said Mr. Burns. "Heaven knows! we have need to have a good deal of charity for ourselves sometimes, to save us from dire humiliation and despair."

"I never thought of that!" said Miss MacIvers. "I did not suppose we had any right to pity and forgive ourselves."

"We have as good right to pity and forgive ourselves, as we have to pity and forgive others. Let us be just."

The train moved on; and at such a rapid and roaring speed that conversation, except in the intervals of stopping at small stations for a minute or two at a time, was next to impossible. Miss MacIvers put her elbow on the window-sill and leaned her cheek upon her hand and looked out; the fresh spring breeze blowing in her face and deepening its delicate rose-color, and fluttering her ribbons and taking liberties with her fleecy gray veil; sometimes fastening it to Mr. Burns's shoulder-straps, and sometimes making it hover over him like a cloud. She had hardly ever, with all her beauty, looked so beautiful as she did now. But Mr. Burns was not looking at her. It seemed that he did not care to look at her, except when he talked to her; he was not in love with her; he sat with his eyes straight before him, thinking; he had an exceedingly active brain, and was always digging into some abstract subject. The little conversation with Miss MacIvers had given him a cue and he was following it up. Miss MacIvers had too much tact to engross him.

When they reached R——, a carriage was waiting for

her, and he helped her into it, pressed her hand cordially but not sentimentally, and said he should soon avail himself of her kind permission to visit her. The carriage whirled away, and he directed his steps at once to the camping-ground, his thoughts pleasantly tinged with recollections of the brief journey.

CHAPTER XXX.

CAPTAIN COURTENAY declined the honor of an introduction to the imperial beauty and belle of R—— (for such Miss MacIvers was considered in her own town), saying, when Mr. Burns mentioned it to him a day or two after his return to camp, enigmatically, "I have more women on my hands now than I know what to do with."

It is true that he was courted most assiduously, though not at all successfully, by the fair sex wherever he went.

Mr. Burns, hotly indignant, retorted, "You need not fear that Miss MacIvers is likely to throw herself on your hands!"

Captain Courtenay smiled cynically, and Mr. Burns caught up his hat and left the tent and made his way over into the town, designing to pay his first visit to his agreeable travelling companion. The sun was barely half an hour high, and the day's heat and bustle and dust were over. Life in the busy city was quieting itself to a subdued hum. From one of the several imposing churches a chime of bells rang out, clear and sweet, calling to evening prayers, and a few belated sisters of some charitable order were hastening away.

"Poor things!" said Mr. Burns, to whom they in passing deigned no glance, but kept their eyes resolutely on the pavement. "I pity them, because they shut out from their hearts and lives so much of this sweet world. But why should I pity them? Their lives are full of something else, of course: of hope in the future,—of faith. No doubt they pity me!" And he smiled and looked about him, and felt with intense thankfulness that he was open to all the joyous influences that could be borne in upon him. He glanced up at the blue sky, and around upon the green earth, and breathed the pure air, and took in the beauty and fragrance blooming inside the pretty garden fences, and honestly thanked heaven that he was as he was; a man free from prejudice and unfettered by superstition; charitable and kindly disposed toward all men; fearless and independent in thought; determined to examine all things and grasp whatever was good, and throw away what was evil. It was characteristic of him that he prosecuted boldly, and without fear of becoming disloyal to Wilma, his acquaintance with Miss MacIvers. He had unbounded confidence in himself. He believed in growth and development and expansion, and was ready to press on and take the consequences.

A river crossed the main street of the city, in the midst of it, spanned by an iron bridge. Many people were traversing the bridge to and fro. Mr. Burns paused midway across it and leaned upon the railing, and looked down into the clear, swift-running water. The sun shone aslant upon it, and was reflected from the shining sides of many a silvery fish that, rising almost to the surface, flapped himself over and darted down out of sight swift as an arrow. Mr. Burns enjoyed such scenes, and felt just now a freedom to enjoy them which he had not often allowed himself in the last few, studious years. He turned away half reluctantly and walked on. He soon passed into a side street, and ascended a long, sloping hill, on whose terraced summit stood the mansion Miss MacIvers had described as her home. The fountain was spouting in front, and on one of the green terraces lay the huge image of a Newfoundland dog. By these Mr. Burns was convinced he had not mistaken the place. He opened an iron gate, and went up the broad stone steps that led to the main entrance. The dewy evening air was heavy with the fragrance of climbing roses that wreathed themselves around the massive stone-work of the portico guarding the door. He rang the bell, and turned to look about him while waiting. The view was fine. Nearly the whole city—with the river, now dark with the gathering shadows, winding through it—was spread out below, and sharply defined in the slanting sunlight that came from behind. Beyond was the camping-ground, on an open, level plain, and the red light shone upon that, too. Mr. Burns was reminded of Little Twin and of Wilma.

" Poor little Wilma !" he said, thinking of her grieved face as the train moved off.

The door opened behind him, and he turned around and felt in his vest-pocket for a card.

" Is Miss MacIvers at home ?"

" Yes, sah.   Walk in, sah," said the ebony black attendant, and showed him through a thickly-matted hall into a high, spacious room that had an air of costly elegance, suggestive of Miss MacIvers herself.   The windows were raised, and through the half-open venetian blinds the wind came softly, swaying the cobweb curtains.   Mr. Burns seated himself and looked about him with pleasure at the beautiful pictures and other gems of art that decorated the room.   His nature was peculiarly receptive ; and just now he gave himself up wholly to the things and circumstances around him, and was willing that the stream of passing scenes and events should flow in upon him unchecked.   As he himself had said, he had given his life to his country and no longer reckoned upon it.   He was broken off from his old pursuits, and felt singularly free from care and responsibility.   It seemed to him that destiny, or Omnipotence,—for he had a happy faith in the conscious love and power of God,—was managing his affairs.   He had come to that place in life where he might simply drift, for a little time.   We know he was energetic, but he did not make himself miserable because his energies, just now, were not needed.   He had no personal dread of war, and his soul was serene and happy.

Miss MacIvers did not keep him waiting.   She came in and swept up to him with her white hand extended and her beautiful face, which blushed so easily and so prettily, animated with a cordial welcome.   She was carefully dressed, though perhaps not with reference to him, and looked altogether elegant.   She was not a soft, luxurious woman ; her face was intelligent, her figure erect, her manner dignified, though she had, also, a good deal of womanly grace. She awoke in Mr. Burns, who probably saw her at her best, a lofty, refined admiration.

"You found the way easily, did you?" she said, drawing up a chair and seating herself near him.

"Oh, yes; one could hardly miss it," said he; "there is no other place like it in the city."

"No other high, terraced hill," said Miss MacIvers. "I have always liked it for the view."

"Yes; I observed it as I came up. It is fine. I see you have the whole camping-ground mapped out over yonder."

Miss MacIvers laughed.

"Oh, yes; and I take my opera-glass and fetch it over here, sometimes, and inspect it at my leisure."

"Do you? But you must drive over some day and see us at close quarters."

"Yes; papa has spoken of it. By the way, where is your Captain Courtenay? I think you promised me an introduction to him."

Mr. Burns's brows contracted.

"I am afraid I was a little presumptuous; the captain doesn't seem disposed to go out much."

Miss MacIvers blushed with chagrin, wishing she had not mentioned the subject. The best she could do was to change it; which she speedily did, and with so much tact that Mr. Burns did not notice her embarrassment. She asked if he would not like to step out on the terrace.

"It is not dark yet," she said. "Indeed, it will not be dark, for the moon is up."

She preceded him and took a light wrap from the rack in the hall and threw it around her shoulders. Outside, on the steps, stood a tall, imposing, elderly gentleman with a narrow, high-bred face and lofty expression. He had clear and rather cold, gray eyes, set close together. A man of integrity and honest convictions, but full of strong prejudices; accustomed to great deference and expecting it. Miss MacIvers introduced him as "papa," and Mr. Burns addressed him as "Colonel MacIvers." He had been a soldier himself, and still carried himself as one. He turned courteously and extended his hand.

"I am pleased to make your acquaintance, sir," he

said, lifting his hat and bowing with dignity. "My daughter spoke of you as being her escort from Crawford, the other day; I must thank you, sir."

"Oh, no," said Mr. Burns, smiling and taking the offered hand cordially, his easy, modern manners contrasting strongly with the elder gentleman's stately bearing; "the obligation was on my side."

"Ah, true!" said the colonel. "It is a pretty even exchange when a gentleman can give his protection in return for a lady's society. I remember the time when I liked nothing better myself."

He turned to his daughter and asked if they could not have chairs out on the terrace. "Or, stay," he continued; "I am afraid it is too damp. Not for you and I, lieutenant; we would make but poor soldiers if we were afraid of a little dew! I was considering Maude."

"Pray don't consider me, papa," said Miss MacIvers. "I am proof against dampness. Let us go around to the south side of the house, there are some rustic seats there."

She led the way and they followed. The colonel seemed to regard conversation as a masculine monopoly, and left little room for his daughter; which, to a young man of Mr. Burns's chivalric nature, was a great annoyance. The colonel related many anecdotes of his soldier life—as what veteran does not? "Many a night," said he, "I have slept upon the frozen ground with only the sky above me. I suppose you will learn to do the same."

"I suppose so," said Mr. Burns.

"The chief thing to dread in war is not the fighting," continued the colonel; "it's the weather."

"Yes; nature is a better mother to all her other children than to us," said Mr. Burns. "She leaves us to our own devices. Is it not so?" turning to Miss MacIvers.

"Well, that is fair, is it not?" said she, "since she gives us intelligence and means. We would hardly exchange our ingenuity to clothe ourselves for the plumage of the bird, would we?"

"No," said Mr. Burns, laughing; "it was an idle complaint.'' And added, after a moment, ''All complaining is foolish, since we find that the balance is struck everywhere throughout nature's domains. I am more and more convinced of the *evenness* of things every day of my life. We have no right to envy—neither do I think we have good reason to pity—our neighbors. We may rest assured that the affairs of each life are properly adjusted somehow.''

''Then that relieves us of responsibility about our neighbors,'' said Miss MacIvers, laughing.

''No, no,'' returned Mr. Burns. ''Of course, the destinies of men are not in our hands. God rules. But He needs us in His providence. He needs to use us in His grand economy. He works for all the suffering and down-trodden through our humanity. We can neither help nor hinder the great events of life; but through our moral nature, through our charity and generosity, we can soften the blow and soothe the pain.''

Having so delivered himself, Mr. Burns felt that the conversation was perhaps taking a more serious turn than the occasion demanded, and got up and looked around. Over beyond the town the moon shone upon the camping-ground, and the white tents looked as if asleep in the valley. How peaceful, in its beginning, seemed this little thread of the war.

''I have hardly seen a finer view than this in my lifetime,'' said Mr. Burns.

''I selected it,'' said the colonel, also rising, ''twenty years ago, when this town was but a little village, on account of the view.''

Soon after they went into the house, and Miss MacIvers played. The colonel explained to Mr. Burns, ''I get quite hungry for music, sir, when Maude's away; she being the only daughter.''

''You have sons?'' said Mr. Burns, to whom it seemed that the colonel's remark left an opening for the question.

''No, sir; no, I have nobody but Maude.''

Miss MacIvers was not an especially brilliant performer, but her music pleased her papa, who, so long as there was no great discord, was not disposed to be critical. He gave Mr. Burns an easy-chair, and reclined his stately figure in another, placed his polished boots on a foot-rest, and leaned back, closing his eyes, and allowed himself to drift peacefully away on the waves of sweet sound. When his musical appetite was appeased, and Miss MacIvers arose from the piano, he at once left his chair, and, after asking Mr. Burns if he would have a cigar, which he declined, he bade the young people "good-night," courteously, and went out.

A little later Mr. Burns took his departure, and walked over to the camp-ground through the still moonlight, filled with thoughts of how beautiful the world was, how many bright nooks and corners it held, how many agreeable people.

"If one will only keep himself open to genial influences," he soliloquized, "one can take in worlds. If we have the magnet of attraction in us, a thousand things will spring up responsive to enlarge and beautify our lives."

When he got back to his tent he sat down and commenced a letter to Wilma, giving her an account of his visit. Miss MacIvers, he said, was pronounced the most beautiful and accomplished young lady in R——, and he accounted it a great favor to be permitted to visit her. He had never calculated upon anything so agreeable in the monotony of camp life. He wondered Wilma had not told him more about her ; she had had so much to say of Miss Percy and Miss Raymond and the preceptress, but so little of this imperial Miss MacIvers.

"I wish you could see her here, Wilma," he wrote ; "she was not properly 'set' in that wretched little boarding-house sitting-room. (By the way, couldn't you find pleasanter quarters in Crawford?) Here, surrounded by all the elegancies and refinements of her beautiful home, she is a princess."

It will hardly surprise anybody that Wilma's heart did not respond, but throbbed despairingly. But Mr. Burns did not mean to hurt her,—never dreamed that he hurt her. He simply wrote, as he had always done, what was uppermost, the things that most pleased and interested him. Had Wilma complained he would have been indignant. He rather prided himself on the purity of his soldier-life compared with the lives of most of his fellow-officers. He stooped to nothing coarse and low any more than he had done in his chaste student life; and few young men had been so blameless in their college career as he.

He got speedily into the habit of spending his evenings with Miss MacIvers. Sometimes he escorted her to the theatre and opera. They never spoke of Wilma. Miss Mac-Ivers ignored her. And perhaps Mr. Burns unconsciously felt that Wilma would not be in keeping with the elegant atmosphere of her home and the society she moved in. Into that society he himself became soon initiated, though without effort on his part, and found himself lionized to an extent that was surprising if not altogether delightful. There was a charm in his youth and freshness and in his originality of thought that won him numerous friends and admirers. Moreover he was so pure, so unsullied. Many brilliant women who courted him felt rebuked for their own unworthy lives by the guilelessness of his. He suspected no evil where there was much deceit and treach-ery, and heart-burning and despair. The world was fresh and sweet to him.

Of course his letters to Wilma took the tone and color of his new experience; and rumors reached her of his popularity at R——, which made her heart thrill with pride while yet it ached with anguish. It was a new de-velopment in her Charley to become a star in the social system. He had always been praised for being talented and scholarly, but never for being brilliant in society and fascinating to ladies. It seemed to her she had never understood him, had never foreseen his splendid possibil-ities. It was selfish, it was presumptuous, in her to feel hurt that she was now often crowded out of his brilliant life, to the extent of his forgetting to write to her at the time which for years had been set apart for writing to her.

It became a dread for her to go to the post-office those days when she ought to hear from him. The agony of suspense, while she stood waiting to see whether the postmistress would hand her out the familiar letter or give her head its little negative shake, was almost more than she could bear. Yet she never blamed him. She exalted him so much above herself that if he should cease altogether to care for her, was it a thing to be wondered at?

Miss Belmont said to her one day, " My dear, you must go home ; you have studied too hard ; you will be sick."

But Wilma could not bear the thought. How dreadful would be to her now the old, quiet, solitary life at Hazelville ! Even Fred, kind-hearted, rough Fred, was gone. He had gratified his patriotism by enlisting as a drummerboy. He wrote to Wilma that he thought he could serve his country as well with a drum-stick as with a musket.

CHAPTER XXXI.

ONE afternoon Miss MacIvers, in company with her stately papa, drove out to the camp-ground and around among the tents. It was warm and pleasant, and the soldiers were lounging about in and out. A number of visitors were upon the ground, and a band was playing and flags were waving. Miss MacIvers put aside her veil, and leaned forward and looked about with interest, it being her first visit to the camp.

" Look yonder, Maude ; there is your friend the lieutenant," said the colonel.

Mr. Burns and Captain Courtenay were walking slowly back and forth before their rather pretentious tent, the captain smoking a cigar. They were the two most distinguished-looking figures upon the ground. Miss MacIvers drew back and blushed deeply in passing. Captain Courtenay removed his cigar and paid a soldier's usual tributary glance of admiration to a pretty face ; though Captain Courtenay's glance was not altogether flattering to women. Mr. Burns gave the beautiful military salute with his own individual grace, and Miss MacIvers bowed. There was this difference between the two young men : Captain Courtenay doubted all women, and Mr. Burns believed in all.

The colonel would have drawn up and spoken to them, but that Miss MacIvers, seeing his intention, urged him in a low voice to drive on.

"So," said Captain Courtenay, pleasantly, in a peculiarly slow, indolent way he had of speaking, "that is your imperial Miss MacIvers?"

"Why, how do you know?" said Mr. Burns, surprised; "had you seen her before?"

"No. I inferred it."

Later in the evening, when Mr. Burns was getting himself ready for his accustomed visit, the captain said, "You asked me some time ago to call with you and get introduced to Miss MacIvers; is it a standing invitation?"

"If you choose to consider it so," said Mr. Burns, a little coldly.

"Then you may take me this evening."

If Mr. Burns had seen any way out of it he would have declined. He admired Captain Courtenay extremely, and saw no flaw in his splendid character except his contemptuous regard for women. He was honorable and proud-spirited, asking no aid of office or rank to lift him up. In his own opinion, fully as much as in the opinion of others, he would have graced any office or any rank. He was a general favorite with the soldiers, whom he treated with a dignified courtesy that won their high respect. He was always elected to take command in drilling and in dress-parade, being accomplished in military tactics and having a marvellous power of commanding.

On the way to call upon Miss MacIvers, he took his handsome black beard in his hand, and turned to Mr. Burns abruptly, and said, "Do not think me curious, but are you in love with Miss MacIvers?"

"No," said Mr. Burns, unhesitatingly. "Why, do you intend to fall in love with her?"

"No. I merely wished to know how the matter stood."

They were let in as usual by the ebony attendant, and Mr. Burns, being a warm and admiring friend of both parties, felt a good deal of anxiety as to how they would impress each other. He had got an idea, somehow (how subtly these things creep into our consciousness!), that there was a sort of antagonism between them; a sort of defiance on Miss MacIvers's part, and a disposition on the part of Captain Courtenay to take it up. And he meant in bringing them together, if possible, to get rid of that, and establish them on an easy, pleasant footing with each other. "Such things can be done," he told himself, "by an adroit mutual friend," and rather plumed himself on his tact,—a quality, by the way, which he did not often exercise. But at the moment of performing the ceremony of introduction between them,—being struck anew by the softness and dignity and gentle deference of Captain Courtenay's manner, and the rare beauty and grace of Miss MacIvers, and the proud bearing of both,—there seemed to flash a challenge between them as their splendid eyes met. Miss MacIvers dropped hers, with a blush that did not die away directly, but settled in her beautiful cheeks, and burned there throughout the evening. Captain Courtenay's visit was a surprise to her, and of course he held the more advantageous position. It occurred to Mr. Burns how well matched they were, either for conflict or harmony.

Captain Courtenay seldom removed his eyes from Miss MacIvers's face; and to Mr. Burns, watching them both narrowly, it seemed that his glance conveyed the most respectful deference and the subtlest flattery that an accomplished man could throw into the finest pair of dark eyes in the world. Miss MacIvers felt the power of it. It penetrated her like music, making every motion of her beautiful, proud form more graceful and rhythmic, and every tone of her sweet voice more sweetly modulated. She played for them, and her fingers, tingling to the very tips with the new, strange something that was infused into her veins, seemed inspired. Mr. Burns had never thought she played well before. The evening passed rapidly and enchantingly. Mr. Burns certainly had the gratification of seeing his two friends at their best; they each exerted a power upon the other to bring out their most brilliant hues.

On their way back to the camp he endeavored to get the captain's opinion of Miss MacIvers, but he evaded all questionings and was unusually silent, which Mr. Burns regarded as a favorable indication. "She will raise the standard of womanhood in his estimation," he thought, with pride in his ladylike friend.

Once Captain Courtenay made this significant remark: "I like proud, high-spirited women who can hold their own."

At first Mr. Burns was not altogether comfortable in the thought of being eclipsed; but detecting himself in that state, he pulled up short and confronted the situation. "Bah! I am not going to enact the dog in the manger," he said. "I'll step aside and give the captain a fair field." He did step aside, and found himself a little lonely and a little low-spirited. He gradually left off going to Miss MacIvers's, and evening after evening the captain went alone. His thoughts turned back to Wilma with some compunction, and he began writing to her with more regularity and at greater length. But to Wilma, who had known him so long, and whose discernment—sharpened by her great affection and her great fear—was so acute in all that pertained to him, there seemed to be little heart in his letters,—very little of that inner life of his that she liked so well. He wrote much less of himself and more of trivial outside matters. There was a lightness, an affectation of levity that she thought was put on to cover up a growing and melancholy indifference. The dread forced itself upon her sometimes, in these sad days, that she must give him up. But it was beyond her strength; she could not. Every tender word he wrote brought tears to her eyes, because she felt that it was *designed* to comfort her, merely, and not written in the fulness of love as he had once written tender words.

A few nights after Captain Courtenay's introduction to Miss MacIvers a grand ball was given in honor of the several regiments encamped there, and Mr. Burns dwelt at some length upon it in one of his letters. He himself had attended it, though not to dance. He wrote to Wilma: "I can't dance. I don't believe I want to learn. I know I should never be a good dancer. The idea of putting on 'pumps' and hopping about over the floor,—well, it ain't my style. I believe you dance (?), and you shall teach me how. We will have a music-box and wind it up, and you and I can dance until it runs down. Would that be nice, or wouldn't it? Well, I am happy to say that once in my life I have attended a grand ball,—like De Quincey,—where the brilliant lights, the enchanting music, the beautiful forms, and flashing jewelry conspired to make a veritable fairy-land. One has to witness such a thing and get imbued with the half sad, half joyous spirit of it to be able exactly to appreciate it. I can't say that I get as deeply intoxicated as some people do; but it is a fact, nevertheless, that all the next day the bewildering music was still ringing in my ears, and bewildering forms were revolving before me in the intricate mazes of certain labyrinthine dances. By the way, I don't know a single figure of any one dance. I don't care to know. I like the mystery of it,—a mystery as beautiful and incomprehensible as the wonderful dresses looped and festooned about the exquisite figures. I fancy I enjoyed the ball as much as anybody else there. There are always a good many ladies who don't dance; and one's uniform is a passport to speedy acquaintance. It doesn't do for people to stand on ceremony with us, because they will only have us such a little while. I have always thought there was a great waste of time in getting acquainted with people. We throw up a barricade of conventionality around us and keep people off, instead of trying to get at them. If a man will open himself to me and allow me to do the same, it won't take long to find out whether we are going the same way and can travel together, or vice versa, and pass on in our respective courses.

"Captain Courtenay escorted Miss MacIvers to the ball, and they were the 'observed of all observers.' Can there be a beauty superior to human beauty when we see it not only in physical perfection, but spiritualized and refined to the highest degree? I think not. By the way, I have not spoken of these two before in the same connection, have I? I suspect Miss MacIvers employed your humble Charley as a stepping-stone to Captain Courtenay, if the sequel proves anything. A pretty long step! But I am not sorry to be the instrument of such a happy consummation. I never before saw a union of such splendid masculine beauty and feminine loveliness. The captain made a feint of asking my permission to take Miss MacIvers to the ball. I told him I stood ready to resign my claims (if I had any) at a moment's warning. From politic motives, partly, I must confess. I would not risk a rivalry with the captain, who is a king and conqueror wherever he goes. Besides, I am too loyal a subject of his to wage war against him even for the smiles of woman, except my own darling's."

Which was a very sweet and tender sentiment to end a letter with. But Wilma had got to be such a sensitive, exacting little wretch—she told herself—that she took exception even to the style of chirography in which that closing line was written, being a careless scrawl across the whole width of the page. It was one of Mr. Burns's characteristics that he always used the largest sized letter paper,—a broad, fair sheet. He felt cramped on a moderate page.

This was quite a long and pleasant and gossipy letter, and Wilma tried hard to make herself believe it was all she could desire. It occurred to her after reading it over many times, until she knew every line by heart, to take it up and read it to Miss Percy, who, at this time, was more of an invalid than she had ever been before, and she had so little to interest her. She reflected, with a pang, that there was nothing in the letter which might not be published in the newspapers as a spicy correspondence, for all it revealed of her own and Charley's relation to each other, excepting in that one line which she would suppress, thinking what a difficult matter it was to invest a love-scene or a love-letter with sufficient dignity to lift it above the ridiculous in the mind of a disenchanted party such as Miss Percy was.

It was not her custom, as we know, to read Mr. Burns's letters to any one; but she began to want to talk about him, and hear others talk about him and praise him to her; she began to want to reassure herself of him by the impressions made upon others by what she, herself, said of him. The fondest deception! Since she gave the utmost bias in his favor, in all that she said, that her great love was capable of.

Miss Percy, lying back upon her pillow, transparent as a waxen image,—and much more beautiful because of the soul within her, which, in spite of its pride and bitterness, seemed at times very noble and lovely to Wilma,—expressed even a greater pleasure and interest in the prospect of the letter than she had expected.

"Raise me up a little, dear, before you begin," she said, and Wilma put her loving arm underneath the fragile form and raised her up. She was not much to lift. Then she sat down by the bed-side and began reading in a low, slightly agitated voice, and had nearly finished when Miss Percy threw up her hands and uttered a cry. Wilma dropped the letter and sprang up and bent over her, trembling. The white face was terribly convulsed.

"What is it, Miss Percy, what shall I do?"

She again slipped her arm under the pillow and raised her up. A little stream of blood oozed from her lips and ran down, staining her white garments and the counterpane with red. Wilma, terrified, laid her down again and ran to the top of the stairs calling for help. Some of the servants heard her and came running through the hall. In a few minutes the whole household was in the room, and a doctor was sent for, and everything was done that could be thought of before his arrival. When he came he could advise nothing but perfect quiet and the closest care.

"Was this hemorrhage brought on by any sudden shock or excitement?" he asked of Mrs. Pettibone.

"Not that I know of; Miss Lynne was the only one who was with her. Do you know of anything, Miss Lynne?"

"No," said Wilma; "I was reading her a letter when she screamed out, and I raised her up and the blood began to flow."

"Was it a letter that she had received? There might have been something in it that affected her," said the doctor.

"Oh, no; the letter was mine," Wilma answered.

"Strange!" said the doctor, and took up his hat and went out. The servants and various members of the family, who had waited to hear the medical opinion, followed him, and only Mrs. Pettibone and Wilma remained.

After a very long time, as it seemed, Miss Percy opened her eyes—her face still contracted as with great inward pain, though whether of body or mind none could say—and beckoned to Wilma, who instantly bent over her, never having left the bed-side. She made some slight, feeble motion with her hand, and when Wilma put hers within it, the slender fingers closed around it, and a more peaceful expression came into the pained face, and the blue eyes closed again. By and by, it seemed that she slept,—the doctor having administered a soothing potion,—though with a continual low moaning, showing that she still suffered. During the day a number of persons, including the preceptress and Mr. Ingraham, came into the hall below and were heard to inquire softly and then go away, no one being allowed to come up. All day and all night she lay, scarcely moving, her eyes closed and taking no notice of what was going on around her. Wilma watched beside her, still holding her hand and never closing her eyes; never, hardly, taking them from the troubled face all the long night. In the morning, Mrs. Pettibone, who was a kindly-disposed, though rather a purse-proud, elderly lady, made her go down to breakfast with the family, and told her she had better slip out and get a breath of fresh air. She put on her hat and went into the garden; she must not go far lest something might happen. She sat down upon a rustic seat, folded her hands idly in her lap, and fixed her eyes vacantly upon the ground. How sad the world seemed, and what a little time it had taken it to change from brightness to gloom. A year ago how happy she was! She thought of Fred away off in the South, of Charley, of Charley's mother, of Miss Percy, and life seemed very, very dark. Some one called her, and she sprang up and ran into the house and flew up-stairs to Miss Percy's room. Miss Percy was dead! The little stream of blood that trickled from her lips marked its way upon her neck, and again stained her white garments and the sheet and counterpane with red.

Wilma threw herself down by the bed-side in violent,

uncontrollable grief, that those who stood about wondered at and could not pacify. Poor child, she was weeping for all her sorrows! She could listen to nothing, hear nothing, until the storm was over. Then she arose and turned away, and went down-stairs and home to Mrs. Woods's, and told them the sad news, and then took a walk by herself, hardly knowing whither her steps tended, feeling, with indescribable anguish, that every day a door was closing against her; for people had been her doors and windows, through which she went out into a great, sunny world of love and trust, and was happy; she had not learned that there are other doors and other windows. Who of us does, until we are locked up within our wretched self and forced to find a way through our suffering out into the light? By and by, she came to the little brook and sat down upon the log, alone, where she and Charley had sat together a short time before, and leaned her aching head against a projecting limb, wishing she, too, might die, and so went to sleep. When she awoke, Miss Belmont was sitting beside her.

"Were you quite tired out, dear?" she asked.

"Why, was I asleep?" said Wilma.

"Yes; I suppose you dropped asleep without knowing it."

"You have heard?" said Wilma, looking up.

"Yes; and I came, immediately, to find you; they told me which way you came. It has been hard for you, my poor child."

"Oh, no," said Wilma; "I was not thinking of that, —of myself."

"I know. But it is right some one should think of you. Mrs. Pettibone told me how faithful you were throughout."

"If it could only have done some good!" said Wilma, her tears falling again.

"It did do good, dear; you did her good all along. You have nothing to reproach yourself with, and so your sorrow can have no bitterness in it. Miss Percy was very unhappy; she had no resources within herself,—I doubt if she ever would have had. Her sorrow, whatever it was, had eaten into her soul like a canker. She has told me, many times, how much she longed for this change, this

L*

rest that has come to her. I was up in her room a little while ago, and she looks, oh, so peaceful! We ought to be thankful that it is all over."

"Oh, but it seems so hard!" said Wilma. "She was so young, and so beautiful and gifted."

"But remember, dear," said Miss Belmont, "it was her life that was hard, not her death. That, it seems to me, is merciful. Shall we not believe it is all for the best? At any rate, she is quite beyond us now,—our help and our tears. But she is in the hands of the Great Father. Can we not trust our dear treasures with Him, my child?"

Wilma remembered what Charley had said; that heaven was a safe place to put one's friends, and the thought, for a moment, thrilled her sad heart. There will be no changes there! everything will be safe and lasting. No death, no disappointments, no loss.

Miss Belmont persuaded her to go back home. She, herself, went with her and spent a part of the day at Mrs. Woods's, and tried to beguile her into a more cheerful mood; and, indeed, thought it strange she did not succeed better. She did not know all the causes of Wilma's dejection. She made, poor child (without knowing it), a cloak of her friend's death—though her grief for that was deep and sincere—to cover other wounds. After Miss Belmont left her she sat down and wrote a line to Charley, telling him of her bereavement; and that gave her more comfort than anything else. She carried it to the post-office, reflecting that he would receive it in a few hours, and perhaps answer it.

Mr. Burns was getting himself ready to attend the funeral of Miss MacIvers's father, who had dropped dead, suddenly, in the street one morning, and was to be buried —being an old soldier—with military honors, when a soldier brought him the sad little letter. He tore off the envelope hastily and read it, his brows contracting.

"What is it?" said Captain Courtenay. "You seem disturbed. Have you had bad news?"

"Yes, rather," said Mr. Burns, going on with his dressing. "A friend of mine writes me of the death of a friend of hers. A singular creature, but capable of inspiring a great deal of affection, it seems to me. There, read it if you like," tossing him the letter.

Captain Courtenay took it up and glanced at it carelessly, changed countenance, and got up abruptly and went out, crushing the letter in his hand. Presently he came in again. "I shall not be able to attend the funeral," he said; "I am obliged to go out of town."

"Why, good heavens!" said Mr. Burns. "What shall we do without you?"

"Get some one else."

CHAPTER XXXII.

THE morning following Miss Percy's death, early,—before it was fairly light in fact,—Wilma arose and dressed herself, and stole out of the house and down to Mrs. Pettibone's. She knew it was her last chance to spend one more hour alone with her friend. In a little while people would be thronging in,—for everybody was curious about Miss Percy,—and would come, like vultures, to devour the lovely, proud face with their hungry eyes, assured that no flashing of the azure orbs could rebuke their curiosity now. She felt, as she hurried along, that she would like to stand between the poor, dead face that could no longer defend itself, and the eager, prying world, and keep it off. But that could not be. The church and the Pettibones had taken it in hand, and there was to be an imposing funeral. Knowing that her friend Bridget was an early riser, she went around to the back of the house, intending to get let in at the kitchen-door.

Bridget had just straightened herself up in bed, and was in the act of twisting up her hair and fastening it with a comb, which she took out at night and laid on the little stand at the head of her bed, when she heard the timid knock.

"Who's there?" she demanded, a little defiantly, pausing in her toilet-making, with her hands up to her head.

"It is Wilma. Will you please let me in?"

She bounced out of bed directly, and hurried out and opened the door without ceremony, revealing herself in her calico night-dress, her broad, bare feet flattened on the kitchen-floor.

"Good gracious me, child! an' what brought ye out i' the night the like o' this?"

"Oh, it is morning," said Wilma. "See! it is almost broad day! I wanted to see Miss Percy once more, Bridget, before they all came in. Will you let me go up?"

"Oh, yes; to be sure. Go right up; ye know the way yerself. The pratty lady!"

Wilma made her way silently through the darkened rooms, and along the hall and up the long, carpeted stairs. She pushed open Miss Percy's door and went in, closing it softly. Everything was changed. The crimson curtains at the windows had been taken down, and were replaced by thick, stiff white ones, that hung in still folds and looked as if chiselled in marble. The bed, smooth and white, was drawn to the farther side of the room, and Miss Percy lay upon it peacefully, all trouble smoothed out of her perfect face and the great stillness of death upon it. Even the little ringlets on her forehead were motionless, unstirred by the faintest breath of air. Wilma approached softly, and looked down upon the sweet face, that soon became obscured by the fast, fast-falling tears. By and by she knelt down and covered her face with her hands, and so lost herself in a sad revery as to be insensible to all external sounds and motions. Sounds and motions there were in the hall and on the stairs; subdued voices, muffled footsteps, and the soft opening and closing of doors; then again perfect quiet.

Suddenly it was borne in upon her consciousness that another presence beside the dead was in the room, and, with a great throbbing of heart, she raised her head and looked up. A tall figure, wrapped in a dark cloak, stood opposite to her on the other side of the bed, gazing down, as she had done, on the face of the sleeper. Presently the cloak was thrown back, revealing a soldier's dark-blue uniform, a shoulder-strap, and a sword-hilt; and a white, beautifully-shaped man's hand was put out to touch, with a curious but gentle touch, the marble forehead and the delicate ringlets of hair. The face looking down was blanched and white as the dead face, with just the difference there is between the whiteness of life and health and the whiteness of death. It had strong contrasts of hair and eyes and heavy brows and lashes, and was the finest masculine face Wilma had ever seen. Its striking beauty, as much as the shock of finding it there when she looked up, held her silent, until the dark eyes, travelling slowly through the dimness of the room, took her in, and widened with surprise and inquiry. Then she arose and stammered, "I—you frightened me, sir; I did not hear you come in."

"You must have been profoundly absorbed," he returned; and though the words were ungracious, they were uttered in a deep voice, exquisitely modulated as though it had been carefully trained to convey the finest and subtlest shades of meaning.

"You are a friend of hers?" Wilma asked, in spite of the awe with which she regarded him, and turning, as she spoke, to leave the room.

"I—yes, I am a friend of hers," he answered. "Pray don't go away; I am about to go myself;" and without another glance at the dead he drew his cloak around him and crossed the room with a gliding, smooth, and noiseless motion, and laid his hand on the door-knob; then stopped and looked back.

"Is the funeral to take place to-day?" he asked, in an indescribably gentle voice; and when Wilma answered, "Yes," he dropped his eyes and murmured something that sounded to her like "My poor Ginevra!" but she was not sure. He went directly down-stairs and out the front door, meeting no one.

The sun was up, but it was Sunday morning, and Crawford was not yet wide awake. A few hours later the church bells began to ring, and then to toll; and Miss Percy's costly coffin (she had left ample means to defray the expenses of an elaborate funeral) was carried into the church followed by a vast procession, at the head of which went the minister, in his sable garments, chanting these words, weighted with the echoes of so many solemn voices, on so many solemn occasions, "I am the resurrection and the life." And so borne about from house to church and from church to burial-ground, and preached over and chanted over, and gazed upon, the beautiful, haughty stranger, whom nobody knew, and whose feet were so weary, was laid to rest, and left for the daisies to bloom over.

CHAPTER XXXIII.

SHORTLY before Mr. Burns's regiment left R———, Miss MacIvers, who had no near relatives, shut up her beautiful home and went away, much to everybody's surprise. She was supposed to be engaged to Captain Courtenay,—they had been so openly devoted to each other,—and it was strange she should go out of town so long as he remained. To be sure (there were those who had watched closely and were posted), he did not visit her at all after her father's death, though they had once been seen walking together in the dusk of a moonless evening. And one shrewd female detective, who could put two and two together, averred that it was by Miss MacIvers's own appointment. She had written him a note, which he had answered, and then followed the meeting. Those who saw her said she was greatly changed. She grew white and thin, and seemed quite broken-hearted, though her step was as proud and her bearing as haughty as ever. Her father's death was a heavy blow.

Mr. Burns, with friendly sympathy, went one evening to see her, but she begged to be excused; saying, in a little twisted note which she sent down to him by a servant, that she was not well. She thanked him kindly, and he was quite touched by her evident deep grief.

A day or two after he heard that she was gone, and asked Captain Courtenay, inadvertently, if he knew where.

"How the devil should I know?" demanded the captain, with unwarrantable impatience.

Mr. Burns flashed up.

"How should you know? Haven't you openly devoted

yourself to her in the face and eyes of this whole community, until it is the universal belief that you are going to marry her?"

"I was not aware of it," said the captain. "The 'universal belief' is a damned nuisance, gotten up to compel people to a stereotyped line of action. I repudiate it."

Mr. Burns had learned in their brief intercourse that there was a certain cold, hard side to Captain Courtenay which it was worse than useless to contend against, and he dropped the subject.

At Crawford Academy there was little attention paid to books in those days. Nothing was studied, even by school-girls, but the national problem; nothing was read but the newspapers. Still, Miss Belmont, the only one of the faculty who stood faithfully at her post, and could see no necessity for neglecting her duty though the whole edifice of government were tottering to its fall, held steadily on with her classes and tried to keep up an interest, though all the time there were tears in her eyes, or just back of them, ready to start and fall whenever her glance encountered a vacant seat. Sometimes a vacant seat became more conspicuously vacant after an announcement by letter or telegram that some one had fallen. Then the girls would make a green garland and lay upon the desk and tie a knot of crape to the chair, until one by one the vacant seats were so marked and consecrated.

Wilma and Miss Allen one day performed the touching little ceremony of the wreath and the mourning-badge, standing weeping beside the chair that had been Mr. Liebenwald's. Gray and Liebenwald were both gone, now. Gray had joined a Western regiment, and fell at Pea Ridge, Liebenwald at Island No. 10.

In the latter part of the second year of the war, Mr. Ingraham and most of the professors threw up their peaceful commissions and entered the army. It was one morning, after prayers, that Mr. Ingraham, tapping the little silver bell on his desk (though that was hardly necessary, the study-hall was always quiet now), in as cheerful a manner and with as much avoidance of sensation as possible, made the announcement that he was about to go. He had waited till nearly all his "boys" had gone, he said ; until many of them had fallen, and he could not sit there looking at those vacant seats any longer.

That was the almost total breaking-up of Crawford Academy. Very few cared to stay after "Prof." was gone. None but those who had held to duty and to Miss Belmont rather than to Mr. Ingraham. Then were shown Mr. Ingraham's personal power and influence. He had bound his students to himself, rather than to principle and to their own best interests. They were half wild at the parting. They clustered around him with streaming eyes, and followed him to the station, and clung to his hands, kissing them, on the very steps of the cars as they were moving off. Oh, it was too bad, they said ; it was too horrible, that that grand head, with its silver hairs, should be made a target for rebel bullets! Even Miss Belmont broke down. She bade him "good-by" at the door of her recitation-room, and then went back and sat down, burying her face in her hands, and wept uncontrollably ; then rallied, and took up sadly, but firmly, the broken threads he had left.

In the mean time, came letters from Mr. Burns. Not regularly, or very often ; but they were enough to make links in the long chain of suspense and sickening, deferred hope. Mr. Burns was becoming disgusted with the whole business of war. Thought it incredible that in this nineteenth century men should stand up and kill one another by the hundreds. Great heavens! would we never get above the savage? What good is all our progress, our refinement, our cultivation? At sound of the trumpet it is all swept away like silken cobwebs, and men are bloodhounds. "Here we are," said he, "some thousands of us, figuring on a great chess-board ; yonder, at Washington, and down below, at Richmond, sit the men who are cunningly playing us against each other. Is this what I have shaped my life for? Is this what I was brought into the world and carefully trained through years of tender infancy and childhood for,—all my teaching and education tending toward the cultivation of a higher nature in me? Is this man's noblest end, most glorious destiny, to

stand and be shot down, himself dealing death to others?
I cannot see it. I had meant to do better things with my
life. War is a fine subject to write about and to talk about;
poets and orators have made the most of it. But practically
—I mean in the everyday details of it—it is an idle, de-
moralizing, cruel thing. Heavens! when I think of these
golden days, spent in lounging about camp by thousands of
men, it maddens me. Why are we not doing something
for the advancement of men, rather than for their destruc-
tion? Even a battle-field is not a sublime spectacle to
me, especially after the battle! I go about among the
dead and dying, see the suffering, the mangled bodies,
and blood, and slain beasts, and I am sickened, horrified.
Oh, God! will it never end? I want to get away from
the battle-smoke and the din of musketry, and shrieks and
wounds, and curses and agonized prayers, and death, and
find some peaceful spot where men are whole, not mangled and bruised and broken, and where women are light-
hearted and gay, and unused to the sight of blood. To
me, the grandest thing in war is the individual heroism of
some brave souls. In a whole army of men, moving and
acting with one impulse, we lose sight of the individual.
But he is here as elsewhere,—each separate, living atom
a world within itself, and the centre, it may be, of another
world. When one man falls the shock is almost sure to
vibrate through some little circle far away; for few of
us are so poor, or obscure, as not to have a place in the
world, and friends. (In my gloomiest moods I sometimes fancy no one is so poor as I in this respect. I have
not one living relative that I am aware of.)

"Do not misunderstand me, Wilma; I do not regret
coming into the army. I would do the same thing over
again to-day, with my eyes wide open to all these horrors.
There is no other way. I only lament that in all these
enlightened, progressive centuries we have not outgrown
such barbarities. Of course I know that out of the blood
spilled now will grow the olive-branch by and by, and
the world will be better, perhaps, that we have fought and
died. I spoke of there being some heroes among us;
Captain Courtenay is one of these. He is the bravest,
best, most indefatigable officer I know,—caring for every-

body, looking out for everybody's comfort.　After every engagement his first business is to inquire who is missing, and to help care for the wounded and bury the dead ; and then to write the tenderest letters to the stricken friends at home,—letters, I suspect, that will be sacredly saved and handed down, yellow with age, a century hence.''

So Mr. Burns continued to write.　But all the time it was pressing upon him, like a nightmare, that his love for Wilma, born in his early boyhood, was dying out.　For many months he struggled against the thought and would not believe it.　Even if there were nothing else to be taken into account,—no consideration for Wilma,—it hurt him that he had miscalculated his own stability of affection.　It touched his honor, his truth, his firm self-confidence.　For Wilma had not changed.　He could find no excuse, outside of himself, for his variableness.

One evening (the army was encamped in a strip of woods bordering a small stream) he went out and took a melancholy walk up and down, thinking life held very little.　The sun was going down, so the world turned round.　To-day, to-morrow, and so on to the end.　Was there anything on which to fasten hope, anything worth planning for and aspiring to?　Gloomier than the duskiness of twilight the shadows gathered in his blue eyes. He went back to the tent.　It was warm, but the curtain was lowered and a dim light burning within.　He raised the curtain and saw Captain Courtenay sitting at a small, improvised table, with his back to the door.　Near him stood a young officer, evidently just arisen from a camp-stool, whom he had frequently seen, but whose acquaintance he had never made, being frustrated in sundry friendly overtures by the officer's reserve and evident avoidance of him.　A slender young fellow, who walked with a proud step, his head bent down, and his military hat pulled low over his eyes.　He was said to be very wealthy ; he had a tent to himself, and a servant who followed him about like a dog.　At this moment the servant was standing a few feet from Mr. Burns.　Captain Courtenay got up and laid his hand on the young man's shoulder, and appeared to be remonstrating with him or demanding a promise from him in some low-spoken words.　His face was pale from strong feeling, and wrought into an expression of combined firmness and gentleness. The other's manner was greatly agitated. Mr. Burns, on the point of retreating, was suddenly surprised by the young man covering his face with his hands and exclaiming, in a muffled voice, "Oh, heavens! what shall I do?" and rushing past him out into the darkness. Captain Courtenay's eyes, following him, encountered Mr. Burns, and in the first flash of surprised glances interchanged he seemed to turn a shade paler. But he recovered himself instantly.

"Ah! have you finished your walk?" he asked.

"Yes. Did I interrupt your interview with Captain Reeves?"

"No; the interview was at an end. The young man is in some trouble."

"So I inferred. Anything connected with his commission?"

"No; a little personal matter."

"It seems to me," said Mr. Burns, smiling, "that you have succeeded better with Captain Reeves than any of the rest of the officers have. I have observed you two walking together several times lately. Raymond and I were speaking of it yesterday; he doesn't notice us poor devils."

"You and Raymond had better let him alone," said the captain, seating himself at the table and drawing some papers from his pocket, his manner plainly showing that he wished the subject dropped. By and by he remarked, "I have not a doubt that our cavalry will be repulsed to-morrow morning if they make an attack, as they propose to do; and in that case the rebels will follow them up and we will probably come to an engagement here."

His prophecy was correct. Before nine o'clock the routed cavalry came flying back in a disorderly retreat, and shouted out, swinging their ragged hats, "Go in and fight now, you infantry; we've had enough of it. The rebels are right after us; they are sure not to halt till they come to that belt of timber over yonder."

"This broad plantation between will make a splendid battle-ground," said a young officer, with swelling chest.

The enthusiasm ran along the lines, and every man caught it. Even Mr. Burns, disgusted, satiated, melancholy, felt electrified. His eyes kindled, his nostrils dilated, his cheeks paled as they always did with passion or excitement. He straightened himself, and threw back his shoulders, and was every inch a soldier. Preparations went forward rapidly, for enthusiasm is a swift worker. About noon the picket-line stationed some rods out in the field was fired upon by the rebel pickets, and a slight skirmishing was kept up until late in the afternoon. A number of officers, grouped together, were drinking coffee and eating a light luncheon.

"I hardly think we shall do any fighting to-night," the colonel of Mr. Burns's regiment had just remarked, and Captain Courtenay, getting up and striking a match to light his cigar, glanced across the plantation and answered,

"Do you think not? It seems to me the firing is getting more brisk along the picket-line. Look! By heavens! there they come."

Simultaneously the bugles sounded, and every man sprang to his place. Out from the opposite stretch of timber arose a dense line of rebel cavalry, with colors flying and drums beating, and advanced at a swift gallop, arms in rest, close up to the Union lines. They were met with a tremendous discharge of musketry and driven back. The battle-smoke slowly clearing away, revealed, here and there, a prostrate horseman in the dust; the rest had all galloped back to the shelter of the woods again. Among the few Union soldiers who had dropped out of their places and lay on the ground, bleeding, was Captain Courtenay's second lieutenant, Starr Raymond. Mr. Burns came up hurriedly, and knelt down beside him; a soldier had raised him up and was putting some water to his lips. He gave a gasp or two, and was still.

"Dead," said the soldier. "Shot right through the side, you see?" showing a rent in the blue uniform.

"Yes; carry him off the field," said Mr. Burns, and moved away, thinking whether the world and humanity had gained anything by this brave death.

There was barely time to carry off the wounded and dead before a rapid advance was made by solid ranks of rebel infantry. They were met as the cavalry had been met, but as fast as they were cut down the living stepped over the dead, filling up the vacant ranks and pressing closer, closer, until the excited command was given, high above the din, "Charge bayonets!" The Union soldiers, overpowered and dismayed, gave way and fled in utter confusion. But reinforcements were close at hand, and before nightfall the enemy were again driven back. The battle had raged barely an hour, and two thousand lives were cut off. Captain Courtenay's roll-call, in the morning, had numbered ninety-seven; to-night a little company of thirty made up his command.

"This is the most disastrous day we have had," he said, walking back and forth in his tent, greatly agitated.

"It was a desperate fight," returned Mr. Burns. "It is the first time I have drawn my sword," taking it from its sheath and examining the blade. "I should have been bayonetted if you had not come to my aid, Burr."

"Yes, I was looking out for you," said the captain; "but I came near being too late."

So intense a feeling came over them both at the recollection of the perilous moment that they silently clasped hands.

A soldier came in on some errand, despatched it, and then lingered to ask: "Did you hear about Captain Reeves?" addressing Mr. Burns.

Captain Courtenay wheeled around. "What about Captain Reeves?" he demanded.

"Shot,—dead," said the man.

"Good God! You must be mistaken, man!"

"No, sir; he fell in that first cavalry charge, and his servant carried him off the field. He's lying in a little hut down here on the river-bank."

Captain Courtenay caught up his hat and started out, exclaiming to the man, "Show me the way!"

Mr. Burns, left alone, was speculating on the violence of his friend's emotion, and wondering what there could be between him and the young officer, when another visitor, one of the college boys, raised the curtain and looked in.

"Hello! lieutenant, alone?"

"Yes; come in, Craig," said Mr. Burns, and motioned him to a camp-stool. "Well, how do you find yourself?"

"Unscathed, thank the Lord," said Craig. "This has been a dreadful day."

"It has, indeed. Poor Raymond!" said Mr. Burns.

"And did you hear about Captain Reeves?"

"Yes; Courtenay has just gone down to see him. Dead, they say."

"But did you hear nothing else?" said Craig, incredulously.

"No. What else?"

"Why, Lord bless your soul, lieutenant, Captain Reeves was a woman!"

"Good God!"

"It is a fact. Bribed her way into the army, they say. It leaked out as soon as she was dead. They have sent for some of the hospital nurses to come and take charge of her."

A sudden suspicion pierced Mr. Burns like a knife.

"Do you suppose Captain Courtenay knew?" he asked, feeling his heart harden against his friend.

"I hardly think so; and yet it might be," said Craig. And Mr. Burns regretted that he had awakened the idea.

"No," he returned, combatting it; "I don't think he knew. It is impossible! Suppose we walk down to that little hut. Is it far?"

"Not above twenty rods."

They stepped out and walked down the river a little way, and came to a rude log cabin, from whose small, square windows a dim light shone. The front door was open, and they entered what appeared to be the main room of the building. It was occupied by soldiers keeping guard. Back of it was another small apartment, and they were told to pass on into that. They expected to find Captain Courtenay there, but the room was unoccupied except by one motionless figure stretched upon a long bench and covered with a flag. Craig advanced and put out his hand to uncover the face. Mr. Burns, into whose heart a sickening fear had crept, grasped his arm.

"Don't do that!" said he. "She is a woman."

"Why, good Lord!" Craig exclaimed, turning round,

"what's the matter? You're as white as a ghost. Sit down and let me run for some water."

He was gone in an instant, and Mr. Burns swiftly and stealthily approached the motionless figure, and, with trembling hand, turned back the flag and looked down on the beautiful face of Miss MacIvers.

CHAPTER XXXIV.

It was an agonized question in Mr. Burns's mind, after that, how he should meet his friend; his faith in him was cruelly shaken. He went back to the tent; the captain was not there. He threw himself on his couch and counted the wretched hours of the night as they dragged on. Toward morning he fell asleep, and awoke when the captain, a little later, raised the tent curtain and came in. His face was white; his heavy, dark hair was wet with dew; he shivered as if with the cold. Mr. Burns, with a groan, turned his face away and feigned sleep. When morning came and he was obliged, almost, to take a stand for or against his friend, he thought it the hardest thing in his life that he could do neither. He avoided meeting his eyes and only spoke when spoken to; and that was very seldom, for the captain was more taciturn than usual, and seemed wholly occupied with what was going on within himself, whatever that might be. Evidently he was oblivious of any change in Mr. Burns. If he suffered, suffering made no impression on his strong physique. In a day he was wholly recovered from the shock of Miss MacIvers's death, so far as looks went.

Mr. Burns, on the contrary, grew haggard, pale, hollow-eyed. He was full of tender humanity, and naturally prone to melancholy; and educated in it somewhat by the suffering around him and the sorrows by which the whole world seemed helplessly burdened. At home, among his books,—associated through them with great minds living on and on,—and intimate with fields and woods and sky and water, studying nature's laws and pursuing her intricate and beautiful paths as science and art and literature traced them, the world and man had seemed far more sublime problems. Of course it was because he was so pressed down and hemmed in by circumstances, and moving without any volition of his own, that he took such a sad view of things. He could not get up and look at his life, or at any life, from an outside standpoint. The whole plan of human destiny seemed small, brief, petty, living in the midst of its boiling and seething. Could a life come out and separate itself, clear and pure, from all this?

In the midst of these gloomy days came a letter from Wilma. He was sitting in his tent, alone, when it was brought to him, and he took it up and opened it with a new weariness. Crises will come. We can no more avoid them in the small affairs of our lives than in the storm that has long been gathering in the heavens. Every line in Wilma's letter tended toward a crisis, though there was a strong effort at cheerfulness in it.

Mr. Burns caught up his hat and rushed out of the tent and took his way down along the creek to a lonesome spot in the woods, where he could give free vent to his excited feelings.

"I cannot bear it! I cannot bear it!" he said, with a groan, crushing the letter in his hand. "I must write to her and tell her that the dream is over. It breaks my heart; but I must. Oh, Wilma! why were we ever so linked together in our tender years, since the chain must be broken? God help me! God help us both! Why does no rebel bullet find its way to me? I am ready, and it would be as good a death as any, perhaps, to die for my country!"

He said it with bitterness, looking back at his old aspirations toward a high, intellectual life. He even felt some pity for himself as he might have felt for another. So young! So full, a little while ago, of the enthusiasm of living; and now, in place of it all, keen disappointment and a probable cruel, bloody death. He bowed his head in his hands and groaned aloud. By and by, he took out his handkerchief and wiped his face, and straightened himself up with an air of resolution, and turned toward the camp ground again and hurried into his tent. There was nobody there, for which he thanked heaven, and sat down to write to Wilma. He told her how long he had struggled and how hard he had tried to be true to her. "God knows," he said, "I meant to be faithful. In the old time, I never foresaw any possibility like this. I thought it was all settled between you and me for all our lives. I did not think anything could change my feeling toward you. I don't know now, why it is changed; I only know that it is. That the old tender love is gone, gone. I can't get it back. And surely, surely, Wilma, the thought that I cannot is as despairing to me as to you. I would to God I could. I esteem and respect, and love you yet, in a certain way, more than any one else I know. I have never met any one I could compare with you in the relation in which you stood to me. I have never met any woman whom I could ask to be my wife but you; and yet I feel that between us the bright dream is over. Oh, Wilma, Wilma! what shall we do?"

There came over him the thought of how Wilma had fastened all good and noble principles and sentiments to him, and believed in them through him, and he had a momentary dread of shaking her trust in them; and he wrote, "I know that you will not believe the less in the truth of mankind because one man has changed to you. I have a strong faith in you and in your power to——". He stopped and drew his pen through the last line. He would not let it seem that he prompted her or suggested to her to bear up under the affliction he himself had brought upon her. Surely it would come from him with a poor grace!

Thinking that he had written all that it was possible for him to write, and that he was powerless to comfort where he had struck such a cruel blow, he abruptly closed his letter with these words, destined to fall as the clods fall on the coffin-lid: "The night is coming on. It rains, and the wind sweeps by, and the shadows gather thickly around me. And so ends the saddest, dreariest day of my life. Oh, Wilma, Wilma, Wilma!"

He did not sign his name; the handwriting was enough. And, hearing the captain coming in, he folded and sealed the letter hastily, and dropped it in the letter-box ; then turned, with sad heart-yearning, toward his friend.

"Burr, tell me, for God's sake ! were you all along aware that Captain Reeves was Miss MacIvers? Was it your doing?"

Captain Courtenay turned upon him with a passion-white face and haughty, gleaming eyes.

"Was what my doing?"

"Getting Miss MacIvers into the army."

"By God ! do you take me for Lucifer let out of hell? I have half a mind to compel you to draw your sword !" laying his hand upon his own.

"You couldn't compel me to draw my sword," said Mr. Burns, sadly. "I want to know about Miss Mac-Ivers. If her death, or her being here, did not shock you, perhaps you cannot understand how it hurt me. But I would like to know the circumstances as you know them."

Captain Courtenay was silent a moment, and then answered, "You doubtless remember giving me the impression that Miss MacIvers was a woman capable of taking care of herself. Upon that supposition I sought her society to vary the tedium of camp-life, taking no thought beyond that. After we left R—— I knew no more of her movements than you did, until one evening in taking a stroll—it was about a week previous to our engagement here—I accidentally encountered Captain Reeves in the wood with his hat removed, and recognized him. I used every means in my power to persuade her to go back home. And that evening when you saw her here in the tent, I told her that if she did not resign her commission within twelve hours I would take measures to compel her to do it. I thought she had. She sent me a note the following morning saying she was on the point of quitting the army. It was just after the cavalry were repulsed. I have not a doubt she wilfully threw herself in the way of death."

Mr. Burns crossed over and grasped his friend's hand ; his eyes were filled with tears.

"I thank God ! I thank God !" he said, in a hoarse voice.

Captain Courtenay's face was deadly pale and his lips

compressed. His hand shook as Mr. Burns's fingers closed around it.

Neither spoke again for some moments. Mr. Burns went back to his place and sat down. By and by he said, in the low, changed voice we all use after a strong emotion has passed over us, "I am sorry—that it got out."

"It did not get out that it was Miss MacIvers," the captain returned, in the same low voice. "The nurses came that night, and I had them dress her in some of their own clothes; and, they accompanying me, I took her to W——, and left her in charge of a minister there to be buried, and told him to write a certificate of her death and send it to a lawyer in R——. I represented that she was a hospital nurse."

"You did all this for her!" said Mr. Burns. "And I thought of nothing beyond the fact that she was dead."

"It was my business more than yours, perhaps, to take charge of her," said the captain.

"True; she loved you," said Mr. Burns; and added, looking up, "and I thought you loved her?"

The captain shrugged his shoulders. "No. I would to God I had never seen her! I'll tell you, Charley, if a man could look beyond his acts to their consequences, he wouldn't blunder so much."

It was a very strong admission for Captain Courtenay to make.

"Still," said Mr. Burns, "certain trees bear certain fruits. We can guide ourselves pretty well by the law of cause and effect; yet,"—thinking of his own affairs,— "it's true we can't foresee results. The best of motives may bring about the saddest consequences."

His letter to Wilma was barely despatched before he began to feel the pain of suspense and anxiety as to how she would receive it and what she would reply. He tortured himself for days with picturing her anguish when she should know for a certainty that all was over between them. The certainty that all was over between them hardly brought any relief to himself, so great was his sorrow for her pain. And he could not fully assure himself, at any time, that he had done what was right and best; especially, as the long months passed and no word

came from her, he began to doubt, and to wonder sometimes, if he were not altogether wrong. He began to
think more tenderly of her. Now that the chains were
broken and he was no longer bound, he began to see her,
as things are seen in the distance, in the vanished, beautiful past. A halo gathered about the gentle head. Then,
as the long silence continued, he began to think she had
given him up easily, and to feel hurt. No doubt (he
thought) he had exaggerated both her affection for him
and her grief at losing him, and it confirmed an old suspicion he used to have in their early love-days that Wilma
could not feel as deeply as he felt. So, perhaps, it was
better ended ; though it saddened him to reflect what
bubbles young loves and hopes are ! He wondered if all
faith, all belief, all enthusiasm would end like this ; if
we must be forever blindfolded, and forever having the
bandages taken off, to be shown the emptiness of things !
He came to the conclusion to make no more plans, entertain no more aspirations, have no hopes or beliefs in anything. He would not be a tool, a toy, a child. He
would not let the beautiful deceits of this world play with
him and toss him aside, bruised and broken. He would
not let himself be puffed up with faith in a bubble that
would explode by and by. He turned a cold, dispassionate eye upon all the rush and swell of life, and looked
with a sort of pitying contempt upon the ambitions and
strivings and enthusiasms of men and women. How far
he had risen above it, an isolated, melancholy spectator !
Sometimes he fancied Captain Courtenay held the same
advantageous position as a sceptical looker-on. And yet,
though he had apparently no faith in the Jack-a-lanterns,
he still pursued them. It was a mystery to Mr. Burns,
who, losing faith, lost all enjoyment. His watch must be
genuine gold, or it was worthless to him ; a woman must
be true, or he took no pleasure in her beauty. But Captain Courtenay could take up a thing, admire it, enjoy it,
throw it away without regret,—without, apparently, feeling of any kind. Mr. Burns had learned, through much
suffering, that the roots of his nature struck deep. In
future he would keep himself high and dry, and not take
root.

CHAPTER XXXV.

WILMA was still living in a faint hope, broken now and then by the intrusive suspicion that, perhaps, it was her duty to herself and to Mr. Burns, and it might be (oh, heavens, what a sickening thought !) that he was leaving it to her to break the slender thread that still held them together. But we cannot put the knife to our own diseased limb ; and in time she came to think it a merciful respite that he did leave it to her. (Though we disinterested parties all know that if a leg or an arm has to be amputated, it is better to use despatch and not consult the patient's sick fancy.) Sometimes pride, even in so gentle a nature as hers, urged to resentment of his coldness. But the uncertainty respecting his real attitude toward her—whether it *was* coldness, or whether the seeming indifference was merely the outgrowth of his changed life—forbade decisive action on her part, and hope still whispered, " Be true to yourself and let time shape the rest," Miss Belmont's beautiful motto.

Miss Belmont was making arrangements, at the close of the school year, to go South and enter a hospital. She had studied medicine and surgery, and thoroughly understood the house we live in ; and felt that she could do good service with her knowledge and skill, and strong nerves and woman's gentleness. So Wilma was thinking about going home, and dreading the pain which the old, familiar scenes would bring to her sore heart.

It lacked yet a week or two of the close of the term when she went one day to the post-office and unexpectedly received Mr. Burns's letter. She hurried home and went into her room and sat down to open it with trembling hands. She read it through, and it seemed as if the wings of death fanned her face. She grew numb and cold and faint. Her eyes were bright and dry, and set in their sockets. Her lips were parted and her breath came hard,—so hard that every breath was a groan. By and by, she got up with eager stealthiness and locked the

door, and felt a kind of secret exultation that the whole
world was shut out and she was alone with this terrible
thing, this devil-fish that grappled her heart. She put the
letter—folded up and crushed back into its envelope with
her shaking hand—down deep in her trunk, as though
she would hide the knife that had stabbed her; and then
fell down with her face upon the floor moaning, but not
realizing what hurt her. Late in the evening she heard
Mrs. Woods come and try her door; she raised her head
and listened with quickened senses, and felt the strange
throb of secret exultation again when she went away,
knowing that she would not again be disturbed. The
moon shone nearly all night long through the uncovered
window, and looked down unpityingly upon her misery.
Now and then she got up and walked about, or knelt beside a chair and laid her tearless face upon it. She never
approached the bed; she could touch nothing but what
was hard and unyielding.

She was glad when morning broke; any change—the
least—must bring some relief. She sprang up at the first
sounds of life and stir in the house, and began rapidly to
make her toilet; pulling down her long hair and brushing
it carefully, and bathing her face. When she came to
look in the glass her face was ashy gray, with heavy
shadows under the eyes. She brightened it up with as
cheerful an expression as possible; she had will-power
enough to do that, and to go out to breakfast looking
much as usual, though her lips and eyes were still dry
and her throat so husky that she dared not trust herself to
speak. Everything seemed strange. Even the clink of
the teaspoons in the cups, as Mrs. Woods served the coffee,
struck her with a new sound. She ate what she could,
and then got up hurriedly and said she was going out.
She remembered that it was Saturday. She went into her
room and put on her hat in great haste and started off to
the woods. Some pent-up power within her seemed hurrying her all the time. She made straight for an old,
unused road she knew of,—where she and Miss Percy used
to go,—with branches of trees meeting overhead. When
she reached it, lying in a deep solitude that was unbroken
except by the notes of a few little birds, and the crack-

ling of twigs under the tiny feet of small, swift, wood
animals, she marked out a "beat" for herself and walked
back and forth upon it, back and forth ; neither thinking
nor feeling much, and yet in a state of intense consciousness. By and by, a thought struck her like a flash of inspiration. She saw a swift way out of this dumb misery.
She would go and drop herself into the big mill-pond ;
she could hear the water roaring over the dam at a little
distance. She darted away through the underbrush,
quickly and stealthily, with her wild, bright eyes, as
though some one might be on her track, and soon came
out on the edge of the pond. Not far off she saw a man
with a gun looking up into a tree, and she sped back into
the bushes before he saw her. What should she do now?
Her heart was throbbing like the heart of a frightened
animal. She must get out of the woods ; the solitude was
dreadful. Soon she found herself on the road to " picnic hill," as it had been called ever since the May-day
party, and she determined to go up there. It was a long
way, but then there was such a good view of the country
from the top of the hill, and she wanted to get up and
look around. She walked at a great rate ; when she saw
any one coming she hid herself among the trees and
bushes along the road-side, thinking that on no account
must she be seen or people would know that something
had happened to her. At last she came to the top of the
hill and stood looking around in her strange solitariness.
If at any time a thought of Charley crossed her mind she
drove it away with a shudder, and walked on faster and
faster, filling her brain with a thousand other fancies to
crowd out the misery of thinking of him. There was no
luxury in this grief, she could not hug it to her bosom and
weep over it. All she thought of was to banish it, to get
away from it.

At last it occurred to her that she was very far from
home and must get back. Half-way back she began suddenly to get faint, and thought perhaps she was going to
die. She sat down on the mossy roots of an old tree
and laid her head back against its trunk, and looked
up through the leaves at the sunny blue sky with fleecy
white clouds floating dreamily across it, and felt that it

would be immeasurably sweet to die,—so sweet, so exquisite, that her lips opened and she laughed aloud. Then her eyelids drooped, and her consciousness began slowly to ebb away. She had a little note-book and pencil in her pocket, the latter a present from Charley, the recollection of which at this moment gave her a scarcely-felt twinge of pain; she thought of taking them out and writing that she would like to be buried beside Miss Percy. But it required too much effort; her hands lay heavy and listless in her lap.

FOURTH BOOK.

CHAPTER XXXVI.

THE High-Water-Mark attorneys had not often been
called upon outside their own county for legal services,
albeit they had something more than a local reputation,
and were highly spoken of in the profession. Some time
after the ball whose history I have recorded some chap-
ters back, an important ward and guardian case was put
into their hands, to be conducted at Hammond Springs,
the county-seat of an adjoining county, distant some
thirty or more miles. There being no regular public
conveyance, they went in their own light, open buggy.
Notwithstanding the season was far advanced, being near
Christmas, the weather was still fine and the roads in
excellent condition. Mr. Burns, who liked travelling
across the country in this manner for the sake of what he
could see and feel of nature in her various moods, took
up the lines and cracked the whip over "Nobby's" ears
and set off in good spirits, the tide of memory that had
swept over him a few evenings back having slowly ebbed
away.

Hammond Springs was a remarkable town, barely half
a dozen years old, but containing a population of over
four thousand, about one-third only being native Amer-
icans, the others gathered from all parts of the earth
almost. As they approached the town, and the houses
and manners and speech of the people began to betoken
the foreign element, Mr. Burns exclaimed, sweeping his
arm comprehensively over the landscape and widening
the range of his inner vision until it took in all the broad
land of Columbia, "What other country under heaven

could stand such a mighty influx of foreign immigration ! could take all these strange chickens under its wings, and clothe and feed and preserve them in harmony with each other?"

"I look upon foreign immigration, when it takes the attitude of a peaceable farming community," returned Mr. Courtenay, "as it appears to about here, as a rather good thing for the country."

Mr. Burns, disgusted at having the wind taken out of his sails, retorted, "Who would dispute that! But it does not always take the attitude of a peaceable farming community. It is oftentimes a seething, boiling, formidable element, fomenting in and throughout our domains. It lifts up its voice in the councils of the nation, and impudently meddles in all our affairs. And yet," he continued, expanding again, "Brother Jonathan goes serenely and powerfully on, carrying forward his mighty projects, maintaining the dignity of his institutions, and holding easily, confidently, and securely the reins of his stupendous government. He is a brewer on a larger scale, is Brother Jonathan, and the scum of his boiling works off in the process of naturalization. America is a grand idea! Human progress couldn't have got along without it."

He paused, and, as Mr. Courtenay made no response (he was going over the impending lawsuit in his mind, and paying little attention to Mr. Burns's eulogies of the nation), he lost himself in contemplation of the sublime picture he had called up.

They drove into town and drew up at the nearest American hotel,—or what by its sign-board and other pretensions purported to be American,—the landlord of which came out in his shirt-sleeves, and, to their inquiry about board and lodging, sorrowfully shook his head.

He could give them a dinner, but not a bed. He "wass werry full; he haf so many boarders und travellers, und de court wass met, und dere wass theater dis veek, und so much beoples." Evidently he regretted his inability to serve them as much as they regretted it.

"We should have written and engaged rooms as they do at watering-places," said Mr. Burns, ruefully.

However, they dismounted and went into the office.

A number of men were sitting and standing about, talking and smoking, and waiting the final summons to dinner. Before Mr. Courtenay had fairly relieved himself of his outside wrappings, a gentleman, stepping in from the street and hastily removing a cigar from his lips, came up and grasped his hand with much more warmth than ceremony. "Bless my soul, Courtenay! is it possible?" he exclaimed.

Mr. Courtenay, who held that a man's personal dignity is apt to be impaired by such hearty familiarity, lifted his eyes a little coldly to the speaker's dark, attenuated face; but travelling back mentally in the space of a second to his college-days, he placed it (somewhat changed) among the best faces of his recollection, and very cordially returned the greeting.

"What, Woodbury!" said he. "How is it I meet you here?"

"You find me at home," said Mr. Woodbury. "I have hailed from this place for the last five years. I did not hear until a short time ago that you were retained on this suit; I have been out of town. I learned some time ago that you were located at High-Water-Mark,—a God-forsaken little hamlet, isn't it?—excuse me,—and always intended running down to see you, but I haven't made it out yet."

Mr. Courtenay introduced Mr. Burns, to whom Mr. Woodbury, who was still holding fast to him, at once transferred his hand.

"I am happy to make your acquaintance," he said, cordially. "You are both employed on this case, are you not?"

"I assist Mr. Courtenay," Mr. Burns modestly returned.

"You are on the right side, but you have strong opposition," said Mr. Woodbury. "The Marchmonts of N—— City are considered the best legal talent we have got around here."

"So I understand," said Mr. Courtenay, and felt his spirits rising. He liked to "lock horns with his equals."

"Parke Marchmont," continued Mr. Woodbury, "expects to be our next congressman; he is working for the nomination already. I wish, for my part, we had some good man to put up against him. By the way, Courtenay, why not you? I always thought you would make a statesman."

"Circumstances have gone against me," said Mr. Courtenay.

"Or, rather, he goes against circumstances," put in Mr. Burns.

"I suspect that is the way of it," said Mr. Woodbury, smiling; "he was always so confoundedly proud. Do you remember how, instead of Courtenay, we used to call you Coriolanus?"

Mr. Courtenay looked as if he did not relish the reminiscence. The bell rang, and Mr. Woodbury accompanied them into the dining-room. Two gentlemen came in presently and sat down opposite to them. Mr. Woodbury looked up, recognized them, and introduced them as the Marchmont brothers; upon which they all conversed together with the freedom and suavity common among men. When they arose from the table, however, the two parties at once separated,—the Marchmonts going off up-street, and the others stepping into the office again.

Mr. Courtenay asked, "Where can we get lodging, Woodbury? We are in a quandary."

"Has our Dutch friend no accommodations?" asked Mr. Woodbury. "I suppose not, though; they seem to be crowded here. Why, damn it! come home with me; we have room enough for a dozen."

It seemed to be a sudden inspiration.

"Then you are a family man?" said Mr. Courtenay.

"Certainly. Why, Lord bless you! I've been married —years. I don't just remember how many; my wife could tell you the exact date. Have I the advantage of you?"

"Of both of us," said Mr. Burns; his question included them both.

"Let me see; are you going up to the court-house?" asked Mr. Woodbury.

They said they supposed so.

"Then I'll send a despatch to Belle,—to my wife,— and go with you."

He went to the desk and scribbled a hasty line, and

gave it to a boy to carry to Mrs. Woodbury, and then they stepped out.

"I dislike to inconvenience ladies," said Mr. Courtenay, regretfully. "Isn't there some private boarding-house,—anything that could give us shelter?"

"Lord, yes! there are a dozen Dutch hovels that could accommodate you right here in this neighborhood. Would you like to look at some of them?"

The young men laughed and declined.

"Smart-looking fellows!" said one of a knot of men clustered around the office-stove as they went out.

"Yes," responded another. "The dark one—that's Courtenay, isn't it—has an eye in his head that I'll wager would hold a jury."

"Humph! the other one has the keenest eye to my thinking," said a third.

"Did you see Parke Marchmont taking the measure of them? Ha, ha! it'll take him to the end of his tape-line, I guess."

"I mean to attend that trial straight through," said the first speaker; "there'll be some sharp practice. I've heard say those High-Water-Mark lawyers would be more than a match for the Marchmonts. I think they have the best side."

"As to right, yes; as to money, no."

"If they win, they'll have money as well as right."

"Ever been to High-Water-Mark?" A runner for an Eastern dry-goods house threw out the question carelessly, and one of the before-mentioned speakers took it up and answered, "No."

"You would be surprised to see such fine birds come out of so shabby a nest," said he.

An elderly gentleman, who had not spoken before, shook his head and replied, charitably, "You can't judge a man by the place he hails from in this Western country. Wait till they have had time to build their nests."

The young men accompanied Mr. Woodbury home in the evening, with a good deal of reluctance, which they tried to cover up, feeling that an invitation so cordially given ought to be accepted with a good grace, especially as there was no alternative.

Mr. Woodbury's residence, a pretty and tasteful frame structure, was situated at the upper end of the town, and a little isolated from other houses; having a large space of ground around it, decorated with trees and shrubbery, and enclosed by a neat picket fence.

"You say you have lived here only five years?" said Mr. Burns, as they walked up from the gate.

"Only five years," said Mr. Woodbury. "I went to work the minute I got here, and built my house, laid out my grounds, and put out the trees and bushes. Back of the house you will find a raspberry patch, a bed of strawberry vines, a grove of wild plum-trees, et cætera."

"You have done wonders!" said Mr. Burns.

"I accomplished all that in one year," continued Mr. Woodbury, "and then I went back East after my wife."

"Oh, then you didn't bring her with you at first?"

"No; bless your soul, she nearly cried her eyes out as it was, over the desolateness of the Western country."

"Burr," said Mr. Burns, "why couldn't we fix up some of our lots in High-Water-Mark? We could put fences around them and set out trees and shrubbery, and so help along the town, besides making the lots more salable."

"We might," said Mr. Courtenay, but his inflection conveyed no strong assurance that the thing would be done.

The hall door, when they mounted the steps, proved to be locked, and Mr. Woodbury rang the bell.

"My wife and her 'help'," he explained, with an amused smile he always wore when he in any way referred to Mrs. Woodbury, "are both cowardly little souls, and protect themselves with bar and bolt, in the absence of the head of the house."

Presently a light step came tripping along the hall, and Mr. Woodbury, with a low, pleasant laugh and a nod to his companions, as much as to say, "It's my wife," tapped a peculiar little tap on the door, and instantly bolt and bar were withdrawn and it flew open, and the daintiest of little women, with coal-black eyes and a smiling mouth, stood to welcome them. One of her small hands found its way into her husband's, which was not lost upon Mr. Burns, who envied men that had sweet wives and pleasant homes.

"Well, wife, here are the gentlemen," said Mr. Woodbury. "Did you get my despatch? Mr. Courtenay; Mr. Burns."

"Yes, I got your despatch," she returned. "How do you do, gentlemen? Mr. Courtenay, my husband, has spoken of you to me many times, and you are welcome to my house."

She extended her hand last to Mr. Burns, making it even between them by leading him toward the parlor door, the others following. As for Mr. Burns, when the light of the suspended lamp in the parlor (for it was dusk) struck her pretty, piquant face, it seemed to him there was something strangely familiar in it, though he could place it nowhere among the faces of his recollection.

"I believe we ought to apologize for intruding upon you," Mr. Courtenay began, with stiff politeness, before seating himself in the chair she wheeled around for him; but she interrupted him with a gesture of her little forefinger.

"Don't speak of intruding; if you had lived as long in the West as I have, and seen as little society, and been as hungry for home faces sometimes, you wouldn't apologize for coming into an old friend's house! Besides," she added, gayly, "I was expecting you; my Tom had the unwonted forethought to send me an *avant-courier!*" Looking up archly at her tall, broad-shouldered spouse, who smiled down upon her with the utmost pride and affection, feeling no solicitude about the impression she might make, fastidious as he knew his friend Courtenay to be.

"But is it not strange," said he, "that I had the forethought to bring them here! eh, wife? My wife, you see, is so eminently hospitable that I have gradually eased my mind of responsibility in that direction, and trust the social matters all to her. So much so that she accuses me of negligence sometimes."

"Mr. Courtenay," said Mrs. Woodbury, "if you are acquainted with my husband you will not be surprised to hear that he has eased his mind of a good many other responsibilities, and handed them over to his wife."

Mr. Courtenay, relaxing wonderfully under her influence, replied, with a laugh, "Tom always was noted for thoughtlessness."

Mr. Burns felt that there was something in the atmosphere of Mr. Woodbury's home, pervaded by the presence of his sprightly wife, which made him appear to better advantage there than elsewhere.

Almost immediately after they were seated, and before they had time to fall into any of the awkward silences which frequently occur after the first gush of welcomings and inquiries, among people who are wholly new and un-assimilated to one another, a little silver bell jingled and Mrs. Woodbury led her guests out to tea, which was served in a small recess opening, by an arched entrance, into the sitting-room. The table, elegantly spread, stood in the centre of the room, and was surrounded by a wilderness of plants and flowers. Delicate vines were wreathed round picture-frames and brackets, and looped in graceful festoons along the edge of the ceiling; some exquisite white statuettes on the mantle peeped out from perfect little bowers of green leaves, and in a miniature grove of fuchsias and geraniums blooming in a bay window, the crimson curtains of which were looped back, hung a canary bird's cage. Mr. Burns, who had a natural affinity for refinements of all kinds, brightened up with his most expansive expression; he took the liberty of congratulating Mrs. Woodbury on her successful creation of a fairy-land.

Mrs. Woodbury blushed at the flattery most fairy housewives are susceptible to, and replied, "Thank you, Mr. Burns; your appreciation does me good. My Tom is blind to the beauties of my kingdom!"

"Wife, you know I used rather to like your flowers," returned Mr. Woodbury, meeting her smilingly reproving glance. "But from practical experience in taking care of them through several severe winters," addressing Mr. Burns, "I begin to fail of seeing any profit in them. Why, sir,"—ignoring the admonitory shake of his wife's little forefinger,—"the fuel those things cause to be consumed, yearly, is no inconsiderable item in this woodless country as a matter of domestic economy. That rose which you see blushing so beautifully yonder, represents to me simply an inestimable amount of care and anxiety, to say nothing of expense, to preserve it intact. And after all," he continued in a way that was highly amusing to his guests, taken in connection with the defiant, pretty face opposite, whose charming remonstrance he seemed to like to challenge, "what is a rose? A pretty, fleeting, evanescent thing! a bit of color and a breath of perfume. The only tangible thing about it is the getting up bitter cold nights to make fires for it."

He ended with his pleasant, half-inaudible laugh, drawing his napkin across his mouth and looking at his wife.

"Don't listen to him, gentlemen!" she said, "for the sake of the future Mrs. Burns and Mrs. Courtenay, who may have a taste for house-plants."

"If they do have that deplorable taste," said Mr. Woodbury, "pray don't encourage its cultivation. I used to bring home all the green things I could find, to please my wife."

"You see, Mr. Burns, he speaks of pleasing his wife in the past tense!" she said. "The way of it is, we have got to have fires all the time, anyhow, to keep other things from freezing. My poor plants are the scapegoat."

There was a piano in the sitting-room, and after tea Mr. Woodbury said, "Belle, can't you give us a little music?"

The invitation was warmly seconded by the visitors, and Mrs. Woodbury seated herself, turned the leaves of a huge book of bound sheet music and began an airy fantasia; and her husband took the young men slyly into his confidence so much as to say that she was considered a very fine performer. After which he bestowed himself comfortably upon the sofa, propped his cheek upon his hand and closed his eyes, shutting out sight for the more complete enjoyment of sound, it might be supposed. Mr. Burns, lying back in an easy-chair, watched the dexterous fingers fly over the keys, and gave himself up to the joyous influence of the musical rhythm. Mr. Courtenay, dimly listening, embraced the opportunity to go over the impending lawsuit again. When the music ceased, Mr. Woodbury arose and stepped into the hall for his overcoat and hat.

"The mail comes in about this time," he said. "Will either of you walk down street?"

Mr. Courtenay arose.

"If you are going, Burr," said Mr. Burns, "I will excuse myself and remain with Mrs. Woodbury, if she will allow me."

"My wife will be very glad of your company," said Mr. Woodbury.

"Indeed, I will!" she exclaimed; and then, as the door closed upon the other two, she added, "Oh, nobody gets so lonely as I these long winter evenings! It is such a calamity to me that the mail comes in at this hour. Mr. Woodbury wouldn't always go down town after supper, if it wasn't for that; and then when he goes and gets among the men, he never realizes how fast the time is going with him and how slowly with me."

Mr. Burns, lying back in his easy-chair, slowly rocking himself to and fro and feeling very luxurious, said, in his heart, that if he were situated as Mr. Woodbury was— such a beautiful home and such a charming wife—the mail and the men down town might go to thunder; he would spend his evenings at home.

"Mrs. Woodbury," he said, suddenly, leaning forward and looking at her, "excuse me, but have I not somewhere met you before? Your face is unaccountably familiar to me."

Mrs. Woodbury laughed.

"I was waiting to see if you would remember me; I thought you would by and by. I recognized you almost immediately. I hardly know how to recall myself to you, without mentioning a mutual friend of ours, Wilma Lynne."

Mr. Burns started and flushed.

Mrs. Woodbury had purposely thrust the name upon him, and watched narrowly, without apparent interest, its effect.

He sat still for a moment and then answered, "I remember. You were Miss Raymond, the governor's daughter."

"Yes; they always called me the 'governor's daughter' at Crawford," said Mrs. Woodbury, smiling, and added (speaking to herself), pathetically, "Poor papa!"

A long pause followed, but not an awkward one. Mr. Burns was too deeply stirred to be conscious, and Mrs. Woodbury's faithful and affectionate memory was recalled to the death of her father, whom she had tenderly loved and whom she still deeply mourned. From thinking of him she passed on to thinking of her brothers, and suddenly burst out with,—"Oh, Mr. Burns, I have just remembered, you were with Starr when he was shot down!"

Mr. Burns slowly gathered up his thoughts.

"With Starr? Oh, yes, yes. I held him up in my arms while he breathed his last gasp. Poor fellow! he hardly knew what hurt him, his death was so sudden."

Mrs. Woodbury's tears were falling fast. Presently she dashed them away and looked up.

"Do you know, it never occurred to me until this moment that my husband's much-praised college friend was this same Captain Courtenay, the head of my brother's company, and your bosom companion! Now, isn't that singular? We used to hear so much about Captain Courtenay, and to think I am entertaining him in my house! I remember asking Mr. Woodbury once if he thought they were related, and he said it was not at all likely. Well, well, what a dice-box the world is! Forever shaking us up and dropping us out in all sorts of attitudes towards each other. They said he and Miss MacIvers seemed to admire each other so much. But she went away before the regiment left R——. And do you know, Mr. Burns," Mrs. Woodbury continued, impressively, "that Miss MacIvers went into the hospitals, and by some means—heaven knows what!—she was killed; and her body, which had been buried, was taken up and brought back to R——, and interred in the beautiful cemetery there, and a splendid monument erected over it."

Mr. Burns sat as numb as a stone and made no answer. He felt as if it was the shaking off of a horrible nightmare when the outside hall-door opened, and he heard the men's voices. He got up and took a turn around the room. His face was so pale that Mr. Courtenay observed it, and asked, when they went up-stairs to bed, "Aren't you feeling well, Charley?" with a solicitude he always showed for his friend, but for nothing else.

"No, not very well. Do you know, Burr, this Mrs. Woodbury is a sister of Starr Raymond's?"

"No; is she? How did you find out?"

"I used to meet her when I went to Crawford Academy to visit a friend, and she remembered me."

"Ah, Crawford Academy! I suspect you had some disturbing conversation then. Did she refer to her brother?"

"Oh, yes; and—and to Miss MacIvers. Her remains, she says, were taken up and removed to R——."

Few words suffice for a subject so fraught with pain and horror, and nothing more was said.

CHAPTER XXXVII.

THE following morning, after breakfast, Mr. Woodbury invited his guests into the library, with the offer of cigars, which Mr. Burns declined.

"Ah! don't smoke? Then perhaps you don't care to accompany us? In which case I have no doubt my wife will be glad to entertain you here. I have an idea you and she are rather congenial, on the subject of flowers,— at any rate," laughing.

Mrs. Woodbury retorted that she was glad to entertain any gentleman who didn't smoke. Mr. Burns was well pleased; he liked women's society; it brought out the truest, tenderest side of him. Mr. Woodbury closed the library door and opened a window a little way.

"My wife is particular about my smoking," he explained. "I am not to light a cigar anywhere about the house but here, and I am instructed always to ventilate a little so that the tobacco-scent will not settle on the books and things."

He drew up an arm-chair for himself, motioned Mr. Courtenay to another, and they sat down with a spittoon between them, their feet elevated at a comfortable angle.

"It takes some time," Mr. Woodbury continued, "to learn all one's matrimonial lessons. My wife, as you may observe, is quite the pink of particularity. I was a good while getting broken in to her exact ways; though now, I flatter myself, I am beginning to run pretty smoothly. How is it you are not married, Courtenay? You came West shortly after graduating in the law-school, didn't you?"

They had talked it all up at the breakfast-table, about Mr. Woodbury's college friend ·being one and the same with the famous Captain Courtenay, whom his wife remembered so well. Mr. Woodbury's last question covered up the first so that Mr. Courtenay saw no necessity for replying to it.

"Yes," said he. "I came West shortly after graduating, and when the war broke out I went into the army. Subsequently, after travelling about a little, I found my way out here."

"And how the devil did you come to settle in High-Water-Mark?" said Mr. Woodbury. "A town without a railroad, or any other advantages, I suppose?"

"It has the advantage of being the finest site for a town of any place I know," returned Mr. Courtenay, with some spirit. And added, with his customary sanguinity touching that point, "Besides, we shall have a railroad before long."

"I don't see," said Mr. Woodbury, knitting his brows, "what possessed you to come West, anyhow! Your chances were good in the East, damn it! You could have held your own with the best of them."

Mr. Courtenay made no answer, but watched the little cloud of smoke he was sending up and, by and by, asked, "Do you practice law?"

"Not much," said Mr. Woodbury. "I am engaged in the land-office business."

"Pays well, doesn't it?"

" Pretty well.   One has a good many chances.   I buy up tax-titles, and that sort of thing.   Don't you speculate any ?"

" No.   That is, very little.   The fact is I hate dabbling in anything outside the profession.   Burns and myself have some land ; we get hold of a piece occasionally ; I suppose we shall make something out of it after a while."

" Oh, yes ; certainly you will, if you hold on to it. The law, Courtenay,—one can't live on the law ! It's a good starting-point ; but you have got to reach beyond it.   I remember you were never practical ; you always let the boys get the advantage of you in money matters. You were cut out for something higher than a financial career.   We used to prophesy you would make a poet or an orator, or something out of the ordinary line.   However, much depends on circumstances.   The present times don't seem to demand a Homer or a Cicero, and so there are no Homers and Ciceros forthcoming.   I have no doubt they would rise up if the exigencies of the day called them.   I suspect it will take some great convulsion to bring you out ; the world will never get the best there is in you until it brings some mighty force to bear upon you."

" It brought the late war," said Mr. Courtenay, " to bear upon me, and I went into it, and came out of it, an obscure captain."

Unwittingly, Mr. Woodbury had touched a chord in his bosom that had vibrated on his life.   It was his one intense and all-absorbing consciousness that there was within him a strong power to be and to do, if occasion came ; and he had been secretly and half-unconsciously preparing himself for the time when all there was in him, —all he could accumulate of brain, of mental power, of culture, would be demanded.   His pride and his reserve, his loathing to take hold of small things (or things that seemed small in comparison with his great ideas) were a sort of saving of himself toward some indefinite, grand end.

" The late war," said Mr. Woodbury, " was not the right kind of force.   I can sympathize with Halleck, who, when asked to write a poem on it, said, ' No, the rebellion was a monstrous mutiny.' Besides, the days when men achieve mighty things with the sword are over. Why don't you go into politics?"

" I am on the wrong side."

" Ah, is that so? Can't you come over?"

Mr. Courtenay shook his head.

" I remember," said Mr. Woodbury, smiling, " you were always a stickler for principle. But do you know I have fancied your principles were hereditary,—handed down to you from an aristocratic ancestry, like your name !"

"You spoke yesterday," said Mr. Courtenay, " about putting up some one against Marchmont in the nomination for Congress. Why not try my friend Burns? He votes your straight ticket."

" Is that so?" said Mr. Woodbury. " Is he posted; can he talk?"

" He can talk with the best of them. I believe he could travel over this Congressional district and win more friends than any other man in it."

" Personal friends; yes, I have no doubt of it. He is prepossessing; I like his address. But political friends, influential friends, are what one needs."

" Yes, I know," said Mr. Courtenay. " Still, I think it might be done; we have some time to work in. Of course, one of the chief things to be done will be to get the people acquainted with him; he is not known."

"Oh, damn it, that's not worth a continental !" said Mr. Woodbury. " When we speak of the people we mean the party, and the party will carry him through safe enough, if by hook or crook we can get his name on the ticket. You get him the nomination in your county convention next spring, and I'll do what I can for him here. I have some little influence in N—— City, too. I don't mind telling you that I entertain a personal spite against Marchmont, and would rather enjoy defeating him."

Mr. Courtenay reflected that he would not explain this latter circumstance to his friend. Mr. Burns was of such a peculiar and fastidious disposition that he would not enjoy (to say the least) taking advantage of any sinister motives on the part of his helpers. He would have all things open and above-board.

"Have you and Mr. Burns talked it up?" asked Mr. Woodbury.

"No," said Mr. Courtenay. "And really, I can't say he would accept the nomination if it were offered to him. It was my own idea."

Mr. Woodbury laughed and said he thought it would be well, before taking any other steps, to find out. He reached for the cigars and passed them again to his companion.

"My father," said he, "was an Episcopal bishop of the diocese of Maryland, as you may perhaps have heard. He never smoked, but I have some pleasant recollections of him connected with my early experience with the weed. His study opened on a wide, grassy lawn, where I used to stroll in the summer evenings, during vacation, smoking my cigar. Often and often he would come to the window, pen in hand,—I can see his tall form yet, a little stooped at the shoulders, and his benign face with its border of thin, white hair blown about by the wind,—and call to me. And, when I presented myself before him, cigar respectfully removed, but knowing very well what would follow, he would say, 'Thomas, my son, you know that I have always opposed your smoking, and that I regard it as a very pernicious and entirely unnecessary practice; but, if you must smoke,—mind, I say if you *must* smoke,—come in here where I can enjoy the odor of your cigar! So, then, I would sit in his easy-chair, puffing away quite as much for his pleasure as my own, while he wrote at his desk. I never knew a man who had a finer taste in the matter of *smoke*, and yet I don't think he ever put a cigar in his mouth."

"Your father is dead, is he not?" asked Mr. Courtenay.

"Oh, yes. He died about the time I was married. I was married in Baltimore. My wife was staying there with her grandmother when I became acquainted with her."

"You are not a member of the Episcopal Church?" asked Mr. Courtenay.

"No, nor of any other," said Mr. Woodbury. "I well remember how, when I went to college, I cut loose from church restraints and declared myself an independent thinker. My father, hearing of my heresy, came up to have a talk with me; the only time he ever visited Harvard; perhaps you remember?"

"Yes, I do," said Mr. Courtenay. "I remember thinking, as he sat beside President K——, looking around upon us with his mild, benevolent eyes, that he was the most beautiful old man I had ever seen! You don't resemble him, Woodbury."

"No," said Mr. Woodbury, "I am like my mother; she was half Spanish. Well, when he came to see me, I told him frankly—we were always open as the day with him, we children—that up to my twentieth year I had implicitly and obediently, and I thought blindly, followed him, and that then I had begun to see that it was time for me to stop and think; and the result was I had sought out a path for myself. 'In which,' said he, 'it seems you have been going at a pretty good jog! Well, my son, I am glad to find that you have a head of your own, and a disposition to investigate and to push forward. But don't you think it is about time for you to stop and think again?' That was all; he was never coercive even in things which he considered of vital importance to us after we were able to reason. Well, I did stop and think, but I never could bring myself into harmony with my father's beloved creed. After a time I don't think it troubled him any. He came to say, ' As you will, Thomas; I see that it is no idle and lawless breaking away from a righteous restraint, but a *growing out of it*, if I may so speak. You have reasoned and arrived at convictions; which is the right of every man. I do not hold you to be an outlaw like one who tramples down the walls of his church and scoffs at even the soul of religion.'"

They had some more conversation relating to "old times," in which Mr. Woodbury was the chief talker; and then came back to politics again, and discussed Mr. Burns's possible chances. After which they spoke of the impending lawsuit, in which Mr. Woodbury was able to post his friend to a considerable extent, as well as to enlighten him respecting public sentiment and the peculiarities of the several parties involved.

In the mean time Mr. Burns and Mrs. Woodbury, after conversing in a lively way upon various topics, pleasant to both,—birds, flowers, books, music,—drifted back to Crawford Academy again; each being anxious to know what was in the other's mind concerning Wilma Lynne, but neither liking to mention her name. Mrs. Woodbury had all a woman's curiosity to learn what had been the causes of separation between the two who had loved each other so tenderly; and Mr. Burns had all a man's anxiety to find out what had befallen the woman whom he had treated cruelly, however inevitable had been his course of action.

"Did you know Miss Belmont?" Mrs. Woodbury asked.

"I knew of her," said Mr. Burns. "She was a remarkable woman, I suppose."

"Oh, a beautiful woman! One of the loveliest characters I have ever known. And do you know, Mr. Burns," said Mrs. Woodbury, lowering her voice to its most impressive key (Mrs. Woodbury was fond of thrilling narrative), "that she was mortally wounded by the explosion of a shell at Gettysburg, where she was taking care of some disabled and dying soldiers."

"Did *she* quit the academy and go into the hospitals?" asked Mr. Burns.

"Oh, yes; and the curious part of it was this: We girls used to believe, though we scarcely whispered it to each other, that Miss Belmont had a strong, secret affection for Professor Ingraham. Not an impure affection; but a kind of grand, reverential love. It used to speak out in her sweet, patient eyes, sometimes; but I think she would have died at the stake rather than give any other evidence of it. Well, when she lay dying, in a large building that had been turned into a temporary hospital, it happened that Mr. Ingraham, who was a colonel then, was brought in, faint and bleeding. Some one remarked, in his hearing, that Miss Belmont was about breathing her last. He sprang up from the couch where he lay, and asked 'Who is that?' They told him 'A nurse; Miss Belmont.' 'Good God!' said he; 'can it be Lucile?' and rushed into the little chamber where she lay, and called her name. The nurse, who stood at the foot of the bed watching her, and who told me the story, said she had thought a moment before that Miss Belmont was dead. Her forehead was clammy, her eyelids drooped, and her form was rigid and cold. But at the sound of his voice her eyes opened instantly, and shone with ineffable light. 'I never before,' said the nurse, 'saw a soul so stand out, as it were, upon a human face.'"

When Mrs. Woodbury finished the story she sat for a minute or two, crying silently; the war had given her many a wound that had not yet stopped bleeding. Mr. Burns got up and walked back and forth across the room; presently he stopped and asked,—

"Mrs. Woodbury, can you tell me where Miss Lynne is now?"

Mrs. Woodbury brushed away her tears with her hands, and looked up with a little hardening of expression. She did not wish to feel kindly toward this man, whom she believed had wrecked her friend's happiness; but somehow, against her will, he had greatly won her tenderness, with his gentle ways, his half-melancholy face, and appealing, earnest, sympathetic eyes. It was not possible to blame him harshly.

"No," she said; "I don't know where she is. The last I heard of her—or from her—she was on the point of going to New York among her father's relatives. They were wealthy, aristocratic people, I believe. You knew, I suppose, that her family was entirely broken up?"

"No," said Mr. Burns.

"You don't tell me!" Again Mrs. Woodbury's impressive manner came into requisition. "Why, her mother and her little sister both died of diphtheria! You know how prevalent it was at one time; and her brother was killed in some battle, I forget where. Of all the lives I have ever known, it seems to me, Mr. Burns, that Wilma Lynne's has been the most cruelly shorn. She founded herself upon her friends; her whole tender nature was rooted in them. And see how they have dropped away from her! I don't know; I think there was enough in her to get above it all; if so, she is a grand woman to-day."

Mr. Burns was deeply stirred, and felt—true to his mercurial nature—an intense impulse to go and find Wilma Lynne, to push aside space and whatever other obstructions divided them, and meet her face to face, heart to heart, again. Of course it was impractical, as many of his impulses were; but it compelled him, for the moment, to strong energy of action. He asked Mrs. Woodbury to excuse him, and put on his hat and went out for a rushing, headlong walk that was one of the habits of his younger days. When he came back, a little exhausted in body and his recollection soothed, the other gentlemen were coming out of the library and said it was time to go down to the court-house.

Their case came on that morning, and lasted through the week, creating intense excitement. There were a multitude of witnesses, and the attorneys were all shrewd and wide-awake, feeling that their own interests in many ways, besides the interests of the parties implicated, depended on the issue.

The day upon which Parke Marchmont arose to plead, the court-room was crowded with an alert, expectant audience. There is something more vitally interesting in the eloquence of the bar than in that of pulpit, stage, or rostrum, because it is concentrated upon a particular case in hand. There is something tangible for it to fasten itself upon. Something depends upon it,—waiting for a public decision that will strongly affect individuals. And say what we will about the fascinations of abstract things when we have risen up so as to grasp them, there is a humanity in us all that makes us pause and look on with keen attention when our fellow-beings are struggling. Mr. Marchmont, to begin with, was very prepossessing in his appearance and manners. He had pleasant, light-blue eyes, blonde hair, and a well-developed figure, such as a certain class of complacent men attain to at forty. His personality was strong, bland, persuasive. He pleaded well; he brought out the claims of his side in the clearest light, and threw those of the other into obscurity. It began to seem absurd, in the most candid minds, that the other side should have set up any pretensions. He sat down, when he had concluded his lengthy and somewhat flowery argument, amid thundering applause, and Mr. Courtenay, who was his especially recognized opponent (Mr. Burns had chiefly conducted the examination and cross-examination of witnesses), arose to follow him. At the first sound of his marvellous voice, so powerful and so thrilling in its rare modulation, not falling upon the ear simply but striking deep into the emotions that are susceptible to the finest things in sight and sound and feeling, the people in the farthest corners of the room raised themselves upon tip-toe to get sight of him. He had an intense personal magnetism which, combined with great mastery of language, his comprehension of men, and his profound knowledge of law, made him the most formidable opponent Parke Marchmont had ever contended against. A few human beings can raise and sway the emotions like the swelling of the sea, and we cannot define the subtle influence that makes the blood curdle, and the hair rise, and the nerves quiver, and the muscles grow tense. Mr. Courtenay had this power, and upon this great occasion it was fully called out.

Mr. Woodbury had the satisfaction of confirming to his wife what he had often affirmed of his admired friend and school-fellow. "I always said," he remarked, "that the force of tremendous circumstances would send him up like a sky-rocket."

"But will he burn out as quickly?" asked Mrs. Woodbury, laughing.

"Oh, yes!" with a shrug. "He'll be the same cold, reserved fellow to-morrow that he was yesterday."

No one in the court-room was more profoundly stirred than Mr. Burns. He felt a strong, new impulse of enthusiastic and affectionate pride in his friend.

Before Mr. Courtenay had taken his seat it was felt, universally, that his cause had triumphed. When he came down people began crowding forward for a nearer view and a hand-shake. But, though he enjoyed a victory and liked the breath of incense when it floated up to him from afar, he hated being lionized and fawned upon. So he had quietly stepped out, and, linking his arm in Mr. Burns's (there was no other man living with whom he would have linked arms), walked homeward. When they reached Mr. Woodbury's gate, Mr. Burns laid his hand upon the latch and paused a moment and said, with feeling,—

"You made a grand plea, Burr, the grandest I ever heard!"

"It annoyed me that there were so damned many women in court," said Burr, and Mr. Burns opened the gate and passed on.

The day following, on the drive homeward, after a silence not unusual between the two friends, Mr. Courtenay remarked, "Woodbury thinks you might stand a chance to get the nomination for Congress next spring."

"I!" said Mr. Burns, to whom the remark had a singular abruptness, the idea it carried having never occurred to him as among the possibilities of his career; though doubtless it had floated through his dreams years ago, as in the case of most American youths.

"Yes," said Mr. Courtenay. "Marchmont isn't very popular, and his defeat yesterday will go against him and in your favor. People like to vote for the best man. You'll have to advertise yourself a little."

"A good deal, I should say," said Mr. Burns, incredulously. But Mr. Courtenay's matter-of-fact way of putting the question began already to inspire him with a remote hope, against which he immediately began to argue by way of clearing up the ground.

"What likelihood is there of my getting the nomination?" said he. "There will be a candidate from every county in the district; and our county doesn't take the lead, even supposing I received the nomination at our convention."

"There will be no trouble about that," said Mr. Courtenay. "And I am convinced you have made a point at Hammond Springs."

"I think it is you who made the point at Hammond Springs," retorted Mr. Burns.

"No matter, it will be known at N—— City as the High-Water-Mark lawyers; and N—— City is the stronghold of your party."

"And the home of the Marchmonts," said Mr. Burns.

"You must recollect," said Mr. Courtenay, "that a man is not always a prophet in his own land. Woodbury thinks there will be nothing to contend against there except a mere local pride ; and he assures me that the people of that thriving town are by no means narrow. They are at least big enough to embrace the whole district and take the best man in it."

"Then I would recommend you to their consideration," said Mr. Burns.

"No," Mr. Courtenay returned. "I was referring to your party. There are none of us broad enough to go beyond party lines. We chain a candidate to our platform as we chain a dog in the back yard. I couldn't be your candidate because you couldn't bring me near enough to get the shackles on my feet."

CHAPTER XXXVIII.

A FEW days after the young men's return from Hammond Springs, an official-looking package was brought into the office by the errand-boy, who had been despatched for the mail, which proved to be from the contractors of a railroad that had been several times surveyed through the country, setting forth a proposition, on their part, to go on and construct the road, and asking aid ; especially soliciting the influence of these very influential attorneys. Mr. Burns came up at once to a high pitch of enthusiasm, and spent several days about town talking up the subject with the prominent men of the place. When in the office, too, he thought and spoke of nothing else, and was a good deal chafed by his friend's non-excitability, as often happened.

"They want money and right of way," he was saying, one evening argumentatively.

"Of course," interrupted Mr. Courtenay, to whom that fact was so clear that it seemed useless to speak of it.

"Well, the question is, how are they to get it? They

must get it *through us.* I was talking with Deacon Clyde to-day."

" And what does the deacon think ?" said Mr. Courtenay, in a tone implying a rather contemptuous regard for the deacon's opinion, whatever it might be.

" He says," returned Mr. Burns, " that it will depend greatly upon you and me whether we get a road or not."

" He flatters us."

" No, it has got to be talked into the people, and we must do the talking."

A few days later, the president of the company, who was an old college friend of Mr. Courtenay's, and who had heard of him through Mr. Woodbury, took a trip up the line and came to see him. A hearty, cordial, corpulent man, to whom Mr. Burns gave his hand with great warmth.

All Mr. Courtenay's school friends had the same high opinion of his intellectual power.

" You are just the man I want, Courtenay," said the president. " I can't talk; never could, except in a blunt, matter-of-fact way. The people, you see, need stirring up; and it takes more diplomacy of eloquence to touch men's pockets than their consciences. They have settled down here on these prairies and have learned to do without many conveniences. They do all their own work, they haul all their grain off to other markets, and they carefully save their dollars. They don't like to pay out money at a venture, and without immediate returns, for a railroad. They are cautious, skeptical, doubtful. Well, you see, their faith must be educated. And you, my friend," laying his hand upon Mr. Courtenay's shoulder, and not perceiving that gentleman's distaste for the flattering insinuation, " must be the educator."

" I think," said Mr. Courtenay, with a slight shrug, at which the hand was removed, " that I must turn you over to Mr. Burns, who greatly transcends me in the kind of ability you require for the furtherance of your project."

A little cooled but not discouraged, the president leaned back in his chair and gave Mr. Burns an examining look with his keen, bright eyes, that seemed to be aided in any

investigation they might make by a high, prominent, per-
tinacious, Roman nose.   The result appeared to be satisfactory.   Mr. Burns and Mr. Griggs (the president) were
soon sailing along on the top wave of railroad enthusiasm.
They took Nobby and drove out into the country, and
paid some flattering attention to a few of the wealthiest
farmers.   They examined the river for bridging and selected a site for the depot, and discussed the whole subject
in all its bearings.   It was a kind of work Mr. Burns particularly delighted in,—it was for the public good.   It is
true, that in his old aspirations toward becoming a benefac-
tor of the human race, he had never thought of railroads.
But who of us go straight to our aim?   We must allow
something for the rush and pressure of circumstances, as the
ocean currents allow for the rotation of the earth.   Where
so many and such great forces are at work outside of us,
we must expect to swerve and bend a little.

Before Mr. Griggs went away he said, confidentially,
" Can't you get Courtenay to work for us?"

" Oh, yes," said Mr. Burns.   " He is as much interested as we are, and will get up and shake his mane, by
and by, but we must wait for him a little."

Before spring was well advanced the railroad excitement
became intense.   There were meetings in town-halls all
over the county, and bonfires in the streets, and warm
discussions upon every hand.   The High-Water-Mark
attorneys were the most indefatigable workers on the line.
After speaking in all the towns and villages, they began
canvassing townships and school-districts, and even visited
farmers in their homes.

Here Mr. Burns had a decided advantage over his
friend.   Familiarity with the people was not to Mr.
Courtenay's taste,—was not in his nature.   His lofty and
polished bearing was extremely out of place in farm
kitchens.   Whereas Mr. Burns could lend a helping hand
to lift a pail of water or put a stick of wood in the stove
for any woman, young or old, pretty or homely, Mr.
Courtenay stood aloof and embarrassed the blushing
farmers' daughters with his admiring glances and grand
manners.   Whether intentional or not, Mr. Courtenay
had a way that inspired people with awe and kept them

N*

at a distance. He could charm and carry away an audience and play upon their emotions as upon a harmonious, many-stringed instrument, but he could not come down and meet his fellow-beings on the broad level of friendly, social intercourse. People applauded him, admired him enthusiastically, were proud of an opportunity to hear him speak, and repeated over and over again in private what he said in public, especially his sharp sarcasms and witticisms. But few approached him. Mr. Burns, on the contrary (except when his mood was bitter or melancholy), was affable, kind, courteous, easy of access. Nobody could doubt his sincerity who looked into his eyes, or whose hand he grasped. He made many friends. Mr. Courtenay intimated to him once, slyly, that he was killing two birds with one stone, his prospects for Congress were brightening. But he flushed angrily and denied any conscious effort in the direction of bettering his chances.

But Mr. Woodbury and other of his friends—and the enemies of the Marchmonts—had not been idle; and his name was beginning to be wafted about in political circles. Some talked confidently and others pooh-poohed. What! a stranger, young, unknown? But then he was a soldier, and had given four years' arduous service to his country; and that fact had weight in those days. In subsequent political gatherings a point was made of this: that whereas Mr. Marchmont had sat in his office gathering rich harvests of gold, his opponent had toiled through wearisome marches, through sickness and battle and danger.

Mr. Courtenay was induced to make one grand, rallying speech for his friend at Hammond Springs. After touching upon the war, and his candidate's faithful service, he said: "But, gentlemen, it is not because Charles Burns was a soldier, brave and generous to the laying of his life upon his country's altar, that I solicit your votes in his behalf. These are not the necessary qualifications for the office to which he aspires. The arduous toils and dangers of war, the rude camp-life would hardly fit a man for a seat among the polished legislators of the nation; but, gentlemen, when Mr. Burns laid down his books and took up the sword the great university of M—— could not boast a more accomplished scholar. The war has been three years ended. Mr. Burns came back wounded, ' tired' (as we used to sing) ' of the war on the old camp-ground,' and gave himself, with renewed zeal, to his books, to his profession, and to a careful study of the times; and to-day," Mr. Courtenay took a step down toward his audience and put his whole soul into the conclusion of his sentence, making an indescribable gesture toward his friend, thrilling all hearts and turning all eyes in one direction, "I would match this *soldier* against any gentleman who has never been deprived of his books and his easy-chair, or had his mind distracted with thoughts of his bleeding country for a single night, in knowledge of law, statesmanship, and acquaintance with all that pertains to government and the affairs of nations."

When the general convention met at N—— City, fate— or the chances of politics—decided in Mr. Burns's favor, and he became the regular candidate of his party, much to his surprise. He could hardly believe it possible that he was really on the road to Congress, with a strong probability of reaching that goal. Things began to take on a rosy hue again ; a little while ago the whole world had seemed faded, and he not thirty yet. Perhaps he had hardly tasted life ; perhaps the richest and best experience of living was yet to come. All that he had gone through seemed a long way off. Of course that was the spring, the seed-time ; and in these last, discontented, apparently idle years, it might be that the seeds were swelling, sprouting, taking root. And now the sun shone, the birds sang, and the green leaves would begin to shoot up.

For the space of a week the opposing wing of the party made no sign, and it was thought that all feeling had died away ; but, at the end of that time, Mr. Marchmont came out, with a flourish of trumpets, as the people's candidate, and the struggle must all be repeated on a larger scale.

Mr. Burns had an instantaneous presentiment, when the news reached him, that it was all over with him. He said as much to Mr. Courtenay, who laughed at the idea and felt his own combativeness rising on behalf of his friend.

"I have a feeling," said Mr. Burns, "that all these

things have transpired once before, sometime in the dim, past ages, and that they ended in defeat."

"You are too visionary," said Mr. Courtenay; and aroused himself and went up to Hammond Springs and made the afore-mentioned speech.

CHAPTER XXXIX.

SUMMER came on apace, reached its climax of heat, dust, listlessness, and prostration, and began to wane. One day a party of individuals—ladies and gentlemen— alighted from a covered conveyance in front of the hotel. One of the gentlemen, throwing the lines to Fred, held a short consultation with the landlord, who had come out on the steps; the result of which was that they all proceeded into the house and up-stairs to the parlor.

"One, two, three, four, five,—how many are there, and who can they be?" said Mr. Burns. He and Mr. Courtenay were just going down to supper. Two of the gentlemen, of middle age nearly, had the air of school-masters, and several of the ladies had a corresponding air. There were two, however, that were probably school-girls; young, pretty, and deep in flirtation with two daintily-moustached young gentlemen, who waited upon them with scrupulous gallantry. Besides all these there were still two other ladies, who, by some indistinguishable line, seemed to be divided from the others, and, you would say, did not belong to the party. Not very young, one was perhaps twenty-five, though slender and girlish-looking, and the other ten or a dozen years older. There was something in their dress and carriage that was not exactly *western*,—they were easy, graceful, evidently cultivated. This much the attorneys, coming in after them and passing on into the office, took note of though they did not see their faces. The landlord bustled out into the kitchen to give orders about the supper and then came back.

"Who air they, an' where air they from?" asked a

dry-goods' clerk, who was vigorously brushing his hair that he had previously made soaking wet at the wash-stand.

" A party o' pleasure-seekers from N—— City; mostly school-ma'ams, I take it," said the landlord. " Except two that they picked up on the way. The stage broke down between here and Winchester, and the two lady passengers got in with these folks and came on."

" Pleasure-seekers, and come here !" laughed the clerk.

" An' why not ?" demanded the landlord, who thought it politic to uphold the reputation of the village as a pleas-ure-resort. " There ain't another town within a hundred miles that's as neatly set down in the bend of a river as this town is ; and as for the river itself, there's no purtier stream on the globe. What with the falls, which is what people comes mostly to see ; and what with the water, as clear as crystal, showing every pebble in the river-bed, I'd like to know where you'd find a more temptin' spot ; and then at this season the maples look jest like so many gorgeous foliage plants."

" Well, it does seem nice, looking at it that way," ad-mitted the clerk ; " like a picture, as one may say ; but livin' right here we don't think much about them things. I expect it's about the same with the folks at Niagara Falls."

The last supper-bell rang, and they all went in and seated themselves in their accustomed places. The party of pleasure-seekers filed in through the hall-door and ranged themselves around the lower end of the long table which was always reserved for the travelling public. All excepting the girlish-looking lady, whose non-appearance was about the only thing the attorneys at the upper end of the table made a note of. Her companion, though middle-aged, was an exceedingly comely and interesting woman. She might not have been even pretty in her youth, having the palest of yellow hair, with eyes and complexion to match. But she was plump and fair, and her cheeks were still rounded, and her face was educated and refined into a beauty of expression very agreeable to see. She was full of a quiet strength and energy that compelled great faith in her capability. She was one whose presence in time of danger would inspire courage, and on whose judgment upon a wide range of subjects one might safely rely. You would hardly limit her; you would expect her to be almost infinite in resources. When she had finished her supper, she said to the girl who waited upon her, "You may bring me a cup of tea, if you please, to carry up-stairs to Miss Stuvysant."

"Is your friend no better, madam?" asked one of the professors.

"No; her head aches badly. She is not very strong."

"She doesn't look strong," said one of the lady professors, sympathetically.

"Stuvysant, Stuvysant! where have I heard that name before?" said Mr. Burns, as they stepped off the hotel porch and went back to the office.

"I think you have seen it in the newspapers," said Mr. Courtenay. "There is a lady reader of that name."

"Do you suppose this is the same?" Mr. Burns asked.

"It may be. Nothing more likely than that she should be travelling across country in a stage, seeing we are limited in the matter of railroads."

"Which we shall not be long, thank heaven!" said Mr. Burns, and they forthwith drifted away on that engaging topic.

Work had already begun all along the line, and before another year the cars would be steaming through High-Water-Mark.

When Miss Stuvysant's friend carried her cup of tea up-stairs, she found her lying across the bed in the little chamber that had been assigned them. She sat up directly and asked, "Why, is your supper over already, Miss Cleveland?" lifting up a face that must be striking to any beholder; not for any distinctive feature,—though the features were all fine: large brown eyes, soft hair, a smooth, dusky skin, a delicate finish,—but for a deep meaning underlying it,—a strong, beautiful soul shining through it. It seemed feverish just now, there being an unnatural, unusual glow in eye and cheek.

Miss Cleveland sat down on the edge of the bed and carefully concealed the anxiety she began to feel as she scrutinized the flushed face.

" Yes, I have finished my supper," she said, " and have brought you some tea. Is your head better?"

" My head? Oh, yes, my head is better. It doesn't ache at all now. But say, listen ! can you hear my heart beat? It throbs so that it moves my whole body. See ! I can't hold my hand still."

" My dear," said Miss Cleveland, " what is the matter?"

Miss Stuvysant laughed, and got up and walked about rapidly.

" The matter? Why, I have heard some news ! and it seems as if my heart will leap right out of my mouth. Did you ever have that sensation?"

She stopped and held her two hands clasped over her heart ; her face was inexpressibly radiant. She unclasped her hands and put one finger upon her wrist.

"I never thought," she exclaimed, "that my pulse would beat like that again !"

She seated herself beside Miss Cleveland, and twined her arms around her.

" Did you ever think there was a secret about me? Well, all these years that you and I, my best of cousins, have been together—am I not an ungrateful creature ?— I have had a secret. Yet not so much a secret, after all, as a motive ; a deep-seated, unswerving motive. Would you think it ?"

"I should think, my darling," said Miss Cleveland, with the utmost tenderness and admiration, "that you had all your life been actuated by something grand and noble and true to make you what you are !"

" Do you indeed think so?" said Miss Stuvysant, tears shining on her eyelashes and in her eyes as she lifted them up. " My egotism and my great reliance upon you make me think that you do. Is it not sweet to accomplish in a little measure what you have earnestly striven to do ? Well, I *have* been actuated by something grand and noble and true,—by a life, by a beautiful life. I have tried to make mine what that was, and what it would come to be, if it continued on this earth, in the distant time when both it and mine should ripen, with silver hairs, for eternity. Oh, my friend, I have lived with one strong purpose and effort to make my life run parallel with that life !"

"You said you had heard some news," said Miss Cleveland, who had a misgiving that her friend's mind was wandering.

"Yes," said Miss Stuvysant, without any explanation. "But I do not know that I have any cause to feel happier for it; yet I do feel happier. Say! would you dare to let yourself enjoy a blissful dream when you *knew* it was but a dream?"

"I am afraid," said Miss Cleveland, "that we all please ourselves with dreams more or less."

Miss Stuvysant got off the bed and went over to the window looking down into the street. Miss Cleveland came and stood beside her.

"Some people assert this," she said,—"that our joys and our griefs are equal."

"Yes," said Miss Cleveland; "if a pendulum swings back, it must swing forward again just as far. I suppose it is so with us."

"If we are evenly balanced," said Miss Stuvysant, looking up; "not otherwise, I think. Some of us are so unhappily constituted that if we swing back we can never get forward again. But there is," she added, thoughtfully, "a grand principle in that pendulum movement. Not many of us would shrink from going down into the depths if we could rise correspondingly on the heights."

Just then Mr. Burns and Mr. Courtenay stepped out of the hall-door directly under the window, which was open, and Mr. Burns made the remark recorded above. Miss Stuvysant listened with an extraordinary brightness of cheek and eye, and exclaimed, "I wonder how they got hold of my name?"

"They probably heard me mention it at table," said Miss Cleveland; "I told the girl to give me some tea to bring up to you. I hope," she added uneasily, "that the stage will be along to-morrow; we have not got very comfortable quarters here."

"But do you know," said Miss Stuvysant, seating herself by the window, and folding her hands on the casement, "I have a fancy that I would like to stop here a little while! I might recover my truant health here, perhaps,

as well as in Denver City.   Look yonder! across the valley; and away over the prairie to the north, and at that
long line of woods circling away.   Is it not beautiful?
And, then," narrowing her gaze, "the village itself is
pretty.   There are a good many neat little cottages, and
there is the school-house!   I never see a school-house
without a thrill of interest.   There must be even more at-
tractions in the place than we can see from this window,"
she added, laughing, "to induce that party of excursionists to spend their holiday here.   They told me there was
a remarkable stream of water running through that body
of timber."

"I do not doubt it," said Miss Cleveland.   "These
Western streams are all beautiful."

"And do you object to stopping here a few days?"
Miss Stuvysant asked, looking up wistfully.

"My dear child! how can we possibly stop here longer
than is just necessary?" said Miss Cleveland, glancing
around the narrow room.

"Oh, not here, of course!" said Miss Stuvysant.
"But maybe we could get lodging somewhere in the
village."

"I hardly believe it.   Still we might.   I could ask the
landlord, I suppose."

"Do, pray!" said Miss Stuvysant.

Miss Cleveland arose at once, and went down-stairs.

The landlord, upon being consulted, said, "I know
of only one place where I think it likely you could git
board, an' that's at Deacon Clyde's.   They take boarders
up there sometimes, if they are the right sort; the deacon's folks are a little stuck up."

"Would you be so kind as to see them for me?" asked
Miss Cleveland.

"Yes; I can do that.   Did you want to go right
away?"

"We would like to go right away, if possible."

She went back up-stairs, and the obliging landlord
posted off to the deacon's, revolving in his mind the
possibility—or impossibility, almost—of entertaining so
many guests in case the deacon could not take these two
off his hands.   After a little family consultation, in which

both Evelyn and Maggie joined, it was decided that the ladies should come.

"It will be nice for a change, Evy," Maggie said. "We can give them the front chamber up-stairs; and of course they will keep to themselves a good deal. And, besides," she added, aside, "he says they are *real ladies,* and I suppose they will be very pleasant company."

Evelyn did not particularly favor the plan, but gave up, as she always did when there was not much at stake, to Maggie.

"I'll have Fred bring 'em up right away," said the landlord. "We're purty full at our house. The stage 'll be along some time to-night, I suppose, and fetch their trunks."

So it was settled; and in less than an hour the two ladies, tired and travel-worn, were taking off their wrappings in the pretty front chamber at the deacon's. The windows, facing the west, commanded a view of the river some rods distant,—or of the strip of timber through which it ran,—and a long line of low, wooded hills, stretching away, beautiful in autumn-tints.

"Isn't this restful?" said Miss Stuvysant, dropping into a low rocking-chair in front of a small wood-stove with isinglass windows through which the fire-light shone out cheerful and red. And then added, laughingly, "I half believe in special providences."

Miss Cleveland, folding up her shawl and putting it away, smiled and shook her head.

"Special providences, my dear, come to those who are looking for them. One might wander along the sea-beach all day without finding a single pretty shell, unless he had eyes for shells."

The following morning was perfect as an Indian summer morning; quiet and still, with a mellow, dreamy, hazy atmosphere, and the sun shining through with agreeable warmth and veiled brightness. Mr. Burns stood in the office door, and felt like a fledgling anxious to quit its nest. The world seemed so broad and inviting outside; the day was so beautiful, the weather so fine, and the air so soft; while everything was particularly dull, dusty, and stupid inside. It was too warm for a fire, and the stove, unblacked and rusty, with a whitish, burnt-out look, and the dead ashes in the grate, was a saddening spectacle.

"Burr," said Mr. Burns, "we haven't been to the river for a month; suppose we take a stroll down that way this morning."

Mr. Courtenay replied with a smile that showed itself in the corners of his eyes, "I am a little suspicious of your motives; that party of school-ma'ams intend to spend the day in the woods and along the river, do they not?—gathering pebbles and snail-shells. I think I heard some such plan discussed among them yesterday evening."

"Upon my honor," said Mr. Burns, with unnecessary emphasis, "I did not think of them. However, there is a mile or two of river circling around the village; we could probably keep out of their way."

"Oh, yes," said Mr. Courtenay, "and I don't know that I object, even, to stumbling in their way; we would doubtless be counted in with the natural features of the landscape."

"Or classed among the animals indigenous to the climate," laughed Mr. Burns. "Though most other animals seek cover at the approach of strangers."

The wind was a little chilly, for all that the sun shone, as they started off; having come up in the last ten minutes, as prairie winds will do. Down in the woods it was much warmer; more hazy and more dreamy. One might easily look at the sun by half shutting his eyes and glimmering at it through his eyelashes. Dead leaves lay thickly on the ground unstirred by the wind. Dry twigs snapped under foot and birds twittered here and there. Rabbits darted into thickets, and squirrels skipped about upon limbs high over head, or disappeared mysteriously in holes and hollow trunks of trees. It was as if nature had dropped into her easy-chair and was taking a nap before bringing out her war-forces for the winter campaign.

The two attorneys sauntered along down the white, sandy road and took a seat upon a log in a sheltered, cozy spot on the river bank. Mr. Courtenay lighted a cigar, and Mr. Burns inhaled its fragrance with a sense of enjoyment. The river rolled industriously along at their feet with a pretty, gurgling sound ; and innumerable small fishes basking in the sun wriggled their small bodies in the shallow water that lapped the white sand at its edge. After a short, dreamy time, in which present surroundings drifted away like a ship at sea, they heard voices approaching.

"That party of school-ma'ams," said Mr. Burns, with a rueful glance back over his shoulder.

"Only two of them, though," he added, "and by the way they are the two who are not school-ma'ams,—Miss Stuvysant and her *chaperon*. I take it she is her chaperon."

Miss Stuvysant had an open book in her hand ; as they came slowly on she closed it, dropped a fine tissue veil over her face, and they turned and walked down the river bank.

"I wish I could see that woman's face," said Mr. Burns, his eyes following them. "She diffuses a magnetic influence through the atmosphere that touches me even here."

"You are very susceptible," said Mr. Courtenay.

"Yonder," exclaimed Mr. Burns, looking back again, "come the excursionists! Shall we move on, or sit here, 'so still among the solitudes that the shy creatures of the woods will think us stumps?'"

"I think it would be as well, seeing they are right upon us," said Mr. Courtenay, "to sit still. It would be undignified to run away."

"Oh, yonder's a boat, yonder's a boat!" exclaimed one of the young ladies whom they called "Kitty."

"But don't you see that it's chained?" called the other one after her, for she had skipped away like a frolicsome young animal and was half-way down the bank.

"I believe I have a key that fits that lock," said Mr. Courtenay, drawing a bunch of keys from his pocket. "It is Fred's boat; we used it one Sunday evening, if you remember."

"Better take the responsibility of loaning it an hour or two," said Mr. Burns. "It places a young fellow in an awkward position not to be able to gratify a lady's wishes under such circumstances."

The "young fellows" had both come up and stood contemplating the chained creature as it rocked to and fro in the shallow water, with an air of idle powerlessness, hands in their trowsers pockets.

"If we knew who owned it," said one of them, giving it a little kick with the toe of his patent-leather boot.

Mr. Courtenay got up and stepped leisurely forward.

"Here is a key, gentlemen, that I think will answer; the boat belongs to one of the men up at the hotel. I don't suppose there would be any objection to your using it."

The young men thanked him and proceeded to unfasten the boat. The young ladies looked up shy and blushing. Mr. Burns arose and, joined his friend, and they strolled away down the river. With a good many little screams and ejaculations the young ladies were helped into the tiny vessel, and the young men shoved it off and sprang in after them. As for the professors and lady teachers, who were evidently the pebble and snail-shell division of the party, they proceeded farther up the bank and went stooping about collecting geological specimens.

"Now wouldn't I thmile," said one of the young gentlemen, who lisped, "if we'd upthet?"

"Oh, my goodness! what should we do?" exclaimed the girls.

"Really and truly, Herbert, what would you do?" asked Kitty, looking up engagingly into the face of the gentleman who lisped.

"I?" said he, smiling down at her. "I think I should thwim out and call for help."

"Oh, you ungallant creature," said Kitty, and turned away with a pout.

Meantime the two ladies who were not school-ma'ams walked down to the falls and stood watching the water splash and toss for a while, and then disappeared in the woods. Discovering which, Mr. Burns lost interest in the day, the river, the stroll, and the pleasure-seekers, and proposed going back home. Towards evening the two ladies walked down to the hotel, past the law-office, to

see about their trunks, which had not been sent up yet.
Mr. Burns standing idly in the doorway stepped back as
they came up, and Mr. Courtenay glancing from the window said, " Ah, the gray lady again !"

" What a finely-poised figure she has !" said Mr. Burns.
" Did you observe it ?"

Mr. Courtenay said yes, he had observed it.

" I am quite sure she is the reader whose name we have
seen in the papers. Her whole person, her attitudes
and movements, are full of language and expression. I
have a strange sort of fancy that she has *felt* the same
things that I have felt myself. It seems to me that there
hangs about her the atmosphere of a Byron, a Tennyson,
a Hawthorne, a Goethe. The rhythm of her motion is
as familiar to me as an old melody."

" You are disposed to be sentimental," said Mr. Courtenay. " Hadn't you better write a little more poetry ?"

" But why," said Mr. Burns, " cannot one get an
' air' from the people he lives with and who attune and
educate his soul even though they might be dead ages
ago ?"

Mr. Courtenay said the subject was one he had not considered ; and that in any case it lay too deep in meta-
physics for his practical mind to fathom.

In the evening, after the deacon's early tea, the visitors
were invited into the parlor. Subsequently, when the
lamps were lighted, Miss Cleveland excused herself and
went up-stairs to write a letter to a long-neglected friend.
After detailing the events of the journey westward, which,
as has appeared, had been undertaken for the benefit of
her friend's health, she said : " And now we are settled
down here in this little village of High-Water-Mark for
—I cannot say how long.

" As you know, it matters little to me ; I am an individualized atom, not adhering to any particular spot. I have
my late magazines, leaves still uncut, a few choice books,
some needlework, my pen, and—Miss Stuvysant. If I
had not the latter, my conscience would prick me sorely,
sometimes, with the hint that I am leading a very idle
existence. But I am comforted with the reflection that I
am needful to her. I am not one of those over-righteous

souls who are afraid to accept ease and rest when they come right in the way. If my Good Shepherd leads me through green pastures and beside still waters, I am content to follow.''

(I am bound to say explanatorily of Miss Cleveland that when her path lay through stony places, through bitter trial and humiliation,—as it had done some ten or fifteen years before,—she did not shrink, but went bravely on and came out one of those glorified victors which we see, here and there, with invisible crowns on their brows.)

"I have told you," she went on, "so much about my dear Miss Stuvysant, and yet I am convinced you can never have a true conception of her until you have seen her for yourself. She is something more than a genius. She has the broadest mental and moral capacity of any one I ever met, and she is perfectly balanced.

"People are apt to be one-sided, you know; to grow only one way. Genius almost always shoots out in a certain direction like the tail of a comet. But Miss Stuvysant radiates on all sides. She is the finest interpreter of the deep and beautiful meanings of other minds, as shown in their works, that I have ever known.

"She might do something grand, herself. I tell her she might be a great writer, but she says the world has not digested the half that is written now ; that there are beautiful things in books that lie unnoticed, year after year, like a pile of goods upon a counter waiting to be shown. And she has the rarest tact and ability to show them. Did you ever think how useless and meaningless words are until a living soul is breathed into them ? Mere empty wineglasses. All that the mighty dead have given us are their thought-moulds ; and if we have understanding and inspiration to fill them we may live as greatly as they.''

Miss Cleveland was going on thus enthusiastically, warming with her theme, when the subject of it came quietly in and got her cloak and hat and passed out again. She looked up, a little surprised, but asked no questions, —she seldom put so much constraint upon her friend as to inquire into her actions and intentions,—and resumed her writing.

Miss Stuvysant wrapped her cloak around her outside

in the hall, and then went softly down-stairs and out of the house. Miss Clyde was playing as she passed the parlor-door. There was no moon, and, being a little cloudy, it was rather dark. She passed swiftly out the gate and down toward the village, the force of a strong determination speeding her on. Not a soul was upon the streets; it was, indeed, a very quiet little village, and all the stores and public places were already shut up, and half the people asleep in their beds. She crossed over, near the hotel, and came up on that side. A bright light shone out through the one window of the law-office. She stopped when she came near it, scarcely breathing, her small hands clasped tightly, and her heart thumping loudly in her bosom. Only one person was visible through the window,—Mr. Burns seated in an office-chair talking to his friend opposite. His hair was tossed back, and he was smiling and a little flushed, as though he were triumphing in a debate, and there was a good deal of his boyhood's beauty and grace upon him for the moment. Miss Stuvysant gazed with her intense soul in her eyes, and wrung her hands silently.

"Oh," she cried out in her heart, at last, "is it, is it possible, after all these dividing years and circumstances, that our two lives have come so close together again? So close that a few steps would bring us face to face! Oh, I knew it would come some time, at some ripe moment. I knew that I *must* see you once more, my Charley, else there is no labor and rest, no trial and compensation, no cross and crown; no even balance of anything in this world."

She stretched out her hands in the darkness, her heart yearning, and her eyes raining tears down her cheeks.

"My darling, my noble Charley, whose pure and grand ambition pointed out the way of life to me, and led me always as by an invisible hand, I have seen your face once more, and I thank God!"

Her head dropped forward upon her bosom, and for a single moment she knelt down upon the pavement, alone in the darkness, then sprang up and sped swiftly homeward. Miss Clyde was still playing, and at the window above still sat Miss Cleveland, bending her calm face over her writing-desk. Miss Stuvysant felt that she could not go in the house just yet. She sat down upon the door-step.

"My Charley, my Charley !" she murmured, with a tender smile on her lips, her eyelashes still wet ; "to think what a little space divides us ! And yet, and yet, oh ! why have I forgotten that it is not space *alone* that divides us, that ever divided us ! If only oceans and mountain-chains, years—ay, death itself, divided us, what sweetness there would still be in the separation ! But this eternal soul-estrangement, this echoless silence that lies between us ! My darling, I have tried to believe that my poor love for you would widen into sympathy with the Infinite Love, and that my great sorrow would unlock for me all sorrowing hearts, and teach me a broader charity and tenderer affection for others than I should ever have felt without it. Yet I did not limit the infinite in worshipping you. I expanded your noble nature to infinity."

She so lost herself in revery that it was some time before her thoughts again took shape, and when they did, the attitude of her mind had changed toward him so that she no longer felt herself to be in communion with him. "How strange," she said, "that now I am so near to him he seems a thousand miles farther away than before ! It is, because seeing him I realize how he has put me away out of his consciousness, out of his life. It flows on without me, unheeding me. I am dead to him ! How would he meet me ? But I shall not meet him ! With all the gathered fortitude of years I could not now undergo that. And yet it is the thing I have hoped for and prayed for, and promised to myself as a crowning reward. But I have seen his face, and is not that enough ? Yet how little, O God ! have I, indeed, this night reached the full realization of this hope upon which I have fed my strength all these long, long years ! And is there nothing beyond ? I have aimed at this, only this, and it has come. What now ?"

She might have sat the night through in the cold and darkness, and with the wind blowing drearily over her, if Miss Cleveland, having finished her letter, had not come down in some alarm to look for her. She had never before brought herself to face the absolute fact that the separation between herself and her lover had been indeed final and effectual.   She saw it now most clearly.

CHAPTER XL.

ELECTION-DAY was at hand, and political excitement had reached its highest pitch.   Mr. Burns's enthusiasm fired his veins like the old ambitions of his boyhood.   It is true that we go all along through life with about the same passions and hopes and impulses, except that they have different objects.   On the eve of election Mr. Courtenay said, "You have grown thin, Charley; this excitement has burned you out pretty fast."

"I know," said Mr. Burns; "I can't help it.   Whether I win or lose, I shall feel vastly relieved when the thing is well over."

"Well," said Mr. Courtenay, "seeing the climax is so near at hand, and you can do nothing more to help on your cause, don't you think you had better be letting yourself down a little so as to be able to meet a possible defeat?"

"I can't let myself down," returned Mr. Burns, impatiently, "until the whole business is over."

"In that case, I am afraid you will fall hard if the worst comes."

"Well, if I fail this time I'll no more of it.   One defeat is all I can stand."

"You show very little pluck, Charley," said Mr. Courtenay.   "Do you recollect the fable about the ant and the grain of corn?"

"Oh, for heaven's sake," said Mr. Burns, "don't bring up any fables!   That wretched insect might have accumulated a fortune, in smaller particles, if he had not stubbornly persisted in trying to carry such a stupendous load."

"He succeeded, though," said Mr. Courtenay.   "I would rather exhaust my life in one grand effort than drib it out in little things."

"And if you fail in your grand effort? I can picture nothing more melancholy than a life devoted to the pursuit of one thing,—giving up all else,—and failing in its accomplishment."

"I don't know why you should regard it as so melancholy," said Mr. Courtenay. "Lives are not so few or so significant upon this earth that the loss of one need be considered lamentable. The loss of one maggot in a cheese might be felt by its immediate neighbors in the way of giving them a little more room, but it would hardly be perceptible to our larger vision."

"What wretched comparisons you make," said Mr. Burns. "You strip man of all his dignity and importance."

"Well, perhaps the figure I used was not attractive," said Mr. Courtenay. "But I have a habit of speculating about how the great mass of human beings must look to some Higher Intelligence whose scope of vision is broad enough to take in the world's millions. I suspect it very closely resembles a nest of wriggling, struggling, quarrelsome vermin, trampling each other under foot and rejoicing in each other's downfall."

"I suppose you mean that as a hint at political contention?" said Mr. Burns.

"Oh, by no means! I meant it quite generally. It holds true in nearly all our relations with each other."

"But it is a fact," said Mr. Burns, "that there is hardly any sort of contest in which there is less praiseworthy emulation. If my election to Congress depended on my making myself worthy—more worthy than somebody else—of the office, I would give my heart and soul to the task. But nothing depends upon myself but skilful management of outside forces and strategic movements against the enemy. It is merely a cultivation, on a little higher plane, of the savage and cunning instincts of our nature. If the high places in the nation were to be won by hard labor and study, by great moral and intellectual manhood, I could push forward with all the forces in me, and feel that I, at least, had a worthy aim."

"You go in for Civil Service Reform, I take it," said Mr. Courtenay.

"I go in for something that calls for the best there is in the men who lead," said Mr. Burns, "and for the best men."

Mr. Courtenay had taken up off the desk two or three little county papers that had lain there a week unopened, and tore off the wrappers. Running his eye over them, he came upon this item in the "Winchester Independent," and, with a laugh, read it aloud for his friend's edification: "Our would-be congressman, Mr. Charles Burns, who waves his sword so gallantly and flaunts his lieutenant's commission in our faces (the only recommendations he shows, by the way), did, we understand, draw four years' soldier's pay and loiter in the rear of the army, in the hands of doctors and hospital nurses, for that length of time; a position, we have no doubt, more in accordance with the gentleman's fastidious taste and delicate constitution than beneficial to the country. A sword is well enough, but we would prefer having it drawn in battle to seeing it paraded on election-day."

"The scoundrel!" said Mr. Burns, red and white by turns with anger. "It is that brainless fop who blows the horn for country dances, damn him!"

Mr. Courtenay laughed. "My dear boy, he handles you gently to what some of your political friends have handled Marchmont. He appears to accuse you of cowardice; did not I, myself, bring pretty much the same charge against your opponent?"

"You did it with more decency," said Mr. Burns.

"You mean I ground my knife down to a finer edge. It probably cut deeper."

"What a detestable business it is," said Mr. Burns. "Run a man for office, and it is like starting up a deer and setting the hounds after it."

The momentous day dawned and faded; a busy, noisy, harrowing day. When the election returns came in—slowly, and balancing pretty evenly for a day or two, now this one ahead, and now that—they showed, at the last, a majority for Marchmont. Mr. Burns staggered a little under the shock, and looked white about the lips and haggard about the eyes, but recovered and bore himself like a man who has the true courage in him. It was a little trying to hear the condolences of his friends, and he waived them off as lightly as possible.

"It is all right, gentlemen; we are beaten and must give up," he said, smilingly, shaking the hands that were held out in useless sympathy, and getting back into the office and shutting himself up with Burr, who was quite cut up on his account.

"It seems incredible, Charley," he said. "Up to this time I thought your chances were absolutely sure. I knew there was a good deal of chicanery going on, but I had no idea they would defeat you."

"Well," said Mr. Burns, "I suppose all I have to do is to settle down to the old routine again."

The prospect seemed dreary enough.

CHAPTER XLI.

THE forerunner of winter—a blustering, disagreeable *avant courier*—came in with a dismal rain; cold, penetrating, and exceedingly uncomfortable. The trees were not yet stripped of their leaves, which hung dripping and wet. The sky gave no hint of any brightness back of its heavy, leaden canopy; and the faith of human nature is not yet so happily grounded in his beneficent majesty, the sun, but that it wavers a little when he hides his face, and we childishly say, "Will it ever shine again?" Mr. Burns, who, in these latter years, had become very susceptible to the moods of the weather, and feeling somehow that the dreary days were more typical of life than the pleasant ones, got out his guitar from under the bed in the back room (he had learned to play it a little while he was in the army), put it in as good tune as he could for the dampness, and sang Longfellow's "Rainy Day," looking out into the bleak, deserted street with the spirit of melancholy brooding in his blue eyes.

Mr. Courtenay, serenely smoking, looked up when he had finished and said, "Now suppose you give us ' Den Lieben, Langen Tag ;' those songs are calculated—upon such a day as this—to put us in cheerful harmony with nature."

Mr. Burns, laughing, said, "I beg your pardon, Burr, I know it's damnable." And got up and put the guitar in its box and shoved it under the bed again.

"What are you doing?" Mr. Courtenay asked. "Don't mind me; if you feel like venting yourself in that way, do so. I haven't the least objection."

Mr. Burns said he had vented himself sufficiently in that way, and came back to his place at the window. He still stood looking out when Miss Cleveland passed by, wrapped in a waterproof cloak and carrying an umbrella. He startled his friend by an exclamation, and the light of awakened interest, or attracted attention, broke athwart his melancholy eyes.

"What is it?" Mr. Courtenay asked.

"Miss Cleveland passing by. Her face, Burr, is a wonderful break in the dreary monotony of a day like this. Did you ever observe what a cheerful, hopeful, animated face it is?"

"No," said Mr. Courtenay, indifferently. He was not in the habit of observing faces that were not young and pretty.

"If I thought I could compass such an act of gallantry," said Mr. Burns, "I would rush out when she goes back and volunteer to carry her umbrella for her. But she seems such a competent sort of person that I am afraid she would think it a superfluous attention."

"Yes," said Mr. Courtenay; "elderly females, I have observed, prefer to manage their own umbrellas. If it was the other one, now,—Miss Stuvysant!"

"We never see Miss Stuvysant," said Mr. Burns. "I wonder if she is hermitizing herself at the deacon's? By the way, Burr, what an age it has been since we called at the deacon's. I had almost forgotten about those ladies, we have been so engaged with that confounded election. I suppose it is really incumbent upon us to go and present ourselves to them."

"The obligation doesn't rest very heavily upon me," said Mr. Courtenay.

"I don't know that it would upon me, either," said

Mr. Burns, "if I had not so often met those pleasant eyes of Miss Cleveland's. I wonder," he continued, "what is the secret of such happy, hopeful, kindly eyes? What have they looked on in this dreary world? What have they found to content them? I suppose we all feel the 'strong necessity of living,' but I can hardly conceive what happy combination of circumstances would make people glad of their life. For me, I am nothing but an hour-glass, through which time sifts his tedious sands. It certainly seems to me, sometimes, that man has been made a sorry jest of."

"In what way?" Mr. Courtenay asked.

"In being endowed with a capacity for things which do not exist! In being deceived a thousand times with bubbles that, before they are in his grasp, promise to satisfy his hungering, but burst the moment he touches them, and float away, leaving him, each time, a little sadder, a little wiser, and with the void in his soul constantly increasing, and demanding something better, larger, higher than the toys which have proven worthless. Thus we go on, from one thing to another,—from the plays of childhood to the grave pursuits of men; from the primer rhymes to the grandest poems; from the twittering of birds and our mother's lullaby to the finest orchestra,— and it is always the same; belief and ecstasy at first, dissatisfaction and scepticism at the last."

"You have not fathomed everything, yet," said Mr. Courtenay. "You have not yet come into the natural and lawful inheritance of man; to which, it seems to me, with your tastes and disposition, you have the clearest title. A man like you ought to marry. Stretch out your hand—in your imagination—and surround yourself with an ideal home; let there be warmth, color, books, music, an atmosphere of perfect refinement; prattling, blue-eyed babes,—pretty little copies of yourself, in whom you could see a continuation of yourself away down through the future,—and a sweet woman with a heart that loved you, and do you still think you would contend that life held nothing worth while?"

A smile crossed Mr. Burns's face, and his inner vision dwelt half tenderly, half painfully, upon the picture,—a

picture that his memory had sanctified as among his ear-
liest, happiest dreams.

"How do I know," said he, "but that even that is
one of the bubbles that would break on my lips? The
way of it is, everything is dazzling, and blinds our eyes
until we grasp it. Yet I do believe," he added, "that
the gratification of the affections does do more toward
reconciling people to existence than anything else."

"You must not, Charley," said Mr. Courtenay, "take
yourself as a type of the great masses of humanity. Look
at the thousands who have a strong interest in living and
working ! Because you have nothing to lay hold of do
not, therefore, conclude that there is nothing satisfactory
to man in this world, and that consequently the world is
a failure."

"'The greatest good to the greatest number,'" said
Mr. Burns, laughing. "Perhaps that is the best law we
could make, and yet it is imperfect. The greatest good
to all men, I would have it. My sympathies have always
been with the few who are crushed for the sake of the
many. One human being, you see, is capable of all the
joy and all the suffering in the world, and if the world
could make all people happy but one man, and he was
left desolate and hungry and cold, it would be a failure."

"I think he would be a failure," said Mr. Courtenay,
"and rather than have my feelings lacerated with sympathy for him I should vote for his extinction."

"You never," said Mr. Burns, "can carry on an argu
ment on legitimate grounds !" and went over and stood
before the book-case and scanned the backs of the books,
all standing upright in military order. It was among his
few occupations to keep them so ; and Mr. Courtenay,
who had careless habits in regard to the books, made it
necessary for him to go over them, dusting and straight-
ening up, once or twice a week. His eye fell upon the
large, handsome, leather-bound volume of Shakspeare,
and he exclaimed, dramatically, "Where are you, William
of Stratford ? You have solved that momentous question
—To be, or not to be—for yourself, but not for us. Burr,
if we *could* believe that all these great, grand souls were
gathered somewhere in the Beyond, and were waiting for

us, we would have something to live for and to strive for,
—a glorious immortality! There are some sweet spirits
here," tapping the books, "that I would much like to
meet; communion with whom would satisfy the utmost
longing of my soul."

"But I strongly suspect," said Mr. Courtenay, "that all
the immortality those sweet spirits possessed they put into
their works and left behind them. Humanity absorbs and
reabsorbs them, and so they live on through the ages."

"That theory cuts off all a man's possibilities," said
Mr. Burns, "and even loses to the world the lesson of
grand lives lived in obscurity. Nothing is of any consequence when it is past, but the leaving our mark upon
time. If our advanced thinkers had not progressed quite
beyond the idea of immortality of spirit, we might, in
this liberal day,—with regard to the life beyond the
grave,—have the most beautiful conception the human
mind is capable of. Theology has taken away so many
of its old restrictions that we are left to wander in Elysian
fields of imagination; and every man can choose for himself out of the illimitable. But alas! we know nothing.
And the fear of there being nothing behind the great
curtain of death palsies our energies, makes us say, If
this is all, how little!"

Presently, Mr. Courtenay got up and put on his hat
and great-coat. Mr. Burns asked where he was going.

"Around to old Shankey's to get a bottle of wine,"
said he. "It may put us into a more hilarious mood."

Mr. Burns did not object, as he often had done. In
spite of his morbid views of life, and his reckless throwing away—or at least wasteful disuse—of energy, he had a
keen consciousness of the dignity of manhood, which lay
like an anchor at the bottom of a stormy sea, on which he
might toss hither and thither but could not quite float
away. When Mr. Courtenay came in with a little puff
of winter about him, and literally shut the door to the
world—locking it—he came forward, almost eagerly, with
the dogged thought, one must do something, and made
at the same time a half-angry resistance to the feeling,
strong within him, that it was contemptible to drink wine
for the purpose of raising one's spirits. The question

o*

came up, was it any worse for himself than for Burr? And some inner consciousness answered in the affirmative. Burr had no evidence about him of any reproving inner consciousness. It was just the time of day, he said, setting the bottle down upon the table and shaking the raindrops from his hair, for a little stimulus to come in and help on the tide that regularly ebbs and flows in the human system once every twenty-four hours; in his case reaching the lowest point somewhere about mid-day, and coming up steadily to high tide from that time until ten or eleven o'clock P.M.

On this day high tide occurred a little earlier than usual, being artificially accelerated, and about dusk the young men had arrived at such a pitch of hilarity as required the guitar to be brought in again. Their two voices—Mr. Burns's treble and Burr's deep bass—made an excellent duet. No matter, now, if the night did close in in utter darkness and the wind, in angry gusts and heavy with rain, sweep round and over them, driving against the windows, rattling the unstable little building and threatening to shake it down over their heads. It had defied worse storms. They had built up a fire and opened the grate, and the ruddy light played over their faces that were soon devoid of melancholy, though from time to time expressive of pathetic emotion as the sentiment of the song waxed touching and appealed to their stimulated susceptibilities. The old war songs were all gone over with intensified recollection of days gone by. Some negro melodies were feelingly rendered, and Sweet Home and Kathleen Mavourneen. The latter, especially, Mr. Burns excelled in; singing it with a pathos bordering on affectation, which, somehow, one rather likes in a man's voice. Then Burr called for Star of the Evening, which was *his* favorite, and conducted the air himself; Mr. Burns giving him a desultory accompaniment and improvising a disconnected alto.

Fred came over from the hotel and said "missus" had been keeping their supper warm for an hour, and wanted to know what was the matter. Mr. Burns, disturbed at the interruption, was about to despatch him back with the good-natured message to let the supper go to thunder;

but Burr, who was always the cooler on these occasions, returned a polite answer to the effect that they were extremely sorry to have occasioned any inconvenience, but they did not care for supper, being very much engaged ; at which Fred glanced with a broad grin at the bottle and the glasses. Mr. Burns poured him out a sparkling goblet and bade him drink to his own good health and life-long prosperity. After which he took his departure, Mr. Courtenay getting up to relock the door.

It was mail-night, and men were splashing along the streets with lanterns and umbrellas. Many of them, hearing the music in the office, paused outside and listened, or peered in at the window; jested among themselves, and reported as a good piece of gossip when they got home that "them lawyers was havin' a jubilee again to-night with their wine an' their singin'." And it is a fact—lamentable or otherwise—that the social standing of the reckless attorneys did not suffer greatly from such reports. I am bound to say in their defence that they had never allowed themselves to become beastly intoxicated ; but they took no pains to contradict various assertions to that effect, and no precautions against their being made. They sang their songs and emptied their glasses in the face and eyes of the whole village ; Mr. Courtenay because he held public opinion in supreme contempt, and Mr. Burns because he scorned secrecy and preferred to take the bad consequences of bad conduct on the spot. It is true some of the more orthodox members of the community gathered their respectable garments around them and passed by with averted faces, meaning to frown down such goings-on. But the large majority looked with indulgent eyes on the little irregularities of these two bright lights.

Deacon Clyde was one who stopped outside in the rain and the darkness, and reported to his family and the two lady guests who were all gathered, as usual during the early evening hours, in the sitting-room, busied with various sorts of light work, that the lawyers were having a concert, and he guessed they were a little tipsy ; adding, "They've got to have a *bout* once in a while, I s'pose, to keep the blues off."

"What kind of a concert?" asked Mrs. Clyde, looking up through her spectacles as tne deacon took out his newspaper and brought his arm-chair up to the light.

"A kind of a private one," said he, laughing.; "anyhow, the audience was all on the outside. Some of 'em tried to get in, but the door was locked. They had their *refreshments* spread out on the table, and Mr. Burns was playing his banjo."

"Oh, uncle! his guitar," said Maggie, looking up and then blushing deeply.

"Maggie knows! he played it under her window one night," exclaimed Mrs. Clyde, with a wink at the visitors, rather proud to mention the circumstance.

"Auntie!" said Maggie, and bent over her work.

Miss Stuvysant, with her hands lying in her lap, turned her luminous eyes upon Maggie's face like one who had received a shock and was struggling silently and with the strong effort of accustomed self-control to adjust herself to a strangely altered condition of things. They had been domiciled at the deacon's a couple of weeks, and she had heard frequent laudable mention of the attorneys: their knowledge, their eloquence, their indefatigable efforts toward getting the railroad, and their growing popularity. During the political campaign, when Mr. Burns's chances for Congress were the universal topic of discussion, she had felt a feverish excitement perhaps greater than his own. And when it was all over, it was a hard thing— one of the many hard things in her painful relation to him—that she could not go and offer a word of sympathy. Though, of course, the bare thought of going to him only crossed her mind when she forgot, momentarily, the great gulf lying between them. It may seem strange, yet it is a fact, that such moments of delicious forgetfulness did come, even after all these years. It is said that when one has lost a limb the sensation of its being still in its place frequently occurs. So when one has lost a friend, the old, sweet sensation of the friendship steals back, and the waking up from these delusions is almost as full of anguish as the first shock.

It was perhaps the saddest thing in poor Wilmingard's case that she felt herself capable of making Mr. Burns's life a complete and perfect life. She knew his proud, sensitive, loving, hopeful, despairing nature so well! She knew just where she could soothe, encourage, cheer, sympathize. She felt that she understood just how time and circumstances had swept between them, causing the estrangement which he himself had at last made final. The thought that he might come, some time, to give the love that had been hers to another woman had never troubled her since the death of Miss MacIvers. It did not seem possible. Neither did she believe he would ever come back to her. What she hoped for and looked forward to was that she might at last stand on a high level with him—above the throbbing passion-world—when recollection had lost its sharpness of pain. This was her religion. She believed that she was following the invisible guidance of his spirit. She had come upon him unawares in this obscure little village, which fact in itself was a shock, because she had always thought of him as mingling in the rush and tide of life and activity. But the stories of his fame and popularity made her heart thrill again with the old pride she used to feel in him. She had never before had a hint of the things she had heard to-night. And it seemed as if the strong current on which she had been borne all these years, up to this moment, was setting back with a mighty revulsion. She felt like letting go the oars she had pulled so long and sinking down. It is pitiful to find that we have built our life upon a delusion! And yet there may be something in the life itself—indeed, there must be if the habit we have acquired is a good habit—to compensate for the shaken foundation.

As soon as she could steady her voice and movements she arose and bade the family good-night, with her usual kindly courtesy, and went up-stairs. Kneeling beside her trunk, she opened it and brought out from its depths a portrait of Mr. Burns, taken in his uniform and with the first flush of his military enthusiasm upon him. She held it in her hand, looking at it passionately, with tears in her eyes.

"Oh, can it be," she cried, "that you have made so little of your noble self? When you were but a boy you scorned such follies as you are engaged in to-night, my proud Charley!"

She recalled Mrs. Clyde's jest and Maggie's blushes, and felt her lip curl; but gazing at the beautiful, boyish face, with its high, proud look, she dropped her head upon her arm, and wept as she had hardly ever wept before.

When Miss Cleveland came up a little later, the light which had beamed in Miss Stuvysant's eyes ever since she had known her—the light which shines from a soul looking up with hope and trust—seemed to have gone out.

CHAPTER XLII.

The following evening being a little less dreary than its predecessor, Mr. Burns, again referring to the deacon's family and their guests, proposed to go up and call upon them. Mr. Courtenay declined, saying, "I have a suspicion that you will not see Miss Stuvysant, and I do not care to make the acquaintance of the elderly lady."

"The acquaintance of the elderly lady is what I particularly look forward to," said Mr. Burns, and immediately prepared himself for the visit. It was cold, and he stepped to the closet, remarking, "I think I had better get out my great-coat."

"Yes, I would," approved Mr. Courtenay; "it does not give you so much the appearance of an invalid as the blue cloak does."

"What shall I say for you," inquired Mr. Burns, "in case they happen to speak of you?"

"You may say that I am indisposed," said Mr. Courtenay. "I'll back up the statement by not leaving the office until you come back. If you are not well entertained, you can make my case pretty serious and come home early."

"You would do for a diplomatic ambassador at the court of France, or some other polite nation. I wonder why you never directed your talents to that end," said Mr. Burns, and went out.

As had happened upon a former occasion, when he was ushered, with a little atmosphere of cold air about him, into the warmth and light of the deacon's parlor, the Kirkwoods and their nephew (the doctor) were there, which again struck him with a not altogether pleasant sensation at first. But they all arose and welcomed him, as before, with so much cordiality that the feeling was dispelled, and he took his place upon the sofa, near Maggie, with a disposition to make himself agreeable. His first quick glance around the room had shown him that the strange ladies were not present. But he did not mind that after a moment, with Maggie's bright face before him, and knowing that her whole being was pulsing with delight that he was near. There is a subtle flattery in the knowledge that our presence gives pleasure which is very soothing, and which makes us turn very kindly towards the one who conveys it.

Maggie at once broached the subject of the strange ladies, having an impulsive way of plunging into subjects.

"Did you know that that Miss Stuvysant, whom Eva and I heard read at N—— City once, was stopping here?" she inquired.

"I supposed it was the same," said Mr. Burns. "I heard you had some visitors. I did not know but I might have the pleasure of meeting them this evening."

"Would you like to meet them?" asked Maggie. "I'll go and ask them to come down!" And before Mr. Burns could protest, she darted away, skipped up the stairs, and knocked at the visitors' door.

They seemed to have settled themselves for the evening. Miss Stuvysant was writing, and Miss Cleveland had some work in her hands.

"We have another arrival down-stairs," said Maggie, a little out of breath and with the color brightening in her cheeks. "And I didn't know but you would come down now. Mr. Burns is here and wishes to see you."

"Indeed?" said Miss Cleveland.

Miss Stuvysant dropped her pen and looked up, her face growing pale.

"Shall we go down ?" Miss Cleveland asked.

"Oh, no; I will not," said Miss Stuvysant. "But suppose you go down ?" she added.

Miss Cleveland deliberated a moment and then arose. "Well," she said, with a little laugh, "I'll smooth my hair and come presently; you need not wait for me, Maggie."

Maggie hastened back.

"Well," said Mr. Burns. "Did you succeed ?"

"Miss Cleveland is coming down," Maggie returned. "But Miss Stuvysant refused. I'm sorry. She is the one I wanted you to see."

"Do you think so much more of her than of the other lady ?" Mr. Burns asked.

"Oh, I like them both," said Maggie. "But Miss Stuvysant is so much—I hardly know what to say,—so much more attractive than Miss Cleveland. She charms you so with her sad eyes and sweet smile."

"Oh, has she sad eyes ?"

"Maybe you would not think so," said Maggie. "Eva doesn't. But when I sit and look at her a long time I always think I see something sad in her eyes. Eva says they are dark and thoughtful, that is all. But I cannot see much difference between 'sad' and 'thoughtful,' can you ?"

Mr. Burns laughed. "There is a philosophy in that," said he, and of course Maggie did not understand.

At that moment Miss Cleveland came in. Miss Clyde being near the door, drew up a chair for her near Mrs. Kirkwood, with whom she immediately fell into conversation, after shaking hands with the minister and bowing to Doctor Webster and Mr. Burns, whose names Miss Clyde mentioned. The doctor and Mr. Burns had each, in turn, arisen and sat down again. Mr. Burns being at some distance from her watched her face, liking it all the better the more he saw of it. Quiet, yet animated, blue-eyed, intelligent.

By and by, when a convenient opportunity occurred (Mrs. Kirkwood being called out of the room by Mrs. Clyde to be shown something in another part of the house), he excused himself to Maggie and crossed over to her. She looked up with a smile and held out her hand to him.

"I think I have met your eyes before, Mr. Burns," she said. "And, besides, you are a person of so much note in the village that one cannot be here long without, at least, getting acquainted with your reputation."

"My reputation," said he, flushing a little at the remembrance of his dissipations, which he knew to be greatly enlarged upon by the village gossips, "I am afraid, will not commend me to you. I must make a strong personal effort to win your favor."

Miss Cleveland laughed.

"Well," she said, "I am so much of an egotist, that I ground my opinions of people upon my own judgment of them rather than upon hearsay."

"Good; that gives one a better chance," said he. "It is not that I pride myself on being a superior lawyer, but I would always rather plead my own cause."

"To be sure," she returned. "You have a vital interest in it, and of course would plead eloquently. But, really, Mr. Burns," she continued, "whatever we hear of people it seems to me that it is right to withhold judgment upon them until we have seen and studied them a little. The soul of a man is an excellent stenographer and takes him down in shorthand upon his face, upon his movements and actions. And a little careful study will enable us to decipher the hieroglyphics which the unseen sculptors are working upon us."

"But that study," said Mr. Burns, "is sadly neglected, as is shown by our being so often taken in."

"And by our sometimes entertaining angels unawares," returned Miss Cleveland, smiling. "Perhaps we as often fail to appreciate as we overestimate. I was admiring, the other day, a fine collection of photographed statuary, and I came across the portrait of an obscure country clergyman that had gotten among the beautiful ideal pictures. It was a homely, intelligent, sympathetic face, with lines drawn all over it, representing thought and feeling, and it struck me that one living, human being who was being carved from within was worth more than all the chiselled marble in the world. That is, that the lesson of his life was worth more than all the lessons wrought in stone. I am afraid we sometimes fail to estimate the value of each single life. There are so many people in the world, there are such crowds wherever we turn, that we mass them together like so many inanimate things. We all like to be individualized. I suppose that is why so many of us struggle for fame and position. We want to be lifted up where people can see that we are one, apart from the many."

"And do you think it of consequence to be one among the many?" Mr. Burns asked. "I mean, do you consider that this brief life of ours is of sufficient importance, even at the best, to induce us to make the most of ourselves?"

"Oh, most assuredly, Mr. Burns! Why, do you doubt it? It seems to me that now, more than ever before in the history of the world, it is worth while to beautify and elevate our lives. And certainly, it has always been of importance that men should make the most of themselves. We can see that very easily—can we not?—by looking back on the steps that have been taken upward from mere animal existence. It is of incalculable benefit to us that men did what they could with their hands and their brains in the past; and what we can do in the present may be infinitely beneficial to future generations."

"Why do you say," asked Mr. Burns, "that the present is a better time to be and to do than the past has been?"

"Oh, because we have so much better light, so much greater freedom. The old shells of prejudice and superstition are crumbling away, and the souls of men are bursting forth with new life. We are at the dawn of a new era of unfettered thought and purpose. I do not envy your sex, Mr. Burns; but I feel this: oh, to be a man in this nineteenth century and alive to the grandeur of it! Is it possible you have not yet waked up to that? If so, I must give you a shake."

"I wish to heaven you could!" said Mr. Burns. "I wish you could rouse me out of the morbid lethargy I have fallen into in this—excuse me—damnable little hamlet."

"I will do my best," said Miss Cleveland, laughing, "and if I prick you hard you must cry out. I wish," she added, "you could meet my friend."

" And can I not ?" he asked.

" I am afraid not. She is something of an invalid just now, and does not wish to meet strangers. However, I will try and persuade her to make an exception of you."

"Do," said Mr. Burns. "Lay my forlorn case before her, and maybe she will take pity on me."

It was a little dinner party, to which the Kirkwoods had been invited, and Mr. Burns, being pressed to remain, did so, chiefly on Miss Cleveland's account. It seemed to him that the deacon's parlor walls were stretching away into infinite proportions with this woman in them whose mind showed such a vast expanse. Her presence was like the out-door air, in which he could take deep, delicious breaths, and feel intensely satisfied. She gave him that comfortable assurance and security that a strong hand-clasp in the darkness gives to a child or a woman. At dinner he had her beside him; Maggie and Dr. Webster sat opposite. The doctor looked across and asked Miss Cleveland the stereotyped question, " Madam, how do you like the West ?"

" Oh, very well, indeed," she answered. " This is not my first visit. I suppose I should not be saying anything original, if I offered an objection to the wind !"

" That depends on what original is," said Mr. Burns. " I hold that anything we discover for ourselves is original."

" Then we must all have a vein of originality," said Mrs. Kirkwood, " for I hardly think any one would fail to make the discovery you speak of who spends any time on the prairies."

Mr. Burns laughed. " Mrs. Kirkwood and I," said he, " discussed the subject of the prairies, on a former occasion, at great length."

As soon as they adjourned to the parlor, Miss Cleveland excused herself, fearing her friend might be lonely, and went back up-stairs, and to Mr. Burns the stimulus of the evening was gone. The parlor walls narrowed down again to commonplace dimensions, and all the faces grew dull and the voices irksome. He felt an impatient longing to get away; and I, his biographer, am obliged to hurry him off as soon as is possible and polite. Bowing himself from the deacon's door-step,—the door Maggie held open, lighting him out and feeling, somehow, that his leave-taking was very unsatisfactory,—he hastened home and found Mr. Courtenay smoking and reading as usual, with a good fire in the stove. He laid aside his book, but kept on smoking. The president of the railroad company had made him a present of a handsome meerschaum pipe, which he took great pride and interest in coloring.

"Well!" he said. "Did you have a pleasant evening?"

"Very, indeed," said Mr. Burns. "You ought to have gone."

"Did you see the ladies?"

"I saw Miss Cleveland."

"The elderly spinster."

"She is a grand woman!" said Mr. Burns, uncompromisingly. "She is a woman with a soul, and to me her face is beautiful beyond description."

"I should have thought her past the stage of beauty," said Mr. Courtenay.

"Of course, I do not mean mere outside, physical beauty. I mean the beauty that shines from within," said Mr. Burns.

"Ah!" Mr. Courtenay took his pipe from his lips and eyed it admiringly. "I see. You are not taken with an image of clay, however exquisitely fashioned. You prefer the meerschaum that grows more beautiful with age and the glowing life within it. I had never thought of applying that to woman."

"Burr," said Mr. Burns, half jestingly and half in earnest, "I am lost in astonishment sometimes that you and I have held together so long, seeing what little similarity there is between us!"

"I suspect that is just the secret of our holding together," said Burr. "Existence would have been too tame if we had not disagreed so well."

CHAPTER XLIII.

Miss Stuvysant had spent the evening in intense
excitement, walking the greater part of the time back
and forth the short length of the chamber, every nerve
a quiver. Now and then she had opened the door and
leaned over the banisters to catch, if possible, the tones
of the voice that had once struck so thrillingly upon her
ear and whose echoes sounded in her memory yet, running
like an undercurrent through all the music—glad or sad,
or gentle or tumultuous—of her life, and which she had
never yet found it in her heart even to try to hush. But
the closed parlor doors shut off all distinct sounds, and
only a confused hum reached her. When her friend came
up-stairs she turned toward her with bright, inquiring
eyes.

"My dear, I am afraid you have had a long, lonely evening," said Miss Cleveland. "I got so deeply interested
in that young lawyer that I could not tear myself away.
I think it would have done you good to meet him ; moreover, I think it would have done him good to meet you."

"Why so?" Miss Stuvysant asked.

"Because I think he needs a little help. He feels so
keenly the social and intellectual poverty of a place like
this."

"Well," said Miss Stuvysant, with a flash of her dark
eyes, "the world is wide and contains incalculable wealth
in those directions. I suppose he was not compelled to
plant himself in the desert. If one deliberately puts oneself in the way of poverty he must accept its privations.
And he ought to do it without complaining."

Miss Cleveland laughed.

"My dear, I wonder if ever one friend endeavored to
prepossess another in favor of a third, and succeeded? I
fully intended you should like Mr. Burns, and I ignorantly
thought I could show him to you just as he appeared to
me. Now to me there was something rather noble in his
taking a stand in these Western wildernesses instead of

hovering, like so many other busy bees, around the sweet cups of Eastern wealth and pleasure. He is not one who must simply gather up from the outside; there is enough *in* him to grow up and make a man. I like that spirit of sturdy independence that cuts loose from the helps that so often prove hindrances, and stands alone. Such natures have a chance to grow broad and strong; and they do. I unwarily admitted that Mr. Burns complained. I have no doubt, my dear, that that grand old oak which you and I observed standing in the midst of a ten-mile stretch of loveliness on the prairie not very far from here, murmurs in its leafy top at its isolation from all its kind. And yet if it had grown among a thousand others it might not have been half so fine. However strong we are, we all want sympathy. Mr. Burns, I think, is peculiarly in need of it. It may be the breakers have not tossed him about much bodily; to outside eyes his life may appear serene enough; but to me he seems to have had a great deal of inner experience. He has fought and suffered, and hoped and despaired, and labored all within himself; there is evidence in his face of fires that have burned fiercely— and smoulder yet perhaps. I fancy that life to him has seemed sometimes—maybe it does now—like struggling in deep water to save himself from sinking down. That is why I said he needed a hand held out to him. *He knows* that he is endowed with a rare nature, and he has a dread of its being wasted. He wants to *do* something, and be something worthy of himself. And this, my dear, is the farthest remove from egotism. I have hardly a doubt that his life here is just the right discipline for something that may come hereafter. It is only in the rebound from the lowest that we reach the highest. Our feet must touch bottom in the dark, deep streams of life if we would have our elastic souls spring up to meet the brightness of a perfect day.''

''Oh, I know that, I feel that!'' said Miss Stuvysant, fervently. ''I do believe with a firm conviction which my own experience has strengthened, that everything which comes to us is for our good. Everything, I mean, except our own sins and mistakes. And even those may be turned to account in bettering our after-lives; though I dislike that thought, there is a sort of exultant selfishness in it ; our sins and mistakes have so close a bearing upon our fellow-beings ! I almost hated the king in Auerbach's On the Heights.''

"But after all,'' said Miss Cleveland, "the only thing left him was to take the consequences of his sin and, as you say, turn them to account in bettering his after-life.''

After a little silence fraught with deep feeling, at least on the part of Miss Stuvysant, she said, "I have never told you much about myself, dear Miss Cleveland ! Long before I knew you there was a time when everything was so dark to me that I longed to die. I did not think of the rest and peace that many people link with the idea of death. I only wanted oblivion. I shrank as much from consciousness upon the other side of the grave as upon this. If I thought of God at all and believed in Him, I believed only that He was good and merciful and would not drag me up into another miserable existence after this was ended. I was a poor little handful of dust animated with suffering rather than with life ; for life means growth and blossom and fruitage, and I did not live in any such sense.''

"But, my dear child,'' said Miss Cleveland, interrupting her, "you lived in the sense in which trees live in winter. The soil in which our souls' growths spring up must have a season of inactivity,—a sort of brooding-time, as it were.''

Miss Stuvysant smiled, though tears were rolling down her cheeks.

"Well, it was a hard, cruel, bitter winter,'' she said. "Oh, I pity myself, even now, in the recollection of it ! I was so little and frail, so borne down and dejected, so rejected and cast down, as though utterly unworthy of all I craved. Oh, it is so hard when, in the ignorance and innocence of youth, you have believed in yourself through the strong assurance of those you loved, to be put aside ! To lose not only your place in the hearts you trusted, but even in your own happy self-confidence ; for that follows when the arm you leaned upon and relied upon as upon the very truth of God, turns and casts you off. Then it is that woman forgets her womanliness, and pride cannot come to her rescue. Then she bows down. Oh, God, pity her! Oh, God, pity her!"

She fell upon her knees by the bedside, and covered her face with her hands in a wild paroxysm of tears. Miss Cleveland knelt down and wound her arms strongly around her.

"My dear child," she said, "do not give way to that feeling! I knew you must have suffered; I knew it because you are what you are. It could not be otherwise. But it is all past and gone now; you have many dear friends who feel your worth, and you are restored to faith in yourself. And it is a truer faith than that grounded in youthful inexperience and in your friends' kindly praise. Can you not look back even now and think that all was for the best? After the smoke of battle has cleared away we can see just where we stood. We may see, too, how the very cloud that oppressed us protected us. Think of this, dear child. What are they that have never struggled and suffered? Their souls' depths have never been sounded. The passionate music that has pulsed along the great world's throbbing heart through all the past has no deep meanings for them. I used to like to repeat, during my own time of trouble,—

> "'In life's goblet freely press
> The leaves that give it bitterness,
> Nor prize its colored waters less;
> For in thy darkness and distress,
>   New life and strength they give.
> For he who has not learned to know
> How false its sparkling bubbles glow,
> How bitter are the drops of woe .
> With which its brim may overflow,
> He has not learned to live.'"

Miss Stuvysant dried her tears and arose.

"It is weak of me to do this," she said. "It is not often of late years that I have felt so broken down as I have to-night."

"You will feel better to-morrow," said Miss Cleveland, caressingly; "go to bed and sleep. These things will come tiding back to us all through life. A great sorrow will never quite fold its wings and lie still in the past."

There had been frequent openings and closings of the

doors below, and all the visitors had departed, and the family had retired to their respective rooms; the deacon and his wife to slumber peacefully, Maggie to divide pleasant and painful thoughts between Mr. Burns's indifference and Dr. Webster's gallantry toward her, and Evelyn to lie awake for hours torturing herself with speculations as to why Mr. Courtenay had ceased his visits.

CHAPTER XLIV.

THE following day, late in the afternoon, a visitor sprang out of a buggy in front of the law-office and came in, carrying a whip in his gloved hand. He introduced himself as Ralph Rosevelt. Perhaps they had heard of him, he suggested, with bland egotism. Oh, yes, they had heard of him, the rich farmer and cattle-buyer living at the extreme northeast corner of the county. Mr. Courtenay set out a chair which Mr. Rosevelt, thanking him, declined, saying that his business was brief. He had come to engage an attorney's services on a trifling lawsuit. He was a large, burly man, showily dressed, displaying a good deal of jewelry about his person, and conveying an idea of wealth and vulgarity. When he spoke of the lawsuit he hinted, with a smirk, that there was a woman connected with it; at which Mr. Burns looked up sharply, and Mr. Courtenay, with a fine sense of decency, dropped his eyes. Mr. Rosevelt, catching Mr. Burns's glance, was disconcerted a little, and moved back his chair and sat down, tapping the floor with the handle of his whip; and thereafter addressed himself chiefly to Mr. Courtenay, the countenance of that accomplished attorney expressing nothing but polite interest as he inquired into the nature of the case. It seemed that Mr. Rosevelt had been proceeded against by the husband of the woman for beguiling her affection away from himself.

"And you wish to prove the accusation groundless, I suppose?" said Mr. Courtenay.

"Of course. What else could a man do?" Mr. Rose-

velt demanded, with a laugh. "And between you and
me it *is* groundless, which is the ugliest part of it, ha, ha.
The fellow's a fool and doesn't know it; he has got the
brightest and most virtuous little woman in the world, and
he doesn't know that, either. Too smart for him by a
damned sight; and so high-strung that she would snap if
you touched her with the tip of your finger."

"I suppose he wants to get some money out of you,"
said Mr. Courtenay.

"Yes,—no, I don't think it's that so much as his
temper. The fool's jealous; which is another way of
saying his wife's too good for him; an acknowledgment
I wouldn't make, for my part, ha, ha."

He glanced at Mr. Burns again, who seemed to have a
subduing effect upon him, for he drew down his face and
arose. At that moment another visitor, having hitched
his horse to a post outside, came in. A small, sandy-
haired, excitable individual, who also carried a whip in his
hand which he clutched nervously as his glance encountered the burly Rosevelt.

"You here, you scoundrel?" he hissed, getting instantly almost beside himself with rage and hate.

Rosevelt grasped his whip as if to strike him, but controlled himself. The new-comer—Marks was his name—
turned to the attorneys.

"Have both you gentlemen agreed to take sides with
that villain against honor and decency? I can tell you
in a few words how the case stands between us. He
wants to beat me in law, while at the same time he exults
over me in his mean soul in the triumph of winning away
my wife. He wants a double triumph, and he hasn't even
the decency to conceal it. He makes a boast of it."

Mr. Courtenay was about to recommend milder language,
when Mr. Burns interposed. "I believe," said he, "that
Mr. Courtenay has agreed to a proposition from Mr. Rosevelt; if you wish, I will undertake the prosecution."

"But I intended to retain you both," exclaimed Mr.
Rosevelt. "You are partners, are you not?"

"No, we are not. And I assure you, sir, you will find
Mr. Courtenay fully adequate for your defence if I prose-
cute."

"When is the trial to take place?" Mr. Courtenay asked.

"Oh, immediately," said Mr. Rosevelt. "Before Squire Blakey, our Briarly Hollow magistrate. I presume the court is already assembled. It is four o'clock now, and we've got a ten-mile drive," taking out a massive gold watch. "You can get right in with me and we'll be off."

"Thank you," said Mr. Courtenay. "I have a conveyance of my own which I would prefer taking, and that will save you the trouble of bringing me back."

"And you," said Mr. Marks, addressing his attorney, "can ride with me, and I will explain the case on the way."

"I am much obliged," said Mr. Burns, a little coldly; "but I presume the case will develop itself when the witnesses appear. I will go with Mr. Courtenay."

Mr. Rosevelt had already gone out and driven off at a fast trot. Mr. Marks followed him, and Mr. Burns went out the back door to harness Nobby, leaving Burr to gather up a few law-books and put them in a valise.

Nobby was a fleet-footed animal, and Mr. Burns took great pride in his gait and carriage; a feeling, by the way, which his companion did not share. Nevertheless it was nightfall when they drew up before Squire Blakey's unpretentious abode with its homely surroundings, rickety stables, straw-covered sheds, and spacious barnyard with cattle lying down and dogs coming up to bark a good-natured welcome. Mr. Burns was about to apostrophize the scene in a line or two of pastoral poetry, when a half-grown boy detached himself from a group in the dooryard and came up to the carriage, examined Nobby with the glance of a connoisseur in horse-flesh, and laid his hand upon the rein with the kindly familiarity which the boy-nature readily assumes toward the lower animals. "Feed him oats, or corn?" he asked, shutting one eye and looking up inquiringly with the other.

"He won't murmur at either," said Mr. Burns, getting upon the ground and stretching his legs. "Rub him down well, my boy; we have given him a pretty hard drive. I suppose," he added, "we shall bring up all right if we follow the path that leads up from this gate?"

"Yes," said the boy, who seemed to have a facetious vein, "it aint much of a trick to find the right door; there's only one,—except another clean round t'other side o' the house."

Thus enlightened they opened the gate and proceeded toward the house. Lights were flashing through the uncovered windows, and showed them a commodious kitchen improvised into a court-room; the squire seated at a table on which lay a pile of books and some writing utensils, and a motley assemblage of people seated upon chairs and benches. The squire himself arose to open the door and received them pompously, never having had the pleasure, as he said, of making their legal acquaintance before. His daughter, a young lady of some pretentions to style and fashion, and with an air of feeling superior to her surroundings, conducted them coquettishly across into the best room to take off their hats and great-coats. Her mother, a spare, elderly woman, in a clean white cap with loosened strings, came in and apologized for having "court" held in the kitchen.

"There's so many that comes stragglin' in at sich a time as this," she explained, "that it would ruin a body's carpet."

"You are quite right," said Mr. Burns, stepping over to the little parlor stove, in which a newly-kindled fire crackled and snapped, to warm his hands. "The kitchen is quite good enough for gatherings of this nature."

The carpet was a rag carpet, and the long, white curtains, looped with scrupulous precision, were coarse muslin; but it was a nice, tidy room nevertheless, and it would have been a pity to bring all those coarse boots and their tobacco-chewing owners into it. As soon as the attorneys got the numbness warmed out of their fingers, for it had been quite chilly riding, they stepped out to the "court-room," and preparations were made for the trial to begin.

The woman who "was connected with it" was a pretty, bright-eyed brunette, with hot, indignant blushes in her cheeks. Mr. Courtenay wondered how she came to be married to the sandy-haired individual, and Mr. Burns was surprised at her reputed preference for the burly Rosevelt. Public sentiment appeared to be in her favor, but that was all, the evidence, such as there was, being upon the other side. Mr. Burns felt himself in a delicate position between sympathy and consideration for the woman, and indignation toward Rosevelt. It appeared to him, as the case developed itself, that Mrs. Marks was the victim of both the accused and the accuser, and that she held them both in disdain for dragging her through the mire of a public lawsuit. Her husband was jealous, irritable, and bad tempered ; and Rosevelt, who admired her and had taken several occasions of forcing his society upon her out of revenge for her contempt of him, had played upon her husband's jealousy and anger, and so, inadvertently, brought the matter before the public, rather glorying in the notoriety, but anxious to throw the costs upon his adversary. The misdemeanors for which he was arraigned were not very flagrant violations of law, and yet sufficient, perhaps, to have turned the tide against him— he having no witnesses and depending wholly upon his lawyer,—had not that shrewd barrister hit upon a device that necessitated an adjournment until the following morning, and then brought the trial to a speedy close. It was this: Opposed to half a dozen disreputable men and women who affirmed that upon several occasions they had seen Mrs. Marks in company with defendant at unseasonable hours and in out-of-the-way places, Mr. Courtenay brought double the number of witnesses to declare under oath that nothing of the kind had ever been seen by them. No amount of questioning or cross-questioning could elicit anything further,—not a particle of evidence was there to bear upon the case in hand,—and Mr. Burns looked upon it as rather a cumbersome joke, and not being in a facetious humor, passed it over, in making his plea, with little comment. His astonishment was extreme when Mr. Courtenay arose and made that absurd testimony the groundwork of a long and able argument. Selecting one of the leather-covered volumes from the kitchen table, he turned the leaves and pointed to a paragraph containing the provision that "Judgment shall be rendered in favor of that side upon which there is a preponderance of testimony." Taking this for a text, and warping it so that a superior number of witnesses was made to appear analogous to a "preponderance of testimony," he drew a striking com- parison between the two sides of the house, and sat down amid boisterous applause.

Mr. Burns arose indignantly, and endeavored to explain the sophistry. "Is it necessary," he demanded, "that the whole neighborhood should witness a theft in order to convict the robber?" He quoted and read law in regard to witnesses and testimony at great length, and got him- self thoroughly warmed up on the subject; and for once, at least, was a match for his ready-witted opponent. Mr. Courtenay replied; parliamentary rules were set aside, and the argument descended to a personal debate, having little reference to judge or jury. Finally, after repeated calls to order from the "court," who felt that its dignity was being disregarded, they sat down, having expended their sharpest sarcasms upon each other; whose subtle- ties, though but imperfectly understood, were loudly ap- plauded by the gaping audience. The squire summed up the testimony, and in his "charge" dwelt at great length upon defendant's preponderancy of evidence (having a leaning toward the wealthy Rosevelt), and the jury brought a verdict in his favor.

Mr. Marks fairly stamped with rage and disappointment, while his opponent indulged in a supercilious quietude of manner, probably for the sake of contrast. Mrs. Marks, of whom Mr. Courtenay had made pathetic mention in his plea, and to whom Mr. Burns had referred in the most delicate and respectful manner as being in no way an- swerable for the charges brought against Rosevelt, and in his opinion uncompromised by them, arose, when the trial was at an end, and approached him with eyes still flashing and cheeks still burning, and thanked him for his kind- ness and consideration.

"I would like to see you on business of my own," she said, with a quivering of her lips. "I mean to get a divorce. I can't live with him after this. Will you come over to my house?"

"Where do you live?" Mr. Burns asked.

"Across the fields, yonder, about a mile from here. I want you to see mother."

"Very well," said Mr. Burns. "I will see what I can do," and she turned away.

Domestic troubles were, of all things that came in the way of his professional practice, the most sickening to Mr. Burns's soul. There were other cases wherein poor men's earnings were wrenched from them by the hard grasp of the law, or where widows and orphans suffered through fraudulent tricks of apparent justice, that had made him wish, many a time, he had chosen some other work to do in the world than seeking to disentangle the threads that vice and cunning and bad nature are forever weaving around the innocent and unsuspecting. But this cutting among the heart-strings that had once thrilled to the sweet music of love, this making of widows and orphans that should be left to the hand of death alone, were most distressing.

To go back to the evening before. After adjournment Mr. Rosevelt invited both attorneys home with him to spend the night, ignoring, in Mr. Burns's case, any unpleasantness in their relations toward each other; showing that somewhere in his coarse nature—at least, so Mr. Burns interpreted it—there was a streak of delicacy and good breeding. Though it might have been mere policy, a man of Mr. Rosevelt's cunning and experience—and success in certain directions—being capable of looking a great way ahead, and keeping a good many irons in the fire ready for future use. There seemed to be no other way; the squire's house was small and overflowing with boys and girls in all stages of growth, and they were constrained to accept the hospitality that offered.

As they were about starting Mr. Rosevelt remarked to Mr. Courtenay, "If it is not objectionable to you or your friend, I would like to have you get in with me, and Mr. Burns can follow us."

"Certainly not," they said.

Mr. Rosevelt's place was not above a mile and a half distant, and was situated in the belt of timber close by the river. The house, however, was approached by a long avenue of maples, very bright just now in their autumn dress. At the end of this there was a wide "clearing" for the buildings, with here and there a picturesque and mighty oak left standing. The house was a large, white Gothic cottage-house, with porticoes and verandas, and green blinds at the windows. It was enfolded lovingly in the arms of two or three of the massive oaks, and had a most homelike and beautiful aspect, bursting upon the sight in the stillness of a perfect moonlight night. It was very late, but there were lights glimmering through the blinds. Long before they reached the gate at the end of the avenue, a deep-mouthed dog began baying loudly and tugging at a huge chain by which he was fastened in one corner of the yard. Two men came out of the rear of the house and took charge of the horses.

"Folks sitting up yet?" Mr. Rosevelt asked.

"Yes, sir," one of them answered, respectfully.

Mr. Burns began insensibly to think better of his host. As they walked up the path to the front door, it struck him that it was the loveliest, most peaceful-looking abode he had seen in the West. Surely the man out of whose brain the conception of it had come, and whose hands had executed it, must have a good side to him. Two small boys, with curly heads and the brightest black eyes, came running to meet him as he opened the door, but backed down shyly at the sight of the strangers. Four other boys, two of them quite grown, were seated round a large centre-table strewn with magazines and papers. A tall woman, with a queenly head and grand, dark eyes, sat among them, but arose as they entered, and the boys all followed her example.

Mr. Rosevelt addressed her as "wife," and presented the attorneys, whom she received with grave but kindly courtesy; starting a little when Mr. Courtenay's name was mentioned, and looking at him sharply.

"And here," Mr. Rosevelt continued, "you see the rest of my family, Frank, the eldest, and Ralph, and Jake, and Ben, and those little urchins under the table, Ned and Joe. They," he added, with a laugh, "are genuine backwoodsmen; never have seen 'society,' ha, ha. Marjory," addressing his wife, "you must take them East next time you make a trip and get them a little used to the world."

"That is a lesson they will learn soon enough," said Mrs. Rosevelt, smiling toward Mr. Burns, whose face, from the first moment, she seemed to like. "I thought I would give nature the first chance with them. They run about the woods and paddle their little boat upon the river, and we teach them all the time without their knowing it, and they are as happy as any other young animals."

"You are adopting the German method with them," said Mr. Burns; and added, laughing, "I shall always regret that I lived my childhood before the days of 'Kindergarten.' I pity myself even now—poor little morsel of humanity!—when I look back on my early schooldays."

"Yes; the world is getting better to the children in many respects," said Mrs. Rosevelt.

"And better for the grown folks, also; is it not, mother?" remarked Frank, the eldest, in a voice so rich and deep for his years,—he could not have been above eighteen,—and, moreover, falling upon Mr. Burns's ears with such a strangely familiar sound, that he started and looked keenly at the speaker, who returned his gaze with a pair of mild but intensely black eyes.

Mr. Burns's thought was, "What a beautiful boy! I must have seen a painting somewhere that looks like him."

Like the other Rosevelts, he had black hair curling all over his head, but his skin was fair and rosy. He was short in stature and rather fleshy; his hands and feet were remarkably small, but finely shaped, his fingers tapering to delicate, shell-tinted tips. Evidently he was not vain of his beauty; it rather embarrassed him. He blushed like a girl under Mr. Burns's continued, admiring gaze. It was easy to discover, in the course of half an hour, that he was the idol of the household, and that he deserved the affection his charming person and manners inspired. He had recently graduated at the State University, and was now about to enter a theological seminary and study for the ministry. He told Mr. Burns, subsequently, that he had hesitated between preaching and teaching. He would have liked to secure a professorship of rhetoric and elocution in some college. "I am a worshipper of language," he said. "I love words better

P*

than pictures or music. They are the more laconic and precise expressions of thought. They have been born of the stress of human needs and polished by the utterance of millions. I love to trace them back to their beginnings; I like to know the circumstances that called them into being. I know language changes, but we can still dive down through all the variations and grasp the old, imperishable roots."

"And have you gone to the bottom of many languages?" Mr. Burns asked, not without a touch of sarcasm; for that had come to be almost a habit of his mind.

The young man blushed, and seemed to draw back a little.

"Oh, no!" said he. "I beg your pardon, if I gave you such an impression."

Mr. Burns, sorry that he had wounded him, hastened to make reparation.

"I suspect you have given some attention to elocution, and I should like to hear you read. Excuse me for saying it, but you have, it seems to me, a very remarkable voice."

"It is a natural endowment, however, Mr. Burns," said Mrs. Rosevelt, who had been a listener to the conversation. "Frank has been too thorough a student to give his time to the cultivation of one faculty, except incidentally. "However," she added, "we all like his reading, and I am sure it will give him pleasure to entertain you."

"Marjory," said Mr. Rosevelt, shortly after they were seated, "can't we have a little music before we retire?"

He seemed, in the midst of his home-circle, greatly influenced by its air of refinement. His coarseness was toned down, and his selfishness and egotism passed into the wider channel of affection for, and pride in, his family. He was very generous, too, as regarded money, spending it lavishly for the comforts and luxuries of life, and for the good of his wife and children. Selfishness was the root and tree of his nature, but it bore some sweet blossoms, nevertheless.

Mrs. Rosevelt went to the piano, an old-fashioned but finely-toned instrument, standing open and loaded with music. The boys all gathered around her and took the different parts in a quartette, making a charming picture as well as a most pleasing harmony. It was after this that Mr. Burns had the before-mentioned conversation with Frank.

By and by Mrs. Rosevelt took the two younger children and went out of the room. Ralph and Jake also said "good-night," and vanished. Mr. Rosevelt and Mr. Courtenay, at a little distance, sat talking together. Mr. Burns was suddenly startled by the appearance of a woman standing in the doorway near him and looking across at Burr, who did not observe her, with a wild, unearthly expression. He had not heard her step, and there was no rustling of the soft, dark garments she wore. In a moment she turned, threw up her hands, and glided away as noiselessly as she came. Mr. Burns looked inquiringly at his companion.

"It is my Aunt Laura, my mother's sister," he explained, with a slight shade of embarrassment.

Mrs. Rosevelt re-entered, and the little circle broke up for the night. The following morning after breakfast Mr. Burns went back to his room to look for some papers he had missed, and, the window being hung upon hinges, he opened it and stepped out on the veranda to look about and to collect his thoughts for the day's business. Burr and Mr. Rosevelt were in the yard below, at some distance, leaning against the fence, smoking cigars. Mr. Burns took a turn around the corner of the house and went down a short flight of steps, at the foot of which was a clump of shrubbery that had not yet lost its foliage, .and came suddenly upon a figure, which he recognized as the apparition of the evening before, crouching behind it, parting the leaves with her hands, and looking with an intense gaze in the direction of the men, from whose sight she was herself safely concealed.

"Poor thing; insane," thought Mr. Burns, compassionately.

Hearing his step she sprang up wildly, stared at him an instant, and then turned and flew away with almost incredible speed and noiselessness.

It took some time for Mr. Rosevelt to gather up his witnesses, and the trial was not resumed until afternoon;

and in the mean time Mr. Burns prosecuted his acquaintance with the Rosevelt family. Frank took him into a long parlor with a high ceiling and entertained him for an hour, with readings and recitations, in the most charming manner, evincing the rare cultivation which proves that the highest art is the perfection of nature. His language was a continual surprise, such as would indicate in an older man years of thought and study ; but at the same time he exhibited the pure guilelessness of a child. He reverenced his mother with an absolute devotion, and informed Mr. Burns with tears of tenderness in his beautiful eyes that he owed everything he possessed, even his capacity of appreciating and enjoying, to her.

"She has never fallen short in anything," he said. "Her mind is so large, her sympathies so broad, that they go beyond me in every direction. I lose myself in her larger world. I think," he added, "it is because of her indomitable energy; she has none of that *inertia* which prevents the most of us from developing our possibilities. You observe that she has a remarkably fine *physique*. She has bodily capability as well as mental. Her sons, with the exception of myself, resemble her."

"But you have vigor," said Mr. Burns.

"I have vitality," said he, laughing. "I am too fat. I have to fight against *inertia*."

The trial closed before nightfall, but there being every appearance of a heavy storm, the attorneys were constrained to accept Mr. Rosevelt's hospitality again. Mr. Burns was the more easily persuaded, as he had it in his mind to see Mrs. Marks again before he went home. Then, too, he had been pressed to come back by Mrs. Rosevelt, who seemed to feel that his companionship was good for her son.

It cleared up about dusk, after a brief but fierce storm of wind and rain, and the moon came out. Mr. Burns, ascertaining that the Marks's cottage was barely half a mile from Mr. Rosevelt's, excused himself for an hour and stepped over there. It was a very small cottage, but white and clean, and the garden and grass-plot around it were protected from the outside world of greedy animals

by a neat picket-fence. Everything about it bore evidence
of labor and care. The walk up from the gate was clean
swept and bordered with flower-beds, though the flowers
had long ago been nipped by the frost.

Mr. Burns knocked, and the door was opened by Mrs.
Marks, who had evidently been crying. An old lady,
whom she very much resembled, and whom she introduced
as "mother," sat rocking a golden-haired child to sleep
in her arms. Another lay on a little bed in one corner
of the room.

"I hope you haven't come to urge Susie on to get a
divorce," said the old lady, bridling a little at mention
of Mr. Burns's name.

"Far from it," said he. "I have come to try to make
peace, and I am glad that heavenly spirit has an advocate
here before me."

"Well, that's right," said the old lady. "Better to
grin an' bear, than to go to getting divorces an' bringin'
disgrace an' hardships on the little ones. It's bad enough
when Providence sees fit to separate parents an' scatter
families, without them taking it in their own hands to do
it. I know it's awful the way John has been going on,
but then he's jealous an' quick-tempered; I always knowed
that, an' so did Susie afore she married him. An' if she
liked him well enough to put up with it then, she ought
to now."

"Oh, mother! put up with all the disgrace? how can
I?" Susie exclaimed, wringing her hands and bursting
out afresh. "I don't know how you, as a mother, can
advise me to it!"

"Oh, Susie! it is because I am a grandmother," said
the poor old lady, stroking with her withered hand the
golden hair of the sleeping child on which her tears fell
fast. "John loves these little ones, and you, too, in spite
of all his faults; and he is fond of his home, and has
worked so hard to make it comfortable for us all. Think
how he has toiled, summer an' winter, an' day an' night
almost; an' all for you."

"Perhaps, Mrs. Marks," said Mr. Burns, who felt that
the mother would be sure to win in the end, "we had
better let the matter rest for a little time. Decisive ac-

tions at such times as this are almost sure to be regretted. Is Mr. Marks about? I would like to have a little talk with him."

"He is out-doors, somewhere," said the old lady, and he took up his hat, bade them "good-night," and went away.

When he reached the gate he found Mr. Marks leaning moodily upon it. He started violently and exclaimed, "What! have you been to see my wife—about getting a divorce?"

"I don't think your wife will want a divorce if you can turn over a new leaf and make a man of yourself," said Mr. Burns, a little sharply. "I have recommended her not to attempt it at present. Not that I have any doubts about her being able to obtain it. I have none. But it is better in almost every case for a husband and wife to hold together if they can, especially if there are children. Children have rights in such matters that ought to be respected; though parents seldom think of that. And now I would recommend you to treat your wife with a little more respect than you have just shown in dragging her before the public in this disgraceful way. Such an outrage is more than almost any sensitive, delicate woman can bear. The proceedings of yesterday and to-day have proved to me, beyond a doubt, that you have a good and virtuous wife; one who ought to be held far above suspicion. Make yourself worthy of her. Go and ask her forgiveness, and her mother's who gave her to you, for your treatment of her. Sell out your property here, and go to some new place and begin over again. That is the best advice, as a friend, that I can give you."

"I would sell to-morrow if I could!" said the excitable man.

"Well, perhaps I may help you to find a buyer," said Mr. Burns. "How much land have you?"

"Only a 'forty.'"

"Very well, I will try what I can do for you."

He said "good-night" and walked away, a little sick at heart, as he always was at any exhibition of the woes of the world.

CHAPTER XLV.

THE night was so still and beautiful that Mr. Burns, as he approached the Rosevelt premises again, felt averse to going in-doors. Besides, he wanted to think over the Marks's affairs and make up his mind how he could help them. He turned off into an ornamental grove—or what had been planned for an ornamental grove—just north of the house, and walked slowly along a narrow path under a row of maple-trees. He soon became conscious of another presence; the faint odor of a cigar was wafted to him from somewhere, and he felt sure that Burr, like himself, had strolled out for an hour of quiet thinking. But how could he have excused himself from the family? It might be that owing to the lateness of the hour the night before when they retired, they had dispersed earlier to-night.

Mr. Rosevelt had said to him when he went away, "If you stay late and we are gone to bed when you come home, you can step into your room through the window, if Mr. Courtenay will leave it unfastened."

He glanced at his watch and found that it was already past ten o'clock. Just then a figure emerged from a path that led from the house a few rods ahead of him and walked leisurely across a broad lawn to the left. He made sure it was Burr, and was about to follow and call out to him when, from the opposite side of the lawn, appeared another figure, which he, by and by, recognized as "Aunt Laura," coming direct to meet him. It looked very much, in that quiet, hedged-in spot, like a contrived plan. He stopped and leaned against the tree in whose shadow he was standing, and felt a strange, but not new, misgiving of his friend. Was it possible Burr had known this lady hitherto?

He flung away his cigar when she approached him, and for once forgot his accustomed courteousness and did not bow or lift his hat. Perhaps there was something in the intense earnestness of her manner that would have made such formality appear trifling. She came up to him in a half-beseeching, half-defiant attitude, her hands extended, but her bearing erect. Burr folded his arms and stood as if hardening himself against appeal. It was plain that it was not a sentimental meeting. Perhaps in some far-away beginning his relations with this strange creature had been sentimental enough, and now had come the hard reality.

Mr. Burns could hear the sound of their voices, but no intelligible words. Presently, as if to favor him, they turned and walked slowly toward him, the woman talking vehemently but in slightly muffled tones.

"No," said Burr, in a low, emphatic voice, "it is useless for you to talk, Laura; I should think your intuition would tell you it is a 'lost cause.' The past is dead and cannot be resurrected. Go back home. Don't stay here in this wilderness."

"Stop!" she cried. "I had something to tell you,—a secret I have kept from you for eighteen years. But your heart is hard as adamant; and now, God forgive me! I will *murder* you, Burr Courtenay."

She sprang in front of him with fierce tragedy, and, quick as thought, drew a pistol from her bosom and levelled it at his breast. But Burr, who was remarkably quick and adroit, when disposed to be, caught her wrist and wrenched it from her and flung it away. It lodged almost at Mr. Burns's feet. Burr held her hand for a moment, and then let it drop. Almost instantly a small, pointed stiletto gleamed in the moonlight. She grasped it in both her hands and made a plunge at him.

"I have waited years for this hour," she cried, "and I am prepared for it!"

But again Burr caught her hands and held them, trying, as it seemed, to subdue the fierce spirit with his magnetic eyes.

"Laura, what are you thinking of, to suppose you could match your poor, little strength against mine? If you wanted to kill me,—and I suppose you did,—why did you not conceal yourself among those trees, and fire on me as I passed along? It would have been much surer, and I do not know that I should have cared much. I am not very tenacious of life; it is not so sweet to me as it was once,—when you and I loved each other, Laura! But I could not let you kill me with my eyes open. I respect the law—of which you know I am an humble representative—too much to allow myself to become an aider and abettor of *murder.*''

She shuddered at the word '' murder,'' and he let go her hands again without depriving her of the knife. She let it drop upon the ground, and burst into tears.

'' There, don't cry, Laura !'' he said, and put out his hand and touched her with a sort of caress, which certainly was more cruel than his harshness to her. '' Go into the house, some one may miss you; and as soon as you can, go back home; you will be far happier there. You have wealth, and that is as much happiness as half the world ask. If it is any satisfaction to you to know that I shall never marry again, why, believe me, I never shall.''

He put her from him gently, and turned and walked rapidly away. She looked after him with streaming eyes, raised her hands imploringly, and then in utter hopelessness and helplessness dropped them and went slowly toward the house, sobbing and moaning.

It was many minutes before Mr. Burns could wake up from the horrible nightmare into which this strange scene had thrown him. His great love for his friend had received another cruel wound, but it could not die. Much as he loathed deceit and heartlessness, he could not loathe Burr Courtenay. The side which he had turned to him had .always been gentle and noble, even self-sacrificing. Burr must surely, all his life, have been the victim of strange circumstances ! The words, '' If it will be any gratification to you to know that I shall never marry again,'' made a startling revelation to him. Had Burr then once been married, and to this woman? What a history had been going on in the soul of his friend all these years that he had known nothing of ! It was a grief to him, which he could not get over, that Burr had, after all, never taken him into his heart, but had kept him always on the outer threshold with the door closed between. And yet, when he thought of it, it had been a good deal so with himself. His own secret had lain, for years, away from Burr's sight. There had been genuine loving-kindness between them, but not the sympathy that discloses all the soul's emotions.

They started home early the following morning, and drove the greater part of the way in silence; Mr. Burns being too heavy-hearted to care to keep up conversation, and Mr. Courtenay too preoccupied. His face looked blanched and hollow, as if he had not slept. For days they lived quite apart from each other, by tacit consent. Mr. Burns had the feeling that in his desponding moods he could no more turn to his friend with the secret assurance of being rallied out of them; for he, too, had his burdens to bear. And there is a kind of generous mockery in trying to lighten another heart when one's own is heavy laden, which he would not subject. Burr to. One thing he was glad of: that Burr seemed to have ceased altogether his attentions to Miss Clyde, and also quite ignored the foolish child, Sarah Jenkins,—not so much as bowing to her on the street. One day he met the former, and was pained to see that she was looking quite white and thin; but she still carried herself with the old, proud bearing. She was one who could suffer death, and not cry out. Burr had always had a preference for these queenly women.

CHAPTER XLVI.

In the midst of Mr. Burns's melancholy depression of spirit, his mind reverted to Miss Cleveland. Her society and friendship—for he felt himself able to grasp that, believing, when he remembered her calm face and cloudless eyes, that there could be no disguises between himself and her—could not fail to be a help to him. He caught at the idea with his customary avidity, and began to carry it into effect. For a week every evening found him at Deacon Clyde's door, asking always for Miss Cleveland, so that Maggie's heart grew sick and she fell back upon

her old resolution again, though perhaps with not so many
tears, for, as I have intimated, Dr. Webster was looming
up in her horizon; dim as yet, like the moon before
the sun has set, but promising to grow brighter, as that
pale beauty does when His Supreme Majesty has veiled
his splendor.

Miss Cleveland always came down and met him with
a cordial face and kindly hand-pressure and beguiled him
away from himself into her own serene, hopeful world,
showing him glimpses of a thousand reasons why it is
worth while to live, without a hint of the didactic in word
or manner.   Miss Cleveland's life was a continual lesson,
and a most pleasing one, with a sort of *Kindergarten* principle running through it; a constant teaching without
seeming to teach, which is the great secret of successful
instruction.   There is a perversity in young human animals
as in young colts; they will eat grass in a green pasture,
but they hate to have the halter slipped around their necks
and be led to the stable where the hay is cut and dried.
Mr. Burns no more dreamed that Miss Cleveland prepared
his lessons for him than the colt suspects his master of
fencing in the pasture field.   But she did.   She knew
that he stood in need of a little wholesome food; some
of the fresh, green grass growing up strong and sweet
above last year's sod.   To him it all seemed the spontaneous, unthinking budding out of the womanhood in her.
There was something, he told himself, in the delicate fibre
of a woman's mind, cultivated and pure, that chimed in
exactly with the organization of his own; which, itself,
had a feminine tone and sweetness that no strong man
need be ashamed of.

One evening—it was cold and raining a little, and Mr.
Courtenay, whose life was flowing on again without any
perceptible ruffling of its unfathomable waters, would have
thought it much too disagreeable to venture out,—Mr.
Burns donned his great-coat and started off up the hill.
It was a little earlier than usual, and when Bridget ushered
him into the parlor it was not yet lighted except by the
coals in the grate, that made a subdued though cheerful
play of lights and shadows upon the walls.   The room
had a soft, penetrating warmth permeated by some delicate

perfume; and seemed all the more inviting with just that glow-worm of fire. Drawn up before it were two low rocking-chairs moving slowly to and fro.

"Ah, is it you, Mr. Burns? Good-evening," said Miss Cleveland's voice out of the soft darkness, as she rose to meet him. "Now I shall have the great pleasure of introducing my two friends to each other. Miss Stuvysant happens to be down-stairs this evening, Mr. Burns."

She took Mr. Burns's hand and carried it on to Miss Stuvysant, who had risen as if electrified, and stood still.

"You will not be able to see each other's faces," Miss Cleveland added, laughing. "Pray be seated, Mr. Burns, and I will go and find a lamp."

She went out, and Mr. Burns took the chair she had vacated. Miss Stuvysant, unable to move, still stood with her hand resting on the back of hers. The firelight shone faintly upon her, and Mr. Burns looked at her inquiringly, and wondered if she were meditating flight.

"I must prevent that," he thought; "at least until they bring a light so that I can see her face." And he made a plunge at conversation.

Miss Stuvysant's lips had tried to form the words, "Will you excuse me, Mr. Burns?" but no sound passed them. To his remark that the night seemed to be getting stormy, she returned, in a low voice, dropping into her chair, "Yes, the wind sounds very wintry."

Bridget came in with a lamp and said, "Miss Cleveland begs ye to intertain each other fur a spell; she has something out here to see to."

She hurried out the moment she had set the lamp on the table, and Mr. Burns met Miss Stuvysant's eyes and sprang to his feet. "My God! it is Wilmingard."

She, too, rose up, and in the moment that intervened before he locked her two hands in his, she regained her strength, and in her face, in her deep, shadowy brown eyes, he saw, by an inner vision, as plainly as we see objects with the external eye, the reflection of the wide gulf which his hand had made between them. The first moment of recognition,—that which she had sometimes, in self-indulgent moods, allowed herself to look forward to as the supreme moment of her life,—fanned into sudden flame his old, boyish loyalty to her. But it faded in the quick-following consciousness of all that had since divided them, and their present relations to each other. Mr. Burns loosened his grasp and she withdrew her hands. She was the first to speak, and though her voice was steady and quite under her control, she showed no affectation of unconsciousness or indifference regarding their attitude toward each other.

"I presume we should both have avoided this meeting if we could have foreseen it," she said. "If you will excuse me, I will go and see if Miss Cleveland will not come in now"

"Wilma!"

He stepped before her and put out his hand as she turned toward the door. His mind was rapidly linking the past with the present, and showing him through what she had gone to reach the height she stood upon now; for her noble, patient, tender face revealed so much to which he alone, perhaps, had the key!

"Do not go!" he said. "Sit down and let us talk. Your life—for I have heard something of it, and I see something of it in yourself, as you stand there—forbids the presumptuousness of my asking your forgiveness, even for the wrongs I have done you. They *were* wrongs, though you may have borne them unharmed, and they left their stain upon me in your mind. Can you forget it in so far as to give me your friendship, Wilma?"

"I have never withdrawn my friendship from you," she said, sinking down in her chair and feeling the dreariness of reaction from a long-deferred hope at last fulfilled.

When we are brought face to face with a reality about which we have had inspired dreams, there is always a disparity which shocks more or less. A broad charity, such as Christ displayed upon the cross, would bid us drop its mantle over even the atrocious Jews crying "Crucify him! Crucify him!" when we remember what a hard thing it would be to bring an ideal religious faith down from the very heavens and fasten it upon a man,—one of ourselves, and very near to us through poverty and lowliness of station.

Miss Stuvysant, with her eyes fixed upon the actual face whose glorified memory had been her guiding-star, sat stupefied with one mighty consciousness; the grand climax of years had come, the sublimest moment she would ever know was passing. She felt that this meeting, which she would have deferred yet many years, was the closing act in the exquisite drama that had united their two lives. She looked, with a shudder and sickened heart, beyond into the blank, blank years that would follow upon this wild night, with no light in the distant horizon. And yet, was it possible that the dream upon which she had fed her life until it grew and widened and blossomed, had its reality in this man? She had placed him so high, and she had climbed so unweariedly to reach him, that now her eyes examined him with a sharp criticism, to find whether she had been deceived. What they saw in the first eager exploration was a form more slender than of old, a whitish face much worn, hair a little thinned at the temples and turning gray, and a mouth with a kind of settled irony. The eyes had their old intensity of expression, but the radiance of youthful hope and inspiration was gone. It is not strange that in the first moments her heart sickened with a terrible disappointment, and a dread that she had lived in a delusion. Charles Burns had almost ceased to be a tangible being to her. Her love for him had widened into a religion. She had worshipped him in all the beautiful and noble things her eye and mind could grasp. Her very life, strongly rooted in the good and true, had grown out of him.

Mr. Burns had no such intense consciousness as hers; the difference between them was this, that she was still living in the dream he had awakened from. His chief thought was, as he contemplated her with eye and mind, "Thank God, I have not ruined her life; she has made a noble woman of herself."

He had proposed that they sit down and talk. But an awkward silence fell upon him which he could not break. She was not embarrassed; the consequences to herself— to her inmost life—that would follow this meeting absorbed her completely. The spell under which she had lived a sad yet half-enchanted life all these years was broken by his actual presence, and it mattered little whether they talked or not.

But two people, whatever their relations, cannot sit and look at each other in silence many seconds. The wind was beginning to rattle the shutters and drive the frozen rain against the window-panes. Mr. Burns got up and walked to one of the windows and stood looking out a moment and then came back.

"It is strange I never thought of its being you," he said. "I knew that your real name was Stuvysant, of course, and yet it never came into my mind that the Miss Stuvysant I read about might be you. You took it when you began your readings?"

"No," she returned; "I took it after the death of my mother and sister, and when I went back to my father's relatives; or, rather, they gave it to me."

"I was shocked when I heard of the death of your mother and little Blanche," said he.

"And Fred, too, is dead. He was killed near Vicksburg," she returned.

There seemed to be nothing more to say. Each realized that though they had come very near to each other in the first instant of Mr. Burns's recognition, the rebound from the shock was sending them farther and farther apart every moment.

"What will be the end of this?" Mr. Burns thought.

Miss Cleveland opened the door and came in; before she had time to close it, the outer hall-door blew open violently, letting in a hurricane of wind and fine snow and sleet, slamming other doors and arousing the deacon and his wife to come and see what was the matter.

"What a terrible night," said Miss Cleveland, as they all started toward the hall.

"It suggests to me," said Mr. Burns, after he had helped the deacon to close and secure the door, "that I had better take my departure. I did not dream of its storming so."

He tossed back his chair with a gesture that Wilma well remembered, and took down his great-coat.

"Oh, you can never face such a storm as this," interposed Mrs. Clyde. "We will give you a bed here. The girls are not at home; they went out to spend the afternoon and did not get back; we have plenty of room for you."

"Oh, no, thank you, Mrs. Clyde," he returned. "I am greatly obliged to you, but I cannot stay. The fact is, I don't like to miss the chance of a battle with this wind. A storm arouses all the combativeness in me, which is a good thing occasionally. I remember it used to be my great delight when a boy to get out and confront old Boreas in his grand high moods."

The sight of Wilma recalled it to him. She stood a little behind the others in the doorway, in order to appear interested in what, for the moment, was a thing of paramount importance, while he buttoned his coat and drew on his gloves. He glanced at her with his old-time smile, and she inclined her head and then stepped back into the room.

After all, what a commonplace meeting it was; the naturalness of it seemed to rob the past of all its romance and mock the strong tension of her life. What a dreamer she had been!

"Well, if you must go," Mrs. Clyde said, "father had better take you out the back way. If we open this door again we shall have another hurricane."

"Oh, yes, certainly," said Mr. Burns.

"I am sorry your visit is cut off so short," said Miss Cleveland. "But you must come again when the weather settles."

"Thank you, I certainly shall," he returned.

The deacon took him out through the kitchen and held a light against the window, so that he could find his way to the gate. He had a hard fight, but it was good for him as he had said. Mr. Courtenay opened the door and let him in, with the snow all beaten into him and frozen in his hair.

"Heavens, what a night it is!" he exclaimed. "I had no idea it had grown so cold. I think my ears are frostbitten."

"Well, it seems to me," said Mr. Courtenay, deliberately, "that a fellow who would venture out such a night as this deserves some such chastisement, especially if he does not try to appease the wrath of the gods by tying up his ears.''

"The wrath of the gods,'' returned Mr. Burns, ''is usually appeased by the precaution of men! But I have always had a prejudice against tying up my ears.''

He took off his great-coat and shook the little icicles from his hair and seated himself by the fire.

It continued to storm through the night, but in the morning the wind dropped down, though it was extremely cold. The snow was piled up along the sidewalks like fine, sifted flour. The more Mr. Burns thought of his meeting with Wilmingard, the more excited and interested he grew. He had not been shaken as she had been. There was no very deep feeling lying in his heart to be rudely awakened; only a painful regret that he had once wounded her. And her manner seemed to show that, though she had felt it deeply, she cherished no hardness against him.

"Some women,'' he thought, "would have met me with a proud, assumed coldness or smiling indifference; but there is not a shadow of affectation in her. She assumes nothing; she ignores nothing. The wreck that I have made of our young loves lies before us, and she neither appeals to me nor reproaches me. She does not seem to see in me the cause of her suffering,—for I can see that she has suffered. She has accepted her share of the world's sorrows without complaint against the instruments of her torture. What a grand charity is that! I fancy she neither despises all men because of me, nor sees an exceptional monster in me. However one might wrong her, I believe she could still give him credit for all the good there was in him. Poor Wilma!'' he apostrophized, ''she has gone through an ordeal such as has burned the life out of many a heart. And she stands strong and delicate and self-poised and womanly.''

Even in the short time they had been together his mind had taken many impressions of her which his memory, dwelling upon, brought out and defined as clearly as stereoscopic views, though perhaps many of them had long ago been unconsciously imprinted on the palimpsest of his boyish appreciation of her, and brightened now in the light of his manhood's discernment. However it might be, he began to realize, with very little present acquaintance, the perfectness of womanhood in her. He grew impatient of another meeting, and yet felt some delicacy about forcing it upon her.

"She would have gone on her way without letting me know," he said ; "and yet, under the circumstances, how could she do otherwise?"

So he took his resolve and planned to see her again.

CHAPTER XLVII.

For two or three days it continued very cold ; so bitterly cold that people did not leave their firesides except from absolute necessity, and the consciences of those who held constant activity to be a duty could offer no reproach for idleness. There are occasional times in the lives of us all when some strong power outside of us takes things in its own hands and eases us, momentarily, of our accustomed burdens. It may even be a suffering and a loss to us, but the loosening of the tension of our lives gives us rest.

One day, quite late in the afternoon, a sleigh, with bells, dashed up to the office-door, and a man, hidden in buffalo-wrappings, sprang out and knocked loudly with the handle of his whip. Mr. Burns hastened to open the door, and the man stepped in and undid the strings of his cap and took it off, and they recognized him as Mr. Rosevelt's hired man.

"There's been awful doings up to our place," he said, hurriedly, "and I have come to get Mr. Courtenay to go up. Mrs. Rosevelt, she sent me. That crazy sister o' hern tried to commit suicide; an' Mr. Rosevelt interfered, an' she shot him, an' it's doubtful if he's livin' by this time. But if he is he wants to make his will; an' if *she* is she wants to make hern, too, I reckon ; anyway, she keeps commandin' them to send for Mr. Courtenay."

Mr. Burns glanced covertly at his friend, and saw his face blanch to marble whiteness.

"I've got to take the doctor with me," the man continued. "They said you would most likely want to drive your own horse. Could you be ready to go right off?"

Mr. Courtenay roused himself.

"Will you go with me, Charley?" he asked, with an appealing look in his eyes that seemed the nearest approach to a craving for sympathy Mr. Burns had ever seen there. His voice, too, faltered a little, and his hands trembled.

"Certainly I will go with you," said Mr. Burns. "But it is just supper-time; hadn't we better go down to supper first? And I will get Fred to harness Nobby and bring him around while we drink a cup of tea."

"Perhaps so," Burr assented.

"Well, then," said the man, tying on his cap again, "I'll drive on; you know the way an' can start as soon as you're ready. The doctor's waiting."

They got ready, speedily, and went down to supper; but owing to some delay on Fred's part they were not able to leave town for nearly an hour after the messenger had gone.

The sun was going down with a red and yellow glare, seen dimly through clouds of fine-sifted snow. The wind had risen, and it seemed to be growing colder. Nobby floundered through deep drifts and galloped over patches of hard, rough ground that the wind had bared of snow.

"It will be a fearful ride," thought Mr. Burns.

After they had got out of town a little way, and were driving along a lane somewhat sheltered from the wind, Mr. Courtenay said, "Charley, this is a wretched time to tell a story, but I wish to give you a few facts of a narrative which I will fill out hereafter in detail. I was once married to this woman whom we are going to see; it was a clandestine marriage contracted when we were at school, a sort of Gretna-Green affair. I was barely eighteen, and she not quite so old. She had a terrible temper, and mine, though not so demonstrative, was equally fierce. We quarrelled one day, and she ran away from me and went home and told her parents. They were greatly enraged and forbade my ever seeing her again, which, indeed, I had no desire to do. They took her to Europe and travelled for a year or two and then came back, and, after a time, took pains to let me know they had procured a divorce, which was false. She—Laura Wallihan was her name—would not give me up, but has always seemed to think she had a wife's claim upon me. I have been evading her for eighteen years. She came upon me once, away down in Florida, when I was on the eve of marrying again,—supposing I was free of her. She broke the heart of the woman I was to marry,—the sweetest, proudest, most sensitive and delicate creature I ever knew,—and poisoned her mind against me. She died—I will tell you where—at Crawford Academy. Your little friend, Wilma Lynne, was her guardian angel, and loved her and cared for her to the last moment of her life, and was the one mourner who followed her to the grave ; though I, myself, was there, concealed in the thick shrubbery of the cemetery."

He paused a moment or two, for the wind, sweeping fiercely across the prairie, seemed to have taken away his breath. Then he resumed. "I used to have lofty aspirations. I wanted my name to ring round the world. At one time, when I was very young, I hesitated between the two splendors of being a great actor and a great statesman. Patriotism triumphed, and I fixed my mark to become another Daniel Webster. But all that changed. Emerson says,—does he not ?—' That whatever we strongly wish will surely come to us.' I believe the contrary ; whatever we feel a strong aversion to, we will, in time, embrace. That was my case. From wishing for fame I went to the opposite extreme, and exerted all the ingenuity I possessed to hide both myself and my name. That has not been difficult since the war. I, in my turn, employed a lie to aid me. I contrived to have Laura informed that I was killed in battle. And she partly believed it until the other day when we were summoned on that cursed lawsuit."

He paused again, and Mr. Burns said, in tones of deep sympathy and sorrow, "Then she is still your lawful wife?"

"She is still my lawful wife," said Mr. Courtenay. "Since I saw her, I have been meditating flight again, and debating in my mind whether I should ask you to accompany me. Charley, my boy, you have been the brightness and the strength of my life for seven years. I dare say you have thought sometimes you were leaning on me, but it was the other way."

They drove on for many minutes without speaking again. Mr. Burns's heart was torn with the strongest emotions: pain, grief, self-reproach, and unbounded veneration for the brave soul that had carried its dreadful burden so long and borne it so well ; that scarcely even now complained. The wind rose higher and higher until it fairly shrieked, and the fine snow drove fiercely against them, and night was closing in. Mr. Burns stood up and tried to peer ahead into the gathering darkness.

"My God! Burr, I believe we're off the road. Whoa, Nobby." Nobby was glad enough to come to a halt. There was no house in sight ; no light, no tree, nor anything but the broad, white plain, with waves of wind and snow sweeping over it. Nobby, in trying to evade the wind, had veered constantly to the right, and so lost the road.

"Do you not think we had better turn back?" Mr. Burns asked. "We shall never be able to get through."

"Yes, let us turn back," said Burr. "This is damnable ! Nobby will surely find the way home."

So they turned him about, and rode on, and on, and on. It seemed as if it would last forever. A horrible fear crept into Mr. Burns's soul. It seemed to him he was being hardened into a marble figure.

"Burr, this is terrible !" he said.

Burr, upright and immovable, answered in a muffled monosyllable.

Some minutes passed.

"Burr, are you very cold ?"

"No ; but I am numb, I can't move. I think we are going to perish here, Charley." The words came thick and at little intervals.

"Oh, no, Burr ; not so bad as that. Not on this bleak, wild prairie, with no house in sight."

On, Nobby, with white fetlocks and foaming nostrils ; snorting, plunging, on, and on, and on.

"Burr ?"

No answer.

"Burr !" with a little shake.

A muffled response.

"Are you freezing, Burr ?"

Mr. Burns's voice sounded strange and weird, even to himself, pitched in a high key to penetrate Burr's dulled ear, and caught up by the wind, and borne off shrieking.

"Burr, are you very cold ?"

"No—not—cold," answered Burr, with slow, difficult enunciation.

Mr. Burns, with his own numbed hands, tried to tuck the robes closer around him. Nobby embraced the opportunity of slackened rein to turn out of the road,—for, at last, they had struck it again,—and the sleigh, striking a prairie-boulder, upset, and something snapped. Nobby, frightened, broke loose, and in a moment was out of sight and hearing, in the darkness and the roar. Mr. Burns got up clumsily and tried to right the sleigh. Burr, also aroused by the shock, staggered to his feet, but sank back upon the ground.

"Burr, in the name of God, what are we to do? Can you walk?"

"No, I think not, Charley. I—I" his voice stopped.

"We are not far from home; Burr; not above half a mile, I think. Come, get up, and let us try."

No answer.

"Burr, let's try to get to town; we'll perish if we don't move on, Burr." He shook him by the shoulder.

"I—I'm quite comfortable now, Charley. I can sleep here very well."

Burr's consciousness was almost gone. He spoke like one who was politely declining a favor.

"You are *freezing*, Burr !" shrieked Mr. Burns. "Here is my hand, pull !"

"I—I can't, Charley. You go. Go, and get home."

"And leave you here to perish? Burr Courtenay, I will lie down here and we'll die together if you don't make an effort to get up."

The severe tone aroused Burr's dull faculties. With Mr. Burns's help he staggered to his feet again, but offered no resistance to the mighty wind. Mr. Burns upheld and steadied him; forced him forward a step; another step, and then he faltered and sank down again, his limbs too stiff and numb to support him. Mr. Burns groaned.

"It's no use, Charley. Don't mind me,—go."

"Go, and leave you, Burr, to die alone? Good God! do you think I would forsake you now?"

"For help, Charley," came almost unintelligibly from Burr's lips, and then, oblivious of the cold, he nestled closer to the ground, like a sleepy child, and the snow drifted over him. No effort of Mr. Burns could arouse him again.

"He is right!" he said, seeing a gleam of hope. "I could never get him home against this wind,—God knows if I can get there myself! But I'll try; I may save him yet."

His whole soul went out in a strong prayer, "GOD GRANT IT!"

As quickly and dexterously as he could with his benumbed fingers, he seized the robes and blanket from the sleigh and flung them over Burr, tucking them closely in around him, and then, bracing his slender form against the fearful storm, he started forward, pressing on step by step, sustained by the strong hope of saving Burr. The cape of his blue cloak, which he sometimes flung on over his great-coat, flapped wildly about him. He gathered it over his head, and with his chin bent in upon his breast, kept his breath in the face of the wind.

CHAPTER XLVIII.

THE landlord of the hotel, together with Fred and Dick Gibson, several boarders, including Dr. Webster, several loafers and two storm-stayed travellers, sat around the bar-room stove, which was kept constantly red-hot.

"Hear it ! it sounds like the disembodied spirits of the accursed," said one of the travellers to the other, not profanely, but in a kind of listening awe.

They were Eastern men, and this was their first experience of a prairie "blizzard."

"Yes," said the other, responsive. "What is it that gives to the elements such unearthly voices? Were you ever at sea in a storm?"

His friend shook his head.

"Well; this is something like it; the creaking, and snapping, and roaring. It would seem that a thousand demon maniacs were careering upon the wind, laughing, cursing, screaming, and battling with each other. There is a weird poem running in my mind;" and the imaginative traveller began repeating it:

> "On such fearful nights as this, 'tis said,
> That vaulted tombs give up their dead;
> That hideous spectres, ghastly and grim,
> Steal stealthily round in the firelight dim;
> And demon birds, borne on wind and rain,
> Flap their black wings 'gainst the window-pane."

"One might easily be persuaded to believe that, to-night," said the other, with a shrug. "That wind would certainly be uncanny if we were not surrounded by these jolly fellows, whose scepticism banishes ghostly delusions."

The "jolly fellows" had been, one after another, telling ludicrous stories to hold up superstition to ridicule. But as the traveller, with thrilling effect, repeated his weird lines, they paused and listened, with cold chills creeping over them and hair bristling on end. Fred, especially, with open mouth and wide-stretched eyes, felt his knees shake.

For a moment or two everybody was silent. Then came a heavy thud upon the door outside. The travellers sprang to their feet; the landlord paused in the act of poking the fire; Fred rolled over on the floor, and Dick Gibson, with Dr. Webster to help him draw the bolts, opened the door. The others, not less startled, sat still and expectant. Something fell forward; a man wrapped in a dark-blue cloak. Every one in the room sprang toward him, and half a dozen voices exclaimed, "Lawyer Burns!"

They lifted him up and laid him on a wide, wooden settee.

"Burr," he gasped. "Go for Burr. He is freezing, dying!"

"Where!" they all cried.

"Out past Jenkins's place. Only a little way. Be quick! quick!"

The struggling voice ceased and the swollen eyelids closed. A little while longer, and Mr. Burns could not have told his errand.

In a moment or two all had started out to look for Burr excepting the landlord, the two travellers, and Dr. Webster, who were tacitly left to take care of the motionless figure on the settee, whose garments were already beginning to drip with melted snow.

"We must remove him from this room at once," said Dr. Webster, who immediately became the recognized authority. "The stove is red-hot, you see. He must be got to bed. Here, help me take off his boots and these outside wrappings."

The travellers sprang to his assistance.

"There's a bed in the sitting-room," said the landlord; "we'll take him in there."

He opened the intervening doors and cleared a passage, and they lifted him up and bore him through.

"He wasn't much to carry," said one of the travellers when they had laid him upon the bed. "I don't see how he stood up against this wind."

"He has got pluck!" said the landlord. "A good

Q*

deal more than the other one has; though the other one's twice as strong."

"He has escaped freezing, marvellously," announced Dr. Webster. "His hands and feet are frozen, but otherwise he is only benumbed and exhausted. He is sleeping heavily, you see; he will lie so for hours. In the mean time we must bathe his hands and feet in cold water."

The landlord hastened to bring it, and they all set to work.

Meanwhile, a sled had been got ready with incredible despatch, and half a dozen men sprang into it and urged the horses forward through the drifts and blinding snow. They drove some distance, and then descrying the lights of the Jenkins's windows—for it was Sarah Jenkins's wedding night, and in every room lamps were glimmering—a man, with a lantern carefully protected by an old blanket he wore around him, got out and went on ahead. Presently he stopped and threw the light forward. It fell on the overturned sleigh. All the others sprang out then and ran on except the driver.

"I don't see anything of him!" shouted the man with the lantern, above the wind. The sleigh was empty and all was white around it.

"Yonder!" cried another. "There's something flapping."

He pressed forward and seized it. It was a tag of buffalo skin. In a moment all hands were pulling at it. Underneath lay Burr. The light of the lantern flashed in his face. It was white as the white snow around it. Some one stooped and laid his hand upon it. It was like marble. He touched the forehead, eyelids, cheek; drew off one fur glove and clasped the stiffened fingers, then looked up, awe-struck, into the others' faces.

They did not take him up at once; they gathered in a little circle around him as if, instinctively, to protect him from the fierce storm, and looked down upon him, silent and speechless. Not one of them but would have risked his life to save him. He had shone like a brilliant star among them and they had worshipped him. They had been wont to boast of him; to think that whatever advantages other towns might have, they had no kingly

Courtenay. But their strong arms and their warm sympathies availed nothing now. The man with the lantern turned away and motioned to the driver to come nearer. They had hastily thrown some straw into the sled-box. Some one spread it out and tried to keep the wind from blowing it away. Others raised him up and carried him and laid him down upon it, and brought the robes and blanket and spread over him reverently, but did not tuck them in as Charley had done; there was no need. Then they drove on, and the pitiless, cold wind blew over him.

CHAPTER XLIX.

It was morning and the sun shone. It was cold, but marvellously calm, as if he who once hushed the winds had spread out his hands again and said, "Peace: be still."

"Burr? Where's Burr?" Mr. Burns, starting up with the familiar name on his lips, looked around upon the strange walls.

Dr. Webster was at his bedside. "How do you feel this morning, Mr. Burns, after your accident?" he asked, with attempted lightness, as if the upsetting of the sleigh and necessitated walking home were the only things to be remembered or regretted.

"*Where's Burr?*" demanded Mr. Burns, with rising impatience and contracting eyebrows, like a child whose question had been set aside.

"He is up-stairs," said the doctor, and added, with professional gravity and authority, "I would advise you, Mr. Burns, not to worry or excite yourself much. You were quite chilled when you got home last night, and I have some dread of fever after the—the exposure."

"What did they take him up-stairs for? Wasn't this bed wide enough for us both?" Mr. Burns returned. It seemed to him that he could not now bear even temporary separation from his friend. Burr's story had come back to

him with his first awakening, and brought the same pain
and tender sympathy he had felt when it was related.

"Burr must be worse off than I am," he added; "he
was out longer, though I covered him up with the robes
and came on as fast as I could, and sent the men. They
found him—*didn't you say they found him?*" turning upon
the doctor with fierce inquiry, as a horrible misgiving
occurred to him.

"Yes; they found him a short distance from town,"
the doctor returned, though he quailed a little under the
intensely questioning gaze.

"Thank God!" Mr. Burns lay back upon the pillow
restfully, and seemed at last satisfied. By and by he
said, with his face averted and speaking partly to himself,
"You have· no idea what a terrible storm it was. I
thought we should perish. Burr thought so, too; only I
could not give up to die there; it was too horrible."

A shudder passed over him.

"I think I will get up now, doctor. My hands feel
queerly—and my feet, too. I'm afraid I can't walk."

He had put his feet out on the floor.

"Were they much frozen?"

"Yes; quite badly," said the doctor. "Here are some
large slippers for you to put on; they are the landlord's."

"Large? I should think they were," said Mr. Burns,
with a laugh, as he slipped his feet into them. "But I
can walk better in them than in my stocking-feet. Now,
if you will have the goodness to tell me what room Mr.
Courtenay is in, doctor,—or show me the way,—I will go
up and see him."

Dressed and standing upon his feet, Mr. Burns recovered
the air of dignity and reserve he habitually preserved in
the presence of strangers. The doctor hesitated. Mr.
Burns, in some surprise, glanced up.

"Good God! he is not *dead!*"

The doctor answered by a look: Dead.

After a time he led the way up into the long, dim parlor. Is that Burr? that long, draped form lying there so
still? Is it Burr's presence that fills the room with such
an awe and majesty? The doctor went forward with
noiseless tread and folded back the sheets, and Mr. Burns

stood and gazed upon the one face that he loved. It was white and beautifully chiselled as the finest marble face; the forehead broad and smooth, the arched, black brows exquisitely pencilled, the long lashes sweeping the cheeks, and the glossy, wavy beard flowing down upon the chest. But the grand intellect beneath was forever stilled.

Some one had carefully brushed back the black masses of hair; there were more white threads mingled with it than Mr. Burns had thought; a few, too, in the glossy beard that he had never noticed before. He took up one of the exquisitely-shaped hands and knelt down, pressing it against his heart.

"Oh, my friend, my Burr!" he cried. "Can it be that you are dead? Would to God that I had perished with you!"

He dropped his head upon the pulseless body, and so remained for many minutes, groaning aloud. Then he arose, and laid the dead hand gently down and turned and grasped the doctor's living hand, his eyes strangely bright.

"Can you tell me, Dr. Webster," said he, "can any intelligence upon this earth reveal to me the knowledge of where my friend is now? There lies the immaculate form of Burr Courtenay! but where, in this vast universe, is the immaculate soul? Shall I ever find it again? You did not know him, Dr. Webster," he added, dropping the hand, and walking up and down the room. "You never saw his eyes beam with tenderness greater than a woman's; or flash in battle when he led his regiment forward in the face of death. How the soldiers loved him! And how tender he was of them, even the least of them! He felt for all their woes and wounds and sufferings; and in the midst of his arduous duties he found time to write their dying messages to friends at home,—tender, comforting letters that could not but soothe the hearts his sad tidings wounded. He told them where their loved ones were sleeping, and marked their graves often with his own hands. And now he is *dead!*"

He ceased speaking, but continued to walk up and down the room, groaning, but shedding no tears. And where was the voice that would have comforted him for its own awful silence ! Had it gone out on the pitiless night-wind calling him—Charley, Charley?—and he had not answered.

Suddenly he thought of the consequences to others (and with a feeling of jealousy that any but himself should have a claim upon Burr) that would follow upon this terrible death. He remembered Miss Clyde, and his heart ached for her. He remembered Laura Wallihan—as Burr had called her, and he could not bring himself to consider her as Burr's wife—with a bitterness that amounted to hatred. One thing he determined upon : if possible he would prevent Burr's history from being made public. Miss Clyde might have the sad privilege of mourning for him if she would, he would take pains that her grief should not be poisoned, by this terrible revelation.

Dr. Webster, seeing that his mind was in some way diverted, asked if he would not now go below.

"Oh, no !" said he. "No, I shall stay here. The time will be short enough."

So the doctor went away and left him.

He sat down in a chair by Burr's side. Cold drops were starting out on his forehead and about his mouth, and there was a strange trembling at his heart as he reflected how utterly alone he was now ; and for the second time in his life he pitied himself. Then he remembered Wilma, and vaguely wondered whether the past might not be bridged over, and they two clasp hands again as in their tender young spring-time, or with even a better understanding and appreciation of each other; for they could both see things more clearly now than in those days. They had both suffered. But when he remembered the grave reserve of her manner, though it was kind and not resentful, he doubted whether anything could be done. And certainly he had not the heart to try. What mattered anything now !

Somebody opened the door and said, "Mr. Burns, there is a lady here who wishes to see you."

Mr. Burns started up, thinking of Miss Cleveland,—there was certainly no other woman in the place who would come to show him a little sympathy,—and asked, " Can she come up here ?"

"Maybe so ; I'll see," said the messenger, and went down.

Presently a tall woman in black entered, and put aside her veil, revealing the noble but much changed face of Mrs. Rosevelt.

" I learn that you have trouble as well as we, Mr. Burns," she said, coming up and giving him her hand, or, rather, clasping his with a strong, sympathetic clasp. " We supposed Mr. Courtenay purposely evaded coming when we sent for him, and it was so imperative that he should come that I came myself to fetch him. I presume you did not know, Mr. Burns, that your friend had a wife and son ?"

"A son ! impossible," said Mr. Burns. " I learned very recently that he had a wife."

"And a son, also," repeated Mrs. Rosevelt, " whom it will surprise you to know is our Frank."

" Your Frank ! Frank Rosevelt."

It required but a momentary retrospection of his brief acquaintance with the young man to enable Mr. Burns to adjust his mind to the startling fact. The next moment he wondered why he had not discovered it for himself. There was every resemblance between father and son ; voice, face, manner, gestures. Except that Frank was a sort of refinement of Burr,—smaller in stature and more delicate in mental and moral organization.

"My sisters will reveal these things to Frank," continued Mrs. Rosevelt, "and I thought it but right that Mr. Courtenay should recognize the son beside the dead body of the mother."

"Then she is dead?" said Mr. Burns, not without a feeling of relief.

"Yes, both she and my husband," said Mrs. Rosevelt.

There was something so touching in the way this grand woman seemed to reserve her own griefs that Mr. Burns silently clasped her hand again.

"Our troubles, if nothing else, ought to unite us, my dear Mrs. Rosevelt," he said. " Is there anything I can do for you ?"

"Nothing, except to let it be known that your friend had a son who will inherit his name."

Mr. Burns drew back. He was thinking of Miss Clyde.

"Is that necessary, Mrs. Rosevelt," he asked. Mrs. Rosevelt looked up with a flash of indignation in her eyes.

"I mean does the young man wish it," he continued.

"I hardly know whether he wishes it," she returned. "But circumstances force it upon him."

"I do not know that I ought to speak of it to you," said Mr. Burns, with an impulse to be frank with her, "but my friend, not knowing that he had a wife living, has for years past been paying attention to a young lady here, in the village. I was thinking that it would be very embarrassing to her to have these things brought to light."

"Hardly as embarrassing for her, I think," returned Mrs. Rosevelt, "as for Mr. Courtenay's son to continue all his life—and consciously, too—in a false position; any disinterested person, Mr. Burns, must see that he, first of all, should receive justice."

Mr. Burns's better judgment decided so, too.

"Where is he?" he asked. "Did he come with you?"

"Yes; he is below, waiting to see his father."

His father!

Mr. Burns thought it was a bitter thing to have his friend wrenched from him in these last hours. He turned and walked to the other side of the room, and while he stood there looking out of the window the young man came in. He heard his voice and started, it was so like Burr's. But he did not turn round. By and by, Frank came up to him, and held out his hand with a gentle courtesy that was also much like Burr's in his softer moods; and his young, beautiful face, now white with intense, sorrowful emotion, was not without a close resemblance to the marble face yonder. Not so proud and not altogether so perfect, but possessing even greater winsomeness, and a fascination equally strong, but not dangerous.

"I have not come to rob you of your friend, Mr. Burns," he said, sadly. "I have only come to mourn with you. I hope you will not think me an intruder."

"No; you have the better right," said Mr. Burns.

"Pray, do not say so!" Frank returned, feeling hurt. "It is mockery. I have no right. He never knew of my existence. I was nothing to him, but he, of necessity, is something to me."

Mr. Burns felt rebuked. A sense of delicacy induced him, by and by, to offer his arm to Mrs. Rosevelt and go below, leaving the young man alone with his dead father. He asked Mrs. Rosevelt if Burr and his wife were to be buried together.

"Oh, no," she returned. "They were not united in life, why should they be in death? My sister will be carried to-morrow to Winchester Cemetery, which is nearer to us; of course we shall leave all this to you."

Burr's funeral was not to take place until the day after.

There were no railroads to connect High-Water-Mark with any other town, but in a few hours the news had spread far and wide. Mr. Woodbury and several other gentlemen drove down from Hammond Springs and delicately consulted with Mr. Burns about the arrangements for the burial, which he begged to entrust wholly to them; the simpler citizens of High-Water-Mark standing back a little in awe of them.

The day of the burial Mr. Burns was unable to leave his room. He sat the greater part of the time with his face buried in his hands, groaning from time to time, but speaking to no one unless especially addressed. Even the first shock was hardly so bad as this fuller realization of his loss. To think that he should be living in the world without Burr! He had gradually let go of everything save this one friend, and now there was nothing to hold to. He listened for hours to the constant stream of people filing up and down the narrow stairs and in and out the long, dim parlor, and felt that it was almost unbearable.

No fire had been kindled in the long parlor, and Burr still lay in all his splendid beauty, not even having lost his awe-inspiring presence. They had dressed him in the blue uniform he had taken off when he left the army; and from all the towns and villages around came squads of soldiers to do honor to him. Scarcely one person in the community but what claimed the privilege of a last look; and none approached him irreverently or gazed upon him without emotion. A few wizen-faced old women, who had been wont to shake their heads at mention of his name, laid their yellow, skinny hands upon his forehead, and wondered how Evelyn Clyde would take it.

Poor Evelyn! in her proud, happy days she had gathered her treasures into her own heart. No mortal shared them. Now they were in ashes and utter ruin, and she turned her heart into a sepulchre and cherished them still. And with the stoicism of a cold, proud nature, whose every feeling and hope were centred upon an object and wrecked in an overthrow, she closed her lips and went about silent and cold and white, almost, as he who had died in the snow.

CHAPTER L.

THE fever which Dr. Webster had intimated as likely to follow Mr. Burns's exposure followed in due course. The torturing ceremonies of funeral and burial were hardly over before he fell into a state of forgetfulness lasting many days.

Frank Courtenay begged leave of her whom he still called "mother" to stay with him. "I will take my father's place to him, in as far as I can," he said, with tears in his eyes. "It must be," he added, "that there was a great deal of good in my father, else a man like Mr. Burns could not have loved him so."

Dr. Webster, also, was especially kind and attentive; and when at last intelligence returned to the long-wandering eyes, and with it the crushed sadness that comes after sickness and grief, these two were beside him. But sympathy from strangers, at first, was so distasteful that he turned away. And then, little by little, their thoughtful presence and tender care won upon him and softened his heart with feelings he had thought would never spring up again. Dr. Webster, who was gaining a small practice, often left him alone with young Courtenay; and gradually they began to speak of Burr; and Mr. Burns recalled and poured into the ears of the deeply-sympathetic son a thousand incidents of his life, until he seemed a hero.

There was a broad charity in the soul of this young man that could look with impartial eyes on the lives of his parents, nor judge them harshly or with reference to the sorrow they had brought upon himself.

Mr. Burns saw it, and came to love the gentle youth whose pure life seemed purged of all the evils that had befallen theirs. Certainly all that was good and noble in Burr Courtenay survived in this son whom he had given to the world. Though he was so young, he was ripe in thought and study; and a strong and deeply-sympathetic imagination in him took the place of experience in older people. He had inherited Burr's eloquence and remarkable command of language. But Burr's personal ambition had been transmitted to him in the broader form of a desire—backed by a strong energy of will—to help others forward. Burr's tender-heartedness led him to do a thousand kindnesses, but his pride kept him always aloof from others. Frank was reserved, but the book of his inmost life might be laid before the world.

Mr. Burns remembered a theory of Burr's; that no good thing, once existing, can ever be lost; and that any being endowed with the life-principle, will give out life in some form for the good of the world,—as Michael Angelo his pictures, as Beethoven his music, as Homer his poems, as Washington his patriotism, and, Mr. Burns added, as Burr Courtenay his son. Sometimes it seemed to him almost as if his friend had passed through some strange transformation and come back to him. And yet the great difference remained that the consciousness of the one was not the consciousness of the other. Showing that no being can slip into another's place, but that each must make his own niche in the world and in the heart of a friend. No one can dislodge another, and himself fill the vacancy; the world is broad and the heart is elastic; and no one being can fill the mould that has been fashioned by another. And so Mr. Burns mourned still for the friend whose history was so interwoven with his own, and with whose soul he had become so familiar in their long years of intimacy. Even after he was able to get up and go about he delayed, many weeks, returning to the office. His wound was too tender to bear, yet, any probing.

One day, about the opening of spring, Frank said to him, "Mr. Burns, I must leave you now and go back to my studies."

"How can I spare you?" said Mr. Burns.

But in the end it was better. The effect of the young man's earnest resolution to take his place in the world and prepare for work was more strengthening to the invalid, who was an invalid in mind as well as in body, than even his tender care of him.

We have many precepts; but those things that stand out like lights upon a dark road, in the long history of the world, are noble lives that have not been turned aside by the little pebbles of circumstance, but have gone straight to a grand aim.

Dr. Webster, in the light and brightness of advancing spring, began to look shabby as to his clothes, which were getting threadbare, and to talk about going back home.

"Don't do that," said Mr. Burns. "You have got a foothold, and we are sure to have better times when the railroad is completed. Come into my office, you are very welcome; and, in the mean time, I will take pleasure in making you a loan of a few dollars. And you shall have the use of my horse for your country practice. Are the inducements sufficient?"

Dr. Webster answered by grasping his hand. "You are a true friend," said he, and added, "I do not know what I could do if I went home; my mother is a widow and poor, and the town in which she lives is already supplied with medical talent. There would be nothing for me there except manual labor of some kind, and I have not fitted myself for that."

"And you shall not do that," said Mr. Burns. "There are more hands in the world than brains."

The doctor had it in his mind to tell him that some time back, when his prospects had seemed brighter, he had thought he might some day ask Maggie Atherton to be his wife; but he did not mention it until several weeks afterward, when they had both gone into the office and the doctor had arranged his medical books beside the ponderous law-books. Then Mr. Burns said, "Why not do it now? My dear friend, if you have a great happiness within your reach, grasp it and hold it close to your heart, or it will vanish from you. Maggie has property, and it seems to me she could get no better security for it than you are able to give."

"Is that really the way to look at it?" said Dr. Webster, doubtfully.

Mr. Burns said, smiling, "It is the way in which I, a man of experience, of gray hairs, and of legal mind, look at it. What more would you have?"

"Nothing!" said the doctor. "And I will take your advice in this, as in many other things, my best friend."

Mr. Burns went with him occasionally to Deacon Clyde's, and offered to poor Evelyn the most delicate sympathy his tender soul could devise, and that came nearer to softening the ice about her heart than any other influence. She came at last to lean upon him a little, and her crushed soul began to send out little tendrils in other directions. She grew kind to the poor, and made a good many homes brighter for her queenly presence in them; and little Maggie, always loving her and admiring her above all others, worshipped her now. She seemed, in some sort, sanctified by having been the altar on which a great fire of love was kindled.

The spring came on apace. Work on the railroad was going forward with a great rush, and High-Water-Mark prospects were brilliant. Earth seemed new and happy, and the world was alive with singing birds and whistling ploughboys; and the green grass waved over Burr Courtenay's grave.

CHAPTER LI.

ONE day, in looking over the papers, Mr. Burns saw a reference to Miss Stuvysant, who, with her friend, had left High-Water-Mark the day upon which Mr. Courtenay was buried, and gone back East.

"She does not need me," said he, bitterly; "and yet, by my own act, she was made independent of me. I was the only thing she leaned upon, and when I wrenched myself away from her she grew up tall and strong. Well, they say the only way to reach our highest possibilities is to have our props taken away! And yet, God pity us all who are left standing alone!"

Dr. Webster had told him a few days before that the deacon had given his consent to his marriage with Maggie, and that the wedding was soon to take place. A part of Maggie's property consisted of a house and grounds not far from the deacon's; and repairs and furnishing had already begun, and Maggie was as happy as a bird, with perhaps the exception of a tender little regret, now and then, over her first love.

"But after all," she would say to herself, consolingly, "Dr. Webster will, maybe, make me happier than Mr. Burns could. For Mr. Burns has never seemed to me to be quite happy himself; and yet," she added, thoughtfully, with a common, egotistic, and yet pretty conceit, "if he had loved me and married me, I might have made him happy. I would have been so good to him, like the poor soul in 'Tender and True.'" And then she would pull herself up sharply, and chide herself for disloyalty to the doctor, who—she told herself severely—never dreamed of her being such a deceitful little wretch.

It had been her great wish from the first hour of her engagement to go on a long wedding-trip, away down East, to visit the doctor's relatives, and to get a glimpse of the mountains and of the great ocean. And so, almost the first Eastern bound train that passed through High-Water-Mark carried away the happy bride and groom, and the white, stately Evelyn, whom Maggie had begged and entreated, with tears, to accompany them. It was in the evening, and Mr. Burns had gone with them to the depot, which was distant nearly half a mile from the centre of the village, and had bidden them "good-by," and waved his handkerchief as the train swept away.

Before returning to the office he went down and walked, by moonlight, along the river bank, recalling,—as only the strongly imaginative can recall,—with vivid memory, his past life, and the friends who, one by one, had dropped away from him. "Is there, then," he murmured, "no reality in these sweet things,—Love and Friendship? Is the practical part of life—the eating and drinking and accumulating—all that is left to us in our latter years? Oh, that a *little* of the poetry and sweetness would linger round us all the way down the long journey !"

Frank Courtenay had written a poem for the Alumni of his *alma mater*, and sent him a printed copy. When he read it, the thought occurred to him that here was a nature that would preserve the best things of life to its very close. He would never lose faith in humanity; he would think it always worth his grandest efforts to work for the bettering of the race.

He had written in one of the many beautiful letters Mr. Burns received from him, "It should be the great effort of each generation to work for the good of itself, and increase the annual aggregate of happiness of its millions. I believe strongly in the present; because it is our one, actual possession." And again, "We are not justified, it seems to me, in cheapening and depreciating this life, as ministers and psalmists often do, by calling it a 'fleeting show,' a 'day of probation,' and so forth. To me it is a noble gift, to be enjoyed and made beautiful. Whatever man's future may be, in his present form and conditions, he is certainly created with directest reference to the world he inhabits; let him get as much good out of the world and give as much to it as is in his nature, and he will have little time to expend in vague speculations of what may come hereafter. I can see so much and enjoy so much, in one little hour, of actual beauty !

Why should I close my eyes and let my fancy revel in the unreal?"

Walking along beside the river-bank, and thinking partly of his young friend and partly of his own youth, when he was hopeful and full of zest, Mr. Burns felt a sudden strong desire to revisit his boyhood's home and his mother's grave. Perhaps something of what he had lost would return to him in that sacred spot. He had never sold his mother's little cottage; and he pictured it standing in its orchard of apple, and peach, and wild plum trees, the flagstones in front covered with moss, maybe, and the grass and weeds growing rank around it. The thought of going back to it, of perhaps making up his mind to spend the rest of his years in that quiet spot, came like an inspiration, quickening the sluggish stream of his life into a strong current. He turned about and walked hurriedly home; packed some clothes into a small trunk, and sat up all night, dozing from time to time in his chair, waiting for the early morning train.

"Let us make haste, Wilma, or the sun will be down before we reach the top of Little Twin, and I don't want to miss it to-night; it's my last chance for a good many months, you know."

The shadows lay upon Hazelview exactly as they had done ten years before; and the sun, throwing his level beams from low down in the west, lighted up the tops of the hills and trees. Mr. Burns was crossing the race alone upon the two logs thrown over it, when these words came back to him exactly as he had uttered them so long ago, as though given back in echo from the low hills hemming in the quiet water. Involuntarily he cast his eyes westward and quickened his steps up the long hill and stood finally upon its summit with uncovered head. He had gazed upon many a grander scene, but none that shed such peace upon his soul,—a peace so tender and sweet that it caused tears to well up in his eyes.

Was it a dream? or had he actually lived those ten years that used to stretch out so gloriously beyond him!

He gazed down upon the changeless water lying far

below, in the shadow, with just the moon dipping into it and throwing a shining pathway athwart it, as it had done so many, many nights before; as it had done on that last memorable night. He stood still and fancied Wilma beside him, looking up with her soulful eyes. Surely, surely, this must be real! The past has rolled back and they stand again, hand in hand, at the entrance of life.

There was a cloud before the sun, purple and crimson and gold. It broke away gradually, and the sun burst forth and shone for a moment gloriously, then went down. Mr. Burns's spirit sank into profound sadness. He stood with folded arms and bowed head, his cloak thrown back over his shoulders. He fancied something touched him upon the arm, and started and looked around. Surely, it must be Wilma's presence that steals upon him in the half-darkness! All at once, upon the perfect stillness of the hour, breaks the tolling of a bell, down below. One, —two,—three,—he counted the strokes mechanically, up to twenty-six. As the lingering vibration of the last mournful stroke died away, he turned and walked slowly back to the village. He inquired of the first person he met,—a stranger,—"Who is dead?"

"A lady, somewhat noted as an elocutionist, who returned here a few days ago after an absence of some years," said the stranger. "I have forgotten the name she went by, but the old settlers call her Wilma Lynne."

THE END.

R   33

What a Boy! Problems Concerning Him. I. What shall we do with him? II. What will he do with himself? III. Who is to blame for the consequences? By JULIA A. WILLIS. With Frontispiece. 12mo. Fine cloth. $1.50.

"Every member of the family will be sure to read it through, and after enjoying the author's humor, will find themselves in possession of something solid to think about."—*New York Christian Union.*

"There is a vein of practical sense running through the story which will be food for old and young readers, and the charming love scenes render the book one of absorbing interest, and the reader must be dull enough not to relish the book from beginning to end."—*Pittsburgh Commercial.*

The Nursery Rattle. For Little Folks. By Anne L. HUBER. With Twelve Chromo Illustrations. Small quarto. Extra cloth. $1.75.

"'Nursery Rattle' is all the better because it generally does not pretend to carry meaning or moral with it, and it has a musical ring in it."—*Philadelphia Inquirer.*

"The best collection of nursery songs from one pen in the language. Simplicity of idea, clearness of expression, brevity of words, and fine humor and sympathy mark the 'Nursery Rattle.'"—*San Francisco Alta California.*

Diana Carew; or, For a Woman's Sake. A Novel. By Mrs. FORRESTER, author of "Dolores," "Fair Women," etc. 12mo. Fine cloth. $1.50.

"A story of great beauty and complete interest to its close. . . . It has been to us in the reading one of the most pleasant novels of the year, and at no time during our perusal did we feel the interest flagging in the slightest degree. . . . Those who admire a love-story of good society, and who especially admire ease and naturalness in writing and character painting, will find in Mrs. Forrester's latest novel a deep pleasure."—*Boston Traveller.*

Pemberton; or, One Hundred Years Ago. By HENRY PETERSON, author of "The Modern Job," etc. 12mo. Extra cloth. $1.25.

"As a historical novel this work is a graphic representation of the Philadelphia of the Revolution, and as a romance it is well imagined and vividly related. The interest never flags; the characters are living, human beings of the nobler sort, and the style is simple, chaste, and appropriate."—*Philadelphia Evening Bulletin.*

"The style is graceful, fluent, and natural, and the various conversations between the different characters are marked with strong individuality."—*Philadelphia Ledger.*

Alide. A Romance of Goethe's Life. By Emma LAZARUS, author of "Admetus, and other Poems," etc. 12mo. Fine cloth. $1.25.

"A charming story beautifully told, having for its subject the romance of a life, the interest in which is and must for a long time be intense and all absorbing.

"This is a tender and touching love-story, with the best element in love-stories, truth. The story is very charmingly told, with rare grace and freshness of style."—*Boston Post.*

The Livelies, and other Short Stories. By Sarah Winter Kellogg. With Frontispiece. 8vo. Paper. 40 cents.

"It is a long time since we have read a more agreeable or better written book. The authoress has a pleasant, racy, lively style, considerable powers of humor, and at times of pathos."—*New York Arcadian.*

"'The Livelies' is a sketch of domestic life made thrilling by the introduction of incidents of the great fire at Chicago.'"—*Philadelphia Age.*

"The tales are pleasantly written, in a bright, taking style, both the plots and characters being interesting. The book is decidedly readable, and will assist materially in hastening the flight of an odd hour."—*Easton Express.*

"There are five admirable stories in this book, all well told and interesting."—*Baltimore American.*

The Fair Puritan. An Historical Romance of New England in the Days of Witchcraft. By Henry William Herbert ("Frank Forester"), author of "The Cavaliers of England," "The Warwick Woodlands," "My Shooting Box," etc. 12mo. Fine cloth. $1.50.

"It is a stirring story of stirring events in stirring times, and introduces many characters and occurrences which will tend to arouse a peculiar interest."—*New Haven Courier and Journal.*

"The story is a powerful one in its plot, has an admirable local color, and is fully worthy to rank with the other capital fictions of its brilliant author."—*Boston Saturday Gazette.*

"The story is well and vigorously written, and thoroughly fascinating throughout, possessing, with its numerous powerfully dramatic situations and the strong resemblance to actual fact which its semi-historical character gives it, an intensity of interest to which few novels of the time can lay claim."—*Philadelphia Inquirer.*

"A romance of decided ability and absorbing interest."—*St. Louis Times.*

The Green Gate. A Romance. From the German of Ernst Wichert, by Mrs. A. L. Wister, translator of "The Old Mam'selle's Secret," "Gold Elsie," "Hulda," etc. *Fifth Edition.* 12mo. Fine cloth. $1.75.

"It is a hearty, pleasant story, with plenty of incident, and ends charmingly."—*Boston Globe.*

"A charming book in the best style of German romance, redolent of that nameless home sentiment which gives a healthful tone to the story."—*New Orleans Times.*

"This is a story of continental Europe and modern times, quite rich in information and novel in plot."—*Chicago Journal.*

Patricia Kemball. A Novel. By E. Lynn Linton, author of "Lizzie Lorton," "The Girl of The Period," "Joshua Davidson," etc. 12mo. Fine cloth. $1.75.

"'Patricia Kemball' is removed from the common run of novels, and we are much mistaken if it does not land Mrs. Linton near the skirts of the author of 'Middlemarch.'"—*Lloyd's Weekly.*

"The book has the first merit of a romance. It is interesting, and it improves as it goes on. . . . Is perhaps the ablest novel published in London this year."—*London Athenæum.*

"'Patricia Kemball,' by E. Lynn Linton, is the best novel of English life that we have seen since the 'Middlemarch' of 'George Eliot.'"—*Philadelphia Evening Bulletin.*

A Family Secret. An American Novel. By Fanny

ANDREWS ("Elzey Hay"). 8vo. Paper cover. $1.00. Fine cloth. $1.50.

"Her novel is as entertaining as any novel need be. . . . There are some character-drawing and life-picturing in the volume which mean a good deal more than mere amusement to discerning readers."—*New York Evening Post*.

"The character sketching and the narrative portions of the work are graphic and entertaining, and show considerable skill in construction on the part of the author. It is a book that will repay the reader's pains, and that is more than can be said of perhaps the average works of fiction."—*Boston Post*.

A New Godiva. A Novel. By Stanley Hope,

author of "Geoffrey's Wife," etc. 12mo. Extra cloth. $1.50.

"'A New Godiva,' by Stanley Hope, is a capital story of English life, abounding in incident of a highly dramatic nature, and yet not overwrought. The plot is somewhat intricate, but it is clearly developed, and is decidedly interesting. The characters are well drawn, and the descriptive parts of the book are spirited and picturesque. There is enough excitement in it to do efficient service for two or three novels."—*Boston Saturday Evening Gazette*.

"It is written with a strong, skilled hand, confident of its strength, and conscious of its skill."—*New York Evening Post*.

"We heartily commend it to our readers."—*New Orleans Bulletin*.

Wild Hyacinth. A Novel. By Mrs. Randolph,

author of "Gentianella," etc. 12mo. Fine cloth. $1.75.

"One of the best novels of our day. No writer of fiction has produced a more delightful and interesting book."—*London Court Journal*.

"This is a clean, wholesome book. The plot, if slight, is very fairly good; the characters of the story are well drawn and skillfully developed; the moral is unexceptionable. . . . We have already said enough to show our hearty appreciation of a book which is excellent in tone and clever in execution."—*London Standard*.

Malcolm. A Romance. By George Macdonald,

author of "Robert Falconer," "Alec Forbes," "Ranald Bannerman," etc. 8vo. Paper cover. $1.00. Fine cloth. $1.50.

"It is full of good writing, keen observation, clever characterization, and those penetrative glances into human nature which its author has a habit of making."—*New York Graphic*.

"It is the most mature, elaborate, and highly finished work of its distinguished author, whose other novels have had an extraordinary success.'—*Philadelphia Evening Bulletin*.

Blanche Seymour. A Novel. By the author of

"Erma's Engagement." 8vo. Paper. 75 cents. Fine cloth. $1.25.

"It is simple and natural in plot, and is admirably told, particularly in its more pathetic portions. The sentiment is gracefully tender, and the characters are drawn with great spirit and discrimination."—*Boston Saturday Evening Gazette*.

"The author's great merit consists in the commendable naturalness of all her characters. She is, too, very amusing with her side remarks and the feminine cleverness which is to be seen on every page. . . . We hardly know a more entertaining little volume than this."—*N. Y. Nation*.

The Heir of Malreward; or, Restored. A Novel. By the author of "Son and Heir," etc. 8vo. Paper. $1.00. Cloth. $1.50.

"This is an English story of ill-assorted marriage and the triumph of good over evil in what seemed to be irretrievably bad. It is a romance of no ordinary power."—*Chicago Evening Journal.*

Article 47. A Romance. From the French of Adolph Belot. By JAMES FURBISH. 8vo. Paper. 75 cents. Cloth. $1.25.

"An able translation of this brilliant and celebrated story, whose thrilling incidents and vivid scenes will amply repay perusal."—*Chicago Inter-Ocean.*
"A translation which created so profound a sensation when presented here in a dramatic form. The story will be read with interest. . . . . It contains some remarkably powerful scenes, spiritedly told."—*Boston Saturday Evening Gazette.*

Edith's Mistake; or, Left to Herself. By Jennie WOODVILLE. 16mo. Tinted cloth, printed ornamentation. $1.25.

"Such a spicy mixture of ingredients as this book contains cannot fail to make an exciting story. The plot is well conceived, the characters well drawn, and the interest well sustained to the end, without degenerating into the melodramatic."—*St. Louis Times.*

Hulda. A Novel. After the German of Fanny Lewald. By Mrs. A. L. WISTER, translator of "The Old Mam'selle's Secret," "Only a Girl," etc. 12mo. Fine cloth. $1.75.

"There is not a heavy page in the entire volume, nor is the interest allowed to flag from introduction to 'finis.'"—*Philadelphia New Age.*
"A book thoroughly German in style and sentiment, and yet one which will command the universal sympathy of all classes of readers."—*Boston Globe.*
"It is rare in these days of mediocre novels to find a work so thoroughly charming as this."—*Norristown Herald.*
"One of the most healthful, fresh, delightful, and artistically-constructed novels that has appeared this season."—*Philadelphia Evening Bulletin.*

One Woman's Two Lovers; or, Jacqueline Thayne's Choice. A Story. By VIRGINIA F. TOWNSEND, author of "The Hollands," "Six in All," etc. 12mo. Fine cloth. $1.50.

"This book must interest and hold the reader, and one will find much besides the plot and incident of the story to charm, as the evident study of nature and love for it shown by the authoress give many scenes of beauty to the book, and picturesque passages abound in it. It is a well written and thought-out story, showing refinement and imagination, as well as a high ideal on the writer's part."—*Boston Evening Transcript.*

Throstlethwaite. A Novel. By Susan Morley, author of "Aileen Ferrers," etc. 12mo. Fine cloth. $1.50.

" 'Throstlethwaite' is the title of a very charming story, by Susan Morley. . . . We commend to novel-readers the story, and feel sure it will more than repay reading."—*Boston Traveller.*

" It is a charming story. The characters introduced are not numerous, nor are the events; but the treatment of the whole is natural and life-like, and the incidental circumstances belonging to the main plot are admirably presented. . . . . It cannot fail to find admirers, as it deserves."—*London Bookseller.*

Her Majesty the Queen. A Novel. By J. Esten COOKE, author of " Surry of Eagle's Nest," " Dr. Vandyke," etc. 12mo. Fine cloth. $1.50.

" The story never flags in interest from the first page to the last. . . . There are many passages of genuine power, the power that comes from a simple, truthful, unostentatious presentation of the facts of life and nature, which is, after all, the highest accomplishment of art. The style of the narrative is eminently pure and pleasing, and in these qualities has not been surpassed by the author."—*New York Home Journal.*

Joshua Davidson. The True History of Joshua Davidson, Communist. A Powerful Satire. By the author of " A Girl of the Period." 12mo. Extra cloth. $1.25.

" The book is written with great power, and its interest is simply entrancing."—*Boston Literary World.*
" The book is a work of remarkable ability, and has made its mark in England, as it will, doubtless, do in this country."—*Boston Evening Traveller.*

Marie Derville. A Story of a French Boarding- School. From the French of Madame Guizot de Witt, author of " Motherless," etc. By MARY G. WELLS. 12mo. Extra cloth. $1.50.

" One of those simple little tales which charm the reader by the very simplicity of the narrative and the eloquent language in which it is told. . . . The author has given us a beautiful picture of faith, charity, self-devotion, and patience, and the translator has fitly set it in a framing of clear and beautiful English."—*Phila. Evening Bulletin.*

Must It Be? A Romance. From the German of Carl Detlef. By MS., translator of " By His Own Might" and " A Twofold Life." Illustrated. 8vo. Paper cover. 75 cents. Fine cloth. $1.25.

" The scene is laid in Russia, and the story is told with great vigor and picturesqueness of style. It has some charming domestic scenes, in addition to a number of intensely dramatic situations. The plot is exceedingly well managed, and the descriptions of Russian character, manners, and scenery are particularly happy. Its striking independence of treatment and its utter freedom from conventionality will prove not the least of its recommendations."—*Boston Globe.*

A Great Lady. A Romance. From the German of Van Dewall. Illustrated. 8vo. Paper. 75 cents. Fine cloth. $1.25.

"*A Great Lady* is an excellent novel from the German of Van Dewall, by MS. The plot is absorbingly interesting, and the story is told with more of the brilliancy and spirit of a French than of a German novelist. Some of the incidents are related with a vivid dramatic power that calls for a high degree of praise. The principal character is drawn with remarkable vigor, and is original both in conception and development. The plot never loses its hold on the reader's attention. The style is terse, rapid, and picturesque."—*Boston Saturday Evening Gazette.*

The Atonement of Leam Dundas. A Novel. By Mrs. E. LYNN LINTON, author of "Patricia Kemball," etc. 8vo. Illustrated. Paper. $1.00. Cloth. $1.50.

"Mrs. Lynn Linton's powerful novel, in which is unexpectedly developed an intensity of dramatic interest."—*Philadelphia Inquirer.*
"Mrs. Lynn Linton's story deserves a high place among sensation novels.

. . . . This is an excellent work."—*London Athenæum.*
"This cleverly written story is one of the most charming contributions to the literature of fiction we have had for some time, and will repay perusal."—*New Orleans Bulletin.*

Philip Van Artevelde. A Dramatical Romance. By Sir HENRY TAYLOR, author of "Edwin the Fair," etc. *New Edition.* 16mo. Cloth extra, red edges. $1.25.

"His dramas show, combined with true poetic feeling, the broad views and knowledge of human nature which have illustrated his long and useful official career."—*London Athenæum.*
"A book in which we have found more to praise and less to blame than in any poetical work of imagination that has fallen under our notice for some time."—*Lord Macaulay,* in the *Edinburgh Review.*

Hubert Freeth's Prosperity. A Story. By Mrs. NEWTON CROSLAND, author of "Lydia," "Hildred, the Daughter," "The Diamond Wedding," etc. 12mo. Fine cloth, black and gilt ornamentation. $1.75.

"It is a carefully executed composition, and as such will be sure to commend itself to those epicures who like to enjoy their novel like their wine, leisurely, holding it up to the light from time to time, that they may see the rich color and mark the clear depth through the crystal. A high, healthy tone of moral teaching runs all through this book, and the story gains upon us as we continue it."—*London Times.*

Under Lock and Key. A Story. By T. W. Speight, author of "Brought to Light," "Foolish Margaret," etc. 12mo. Fine cloth. $1.75.

"To all who are fond of exciting situations, mystery, and ingeniously constructed plots, we unhesitatingly recommend this work. The characters are strongly drawn and individualized, the style is good, and the interest absorbing and unflagging from beginning to end."—*Boston Globe.*

Charteris. A Romance. By Mary M. Meline, au- thor of "Montarge's Legacy," "In Six Months." 12mo Cloth. $1.50.

"The story is one of great interest, the plot being worked out with a degree of elaboration that holds the reader in a condition of expectancy to the end."—*Allentown Herald.*

The Romance of the English Stage. By Percy Fitz- gerald, M.A., F.S.A., author of "Life of Garrick," "The Kembles," etc. 12mo. Extra cloth. $2.00.

"The work shows great reading, and good selection from remote and unfamiliar, and, in some cases, inaccessible authors. It is sprightly and entertaining, and whoever loves Pepys, or Lamb, or Walpole; Boswell, Greville, or Holland, will be pleased with Mr. Fitzgerald's chronicles."—*Philadelphia North American.*

"'The Romance of the English Stage,' by Percy Fitzgerald, tells of both the lofty and the lowly in those olden times. . . . A picture with bright lights and sombre shadows, it is attractive as the representation of days long past, which we nevertheless rejoice to know can now only exist as history."—*Boston Transcript.*

Life's Promise to Pay. A Novel. By Clara L. CONWAY. 12mo. Fine cloth. $1.50.

"This story is pleasantly written, has an ingenious plot, and is both clever and entertaining."—*N.Y. Daily Graphic.*
"She shows the capacity to deeply interest the reader, and also exhibits promising skill in character-drawing and plotting for the best effects."—*St. Louis Republican.*

Starting Out. A Story of the Ohio Hills. By Alex- ander Clark, author of "Schoolday Dialogues," "The Old Log Schoolhouse," etc. Illustrated. 12mo. Fine cloth. $1.25.

"Something lively for winter evenings. It is a stirring, racy story, illustrated by a dozen original designs, and beautifully printed and bound."—*The Steubenville Gazette.*

"The simple announcement of the issue of the work is enough to create a general desire to read it."—*Springfield, Ohio, Republican.*

German University Life. The Story of My Career as a Student and Professor. With Personal Reminiscences of Goethe, Schiller, Novalis, and others. By HEINRICH STEFFENS. Translated by WILLIAM L. GAGE. New Edition. 12mo. Fine cloth. $1.25.

"The volume will be intensely interesting to all who take an interest in the great men and rich literature of Germany."—*St. Louis Republican.*
"It affords an inside view of a peculiar life and a striking circle of men. Its portraits of great and famous thinkers and teachers will be studied with rare enjoyment by every one of their disciples. And its graphic picturing of scene and incident at a most stirring juncture of European affairs possesses a positive interest for us all."—*Boston Congregationalist.*
"The book is absorbing, and we could not lay it down unread, not only on account of the interest of the life speaking through it, but for the brilliant constellation around it."—*The Philadelphia Presbyterian.*

THE WORKS OF E. MARLITT.

TRANSLATED BY MRS. A. L. WISTER.

AT THE COUNCILLOR'S;
OR, A NAMELESS HISTORY.

Sixth Edition. 12mo. Fine cloth. $1.75.

"Pure in tone, elegant in style, and overflowing with the tender and openly-expressed sentiment which charac- | terizes human romance in Germany."—*Worcester Spy.*

THE SECOND WIFE.

Twelfth Edition. 12mo. Fine cloth. $1.75.

'A German story of intense interest by one of the best-known writers of | romance of that country."—*Washington Chronicle.*

THE OLD MAM'SELLE'S SECRET.

Eleventh Edition. 12mo. Fine cloth. $1.50.

"It is one of the most intense, concentrated, compact novels of the day. . . . And the work has the minute fidelity of the author of the 'Initials,' | the dramatic unity of Reade, and the graphic power of George Eliot."—*Columbus, Ohio, Journal.*

GOLD ELSIE.

Ninth Edition. 12mo. Fine cloth. $1.50.

" 'Gold Elsie' is one of the loveliest heroines ever introduced to the public."—*Boston Advertiser.*
"A charming book. It absorbs your | attention from the title-page to the end."—*The Chicago Home Circle.*
"A charming story charmingly told."—*Baltimore Gazette.*

THE LITTLE MOORLAND PRINCESS.

Sixth Edition. 12mo. Fine cloth. $1.50.

"A charming story."—*New York Observer.*
"The plot is admirably contrived."—*Philadelphia Evening Bulletin.* | "Delightful for the exquisite manner in which its characters are drawn."—*Boston Evening Traveller.*

COUNTESS GISELA.

Sixth Edition. 12mo. Fine cloth. $1.50.

"One of the very best of its class, and is a genuine representation of court, burgher, and rural life in Germany. The translation is spirited and faithful."—*Philadelphia Press.* | "There is more dramatic power in this than in any of the stories by the same author that we have read."—*N. O. Times.*

TRANSLATED BY MRS. ELGARD.

OVER YONDER.

Fifth Edition. 8vo. With full-page Illustration. Paper. 30 Cts.

" 'Over Yonder' is a charming novelette. The admirers of 'Old Mam'selle's Secret' will give it a glad reception, while those who are ignorant of the | merits of this author will find in it a pleasant introduction to the works of a gifted writer."—*Daily Sentinel.*

MAGDALENA.

Together with "THE LONELY ONES," by Paul Heyse.
Fourth Edition. 8vo. With two full-page Illustrations. Paper. 35 Cts.

"Paul Heyse's 'Lonely Ones' is an Idyl—a perfect little picture in its way."—*Baltimore Statesman.* | "Both of these stories are exceedingly clever and entertaining."—*Richmond Enquirer.*

THE "WIDE, WIDE WORLD" SERIES.
The Works of the Misses Warner.

The Wide, Wide World. 12mo. Two Steel Plates 694 pages. Fine cloth. $1.75.

Queechy. 12mo. Two Illustrations. 806 pages. Fine cloth. $1.75.

The Hills of the Shatemuc. 12mo. 516 pages Fine cloth. $1.75.

My Brother's Keeper. 12mo. 385 pages. Fine cloth. $1.50.

Dollars and Cents. 12mo. 515 pages. Fine cloth. $1.75

Daisy. 12mo. 815 pages. Fine cloth. $2.00.

Say and Seal. 12mo. 1013 pages. Fine cloth. $2.00.

☞ *Complete sets of the above volumes, bound in uniform style, can be obtained, put up in neat boxes.*

The sale of thousands of the above volumes attests their popularity. They are stories of unusual interest, remarkably elevated and natural in tone and sentiment, full of refined and healthy thought, and exhibiting an intimate and accurate knowledge of human nature.

THREE POWERFUL ROMANCES,
By Wilhelmine Von Hillern.

Only a Girl. From the German. By Mrs. A. L. WISTER 12mo. Fine cloth. $2.00.

This is a charming work, charmingly written, and no one who reads it can lay it down without feeling impressed with the superior talent of its gifted author.

By His Own Might. From the German. By M. S. 12mo Fine cloth. $1.75.

"A story of intense interest, well wrought."—*Boston Commonwealth.*

A Twofold Life. From the German. By M. S. 12mo Fine cloth. $1.75.

"It is admirably written, the plot is interesting and well developed, the style vigorous and healthy."—*Boston Saturday Evening Gazette.*

TWO CHARMING NOVELS,
By the Author of "The Initials."

Quits. By the BARONESS TAUTPHŒUS. 12mo. Fine cloth. $1.75.

At Odds. By the BARONESS TAUTPHŒUS. 12mo. Fine cloth. $1.75

NOW COMPLETE, IN FIFTEEN VOLUMES.

THE

NEW STANDARD EDITION

OF

PRESCOTT'S WORKS

WITH THE

Author's Latest Corrections and Additions,

EDITED BY

JOHN FOSTER KIRK.

AS FOLLOWS:

HISTORY OF FERDINAND AND ISABELLA,
3 Volumes.

HISTORY OF THE CONQUEST OF MEXICO,
3 Volumes.

HISTORY OF THE CONQUEST OF PERU,
2 Volumes.

HISTORY OF THE REIGN OF PHILIP II.,
3 Volumes.

HISTORY OF THE REIGN OF CHARLES V.,
3 Volumes.

PRESCOTT'S MISCELLANEOUS ESSAYS,
1 Volume.

This Edition is Illustrated with Maps, Plates, and Engravings. Price per volume, 12mo, in fine English cloth, with black and gold ornamentation, $2.00; library sheep, $2.50; half calf, gilt back, $3.50.

"It would be difficult to point out among any works of living historians the equal of those which have proceeded from Mr. Prescott's pen."—*Harper's Magazine.*

"We would gladly do our share towards making acknowledgment of the debt of gratitude we all owe to Messrs. Lippincott & Co. for the superb and even monumental edition of the *Works* of William H. Prescott, which they have at last brought to completion."—*New York Christian Union.*

"The typography, indeed the entire mechanical execution, of these books is exquisite; and we unhesitatingly pronounce the series not only the best edition of Prescott's Works ever published, but one of the handsomest set of books the American press has given us."—*Boston Journal.*